More praise
Shell Game

"There are genuine moments of slapstick humor . . . As usual, supporting characters . . . are the spice in O'Connell's mystery stew." —*Milwaukee Journal Sentinel*

"This is the sixth Mallory mystery . . . and it's one of the best. The characters are intriguing, and the plot's hairpin twists and turns are dazzling. Highly recommended."
—*Library Journal* (starred review)

"O'Connell achieves a nuanced portrait of the increasingly antisocial Mallory, who . . . understands the darker chambers of the human mind." —*The Atlanta Journal-Constitution*

"O'Connell . . . packs *Shell Game* with visual spectacles . . . [her] sure writing and sense of suspense never falter."
—*The Christian Science Monitor*

"Mallory . . . retains all her feral, sullen, paradoxically endearing components." —*Kirkus Reviews*

"O'Connell is at her best in creating a host of intriguing and even inscrutable characters . . . The novel is rich in description and the dialogue builds suspense."
—*The Florida Times-Union*

continued on next page . . .

Mallory's Oracle

"*Mallory's Oracle* is a joy . . . Exciting, riveting . . . Kathy Mallory is a marvelous creation."   —Jonathan Kellerman

"A classic cop story . . . one of the most interesting new characters to come along in years."   —John Sanford

"Kathy Mallory, NYPD, is one of the most unique, interesting, and surprising heroines you've ever come across in any work of fiction."   —Nelson DeMille

"A story and an author who really involve you, and make you care—and that is so rare! Carol O'Connell will have to skip being a cult author . . . *Mallory's Oracle* is so good it will launch her career in bold stroke." —James B. Patterson

"Wild, sly, and breathless—all the things that a good thriller ought to be."   —Carl Hiaasen

"One of the most stylishly innovative and witty mysteries in years."   —*San Francisco Chronicle*

Killing Critics

"Mallory is one of the genre's most original and intriguing characters, and her third adventure should be gulped down at one sitting."   —*The Cleveland Plain Dealer*

"Darkly stylish, with a highly original protagonist and expertly drawn characters. This is great fun."

—*Chicago Tribune*

"[A] crafty page-turner."   —*People*

"A tight, twisting mystery."   —*Newsday*

The Man Who Cast Two Shadows

"Beautifully written . . . [Mallory] is both mysterious and as real as a fist in the face." —*Harper's Bazaar*

"Chilling . . . fascinating . . . The suspense along the way is excruciating." —*Detroit Free Press*

"After the raves garnered by *Mallory's Oracle*, it's hard to believe the author could produce another book that's just as intense, powerful and affecting. But she has. Three cheers for O'Connell, who has moved from neophyte writer to established literary superstar." —*Booklist* (starred review)

"Even more satisfying than *Mallory's Oracle*. And that's high praise indeed." —*People*

"A gifted storyteller . . . prose that is rich in nuance with cunning plot lines . . . a complex, stunningly unique protagonist, who not only commands our attention, but stimulates the imagination." —*Milwaukee Journal Sentinel*

Stone Angel

"Mallory makes a hard-edged, brilliant, and indomitable heroine. *Stone Angel*, as much Southern novel as mystery novel, is rich in people, places and customs vividly realized, with mordant humor, terror, and sadness."
—*San Francisco Chronicle*

"O'Connell conjures up a world of almost Faulknerian richness and complexity. In *Stone Angel*, her imagination truly takes wing." —*People*

continued on next page . . .

Judas Child

"Breathtakingly ambitious suspense . . . A brilliant twist . . . mesmerizing." —*Minneapolis Star Tribune*

"Her most stunning novel yet . . . more chilling, twisted, and intense with each page . . . [a] soul-shattering climax." —*Booklist* (starred review)

"More than enough darkness and tension to make fans of Mallory take notice . . . Solidly crafted . . . a compelling tale." —*Chicago Tribune*

"O'Connell has created some truly enigmatic and interesting characters . . . [She] is a writer of uncommon talents." —*Milwaukee Journal Sentinel*

"A chilling tale." —*Publishers Weekly*

"Every bit as intense as O'Connell's acclaimed Kathy Mallory detective stories . . . The characters are so painfully real . . . that you're hard-pressed to take anything for granted in this grisly, poetic tale." —*Kirkus Reviews*

"Powerful . . . complex . . . gripping in suspense." —*Library Journal*

Shell
Game

Carol O'Connell

BERKLEY BOOKS, NEW YORK

SHELL GAME

A Berkley Book / published by arrangement with
Hutchinson

PRINTING HISTORY
G. P. Putnam's Sons hardcover edition / July 1999
Berkley paperback edition / August 2000

All rights reserved.
Copyright © 1999 by Carol O'Connell
Cover art and design by Tony Greco
This book may not be reproduced in whole or in part,
by mimeograph or any other means, without permission.
For information address: G. P. Putnam's Sons, a division of
Penguin Putnam Inc., 375 Hudson Street, New York, New York 10014.

The Penguin Putnam Inc. World Wide Web site address is
http://www.penguinputnam.com

ISBN: 0-425-17603-7

BERKLEY®
Berkley Books are published by The Berkley Publishing Group,
a division of Penguin Putnam Inc.,
375 Hudson Street, New York, New York 10014.
BERKLEY and the "B" design are trademarks
belonging to Penguin Putnam Inc.

PRINTED IN THE UNITED STATES OF AMERICA

10 9 8 7 6 5 4 3 2 1

Acknowledgments

Dianne Burke of Search and Rescue Research Ltd., Tempe, Arizona.

Peter Gill, Peerless Handcuff Company, Springfield, Massachusetts.

Law Enforcement Equipment Company, Kansas City, Missouri.

Special thanks for the inspiration of an unknown Polish artist, who created a political poster with the legend "War, what a woman you are." I saw it many years ago and could never forget it. If I ever track this artist down, the name will appear in subsequent editions.

This book is dedicated to a generation and an era of jazz babies and cigarette smoke, Nebraska farmboys in Paris, women in uniforms and women in sequins, bombs bursting in air, Gershwin tunes and Billie Holiday, rows upon rows of gravestones all over the earth, the cities that fell and the people who prevailed.

Prologue

THE OLD MAN KEPT PACE WITH HIM, THEN RAN AHEAD IN A SUD-
den burst of energy and fear—as if he loved Louisa more.
Man and boy raced toward the scream, a long high note, a
shriek without pause for breath, inhuman in its constancy.

Malakhai's entire body awoke in violent spasms of flailing
arms and churning legs, running naked into the real and solid
world of his bed and its tangle of damp sheets. Rising quickly
in the dark, he knocked over a small table, sending a clock to
the floor, shattering its glass face and killing the alarm.

Cold air rushed across his bare feet to push open the door.
By the light of a wall sconce in the outer hallway, he cast a
shadow on the bedroom floor and revolved in a slow turn, not
recognizing any of the furnishings. A long black robe lay
across the arms of a chair. Shivering, he picked up the unfamiliar garment and pulled it across his shoulders like a
cape.

A window sash had been raised a crack. White curtains
ghosted inward, and drops from a rain gutter made small wet
explosions on the sill. His head jerked up. A black fly was
screaming in circles around a chandelier of dark electric candles.

Malakhai bolted through the doorway and down a corridor
of closed rooms, the long robe flying out behind him. This
narrow passage opened onto a parlor of gracious proportions
and bright light. There were too many textures and colors. He
could only absorb them as bits of a mosaic: the pattern of the

tin ceiling, forest-green walls, book spines, veins of marble, carved scrolls of mahogany and swatches of brocade.

He caught the slight movement of a head turning in the mirror over the mantelpiece. His right arm was slowly rising to shield his eyes from the impossible. And now he was staring at the wrinkled flesh across the back of his raised hand, the enlarged veins and brown liver spots.

He drew the robe close about him as a thin silk protection against more confusion. Awakenings were always cruel.

How much of his life had been stripped away, killed in the tissues of his brain? And how much disorientation was only the temporary companion of a recent stroke? Malakhai pulled aside a velvet drape to look through the window. He had not yet fixed the day or even the year, but only gleaned that it was night and very late in life.

The alarm clock by his bed had been set for some event. Without assistance from anyone, he must recall what it was. Asking for help was akin to soiling himself in public.

Working his way from nineteen years old toward a place well beyond middle age, he moved closer to the mirror, the better to assess the damage. His thick mane of hair had grown white. The flesh was firm, but marked with lines of an interesting life and a long one. Only his eyes were curiously unchanged, still dark gunmetal blue.

The plush material of the rug was soft beneath his bare feet. Its woven colors were vivid, though the fringes showed extreme age. He recalled purchasing this carpet from a dealer in antiquities. The rosewood butler's table had come from the same shop. It was laid with a silver tray and an array of leaded crystal. More at home now in this aged incarnation, Malakhai lifted the decanter and poured out a glass of Spanish sherry.

Two armchairs faced the television set. Of course—one for the living and one for the dead. Well, that was normal enough, for he was well past the year when his wife had died.

The enormous size of the television screen was the best clue to the current decade. By tricks of illness and memory, he had begun his flight through this suite of rooms in the 1940s, and now he settled down in a well-padded chair near the end of the twentieth century, a time traveler catching his breath and seeking compass points. He was not in France anymore. This was the west wing of a private hospital in the northern corner of New York State, and soon he would remember why the clock had sounded an alarm.

A remote control device lay on the arm of his chair, and a red light glowed below the dark glass screen. He depressed the play button, and the television set came to life in a sudden brightness of moving pictures and a loud barking voice. Malakhai cut off the volume.

Something important was about to happen, but what? His hand clenched in frustration, and drops of sherry spilled from his glass.

She was beside him now, reaching into his mind and flooding it with warmth, touching his thoughts with perfect understanding. A second glass sat on a small cocktail table before her own chair, a taste of sherry for Louisa—still thirsty after all those years in the cold ground.

On the large screen, a troupe of old men in tuxedos were doffing top hats for the camera. Looming behind them was the old band shell in Central Park. Its high stone arch was flanked by elegant cornices and columns of the early 1900s. Hexagonal patterns on the concave wall echoed the shape of the plaza's paving stones, where a standing audience was herded behind velvet ropes. Above the heads of the old magicians, a rippling banner spanned the upper portion of the shell, bright red letters declaring the upcoming Holidays of Magic in Manhattan.

The preview—of course.

So this was the month of November, and in another week, Thanksgiving Day would be followed by a festival of magicians, retired performers of the past alongside the present flash-and-dazzle generation. Beneath the image of a reporter with a microphone, a moving band of type traveled across the width of the screen to tell him that this was a live performance with no trick photography. The cameras would not cut away.

Malakhai smiled. The television was promising not to deceive the viewers, though misdirection was the heart of magic.

The plaza must be well lit, for the scene was bright as day. The raised stone floor of the band shell was dominated by a large box of dark wood, nine feet square. Malakhai knew the precise dimensions; many years ago, he had lent a hand to build the original apparatus, and this was a close replica. Thirteen shallow stairs led to the top of the platform. At the sides of the broad base step, two pairs of pedestals were bolted into the wood and topped with crossbows angling upward toward a target of black and white concentric ovals. The camera did not see the pins that suspended the target between the tall posts, and so it seemed to float above the small wooden stage.

Memory had nearly achieved parity with the moment. Oliver Tree was about to make a comeback for a career that never was. Malakhai leaned toward Louisa's empty chair. "Can you find our Oliver in that lineup of old men?" He pointed to the smallest figure in the group, an old man with the bright look of a boy allowed to stay up late in the company of grown-ups. The scalp and beard were clipped so short, Oliver appeared to be coated with white fur like an aged teddy bear.

"Where has he been all this time?" Even as Malakhai spoke these words, he recalled that Oliver had spent his retirement years working out a solution to the Lost Illusion.

The crossbow pedestals were made of giant clockwork gears, three intermeshing toothy circles of brass. Soon their weapons would release arrows in mechanized sequence, four time bombs set to go off with the tick of clocks and the twang of bowstrings. All the sights were trained on the oval target. The television camera narrowed its field for a close look at the magazine on one crossbow. This long narrow box of wood was designed to carry a load of three arrows.

The camera pulled back for a wide shot of two uniformed policemen on top of the platform. One of them held a burlap dummy upright while the other officer manacled its cloth hands to the iron post rings. Then they both knelt on the floorboards to attach leg irons to the widespread feet. And now the mannikin was splayed out across the face of the target. Standing below on the floor of the band shell, the newsman was speaking into his microphone, probably giving the history of the Lost Illusion and its long-deceased creator, the great Max Candle.

Malakhai inclined his head toward Louisa's chair. "I never thought Oliver would be the one to work it out."

Indeed. The retired carpenter in magician's silks had once been the most ordinary member of the troupe, a boy from the American heartland, stranded in the middle of a world war and without a clue to get himself home. So Oliver had only made it as far as New York City. Perhaps Paris had spoiled him for the midwestern prairies that spawned him.

And now Malakhai remembered one more thing. He touched the arm of the dead woman's chair, saying, "Oliver made me promise you'd watch this. He wanted you to see him in his finest hour."

The camera was panning the plaza. "There might be a thousand people in that park. Millions more are watching this on television. No one in our crowd ever had an audience that size."

Oliver Tree had surpassed them all.

More lost time was restored to Malakhai as he reached down to the cocktail table and picked up the formal invitation to a magic show in Central Park. He read the words in elegant script, then turned to the woman who wasn't there. "He's dedicating this performance to you, Louisa."

The rest of the text was a bit cryptic for Oliver. A hint of things to come?

Malakhai faced the screen as the two policemen finished cocking the crossbow pistols. The gears of the pedestals were all set in motion, toothy brass wheels slowly turning. A clockwork peg rose to the top of its orbit and touched the trigger of a crossbow. The first arrow was launched and flying too fast for the eye to track it. In the next instant, the burlap dummy was losing stuffing where the metal shaft had torn its throat. The next bow fired, and the next. When every missile had flown, the cloth effigy was pinned to the target by shafts through its neck, both legs and that place where the human heart would be.

The uniformed officers climbed to the top of the platform, unlocked the irons, and the demonstration dummy fell to the floorboards. They picked it up and carried it between them. The sawdust bled down the stairs in their descent. They made one last tour of the pedestals, cocking the weapons, allowing more arrows to drop from the crossbow magazines.

Oliver Tree stood at the base of the stairs and handed his top hat to another magician. Then he donned a scarlet cape and pulled the monk's hood over his white hair. As he slowly climbed toward the target, the long train of material flowed over the stairs behind him.

When the old man reached the top of the staircase, he stood with his back to the crowd and raised his arms. The cape concealed all but the top of the oval target. The scarlet silk sparkled and gleamed with reflections of camera lights. Then the cape collapsed and fell empty to the wooden floor. In that same instant, as if he had materialized in position, Oliver was revealed facing the crowd, spread-eagle across the target, bound in chains by hand and foot, himself the target of four armed crossbows. The gears of every pedestal were in motion. Soon the arrows would fly.

Malakhai clapped his hands. So far, the timing had been flawless. If the volume had been turned up, he might have heard the first round of applause from the audience in the plaza. Oliver Tree had grown old awaiting this moment.

The magician jerked his head to one side—the wrong side—as the gears on the first pedestal stopped and the bow released its arrow. Oliver's face contorted in a scream. There was blood on his white tie and collar. His mouth was working frantically, no doubt begging his captors to stop the rest of the crossbows from firing their arrows and killing him. Oliver's cries for help went ignored by the policemen and the reporter. They had apparently been informed that the great Max Candle had used these same words in the original act— just before dying in every single performance.

Another arrow flew, and another. While Oliver cried out in

pain, the young reporter was smiling broadly for the camera, perhaps not understanding that the old man high above him on the platform was mortally wounded. Possibly this grinning child of the television era did not realize that all blood was not fake blood, that the arrows pinning the old man's legs were quite real.

The crowd was staring agape. Though uninitiated in the art of magic, they knew death when they saw it, when it came with the final arrow swiftly ripping a hole through Oliver's heart. The old man's screaming stopped. He dangled from his chains, not struggling anymore. His eyes were wide, unblinking—fixed in fear.

Malakhai had much experience with death. He knew that it never came in an instant. Perhaps, just for one moment, Oliver was aware of a few people in the crowd moving toward the platform, coming to help him—as if they could.

The newsman was laughing and waving these rescuers off, yelling and gesturing, no doubt assuring them that death was part of the show, a special effect for their viewing enjoyment. Then the reporter looked up at the chained corpse, and he lost his professional smile, perhaps realizing that trick photography was not an option here.

This was what death looked like.

The police officers, better acquainted with mortality, had already reached the top of the stairs. They unlocked Oliver's manacles and gently lowered the body to the wooden floor. Women covered the eyes of their children. The cameraman was ignoring the wild, waving hands of the reporter, who was mouthing the words to make him stop the pictures. But the lens was so in love with its subject, narrowing the focus, closing in on the fear-struck face of the dead magician and his true-to-life blood.

Louisa's sherry glass fell to the floor, and the dark red liquid spread across the pattern of the carpet.

Malakhai's hands were rising of their own accord. It was an act of will to keep one from touching the other, so as not to harm Louisa with a sound that aped applause. His lips spread wide with a silent scream, a parody of Oliver, whose volume had been turned off even before his life was ended. Then Malakhai's hands crashed together, slapping loudly, again and again, madly clapping as tears rolled down his face and ran between his parted lips in warm salty streams.

What a worthy performance—murdering a man while a million pairs of eyes were watching.

One

SOMETIMES HE WONDERED WHY THE CHILDREN DIDN'T CRY TO
see such monsters in the world—a giant blue hedgehog, a
huge fat worm, a cat the size of a floating building. And there
were more fantastic creatures that Detective Sergeant Riker
could not identify.

The morning air was freezing cold. All the boys and girls
were swaddled in woolen scarves and down coats. They sent
up soft choruses of oohs and aaaahs when the cat with a
sixteen-foot bow tie emerged from a side street. Its stovepipe
hat could house a bodega. The grinning helium balloon was
bound to the earth by long ropes in the hands of marching
Lilliputian humans. The wind was high as the great looming
cat dragged his rope handlers along with him, and it was no
longer clear who was tethered to whom.

The balloon was being sandwiched into the parade route
between two earthbound attractions, a Conestoga wagon
drawn by four live horses and a float pulled by a car and carrying the world's largest peanut on two legs. Other wildly
fanciful floats were backed up to 85th Street. They awaited
instructions to alternate with the helium giants held down by
sandbags and corralled in the cross streets on either side of
the Museum of Natural History.

Wooden blue sawhorses barricaded the crush of onlookers
along Central Park West. The crowds would be fifty-people
deep at the midpoint of the parade route, and denser still
in Herald Square, where Broadway performers were tap-

dancing their hearts out to keep warm. But here on the Upper West Side, where it all began, the crowd was only a thick band of spectators lining the park side of the boulevard.

The detective sat on the edge of the magicians' float, his legs dangling from the wide brim of a top hat scaled for King Kong, and he wrapped his coat tighter against the high wind. Riker had the best view in town for the Macy's Thanksgiving Day Parade, and he blamed his partner for this. He turned to the young blonde behind the aviator sunglasses. "Mallory, tell me again. What am I doing here?"

"You're earning a turkey dinner at Charles's place." Detective Mallory lowered her dark glasses to glare at him properly, to make it clear that she was not up for a rebellion this morning. A deal was a deal.

In the long slants of her sunlit eyes, there was a perverse green fire with no warmth. Riker found this standout feature slightly less unnerving in her adult face. As a little girl, she had frightened people.

Ah, but she still frightened people, didn't she?

Well, to be fair, Kathy Mallory was taller now, five ten, and she carried a gun. Fifteen years ago, the street kid had cleaned up well after only one bath, revealing luminous white skin in sharp contrast to a red pouting mouth. And even then, the delicate bones of her child's face were sculpted for the high drama of light and shadow.

This morning, she wore a long trench coat. The black leather was too light to offer much protection from the weather, but she seemed not to feel the bitter chill in the air. And this fit well with Riker's idea that she was from some other planet, dark and cold, farthest from the sun.

"Mallory, this is a waste of time. Even Charles thinks it was an accidental death. Ask him. *I* did." He knew she would never ask. Mallory didn't like to be contradicted. However, the other eight million New Yorkers believed Oliver Tree had died because of a magic trick gone wrong.

He turned around to look at the giant playing cards set into the enormous hatband of bright metal. Between an ace and a deuce, the center card was a portrait of the great Max Candle, who had died thirty years ago. Twelve feet above the top hat's brim, the late magician's younger cousin was standing on the crown with two other men in red satin capes and black tuxedos. Six feet four without his shoes on, Charles Butler created his own scale of gianthood on the high circular stage.

Though Charles was not a real magician, it was easy to see why he had been invited to appear on the float. The resemblance to his famous cousin was very strong. At forty, Charles was near the age of the man in the photograph. His eyes were the same shade of blue, and his hair was also light brown, even curling below the line of his collar in the same length and style. Both men had the same sensuous mouth. But thereafter, the similarity was distorted. The late Max Candle had been a handsome man. Charles's face was close to caricature, his nose elongating to a hook shape with bird-perching proportions. The heavy-lidded eyes bulged like a frog's, and his small irises were lost in a sea of white. Max Candle had had a dazzling smile. His younger cousin smiled like a loon, but such a charming loon that people tended to smile back.

Charles Butler was Max Candle trapped in a fun-house mirror.

And now Riker caught his own reflection in the wide hatband of polished metal. He stared at his unshaven face and veined eyes. Graying strands of hair whipped out beneath the brim of his old felt hat. He was wearing a birthday present from Mallory, the finest tweed overcoat he had ever owned, tailored for a millionaire—which explained why he looked a homeless bum in stolen clothes.

He turned to his partner, intending to thank her again for these wonderful threads, to say something sentimental and foolish.

Naw.

"You're really off the mark this time, kid." Sentiment would have cost him too many points with her.

"You don't know it wasn't murder," said Mallory.

Yes, he did. "I trust the West Side dick's report. He said the machinery checked out. The crossbows did what they were supposed to do. The old guy just screwed up the act."

She turned away from him, for this was heresy, and she was not listening to any more of it.

Riker craned his neck to look up at the circular stage. Charles Butler was juggling five red balls. The other magicians were making birds and bouquets of flowers disappear and reappear to the applause of sidewalk spectators. Charles was clearly enjoying himself, an amateur mingling with some of the most famous magicians in memory, albeit an old memory of another time, for his companions were of the World War II generation.

Riker turned back to Mallory. She was focused on the crowd, watching for the first taxpayer to do something criminal.

"Well, kid, maybe Oliver Tree *wanted* to die."

"You never know," said Mallory. "But most suicides prefer the painless route over four sharp arrows."

The members of a high school marching band were warming up their instruments on the sidewalk. The trombone nearly decapitated a pedestrian as the musician turned sharply, unmindful of the press of people all around him. The French horns and the tuba were at war with the clarinet, and the drummer was in a world of his own, bored and bent on annoying everyone within earshot.

Damn kids.

A cadre of sequined baton-twirlers walked by the magicians' float. Two pretty girls waved at Riker, giving him a better opinion of teenagers as a species. In their wake, another giant was joining the parade. Riker grinned at the chubby airborne effigy of a fireman. This was a balloon he remembered from atop his father's shoulders when he was five years old. Fifty years later, many new characters had replaced his retired favorites. Ah, but now another old familiar fellow was queuing up along the cross street.

Through a spiderweb of bare tree branches, he could see the gargantuan Woody Woodpecker balloon lying facedown and floating just above the pavement. The great arms and legs were outstretched, and one white-gloved hand was covering an automobile. All of the balloon's personal handlers were dressed in woodpecker costumes, but they had the scale of scurrying blue ants with red hair and yellow shoes as they pulled back nets and removed restraining sandbags from the bird's arms and legs.

"Hey, Mallory, there's Woody, your favorite. Remember?"

She looked bored now, but when she was a child, this same giant balloon had made her eyes pop with wonder.

"I never liked that one," she said.

"Oh, you *liar.*" Riker had the proof, clear memories of that parade, fifteen years before, when he was still allowed to call her Kathy. The ten-year-old girl had stood by his side on a cold day in another November. She had resembled an upright blond turtle, for Helen Markowitz had cocooned her foster child in layers of sweaters, woolen scarves and a thick down coat. That was the day when they had to peel little Kathy Mallory's eyes off the gigantic woodpecker, resplendent in his fine mop of red rubber hair and that magnificent yellow beak.

Riker raised his eyes to see the handlers letting out the ropes, and the horizontal balloon was on the rise. At last, the mighty bird was standing sixty feet tall, looming above the crowd and blocking out a good portion of brilliant blue sky. If Woody chose to, he could look into the upper windows of the museum and even examine its roof.

"You loved that balloon," said Riker, insistent.

Mallory ignored him.

He looked down at his scuffed shoes, lowering the brim of his hat against the strong light of morning sun. He was feeling the slow onset of pain. Nostalgia always brought on a fresh spate of grief during the holidays. He missed his old friends. Sweet Helen had died too soon, too young. And following another untimely funeral, Inspector Louis Markowitz had been buried beside his wife.

Privately, Riker believed that Lou Markowitz had not gone to his eternal rest, but was probably having a very tense death. Sometimes he could almost sense the old man's spirit hovering near Mallory, trembling in wait for his foster child to revert into the feral creature found running loose on the city streets.

As if she had changed all that much.

Woody Woodpecker grandly sailed down Central Park West, dwarfing every tree and tall building along the boulevard, and Riker was reliving Kathy Mallory's first parade. That day, he had gamely volunteered for midget duty—police code for keeping an eye on the brat—so that Helen and Lou could say hello to old friends in the crowd. Her first year in foster care, Kathy could not be introduced to innocent civilians, lest they lose a hand while patting her on the head. It was fortunate that Helen had bundled the child so well, for this had restricted Kathy's movements and slowed down her tiny hands. That day, it had been easy for Riker to catch the baby thief boosting a wallet from a woman's purse. Forgetting whom he was dealing with, he had bent down low to scold her in a tone reserved for small children—*real* children. "Now, Kathy, why would you do a bad thing like that?"

The little girl had looked up at him with such incredulity, her wide eyes clearly stating, *Because stealing is what I do, you moron.* And this had set the tone for their relationship through the years.

He shook his head slowly. Lou Markowitz must have had a heart attack when his foster daughter quit Barnard College to join up with the police. Now Riker looked down at the magnificent coat she had given him to replace the old threadbare rag that more closely fit his salary—and hers.

He turned to face Mallory with another idea for needling her. "The papers said the old guy wasn't even a real magician. Just a nobody, a carpenter from Brooklyn. Maybe Oliver Tree didn't know how—"

"Charles says the old man performed with Max Candle. So I figure he knew what he was doing." She turned away from him, a pointed gesture to say that her mind was made up; this conversation was over.

So, of course, Riker went on with it. "The man was in his seventies. Did you consider that his timing might be a little off?"

"No, I didn't." Her voice was rising, getting testy.

Good. "Like you're the expert on magic?"

"Magic is a cheat," she said. "There's no risk. He shouldn't have died."

Was she pouting? Yes, she was. *Better and better.*

"No risk, huh? Never? Charles didn't tell you that." The younger cousin of Max Candle owned more magic illusions than a store. "You never even asked him, did you, Mallory?"

No, of course you didn't. He leaned in close for another shot at her. "What about senility? Suppose the old guy was—"

"There's no medical history of senility." She turned her back on him, as if this might prevent him from having the last word.

It would not.

Riker would bet his pension that she had never seen a medical history on the dead man. He knew for a fact that she had not even read the accident report. Mallory liked her instincts, and she ran with them.

And now he understood his own place in her schemes. She had only wanted him along today as a show of force. She was planning to turn Charles's holiday dinner party into an interrogation of elderly magicians—all witnesses to a damn *accident.*

"I still say it ain't right, kid. You can't go drumming up new business. Not when NYPD has a backlog of dead bodies."

Mallory had tuned him out like an off chord in the nearby marching band, which was playing loudly but not together. She was intent on the faces along the barricades.

Riker threw up his hands. "Okay, let's say it was a real homicide. How do you make the stretch to an assassination during the parade?" She could not, and he knew that. She was making up this story as she went along.

"My perp loves spectacle." Mallory faced him now, suddenly warming to the conversation. "He killed a man on local television. This parade is televised all over the country. If he's gonna do another one, today's the day."

Her perp? So she was already racing ahead to the moment when she claimed the case file and the evidence. "Mallory, *before* we assume the killing is an ongoing thing with a pattern, most of us wait till we got at least two homicides in the bag."

"Suppose the next homicide is Charles?"

A good point, though stretching credibility beyond all reason. She had been wise to con him into doing this baby-sitting detail on his own time. Lieutenant Coffey would never have bought into this fairy story nor given her one dime from the Special Crimes budget. And she would never have forgiven the lieutenant for laughing. Mallory could not deal with ridicule in any form.

But this is such a crackpot idea. And, for a gifted liar, it was pretty lame. But he decided she was only having an off day.

Yet Mallory's instincts were usually good. It might not be a total crock. He had to wonder why Oliver Tree had taken such chances. The daredevil stunt was a young man's trade. Maybe Mallory was right. The apparatus could have been foiled. Though the trick was very old, only one long-dead magician had known how it was supposed to work. According to Charles Butler, that was why they called it Max Candle's Lost Illusion.

A balloon in the shape of a giant ice-cream cone smashed into a sharp tree branch and deflated to the cheers of jaded New York children.

And now Riker realized why Mallory hadn't asked for the case file on the fatal accident. She did not plan to challenge the work of another detective until she had something solid. So she was finally learning to play nicely with the troops. Well, this was progress, a breakthrough, and it deserved encouragement. He vowed not to bait her anymore.

"I still say it was an accident," he said, baiting her only a little.

Oh, shit.

Mallory had targeted a civilian. Her eyes were tracking him in the manner of a cat that had not been fed in days and days.

But why?

This youngster on the pavement was dressed like the men on the top hat stage. The lone magician seemed less out of place, not half as suspicious as the stilt-walkers and the strolling people in banana suits.

Mallory had locked eyes with her suspect and stopped him

cold. Could the boy tell from this distance that every muscle in her body was tensing to jump him? The young magician melded back into the mob of pedestrians; Riker remembered to exhale; and Mallory stood up, the better to keep track of her new pet mouse in the crowd.

Men and women of the mounted police had joined the parade astride seven trotting horses. The officers made a smart appearance in helmets, black leather jackets and riding boots. They carried poles bearing unfurled banners of police emblems. As they reined their mounts in a line across the boulevard, the banners whipped and cracked in the wind, and the horses snorted white clouds of breath.

The kamikaze pilot of a golf cart drove toward the center of this lineup, perhaps believing the horses would stand aside for him. They did not. The driver slammed on his brakes two feet from a stallion's knees. Riker winced as the self-important fool stood up behind the wheel of the cart. Puffing out the breast of his parade-staff jacket, he gestured with one waving arm, ordering the riders to move out of his way.

The mounted police officers turned their dark glasses down toward the general direction of the civilian and his golf cart. They were not focusing on him, but seemed only mildly distracted. All of them were dead still in the saddle. Formidable wooden truncheons hung from their belts, and heavier weapons rested in holsters. And now the riders turned their faces up to the sky. Cops only took orders from cops. Their unspoken message was clear: *If we notice you, we'll have to shoot you, won't we?*

The golf cart ran over the curb of the sidewalk in a hasty effort to get around them.

Tiny Santa's elves, with pointed ears and long red stocking caps, gathered around the mounted police, and the children's hands reached up to pet the horses. Nearby, a camera crew was setting up to shoot the top hat float, their lenses competing with roving civilian minicams. The news camera was turned toward the corner of the museum, where another balloon was caught up in a crosswind and dragging its handlers.

In the apartment building on 81st Street, children were

hanging out of windows, screaming and waving to a gigantic floating puppy, having recognized the bright golden character from their best-loved cartoon show. Even the elves had broken off their horse petting to jump up and down, pointing, yelling and waving to the balloon looming over them and casting a shadow as big as a circus tent. And he *was* magnificent, his great size trivializing all life on earth. Riker guessed the dog's collar must be thirty feet wide. The tail was easily the length of three limousines wagging in the wind and grazing a tenth-floor window.

The nearby gang of two-legged Christmas tree ornaments must also be children in disguise, for they were spooking the horses by spinning madly and leaping high in the air with excitement. The children's squeals vied with the cacophony of two marching bands, yet Mallory was undistracted from her suspect in the magician's costume. The boy had retreated behind the blue barricade on the sidewalk near a more familiar figure closer to Riker's age.

He waved to the chief medical examiner, who stood with his wife and young daughter. The man returned the wave and left his family to duck under the barricade.

"Morning, Riker." As Dr. Slope walked toward the float, he had the distinguished bearing of a stone-faced general, and he was just as brave. "Kathy," he yelled, risking a bullet to call her by her first name in front of all these cops. "The poker game is tomorrow night at Rabbi Kaplan's house. Can you make it?"

Mallory turned her face away from the suspect to look down at the medical examiner. "Are you old ladies still playing for chump change?"

Dr. Slope never missed a beat. "Are you still palming cards?"

"I never did that," said Mallory.

"We never *caught* you doing it," Dr. Slope corrected her. He turned around and cracked a smile for Riker. "She was thirteen the last time she took a chair in the game."

Riker grinned. "I heard about that little red wagon Markowitz bought her—so she could carry all her winnings home."

Dr. Slope feigned sudden deafness and turned back to Mallory. "Rabbi Kaplan wants you to come. Eight o'clock sharp. Can I tell him you'll be there?"

"I'm not playing any games with cute names or wild cards," said Mallory. "Straight poker or nothing."

"You got it," said Dr. Slope.

The wind pushed the golden dog balloon, and a platoon of handlers drifted with it, tiny ant-size leash holders trying to restrain the giant animal's gambol into the parade route. The wind bustled the dog into the lifelike enthusiasm of a real puppy. Legs with outsized paws stretched out in a goofy gallop. His bright red tongue hung low, and his eyes were wide. The huge mouth was fashioned in a joyous rubber-puppy grin.

On the stage of the top hat float, one of the old men was on his knees, arms extending toward a child, tossing out a yellow ball which had just materialized in his hands.

Riker and the camera crew were watching the balloon dog in the instant when an arrow hit the side of the giant top hat and shuddered with the vibration of sudden impact. The featherless metal shaft pinned the old man by his coattail.

A crossbow pistol disappeared under the red cape of the lone magician in the crowd. So the boy had come stealing back while they were distracted by Dr. Slope.

In the next second, Mallory's running shoes had hit the ground and she was gone.

Riker jumped off the edge of the float, jarring his bones on hard pavement. He was in motion without a prayer of catching up to his young partner. He kept track of Mallory and her fleeing suspect by the jerking ropes of balloon handlers being knocked aside like ninepins.

A gunshot banged out.

What in hell?

His stomach rose up and slammed down hard. With a rush of cold adrenaline, he put on some speed. What was Mallory thinking? She knew better than to fire a weapon in a crowd. Even a bullet shot into the air could take out innocent life, falling back to earth with enough velocity to penetrate a human skull.

All these little kids—Jesus.

Riker's heart was hammering against the wall of his chest, and his lungs were on fire. He slowed down to catch his breath, and now he could see a few out-of-towners in the crowd, mothers who held their children a little tighter. The real New Yorkers had not blinked when the gun went off. It was already forgotten, displaced by the racket of yet another high school marching band. The tiny screaming fans of the humongous dog were chanting, *"Goldy, Goldy, Goldy."*

When he caught up to his partner, she was sitting on top of the rogue magician and cuffing his hands behind his back. The crossbow lay on the pavement, harmless without its arrow. Her trench coat was wide open, flapping in the wind, and Riker could see that her revolver was already back in its holster. So her hunch had panned out. But there would be hell to pay for the gunfire. And something else troubled him.

What's wrong with this picture?

A police chase was the stuff of a New York sideshow. Every collar on the street was guaranteed an attentive audience. So Riker thought it odd that the crowd was staring up instead of down.

"Look at the puppy!" yelled a five-year-old boy from the sidewalk, and Riker obediently sought out the golden balloon. The behemoth's tail was losing air and hanging between the hind legs in a limp and mournful attitude. The great body listed to one side, leaning against the granite face of an apartment house. Tiny people on the balconies were running indoors, as though under attack, and Riker supposed they were. This tableau had all the makings of a vintage monster movie.

In a last act of lifelike animation, one wounded rubber paw reached out for a balcony, then lost its purchase and dipped low to graze the upper branches of a tree. The puppy's great head sagged against the twelfth floor of the stone facade and then lowered, flight by flight of windows. The rubber dog was going down, deflating, dying.

The five-year-old was pointing at Mallory. *"She* did it— the one with the big gun. She *shot* Goldy. She *killed* him!"

Mallory glared at the little boy, and Riker was treated to a glimpse of the ten-year-old Kathy he used to know. In her face was a child's rejoinder of *I did not!* The boy on the sidewalk wisely conceded the argument and hid behind his mother's coat.

A mounted policeman galloped up to Mallory and her prisoner. The cop was grinning as he reined in his horse and pointed to the damaged balloon. "Nice going, Detective."

The handlers were not holding the balloon down anymore, but running to get out from under the giant puppy as he lost helium and altitude.

"Yeah, Mallory," said the cop on horseback. "I never shot anything that big."

Riker stepped up to the mounted policeman and pulled rank. "Shut up, Henderson. That's an order. Just move along before she shoots your damn horse."

Mallory spoke to Riker's back. "I didn't do it."

Well, it was predictable that she would try to lie her way out of a suspension. Discharging firearms in a crowd was a serious violation, but shooting a balloon would cost her a great deal more. She was about to become the joke of NYPD, and Riker was already sorry for her.

The rest of the mounted officers converged on the scene, the hooves of six horses clattering on the pavement. Two men dismounted and took the prisoner into custody. They had missed Mallory's humiliation, but were just in time to witness Henderson's. His horse could cope with gunshots, but the sight of a huge dog falling from the sky was more than the startled animal could bear. The stallion reared up and dumped his rider on the road.

Two small children on the sidewalk were taunting Mallory, pointing their mittened fingers at her and chanting, *"You killed Goldy, you killed him, you killed him, you—"*

Mallory pulled out her .357 Smith & Wesson revolver.

The children stopped chanting.

She held out the weapon on the flat of her hand. "Touch it, Riker. The metal's cold. I *didn't* fire my gun. It never left my holster. There's a shooter in the crowd."

He did touch it. The metal was not warm. But the wind-chill factor of hard-blowing frigid air had tumbled the temperature below zero. How much time had elapsed? How long could a gun hold its heat?

He looked out over the faces in the dense crush of civilians behind the police barricades.

So many children.

Suppose Mallory was *not* lying?

Slowly, he turned his eyes to the thousand windows overlooking the parade route. A shooter in the crowd—but where? And where was that gun aiming now?

Two

THE UPPER HALF OF THE OFFICE WALL WAS A WINDOW ON THE squad room of Special Crimes. The environs were bleak. Gray file cabinets lined one grime-white wall, and a bank of dirty windows overlooked the SoHo street. Yet the atmosphere was suspiciously festive. There were no civilians in the house, not even clerical staff—only men with guns, milling around steel desks topped with computer monitors and piles of paperwork on fresh homicides.

Believing that his people worked better without a superior officer's eyes on them, Jack Coffey usually kept the blinds drawn—but not today. The lieutenant watched as ten grinning detectives gathered around the punch bowl on the center desk. Only five of them had been scheduled to work this holiday shift. None of their conversations penetrated the thick glass, but the tension came through. It hummed, it reeked.

What were they going to do to her?

Lieutenant Coffey was a man of average height and average features. Even his hair and eye color were in the middle range of brown. However, at thirty-six, he was uncommonly young for a command position, or so the brass at One Police Plaza had argued. Over the past year, stress had made inroads on a bald spot at the back of his head; he had acquired deep worry lines and a world of trouble in his eyes; and now his appearance was older, more appropriate to the job.

At the back of the private office, another man struck a

match and added a whiff of sulfur to the air, followed by a stream of gray smoke.

It would be nice if once—just once—Detective Sergeant Riker would ask for permission to light up a cigarette. Lieutenant Coffey bit back a reprimand as he stared at this detective's reflection in the glass. Riker was standing at attention, telegraphing the strain of the morning—waiting for the show to begin.

In the squad room beyond the window, men in shirtsleeves and shoulder holsters were ladling eggnog into paper cups and opening containers of Chinese take-out food. On the far side of the room, a pair of uniformed officers were keeping their distance from the detectives.

And that was another odd note.

The two men in uniform exchanged uneasy glances. Perhaps they also wondered why they were here. Patrol cops never partied with detectives; they wouldn't even drink in the same bars.

Invited as witnesses? Yes, that would fit, for now a detective was unwrapping a furry stuffed toy. It was a replica of the puppy Detective Mallory had recently dispatched to Balloon Heaven.

Lieutenant Coffey glanced over one shoulder. Detective Riker was leaning against the back wall, as if suddenly very tired. A hat brim shaded his eyes from the overhead lights. Riker must have plans for Thanksgiving dinner. He was stealing glances at his cheap watch, and he had not yet removed his new coat, which was not at all cheap.

"Nice material," said Coffey, whose own coat was from a discount store in New Jersey. "Very expensive. People will say you're on the take."

Riker smiled as he brushed a cigarette ash from the tweed lapel. "Mallory gave it to me."

"Don't tell *anyone*." There were enough rumors going around about his only female detective. Coffey turned back to the window on the squad room, where his detectives perched on the edges of desks, sharing foxy smiles and watching the door. The two patrol cops traded looks of deep discomfort. Coffey knew they would rather be downstairs with the other uniforms.

He could roughly guess what was going to happen next. Without looking away from the glass, he spoke to the man behind him. "You know she won't get off easy this time."

"Mallory says she didn't do it."

"I expected that from her. But what about you, Riker? You know better. She's lying."

"The gun was cold."

"The day was cold." Coffey turned around to face his sergeant. "Even if the gun test comes back negative, that won't clear her—not with me. You never searched her for a backup piece, did you?"

Riker's slow smile said, *Silly question.*

In the squad room on the other side of the glass, a man grabbed up the telephone, listened for a moment, then made the thumbs-up gesture to the other detectives. And now they were all converging on the stairwell door.

Ambush.

The desk sergeant must have warned them that Mallory was on her way upstairs.

Show time.

Today the world would stop revolving around Markowitz's daughter. She had gone to the limit of her old man's influence.

Detective Riker walked over to the window and followed the action with his eyes. He would do nothing to warn his partner. Even the late Inspector Markowitz would not have tried to stop this. It might be Mallory's last chance to come into the fold. So much depended on how she reacted.

She had no friends among those men lying in wait by the door. They saw her as an outsider, never drinking or breaking bread with other cops. Perhaps the worst offense was keeping her own counsel; her silence fueled their paranoia. In the tight community of police, every loner was suspect.

The two uniformed officers were hanging back, wanting no part in this.

Why?

The stairwell door was opening. He could see curls of blond hair beyond the tight press of bodies. The wall of armed men parted to form a gauntlet, giving Coffey a clear view of the toy dog, a perfect replica of the Goldy balloon. It lay on the floor, bleeding catsup from a mortal wound. A white chalk mark had been drawn around the furry body—all decked out like a corpse at a crime scene.

Mallory was looking down at the stuffed animal when the detectives screamed in unison, "I didn't do it!"

Mallory's slogan.

Her head remained bowed, eyes fixed on the toy. She stiffened slightly when a detective taped a giant paper star on her shoulder. The bold print of a felt-tip marker read: "The only good puppy is a dead puppy."

Any second now, she would explode—or she would work it out. The men were popping off the balls of their feet, finding this tension delicious, God's gift to all the detectives of the Special Crimes Unit. A true day of thanksgiving.

Aw, Mallory, no.

She was looking up at them now, wearing a broad smile that was radiant—and pure Markowitz, a damn ghost of the old man. There had been no resemblance between father and foster child—absolutely none. Yet this was the inspector, back from the grave and charming everyone in the room.

Oh, Jesus, this is criminal.

Mallory had even captured mannerisms, tugging on her right earlobe as she focused on every man in turn, making each one the center of the universe and special in her eyes—Markowitz's eyes. How many hours had she labored in front of a mirror, coldly perfecting this impersonation—and why?

Coffey stared at his detectives, all but Riker, who had turned away from the window, not wanting to see this anymore. Her cheap magic act was working on all the others. Their faces were full of delight, their own smiles saying, *Well, hello again, old man.*

It was shocking to see Markowitz alive in Mallory—and obscene. How conniving and maniacal.

How smart.

She might learn all her lessons the hard way, but she did adapt with inhuman cunning and speed.

The men were grinning, all cops together now, laughing and slapping backs, aiming light, good-natured punches to her arms. Mallory the loner had won them over with charisma stolen from a dead man. The only woman on this squad was finally one of the boys—just what Coffey had hoped for, and he damned her to hell for the way she had pulled it off.

He threw open the door and yelled, "Mallory! Get your ass in here!"

The mood of the room shifted abruptly, and he was met with sullen glares from every cop, including the pair in uniform.

Oh, great. Just great. Now it was all of them and Mallory against himself. Ah, but payback, fresh ridicule, was only as far away as tomorrow's press release. And now he looked forward to telling her about the crossbow shooter.

She walked toward the door, taking her own time, so as not to give the impression that she was acting on a direct order from a commanding officer. The smile dropped away as she crossed the threshold of his office. The show was over.

He slammed the door and sat down behind his desk. "Mallory, you're going to take a little vacation for a while."

She removed the paper star from her shoulder. "I don't have any vacation time left."

"I know that." He made a show of moving papers around on his blotter, unwilling to meet her eyes until his anger subsided. "Call it a little gift from Commissioner Beale." Over the edge of his desk, he watched the legs of her designer jeans folding into the chair beside Riker's. She wore new running shoes, and he knew that brand—two hundred dollars a pop. The long leather trench coat parted as she crossed her legs. And how much had that tailored item cost?

"I can't take any time off." Mallory shot the crumpled paper star into the wastebasket next to his desk. "I'm working a full caseload."

Her voice was too confident, and he was about to change that. "Not anymore."

His attention shifted to the long ash on Riker's cigarette. It was perilously close to dropping on the floor. It had taken three months of requisitions to get the new carpet. A cloud of smoke drifted across the desk, and he wondered if Riker was deliberately distracting him with this flanking maneuver of fresh aggravation. Coffey turned to Mallory. Her face was absent the sham warmth of Markowitz.

If a machine had eyes . . .

"You're off duty until this shit dies down, and that may take a while." He picked up a sheet of quotes from the parade broadcast and handed it to her. "America's most famous cartoon character was gunned down in the street—by a cop. Parents are gonna use your name to scare their kids into behaving."

"Yeah," said Riker, rousing from lethargy. "I can hear the mommies now—'Clean up your room, or Detective Mallory will shoot your dog.' "

The phone jangled, and Coffey picked up the receiver midring. This was the call he had been waiting for. He listened for a moment, then said, "Put him through." And now a technician was delivering a dry recital of test results produced in record time. Normally, Special Crimes only got this kind of service when a cop killed a human.

Mallory was reading the quotes of the newscasters. Was her stomach knotting up? He hoped so.

"This is bogus," she said. "I did *not* fire my gun in—"

"Oh yeah?" Coffey covered the phone's mouthpiece with one hand. "There's a bullet missing from your gun." He turned to her partner and tossed a sheaf of stapled, badly typed text into the sergeant's lap. "Riker, you forgot to mention that little detail in your report. Fix it." He spoke to his caller: "What else? . . . Hold on." He cupped the receiver again. "The tech says the gun was fired recently."

Riker looked up from his paperwork. "I bet they can't pin it down within twenty-four hours."

Coffey pretended not to hear that, because it was true. As he thanked the technician for the holiday overtime, he was making a mental note of what Mallory was costing the Special Crimes budget.

"My gun was fired yesterday," she said. "Not this morning."

"What were you—"

"Lieutenant?" Riker slowly shook his head. "You don't want to know."

"The hell I don't." Well, actually, he didn't. There was a lot to be said for deniability in copland politics. Coffey turned his attention back to Mallory. "Out of all the balloons in the parade, why did you have to shoot a dog—a *puppy,* for Christ's sake."

"Yeah, Mallory." Riker's head was bowed over the papers in his hand. "That was cold. Why not shoot that annoying woodpecker you never liked?"

"I *didn't—*"

"Right." If NYPD could not prove it, she did not do it— Coffey knew that old song. But this time he had witnesses. "I've got statements from people who saw you fire your gun."

"Damn civilians." Riker's pencil was moving over lines of text. "They hear a car backfire, and then they see a gun that isn't there." He looked up at Coffey. "And who says the balloon was shot? Another balloon went down when a tree branch ripped it."

The lieutenant opened the center drawer of his desk and pulled out a videotape. He held it up to Riker. "For a joke, one of the reporters asked Dr. Slope to examine the dead balloon. Well, his kid's with him, right? I guess he thought it might be fun for Faye. So, to quote our chief medical examiner, 'Yup, that's a bullet wound all right.' " Coffey dropped the tape in the drawer and slammed it shut. "They've got film of Dr. Slope bending over this pile of rubber, explaining how the edges of the holes are more consistent with bullets than trees."

"Good," said Mallory. "That backs me up. The guy with the crossbow wasn't the only shooter in the crowd."

This was the moment Coffey had been waiting for. He leaned toward her, not even trying to suppress his happiness. "The crossbow shooter was hired by the magicians on the float. The kid was part of the act, Mallory—a publicity stunt. The old guys *paid* him to do it."

It was not hard to read her face. She reminded him of the children on the parade films, eyes turned skyward, watching the giant puppy deflate—a startled wide-eyed look followed by an expression of *Oh, shit.*

Two screwups in one day.

She was shaking her head in denial. "No. If it was faked, Charles Butler would've—"

"Charles didn't know," said Coffey. "I talked to him myself. The old guys didn't tell him what was coming. Said they didn't trust him to act surprised. They wanted the genuine article for maximum effect."

"That fits," said Riker, nodding. "Charles can't hide a thing with that face of his. The way that poor bastard loses at poker. Behind his back, Dr. Slope calls him *the bank.*"

"I want to see that crossbow shooter," said Mallory.

"Too late." Coffey was not smiling now. "The West Side dicks kicked him loose twenty minutes ago. We'll be lucky if he doesn't sue the city. So you don't go anywhere *near* the kid." He rapped his knuckles on the desk to make sure she was paying attention. "That's an order, Mallory. Don't even think about crossing me. You can't afford one more violation."

Her voice was almost mechanical, giving equal weight to every word. "There was another shooter in that crowd."

"What if there was?" Coffey shrugged. "The parade has passed by. It's over. Who the hell cares?"

Well, *she* cared. That was obvious. Mallory was shredding the sheet of press quotes into tiny pieces. Not one scrap escaped the lap of her cashmere blazer. She was freakishly neat.

"There must be a witness on my side. I never drew my gun." Mallory stood up and deposited the confetti in his wastebasket, and she also took this opportunity to scan everything on his desk.

He riffled through the paperwork and picked up an affidavit signed by a taxpayer. "This is my personal favorite." Riker's report had described the witness as a punk kid with too many earrings and a bad attitude toward cops. "This guy swore he saw you aim the gun at the balloon. And then he heard you say, 'Take that, you evil puppy from hell.'"

Mallory did not get the joke, but Coffey was grinning, his life was complete. She had no more possible comebacks.

He had not anticipated a sniper shot from her partner.

"She had good reason to go after the kid with the crossbow. It wasn't a toy," said Riker. "Crossbows are illegal in—"

"He had a performance permit signed by the damn mayor." Coffey waved the paperwork faxed from the West Side precinct.

"And she was supposed to read that through his back pocket while he was running away? And what about that old guy who died last week? The Central Park magic show? He was killed with crossbows—*four* of 'em."

"Okay," said Coffey. "The arrest was a righteous call. But don't tell me you're going for a connection to the park accident."

Mallory sat down and leaned back in her chair, suddenly more cheerful—always a bad sign. "What if it wasn't an accident? Suppose I can prove Oliver Tree was murdered?"

Coffey had a problem with that. Mallory was too hot to get clear of the balloon assassination. She might cheat the pieces to come up with a diversion. "No way. It's a closed case. Accidental death, cut and dried."

"When did anyone *ever* die in a cheesy magic act?"

She had a good point, but he would never admit it—not to her. "There's no reason to question another detective's report, not unless you enjoy making enemies. So forget it. And now there's still the little matter of a bullet missing from your gun."

"Mallory fired her gun yesterday," said Riker, with great reluctance. "I found four witnesses, all patrol cops."

Coffey made a rolling motion with his hand. "Come on, what's the rest of it?"

"She killed Oscar the Wonder Rat. Picked him right off the top of the candy machine in the lunchroom." Riker pointed one finger like a gun barrel and cocked his thumb to fire. "Single shot."

No, no, no!

Coffey stared at the ceiling for a moment, outwardly

calm, inwardly screaming at Mallory, *Are you nuts? Totally nuts?*

"Okay, Riker. Leave the missing bullet out of the paperwork. I don't want the reporters to know she gunned down a rat with a pet name."

He had to wonder about those four uniformed officers who had watched her pull a weapon inside the station house. What had gone through their minds when they heard a gunshot in the one place where they were supposed to feel safe? Most cops would have twenty-year careers without ever firing a gun on duty.

Had the uniforms downstairs already pegged her as a loose cannon? In that paranoia unique to cops, were they watching her more closely now? And how long would it be before the rat story crossed the line between the patrolmen and his detectives?

And now he understood why those two men in uniform had not taken part in humiliating Mallory. Cop, accountant or postman, the rules were the same: It was not a sane idea to antagonize a dangerous coworker.

The uniforms would find another way to deal with her.

Mallory was pulling papers from the deep pockets of her trench coat. She unfolded a sheet of text and set it on his desk blotter. It bore the masthead of the tax assessor's office, and by the date, this information was a week old.

"Oliver Tree left an estate worth millions," she said. "That's just the tangible property. I haven't even looked for cash holdings yet."

In Malloryspeak, this meant she had the bank statements, but he would not like her method of acquisition, and neither would the bank appreciate her computer skills, her high-tech lock-picking.

Riker was leaning forward to stare at the list of property holdings, clearly surprised by this information. So Mallory was a week late in sharing the money motive with her own partner. Well, that was typical.

She tapped the sheet with one red fingernail. "Forty years ago, the old man bought up a row of condemned brownstones. Got them for a song and did the renovations himself.

He still owned three of them when he died. And he owned a small theater in a prime real estate location." On top of this paperwork, she laid down her own report on the parade shooting. "The crossbow shooter was related to Oliver Tree. I don't know how he figured in the old man's will—not yet."

By the look on Riker's face, he was also hearing this for the first time.

Coffey scanned the lines of text underscored in red ink. The bowman's name was Richard Tree, nephew of the magician who had died a week ago—killed by four arrows.

She laid a three-year-old arrest report on top of this sheet. "The nephew has a juvenile record for drugs. Maybe the parade stunt was a fake. But a junkie would kill his own mother for cash, and that kid was in the park the day his uncle died. So I've got motive and opportunity." And then, as if she had read his mind, she added, "I didn't raid sealed juvie records. I talked to the cop who busted him."

Of course, she had found that officer's name in a raid on sealed juvenile records, but Coffey let that slide.

"I like money motives, too." Riker was looking at his wristwatch again as he stood up and buttoned his coat. He averted his face, hiding the anger from his partner. There were many lessons that Mallory had yet to learn, but apparently Riker intended to handle this one privately. One hand was on the doorknob when he glanced back at Coffey. "I'm sure the mayor's office wants the park death to stay accidental. High murder stats are bad for tourism. But you know she's got something here."

Coffey sat back in his chair, not surprised that Riker would back his partner, even if he thought this was crap, and he probably did.

"Mallory, we're running late," said Riker.

She looked down at her pocket watch, not trusting him with the time of day. "I need the West Side report on Oliver Tree. Everything from the detective who caught the case. I want statements, evidence—"

"Not so fast." Coffey pushed her sheets back across the desk. "First you check out these leads—discreetly. Riker will do *all* the interviews. Officially, you're on vacation. You got

that, Mallory? You don't interrogate *anybody*. If you get anything solid, *then* we'll talk about stepping on toes in another
precinct. Oh, and I'm keeping your gun for a while."

Mallory didn't like that, but she was clearly going to eat it.
And why not? She had other guns at home. He believed she
only carried a private cannon because the police-issue .38
didn't make big enough holes. She stood up and cinched the
belt of her trench coat, electing not to press her luck by staying any longer.

"Sit down, Detective," said Coffey. "I'm not done with
you."

Between a dead rat and a punctured balloon, Mallory had
done herself a lot of damage, but she couldn't see it yet. She
was standing too far outside the closed society of cops.

He waited until she had settled back into the chair, then
slammed his hand on the desk with enough force to send
pencils and pens rolling off the edge. "Don't you *ever* pull a
gun inside this station house again! Even if you don't get off
one bullet—if you only pull the gun out of your holster—I
will *fire* your ass!"

Behind her back, Riker's face was solemn as he nodded in
rare agreement with Coffey. Mallory could not afford to learn
every lesson by hard experience. She would not survive.

Coffey let his words settle in for a moment and then
pressed on. "That stunt with the rat? That's gonna come back
on you. You *don't* want the reputation of a gun-happy
screwup. It makes other cops nervous. Those uniforms who
watched the rat get shot? Now they're gonna be watching
you, Mallory—waiting for more evidence that you're dangerously nuts. And then, one day, you'll be in trouble. You're
gonna look around for backup from the uniforms—and they
won't be there."

Fellow cops might hear her calls for help on the radios of a
dozen police cars, but they would turn stone deaf and let her
die alone—waiting for them.

"No cop will raise a gun to you," said Coffey. "They'll sit
back and let some perp do that part. But you'll be just as
dead."

Welcome to the darker side of NYPD.

Mallory was angry now, taking this as a threat. And she was right about that. Coffey turned to his senior detective for another kind of backup.

Riker came at Mallory from behind as she was rising. His hands pressed on her shoulders to gently force her back down to the chair. "You'll appreciate this, kid—since you're such a fanatic about neatness." Head bent low, his voice was soft, almost a whisper. "Back when I was in uniform and a cop went down that way—we called it 'good housekeeping.' "

Three

A WHITE TIE HUNG LOOSE AROUND CHARLES BUTLER'S OPEN collar. The sleeves of his dress shirt were rolled to the elbow, and his foot tapped in harmony with a Vivaldi mandolin concerto.

The kitchen was his favorite room, and today it fed all his senses. Sunlight brightened the yellow walls, set copper pots to gleaming and sparkled off chrome pans and spice jars. The air was ripe with the smell of fresh-baked bread slathered in garlic butter, and the aroma of roast turkey wafted up from the oven door. As Charles reached for the basting brush, he realized that his guest held an empty glass.

"Sorry, Nick." He searched the countertop, hunting for the recently uncorked wine amid the jumble of jars and plates, but the bottle was gone. Perhaps someone had taken it into the front room. He reached for another one from the case on the table.

"No need, Charles." The older man shook out a large dinner napkin, laid it on the chopping block, and as he delicately used two fingers to draw up the material, an open bottle of red wine materialized at the center of the wooden square.

Just like old times. Charles had been a small boy the last time Nick Prado came to dinner. Thirty years ago, this man's hair had been lustrous black. Now it was a sparse iron gray. And his dark Spanish eyes had faded to an ordinary brown.

"When is Malakhai coming?" Nick's Latin accent was gone without a trace, and this was another disconcerting effect of time. The flavor was leaving every aspect of the man.

"Malakhai phoned his regrets." Charles filled two wine-glasses. Though he towered over most people, it felt odd to be looking down at Nick, trading statures with the elder man who had once bowed his head to speak with a child-size Charles.

Nick turned to the wall rack of cooking utensils and admired his reflection in the chrome of a frying pan lid. Though he could well afford cosmetic dental work, he still had his natural teeth, evidenced by the gaps of receding gums and the yellow stains of a lifelong tobacco habit. Judging by the smile that showed every tooth to the frying pan lid, he must perceive his aged enamel as a sign of continuing virility, for despite the fading, the graying and the yellowing, this was still authentically Nick Prado in all his original parts. Apparently, the paunch at his belt line did not adversely affect this good opinion. He patted it now in a compliment to himself.

Another guest appeared in the kitchen, but only his head and a stretch of neck as he checked round the edge of the door to see that no one was there before he opened it wider. Franny Futura smiled, and his eyes became slits of gray, disappearing into the folds above them and the bags below. He stepped into the room and lightly tap-danced across the tiles, as if the floor might be hot. He was led to the oven by an upturned sniffing nose. "Oh, Charles, it smells wonderful." On a sadder note, he added, "We're out of hors d'oeuvres again."

The Frenchman spoke perfect English. And he was such a clean man, as if some insane housekeeper had been at him with an arsenal of solvents and powders, scrubbing his skin to a raw pink and scouring his dentures until they were too white to pass for the real thing.

Charles had met him only one week ago, but he guessed there had never been much of a chin to support Franny Futura's face, and now the flesh fell past it to hang in a loose wattle. The slicked-back hair of his scalp was white, but his thick eyebrows had been made young again with black dye.

Franny stood at the kitchen counter, refilling his wineglass and carefully rolling the bottle to avoid spilling a single drop. "That lovely girl has disappeared."

"Mallory?" Charles dipped his basting brush in a pan of melted butter. "She's probably in her office across the hall. She'll be back."

"An office across the hall?" Nick Prado reluctantly turned away from his reflection. "But you said she was a *real* police detective. What's she—"

"She's a silent partner in my consulting firm." Of course, the word *silent* stood for *covert*. NYPD frowned on moonlighting and flatly forbade outside employment that required investigative skills.

"So, Charles, how does that work again?" asked Nick. "This business of yours?"

"Well, institutes and universities send me people with interesting gifts. I evaluate them, and Mallory does all the computer work and background checks. She takes the raw data and—"

"Fascinating," said Nick.

But Charles could tell it was not at all interesting to either man. He was boring his guests. "Now Mallory's regular job is miles more intriguing. She's a—"

"Pretty girl, fabulous eyes," said Nick. "And that hair. I've always been partial to blondes. Is she married?"

"Oh, right, you old fool." Franny Futura grinned. "As if you had a shot."

Charles hoped they would not speculate on his own chances with Mallory. He could imagine the sad shake of their heads as they estimated the great size of his nose in inverse proportion to his slim prospects. Not that he was overly sensitive about the large hook growing in the center of his face, but he was constantly aware of it. No matter where he turned his eyes, there it was.

Nick Prado was uncorking another bottle. "So, why didn't you introduce her last week? At Oliver's funeral?"

"What?" Charles turned away from the chore of basting. "I didn't see her there." And since she had never met Oliver Tree, he had to wonder *why* she was there. "Are you sure it was Mallory?"

"Oh, yes. I saw her, too." Franny opened the door. "She was in the back of the crowd taking photographs."

Nick picked up the wine bottle as he followed his friend out of the room, saying, "I wonder if she got any good pictures of me."

When Charles had finished with the turkey and closed the oven, he glanced through the open doorway for a narrow view of the dining room. Mallory had returned. She was walking around the long table. He watched her resetting the plates and silverware with machine precision. If he took a ruler to the place settings, he knew they would be equidistant to within the smallest fraction of an inch. And all the knives, forks and spoons would make perfect right angles with the edges of the lace tablecloth.

Nick Prado approached Mallory, holding a full wineglass in each hand. He sucked in the paunch at his belt and vamped her with a slow smile, displaying all the gaps between his nicotine-stained teeth, no doubt believing that she would find this attractive, possibly seductive, for they were his own teeth, weren't they?

Mallory accepted a glass of red wine, then resumed the chore of compulsive silverware straightening.

"May I call you Kathy?" Nick was asking.

"No one calls me Kathy." Done with the silver, she turned her back on him and walked away, probably off to straighten the picture frames in the next room.

The smile evaporated. Nick must see Mallory's behavior as incomprehensible rudeness. When he got to know her better, he might appreciate the fact that she had used five words instead of the standard *no*. She was evidently on best behavior for the holiday.

Charles waited a tactful minute for the older man to recover his dignity, to rationalize away her rejection, perhaps assuming that the woman who owned three guns was merely shy. When Nick had walked off to rejoin the rest of the company, Charles carried a plate of appetizers through the dining area and into the front room. Four tall windows flooded the parlor with afternoon light, enriching the colors of Tiffany lampshades and the Oriental pattern of the carpet. Large canvases of abstract art hung on every wall, blending remarkably well with the antique furnishings.

Detective Sergeant Riker sprawled at one end of the Belter sofa, all settled in with his beer and cigarettes. He looked more natural now that he had undone his tie and further creased his suit. Half an hour ago, when Charles greeted him at the door, the policeman's fine new coat had created the immediate impression of a rich man whose hat and shoes had been in a terrible accident.

Pointedly ignoring Riker, Mallory settled into an armchair opposite the couch. Charles wondered if he was reading too much into the strained behavior of the two detectives. They had arrived together and not—awkward as strangers meeting in a hallway for the first time.

Mallory was speaking with Franny Futura. She had already trained him to call her by her last name, sans Miss or Ms. "You were the one who did the parade stunt with the crossbow." This was not phrased as polite conversation.

"Well, I staged it, yes." Franny's head wobbled a bit, suddenly insecure on its pinion. He had no way to know that Mallory was egalitarian, regarding everyone with equal suspicion.

"Why a crossbow?"

"You think it might have been a bit much?" Franny moved back, pressing his body into the couch upholstery. "I mean— the similarity to Oliver's death."

"That was the idea, wasn't it?"

Franny flinched, as if she had accused him of something more heinous. Charles hovered over the man's chair, wondering if he should run interference. Mallory had a difficult time switching out of the interrogation mode for social occasions, so she never bothered to try.

"But the stunt wasn't *my* idea," said Franny. "Nick hired him. The boy was supposed to aim the crossbow when the float rolled past the first television camera. But then this camera crew set up right next to the . . ." His words trailed off as she looked away, losing interest in him.

Nick Prado was her new target. He was settling into the

chair next to hers when she turned on him. "Why did you hire
that crossbow shooter?"

"Considering the way Oliver died, that *was* in poor taste,
wasn't it?" He smiled in self-congratulation. "I've prostituted
my talents as a publicist." Indeed, Nick was a self-described
publicity whore and the owner of the largest public relations
firm in his hometown of Chicago.

"You knew he was Oliver Tree's nephew," said Mallory, as
if she had already caught him in a lie.

"Of course I did," said Nick. "The boy needed money. And
the stunt gave his uncle a few more minutes of fame on the
evening news." He leaned toward Mallory with a delicious
stage leer.

This was a tense moment for Charles. Nick's face was
entirely too close to Mallory's. With great relief, he left the
room to answer the doorbell. When he returned to the parlor with the last dinner guest, another Frenchman, Nick
Prado was still alive, and Mallory was focused on Franny
again.

"You were the one who got hit by the arrow." This was a
fact, but she had fashioned it into an accusation.

"Was he?" The late arrival, Emile St. John, entered the circle of conversation, looming over everyone but Charles. This
was the eldest magician, close to eighty, but he seemed
younger than his two friends. A deep tan and the faint outline
of ski goggles gave him a look of robust good health.

There had been no time for formal introductions at the
parade, and now, as Emile shook hands with Riker, Mallory
was frankly appraising the man's silver hair styled by a master barber, and he had changed his parade costume for a gray
suit tailored by another maestro.

Emile sat down in the George III side chair, creating a
buffer between Mallory and her interrogation subject. His
placid blue eyes settled on Franny with a smiling benedic-
tion, instantly calming the smaller man. "I thought Nick was
supposed to get shot this morning."

"Well, he wouldn't get up on the stage," said Franny in a
voice of complaint. "So *I* had to do it." He offered Mallory a

weak smile of solicitation, seeking only to appease her. "The crossbow trick was perfectly harmless—really it was. We weren't being reckless with public safety." His hand drifted up to his mouth. "Oh, sorry." Apparently, he had just remembered that the young detective stood accused of being wildly reckless in public.

Nick Prado edged his chair closer to Mallory's. "You upstaged us with that chase scene. It was wonderful publicity for the magic festival."

"Oh, yes." Franny brightened. "And when you shot the balloon—"

"I *didn't* shoot the balloon," said Mallory.

"No, of course you didn't." Franny inched down the sofa toward the more amiable Riker. "So sorry to have brought it up."

Mallory faced Nick. "You weren't on the float when that gun went off. What did he mean when he said you wouldn't get on—"

"Am I a suspect?" Nick seemed delighted at the prospect. "All right, *I* shot the big puppy. I'm yours." He held out his wrists, awaiting manacles. "Take me away—please? No?" He grabbed up her hand with the intention of kissing it, but she was faster, jerking her arm back.

For a moment, Charles feared that Mallory would wipe her hand on a cocktail napkin. She seemed to find the man that distasteful.

Smiling and serene, Emile St. John looked up as Charles passed him a plate of hors d'oeuvres. "Malakhai's not here yet?"

"He'll be in late this evening." Charles sat down beside Nick Prado and worked over the cork of another wine bottle.

Birdlike, Franny Futura cocked his head to one side. "*Why* is Malakhai coming?"

"He was invited to the festival." Nick reached over Mallory's lap on the pretext of robbing the hors d'oeuvres plate. His arm brushed her thighs. Her expression was lethal, but she did nothing to harm him.

"Well, he's always invited to these things," said Franny. "But he never actually shows up."

"Malakhai?" Riker roused from his comfortable slouch and leaned into the conversation. "I know that name—Charles's friend. He lives in the bughouse, right?"

"Please don't call it that." Charles freed the cork and poured out a glass for Emile St. John.

"Sorry—the *nut*house." Riker smiled at Mallory. "And you thought I wasn't well brought up."

She had yet to acknowledge, by glance or word, that Riker was in the same room.

"Malakhai owns the building," said Nick. "Quite an impressive old mansion. He leases it to a private hospital and keeps a suite of rooms for himself. Lives there with his dead wife."

Riker sipped his beer. "So he's still crazy."

"No!" said Charles.

"Oh, yes he is." Nick laughed. "Mad as they come, but in a very original way. The dead wife was part of his magic act."

"Neat trick," said Riker. "But highly illegal."

"There was no corpse on stage." Emile St. John set his glass on the coffee table. "The audience couldn't actually see Louisa."

"An invisible woman." Riker slugged back the last of his beer. "Crazier and crazier." He wandered off toward the kitchen in search of the six-pack he had brought with him.

Franny called after Riker, "He knows Louisa is dead. It's an act."

"Is it?" said Nick. "You haven't seen Malakhai since the war, have you? He lives with that dead woman. He sleeps with her, too." He inclined his head toward Mallory and flashed a wide smile. "He even makes love to her. She's younger than you are, and he's well into his seventies. It gives one hope."

Riker returned with a full beer can and sat down beside Franny on the couch. "How long has this been going on?"

"As I recall," said Emile St. John, "he put Louisa into the act right after the Korean War."

Mallory inched her chair away from Nick and closer to Emile. "Charles said the wife died in World War II."

"Oh, she did," said Emile. "But years later, Malakhai found her again in a Korean POW camp."

"Korea. That was my dad's war," said Riker.

Mallory stared at Emile, still behaving as though Riker did not exist. "What do you mean he *found* her?"

"Torture," said Riker, insisting that he *did* exist on the same planet with Mallory. "My dad came out of one of those camps with a few strange quirks. So that's how Malakhai lost his marbles. Poor bastard."

"Perhaps." Emile seemed to ponder this. "But I might argue that he's saner now. At least, he's more at peace. Between those two wars, Malakhai was the saddest man on earth." He turned to Mallory. "It's hard for an American your age to imagine the aftermath of a global war. Your cities didn't turn into craters, did they? None of your roads or landmarks disappeared."

Emile paused to sip his wine, and the rest of the company waited on him. Even Mallory recognized the authority of a natural storyteller. It was as old as the cave.

"In postwar Europe, so many souls were unaccounted for—misplaced in relocation camps, dead—or wandering. Refugees were on the road for years, hunting family members. You might be walking down a busy street in London or Rome, and you'd see one of these people staring into every face on the sidewalk—looking for someone lost in the war.

"Malakhai was like that in the late forties and early fifties. It was painful to watch him perform on stage. Sometimes he just stared at the audience. He'd gone blank, lost his place in the act. And then I knew he'd seen some red-haired woman sitting out there in the dark. Louisa was long gone by then, years dead, and he knew that. But he was still looking for her in every crowd.

"In the next war, he found her in a North Korean prison cell, five feet square. No room to stand up or lie down. They kept him in that cage for a year. He went into it alone and came out with the lovely Louisa. What a wonderful magician."

Franny was nodding. "She was lovely, wasn't she?" He turned to Riker. "And a musical prodigy. Thank God, her concerto survived the war." He lifted his glass. "I propose a toast to Louisa and her music."

"And to increased record sales," said Nick. "May *Louisa's Concerto* pay royalties forever."

Mallory joined the toast, still nursing the same wine that Nick had fetched for her. She never drank more than an ounce of alcohol at one sitting. Charles guessed she was unwilling to lose any amount of control to inebriation.

"Oliver loved Louisa, too. He adored her." Emile's glass was rising again. "To unrequited love."

Charles lifted his own wineglass to Mallory, hoping the gesture would be lost on her, for she had been known to laugh on two or three occasions. Though she never laughed loudly, not with a fully involved set of lungs. Another control issue, he supposed.

Riker hoisted his beer in salute, and then let it hang in the air for a moment. He had suddenly remembered to ask the eternal policeman's question. "How did Louisa die?"

"No one knows," said Nick. "She could've been shot for a spy or hit by a bus."

Riker was incredulous. "You never asked?"

Mallory showed no more interest in this conversation. She had already heard the punch line to this setup. Charles had told her long ago, and now he repeated it for Riker. "No use in asking. Malakhai can't tell anyone how his wife died. That's spelled out in his recording contract. The music company thought a mystery would sell more copies of *Louisa's Concerto*."

✛   ✛   ✛

When they were all gathered in the dining room, Charles sat at one end of the table, directing the traffic of bowls, platters and bottles of wine. Emile St. John sat at the other end, which instantly became the head of the table. The man had an aura of authority that did not fit the magician's trade.

Leaving this puzzle for the moment, Mallory looked across the table at Riker. He was only picking at his food, shifting with discomfort and looking sad.

Well, good.

Though never one to complain about betrayal, Mallory did

keep score. She was done punishing him for siding with Coffey and the dead rat, but she would be slow to forgive. As he passed her a platter of dark meat, she met his eyes for the first time this afternoon. "That was real smart, Riker—wearing a pre-spotted tie to dinner."

"Yeah." The detective looked down to admire the red stain, a souvenir of another meal. "It takes all the work out of being a slob." He was relaxing now, taking her sarcastic overture as a truce. He turned to Emile St. John, who was flanked by Franny Futura and Nick Prado. "So they're letting Malakhai out of the nuthouse. Is he bringing his dead wife to town?"

"He never goes anywhere without her." Emile passed a salad bowl to Mallory. "She was a gifted composer, a wunderkind. I'm sure Charles has mentioned *Louisa's Concerto?*"

She nodded. Charles had done more than mention it. He had raved about it, going on at great length, believing that she might be paying attention. He loved only classical pieces. She loved everything else. Thanks to her insanely musical foster father, Mallory could name every bandleader of the swing era, every jazz musician of note, all the blues artists and the stars of rock 'n' roll, but she did not know a concerto from a sonata. If one could not dance to the music, it was not in Mallory's vocabulary.

"I knew Louisa during the war," said Nick Prado. "World War II, now that was a time. Oh, Emile, you'll love this. Malakhai's doing his old act at Carnegie Hall. A symphony orchestra is going to play the concerto."

"But Malakhai wasn't mentioned in the advance publicity," said St. John.

"Late booking." Charles rose from the table. "Some diva caught a cold and canceled a performance. Back in a minute. I'm just going to change the record."

Mallory was watching Riker's face. She could guess what was going on behind his bloodshot eyes. He was probably mulling over the events of the day. Had he put it together yet, the conflict of motive and style? The money motive for Oliver Tree's nephew, who loved drugs, didn't fit her earlier profile of a thrill kill for the love of spectacle.

Her partner must be wondering if she had spun him a story during the parade this morning. Or did she spin one for Lieutenant Coffey this afternoon? Might both versions be fairy tales?

Confused, Riker?

The music was playing at the low level of a backdrop for dinner conversation. The ancient record player had been brought up from the basement so Charles could play requests from Max Candle's store of vintage albums. She dated the last Artie Shaw album to 1943. Now she was listening to *Lady Sings the Blues,* automatically crediting lyrics to the singer Billie Holiday, and the music to Herbie Nichols.

"For Malakhai," said Charles, returning to the table. "This is one of his favorites."

Apparently, the absent Malakhai had a penchant for dead women, but he had at least ventured into the fifties. Mallory could place this recording in the autumn years of the artist's short life.

Franny Futura had downed two glasses of wine and lost his nervous mannerisms. With a table between himself and Mallory, he was less the mouse. She handed him a peace offering, a bowl of cranberry sauce.

"Tell me how long you've known Oliver Tree." She had softened her voice to make this sound less like an order.

"I knew him when we were teenagers in Europe."

"Europe?" Riker turned to the man seated beside him. "I thought the little guy was a carpenter from Brooklyn."

"Yes, by way of Paris," said Futura. "But Oliver was originally from Nebraska. When his parents died, he was sent to France to live with his grandmother, Faustine. We all started out at Faustine's Magic Theater. Max Candle and Malakhai too."

"So Oliver Tree had a lot of experience in magic." Mallory directed a condescending smile at Riker. This killed his theory of death by incompetence. "He was a good magician."

"Oh, no. He was the worst," said Nick Prado. "A good carpenter. He made fine props. But Oliver was terrible at magic."

And now Riker was smiling, and Mallory was not.

"Right you are," said Futura. "Oliver never could get the timing right for a stage illusion. Couldn't do sleight of hand either."

"The crossbow—the one from the parade stunt," said Mallory. "Wasn't that a prop in his act?"

Futura seemed confused by the shift of context. "Oliver's act? Oh, you mean Max Candle's Lost Illusion? Oh, no. That routine uses repeaters. But I'm sure the single-fire crossbow was one of Oliver's. Of course, his collection was nothing like Max Candle's. Years ago, I wanted to buy a few props, mementos from the old days. But Max's widow wouldn't sell."

"Dear old Edith." Nick Prado's acid tone implied anything but endearment. "Is that woman dead yet?" And now he wore a pained expression. "I'm sorry, Charles. I'm sure you were very close to her."

"No need." Charles didn't seem shocked. Apparently, he knew that his cousin's wife had no admirers in this gathering. "And yes, she's dead. A heart attack. It happened a month ago."

The old men seemed pleased with the death, barely suppressing smiles all around the table. Prado was the most cheerful. "Charles, I hope you inherited the lot—all the stuff in the basement. You've got Max's platform, right?"

"Yes, but it hasn't been out of the crate in thirty years." Charles turned to Mallory. "Oliver's platform was very faithful to the original. Max totally mechanized it to do away with assistants and human error."

Riker looked up from his plate. "So the cops weren't in the original routine?"

"Well, yes," said Prado. "But they're just window dressing. A police presence assures the audience that the weapons and handcuffs are real. Charles only means that Max did away with Edith. She was his assistant when he had that accident in Los Angeles. Remember that, Emile? It laid him up for a year. That's when he built the platform."

Mallory sat up a little straighter. "You think Max's wife tried to do him in?"

Prado seemed to be considering this. "That would explain a lot."

Charles's knife and fork clattered to the plate. "Mallory, that's enough. First Oliver, and now Max. Sometimes people *do* have accidents."

Mallory wasn't listening. She was assessing her suspects by their tailoring or the lack of it. Nick Prado was obviously doing well, and so was Emile St. John. But Franny Futura's tuxedo did not fit him properly. Perhaps it was rented. He might be hard-pressed for cash. She loved money motives best of all.

"So none of you liked Edith Candle," said Riker.

"Well, no." Prado sipped his wine. "But I'm not sure Max liked her all that much either. Sorry again, Charles." He lifted his glass higher. "It's the wine talking."

"But Max stood by her," said Futura. "He was very big on keeping promises—vows. Deserting a wife wasn't his style."

"Well, he did have an affair with another man's wife," said Prado. "He was no saint."

Charles dropped his fork again. This was news to him.

St. John pushed his chair back from the table. He pulled a platinum cigar case from his breast pocket and tactfully changed the subject. "Mallory, I gather you don't think Oliver died by accident. Can you prove it?"

"It would help if I knew how his crossbow trick was supposed to work."

"But nobody knows," said Futura. "The Lost Illusion was only performed one time." He pulled out a cheap cigarette lighter for his friend's cigar. "That was what, Emile? Forty years ago?"

St. John nodded, exhaling blue smoke. "A lot of magicians tried to trace that performance, but Max was very careful about staging out-of-town tryouts. The ideal town would be remote and too small to support a newspaper. Sensible precaution—no critical reviews while he was working out the bugs in a new act."

Smoke was swirling in shafts of late-afternoon sun. Mallory sipped her wine and watched the white-haired men. They were full of food and wine, content and drowsy—vulnerable.

"Did anyone think Oliver's invitation was a little strange?"

Mallory had their attention as she feigned a moment of forgetfulness. She pulled Charles's copy from the pocket of her blazer and read the lines aloud, as if she had not memorized them, " 'You are invited to the solution of Max Candle's Lost Illusion, and more than one deadly mystery will be revealed.' The wording is odd, isn't it?"

And ominous?

Obviously Riker thought so. He was staring at her, not too happy at the moment, his suspicious eyes saying, *You've been holding out on me again.*

Mallory shrugged a silent, *Yeah. So?*

He shook his head to tell her he didn't deserve this, not from her. They were partners.

But where had her partner been when she was left hanging and twisting in the squad room today? He had been with Jack Coffey behind the glass—*watching* the show.

"This invitation." She turned to the old men at the other end of the table. "What does it mean? What's the other mystery?"

"Nothing odd about the wording," said the unflappable Emile St. John. "Oliver worked out quite a few of Max's old routines, and they were all deadly. He gave them away as gifts to old friends. I got instructions for the hangman illusion and a replica of Max's old gallows."

"I got a set of plans and crate of props," said Nick Prado.

Franny Futura was nodding. "I got Max's pendulum illusion. I'm going to do it in Oliver's little theater."

Mallory's partner smiled to say, *There goes your new theory—endgame.*

Not yet, Riker. "But the illusions were left to you in Oliver's will." Mallory was not asking them, she was telling them. "None of you knew what the invitation meant—not till after he died." She looked at Riker, ripping her game point back from his side of the table.

"Oh, I knew what it meant," said Nick Prado. "That invitation is months old. The instructions for my illusion arrived long before I left Chicago."

The others were nodding in agreement. So they had also received the explanatory letters and illusions before Oliver

died. Well, maybe one of them was lying—or all of
were.

"Of course," said Futura, "I can't do the pendulum illusion
with Oliver's plans. I'm afraid he botched it—just like he
screwed up the trick that killed him."

Without looking at Riker, she knew he was grinning, a
prelude to laughing out loud. He must be loving this, watching her get everything wrong. But he was at a disadvantage:
he didn't know there was a gunman at the parade this morning. If he had believed her, he wouldn't have confiscated her
favorite revolver.

And Riker wondered why she didn't like to share.

Now she did look at him, surprised that he was not smiling
as he stubbed out his cigarette. "You can't win 'em all, kid."

Mallory nodded. *Yeah, right.* Did he really believe she
would take the fall for the balloon shooting and face a charge
of reckless endangerment? *Not a shot in hell, Riker.*

She moved on to another prospect for her gunman, the
man missing from this company, the one who lived with a
dead woman. Though lunatics seldom made her short list,
she was already planting the blame on Malakhai. *How did
your wife die, old man? And where were you when that gun
went off this morning?*

Four

THIS MORNING, IN A RARE DEPARTURE FROM HIS HARVARD CLUB uniform, Charles Butler was not wearing a three-piece suit and tie. His blue jeans and denim shirt were a concession to practicality; wading through three decades of dust would be a dirty job.

Mallory pushed up the sleeves of her sweatshirt. Because firearms made civilians nervous and she wore no blazer to cover the holster, she had left her police-issue .38 in the upstairs office. This was a severe breach of her own dress code, which usually included a larger gun.

The rectangle of harsh light from the stairwell extended across four feet of the basement floor, and beyond that was impenetrable darkness. Mallory continued their yearlong argument. "Why don't I just rewire the wall switch?"

"All that trouble? What for?" He reached up to the top of the fuse box and pulled down a flashlight. "I think it's charming this way."

Yeah, right.

Charles the antique lover thought every broken old thing was charming, even the electrical wiring. Mallory decided to refrain from any more suggestions. It was better to simply wait for him to trip and break his neck in the dark. She was that patient with her friends.

Guided by the flashlight, they walked down a haphazard corridor of packing crates and trunks. The yellow beam roved over a broken rocking chair, which might be the source

for a trace of wood rot in the air. The smell of dust was everywhere, and now she detected a whiff of mold. Stacks of barrels and cardboard boxes massed in dark towers on all sides.
As she skirted around a headless dressmaker's dummy, part
of her mind was still working on the wiring problem.

Originally, this space had been a manufacturing plant with
the proportions of a hotel ballroom. But Charles, the giant
hobbit, longed for cozier human scale. Maybe he preferred to
use the flashlight because it didn't show the true size of the
basement.

"I pulled out the crates last night," he said. "All the major
parts are accounted for. I couldn't find the leg irons, but I'm
sure they'll turn up. The platform has to be assembled. That
might take a while."

"I've got lots of time. Jack Coffey put me on indefinite
leave." She didn't mention that the lieutenant had also taken
away her favorite gun. That was still a source of humiliation.

"Not a vacation, I take it."

"No, but we're calling it that." She followed him to the
wall of tall wooden panels joined by hinges. It spanned the
entire basement and closed off the area where Max Candle's
illusions were stored—and where the electricity still worked.

Charles stood before the two center panels that passed for
a doorway. They were chained together and padlocked. "The
platform hasn't been unpacked since Cousin Max died. That
was thirty years ago. The mechanisms may not be in very
good shape."

Mallory stared at the lock with disdain. It was an oversized
antique as large as an alarm clock. "I just want to see how the
trick works."

"I can't help you with that." Charles worked a key in the
lock, and the freed chains slid through circles in the wood.
"No one knows how the trick was done. That's why they call
it the Lost Illusion."

He used both hands to spread the pleated segments of the
wall. The panels creaked as they shifted back on metal tracks,
accordion style, opening to a cavernous space. A gray diffu-
sion of morning light came from a window set high in the
wall and level with the floor of the air shaft. Beyond the dirty

glass and the iron bars, trash cans of a neighboring building were spilling over with garbage—rodent heaven. One small dark animal slithered up to the window for a better look at her. This creature was too bold to go on living, and Mallory resolved to continue another argument with Charles over the traps that would break this rat's back.

"There was only one performance with all four crossbows in play," said Charles. "That was the out-of-town tryout."

She turned away from the dark thing at the window. "So it was a bad act?"

"A dangerous act." He bent down and touched a globe. It came to life with a soft yellow glow. Alternating current made it grow bright and dim in the natural rhythm of breathing. Above the globe, a painted dragon flowed across three rice paper panels of a folding screen. By a trick of oscillating lamplight, the dragon's breath was a flickering fire.

Twenty feet away, in a shallow canyon of shelves and cartons, a vertical row of tiny stars were shimmering, forming a bright crack in a patch of solid black shadow. While Charles walked around the dragon screen, Mallory drifted toward the sparkles. Pausing by a floor lamp with a fringed shade, she pulled its chain to cast a circle of light around an old wardrobe trunk standing on end. It had been opened to expose a narrow slit of flashing sequins. Its cracked leather exterior was papered with the faded colors of foreign shipping labels.

The cover of an old record album lay over the opening at the top of the wardrobe. Judging by the even coat of thick grime on the rotting cardboard and the surface of the trunk, neither had been disturbed in decades. At her feet were impressions of large squares. Their wide, hard-edged tracks led off across the floor to the area behind the screen, where Charles was turning on more lamps. So the narrow opening had been protected by the crates he had moved last night. That would explain why the sequins still shimmered, when they should be dulled with a film of dust.

Mallory put her hands into the opening of the wardrobe and spread the sides, using force, for the hinges were frozen with rust. Inside the left half of the trunk was a narrow chest of drawers, and on the right was a rack of tightly packed clothing on hangers. Her eyes passed over gaudy colors and spangles to settle on the plainest material. She pulled a suit from the rack and held it up to the light of the floor lamp. The off-white satin had not yellowed, but it did seem richer for the aging. The jacket and trousers were styled for a man, but altered and refitted to a slender figure with a small waist. She looked at the stitching. This was the work of a very good tailor. It rivaled every bit of clothing in her closet.

Charles was walking toward her as she pressed the suit against her own tall body. "Lovely," he said. "Where did it come from?"

She nodded toward the trunk. "I know it didn't belong to your cousin's wife. Edith was too short."

His hand grazed one of the shipping labels. "Faustine's Magic Theater. I remember this. It was part of a large shipment from an abandoned theater in Paris. Max bought up the entire stock after the war. The costumes must have belonged to one of the performers. When I was a little boy, this trunk was always locked."

Mallory riffled through the lingerie in the top drawer. Her hand touched a flat object, and she pulled out a passport. The name on the inside page was clear, but the photograph had been mutilated, the face scratched away with a sharp object. Turning to the other side of the trunk, where the clothes were racked, she prowled through them, pocket by pocket, until she found a card with French text and the same name. "The trunk belonged to Louisa Malakhai. I wonder what Edith thought of her husband keeping another woman's clothes?"

"If you're thinking she might have been jealous, you couldn't be more wrong," said Charles. "Louisa died years before Max even met Edith."

"Another accident?" Mallory looked down at the lock. It had been forced, but long ago. Rust filled the marks made by a tool twisting the metal catch. Charles had said it was always locked when he was a child, but perhaps Max Candle was still alive when his wife had broken it open.

She casually handed him Louisa Malakhai's open passport. As he looked down at the inside page, his face was suddenly grim. Perhaps he was drawing his own conclusions about who had vandalized the photograph and why. And now he was looking at the obvious damage to the lock. His freakish brain could add up evidence faster than hers.

"Accidents happen," said Charles, setting the passport on the top of the trunk, pretending he had not seen that bit of wifely violence in the scratches across the face of another woman. "In fact, that's why Max retired the crossbow trick after one performance. Someone died attempting it."

"But it's all a cheat," said Mallory. "You'd have to work at it to get killed in a magic act."

"In *most* cases, you'd be right," said Charles. "Even Houdini was no Houdini. But Max wasn't like any other magician."

She followed him to the other side of the dragon screen, where more globe lights and another old floor lamp illuminated the plastic drapes of metal wardrobe racks. Inside the protective cover of cellophane, a thousand rhinestones threw back a riot of light. Silk and satin materials gleamed in every color. Beyond the racks were rows of sturdy metal shelving material, and this was all that Mallory approved of. She cared nothing for the contents of the shelves, the dust-gathering clutter of leather hatboxes and giant playing cards, ornate painted canisters and small trunks. There were so many cartons and loose goods spread across the rest of the floor, it would take years to inventory Charles's inheritance.

The lamp farthest from the dragon screen illuminated the familiar guillotine. High in the air, a wicked metal blade hung waiting between tall stocks of wood. She pointed to it. "I know that's a cheat."

"Well, Max created the guillotine back in the days when Edith was in the act, losing her head every night. She wasn't inclined to take risks."

Charles looked over the large wooden boxes ganged together on the floor. Tall panels of thick wood were propped up against one wall of shelves. "As I recall, the platform is peg-and-groove construction, like a giant Erector set."

Two hours later, the shell had been assembled into a box nine feet square and fronted with stairs. The other three sides were paneled in dark rosewood. Thirteen steps led to a stage and two standing posts of light maple. Mallory looked up at the oval target hanging between them. The pegs at the sides of the target were painted black, and so it appeared to float in space. "Looks just like the one Oliver Tree used."

"It should." Charles stood by the side of the platform. "Oliver did most of the work on this one. He was a fine carpenter. There is one difference in the target—the pegs that fit into the post slots. Max's are wooden. Oliver's are steel."

She looked down at the square metal wells sunk into the first step, a pair on each side. They were made to receive the matching brass posts at the bases of the four pedestals. "That's different, too. In the news clips from Oliver's act, it looked like the pedestals were bolted down."

"He was always improving on things. Probably thought it was safer that way. From what I saw of his replica, everything else was the same. But I never had a look at his interior room." One hand brushed the center panel of a side wall to the right of the staircase. "The pressure lock should be here."

He pushed on a slat of wood. The panel opened, and now they could see into the hollow heart of the platform. Overhead, the open trapdoors provided dim light. Charles walked in and pulled the chain of a hanging lamp. The round metal shade cast a bright circle of light on the floor and left the ceiling in shadows.

"Amazing," he said. "That bulb is at least thirty years old."

Mallory leaned into the small room and surveyed the walls of slots, pegs and grooves awaiting their matching parts.

"I never saw Max load the mechanisms." Charles stood in the doorway looking over the stacks of unopened crates. "It's going to be a bit like assembling a Chinese puzzle block." He walked over to the nearest box and read the label. "Lazy tongs. I know where this one goes—under the center trapdoor. No other place for it."

Mallory walked around to the staircase as Charles and the box disappeared into the shell.

He called out, "If you're ever down here alone, remember there's no knob on the inside. I got locked in once when I was a little boy."

"What about the trapdoors?"

"You can't work them from the inside. They open with the foot levers on the stage."

"Sounds like careless carpentry."

"Well, if there is another way to open them, Max never told me. He didn't want me playing down here alone. Too dangerous, he said."

Yeah, right.

Mallory was halfway up the platform steps when she heard Riker's voice calling out, "Hey, where *is* everybody?"

At this height, she could see over the top of the dragon screen. Her partner was standing on the other side in a sorry mismatch of new and old clothes. Mallory resolved to steal the man's hat so it could be brushed and blocked. The scuffed shoes would pose a more difficult problem in her project of cleaning Riker.

He rounded the screen and stood before the platform, pointing back toward the dark opening in the accordion wall. "I almost broke my neck out there."

"You're late." She glanced at the paper sack in his right hand. It was large enough to hold her .357 revolver.

"I stopped to buy a newspaper." Riker held it up to display the large block print on the front page. "Congratulations. It's the longest headline this rag ever ran. 'Cop slays puppy as a thousand children watch.' "

And now that he had the desired reaction—she was pissed off—he folded the tabloid into the deep pocket of his coat. "Lucky they only ran a photo of the balloon. Now all those little kids won't recognize you on the street—and pelt you with their beer cans." Riker was grinning.

Mallory was not. "So what did Coffey say? Does he still think I'm dangerously nuts?" *Is that what you think, too?*

"What?" A surprised Charles was standing by the side of the platform. "Jack Coffey said that?"

Riker shrugged. "Naw, she's exaggerating again." He looked up at Mallory, six steps above him on the staircase. "The lieutenant never said you were crazy. He just didn't want the other guys to find out you were seriously gun-happy. There's a difference."

She looked down at Riker, eyes narrowing. "So, you're still backing Coffey."

"You mean his little spiel on dead cops? That was part of your education, kid. You needed to hear it." He climbed the steps to join her on the staircase. "But I'm on your side. Always have been."

Not always, not yesterday.

Charles had disappeared back inside the platform room. And now a tangle of twisted metal was slowly rising from the square opening in the floorboards. It resembled mangled umbrella bones as it hovered for a moment before toppling over in a crash of wire and steel. Then it was dragged back down again, and Charles's smiling face popped out of the opening. From Mallory's position on the stairs, it appeared that his head had been severed and carelessly left on the floorboards.

"Still has a few bugs to work out," said the grinning head.

As Charles slowly sank below the level of the stage floor, Riker whistled in appreciation. "Now that's cool."

Mallory was staring at the paper sack clutched in the detective's hand. "Did you get my gun back from Coffey?"

"You mean the cannon?" He shook his head. "The lieutenant says you'll have to make do with your .38. Remember the one the department gave you when you signed up? The *legal* gun?"

"Does he think I'm going to run amok through another crowd?"

"No," said Riker. "I think he's still holding a grudge for the rat shooting. Some people are buggy about dogs. The lieutenant's gone soft on rats with pet names."

Charles's head reappeared at the square opening in the stage floor. "You shot the man's pet rat?"

Mallory turned on the talking head. "Charles, don't start with me."

He ducked down into the platform, and she could barely hear his muffled muttering: "I'm sure the rat had it coming."

Riker climbed to the top of the platform and crouched down by the trapdoor. Leaning over the opening, he said, "The rat was named Oscar."

"Could've been worse," Charles's voice called up from the hole. "It's not like she shot Coffey's *dog*."

Mallory looked up to the high ceiling. After a quiet moment of self-censorship, she faced her partner. "Did you get *anything* useful?"

"Hey," said Riker, walking back toward the staircase. "Would I come empty-handed?"

Charles remained undercover, saying, "Not while she still has two guns left."

She climbed to the top of the stairs and stood next to Riker, ignoring the other face smiling up at her from the dark square in the floor. "Did you at least get the files on Oliver Tree?"

"Don't need 'em." Riker dipped one hand into his paper sack and pulled out a manila folder. "The West Side cops got tired of being ambushed by reporters, so they issued a press release. It's all in here. The papers will get it in the morning."

She took the folder from his hand and opened it to see only two sheets of spare text. *Not good enough.* "You didn't talk to the West Side detective, did you?"

"Lieutenant Coffey nixed that idea. Remember? But it doesn't matter." He tapped the folder in her hand. "You got all the facts. Nothing wrong with the crossbows. They all checked out. The handcuffs belonged to the cops in the act. Nobody could've tampered with 'em. What got the old man killed was his own cuff key. It was broken off in the handcuffs."

Mallory was unconsciously crumpling the sheets in her hand. "What about Oliver Tree's executor? Did he give you the breakdown on the will?"

"Never talked to him. He's on a cruise ship for the next three days."

So Riker had not done either of the scheduled interviews. Yet he seemed pleased with himself. "That's it, Mallory. Accidental death. If the key hadn't broken, the old guy would still be alive."

"For a few million dollars, somebody might've tampered with it. I need the executor's copy—"

"It's an old piece of metal. You don't have to spend good money on lab reports to see that. No marks, no cut points."

"Did you get the name of the executor's cruise line?"

"What for? It's an accidental death. We can't lean on the executor for information, and we sure as hell can't drag him off a cruise ship. It was a waste of time anyway. Fat chance a lawyer would give me the time of day without a warrant." Riker handed her the brown paper bag. "That's a present from one of the cops in the old man's magic act."

She pulled out a pair of handcuffs. "No evidence bag? No paperwork?"

"Kid, they never get that fancy for an accidental death."

For Riker's benefit, she made a show of studying the handcuffs. A week ago, she had made a more careful examination while this evidence was shackled to the wrist of a cadaver on Dr. Slope's autopsy table. But she had neglected to mention that morgue visit to Riker.

Mallory pointed to the broken shaft of metal protruding from the lock. "Where's the rest of it?"

"Never satisfied, are you? The uniforms never found the other piece." Riker unbuttoned his coat, preparing to stay awhile. "Now the cop who owns those cuffs—he'll keep his mouth shut. Coffey won't know we've been talking to anybody in the uptown precinct."

As if I care. So the manacles had never been processed. "No paper to show a chain of possession. Useless for court evidence."

"Look at them, Mallory. There's a broken key jammed in the damn lock. That cinches the accident finding."

She descended the stairs and stood by a floor lamp, holding the manacles close to the bulb. The broken section of metal was both bright and dark. "This is evidence of murder—or it would've been if anybody'd done their job right." And Mallory included Riker in this defamation.

Last week, she had been the only cop to attend the postmortem for Oliver Tree. Dr. Slope had closed the little man's frightened eyes and denied her request, calling it unnecessary and ghoulish. The medical examiner had not even cut into the body, for accidents did not merit full autopsies. Finally, Mallory had done the job herself. She had taken up Slope's hammer and broken the little carpenter's hand, rather than damage evidence by removing the broken key or sawing through the metal bracelet.

And after she had so carefully and ruthlessly preserved the handcuffs, what had the West Side detective done? He had tossed them back to the cop who owned them—a damned souvenir.

What could she salvage? "If I give these cuffs to Heller, he'll say it was an old key shined up to—"

"Heller's not gonna say squat." Riker came down the stairs, stepping slowly and shaking his head. "Forensics isn't gonna waste time or money on this. And your favorite suspect? You really think that old man left his money to a junkie? Think about it, kid. Why would the nephew kill to inherit millions, and then take a hundred bucks to do that crossbow stunt in the parade? Does that sound like a hot murder suspect with a money motive?"

No, but the nephew was still useful. "You're not planning to mention that little detail to Coffey, are you?"

Now Riker had the look of a man discovering that his drink had been watered down. "You *never* liked that junkie for a suspect. You scammed Coffey, didn't you?"

Mallory was rigid, silently waiting for her anger to pass off. If Riker had only believed in the gunman at the parade, she wouldn't have needed a scam to keep her in the game.

"Maybe you're both right." Charles was fitting the base of a pedestal into a steel well on the staircase. Three clockwork gears of tarnished brass formed a column four feet tall. "The Lost Illusion was dangerous. Suppose Oliver compounded his risk by using an old key?"

"I don't think he was that stupid." Mallory teased the piece of broken metal out of the lock with her fingernails. "But planting an old key was a good idea for the killer. A weakness in a new key would stand out in a test for metal fatigue."

And now the metal was free of the lock. She stared at the odd detail of the slotted shaft. "I say the metal was shined up to look like new. So who has an old cuff key lying around? I got it narrowed down to cops and magicians."

Charles walked up behind her and looked over her shoulder at the broken bit of metal in her open hand. "There's nothing wrong with the key plug. It's only the extension that's broken."

"Key plug?" Now she saw the joint line in the metal between the tooth of the key and the slot. She looked up at Charles. "You've seen this before?"

"Yes, it's just like Max's. Elegant thing. It might be the only design that Oliver couldn't improve on." He walked back to the platform and knelt down to search through a box of tools. "There are all sorts of ways to open handcuffs. You can even do it with a wire."

"Not NYPD cuffs," said Riker. "They're the best."

"Well, *most* can be opened with a wire or a pick," said Charles. And Mallory knew he was being tactful. Riker's knowledge of locks did not extend beyond the aluminum tabs that opened his beer cans.

Charles pulled a green velvet pouch from the toolbox. "But if your life depends on it, and you're really pressed for time, it's always wise to use a key."

Mallory hunkered down beside the toolbox and stared at the embroidered *F*. This was a twin to the small bag Slope had removed from Oliver Tree's clothing. She wondered what the brilliant West Side detective had done with *that* piece of evidence.

Charles opened the pouch and pulled out a collection of short metal posts dangling from the narrow opening in a four-inch rod. "See the slot? It's identical to what's left of yours."

She stared at the fringe of metal posts. Some were hollow and a few were solid. They had the thickness and the teeth of handcuff keys, but they were too short to be of any use.

"This is an old souvenir from Faustine's Magic Theater." Charles unscrewed a ball at one end of the slotted rod and emptied a dozen key plugs into his hand. "Some of these are antiques." He pointed to one of them. "This is the key Houdini used to open English handcuffs. I think they were called Darbys." He held up another post with teeth on both sides. "And this one opens Martin Daley bottleneck cuffs. One of these is a master for the Boer War model, like the old padlock on the accordion door. And the rest are—"

"Masters?" Mallory stood up to hold one plug closer to the

light. And now she noticed the detail of fine grooves on its head.

Riker took the broken key from her hand and unscrewed it from the shaft. He looked back at the plug she was holding. "They're all master keys?"

"Yes," said Charles. "One of Faustine's many husbands was a toolmaker." He screwed a key plug into the end of the rod. "This extends the reach, so you can work a lock with one cuffed hand." He stood up and pointed to the manacles in Mallory's hand. "May I?" He picked them up and turned his back for a moment. Then he faced her again, holding them out to her. "Here, lock up my right hand and don't let go of the other bracelet."

She obliged, slipping one manacle over Charles's wrist and locking it shut. He raised the cuffed hand above his head, dragging her arm upward by the chain connected to the bracelet's mate. When he lowered his hand again, the metal fell from his wrist, open and dangling from the handcuff Mallory was holding.

Startled, Riker took Charles's key and held it up to the broken one. "How did you do that so fast? I swear, I never saw you work the lock."

"Nothing to it." Charles looked at Mallory, almost apologetic. "Oliver might have been killed by sentiment—using his old key from Faustine's."

"And he used the wrong key plug," said Riker. "Charles's key doesn't match the broken one. Sorry, kid. There goes your case. The metal broke because the old guy was forcing the wrong plug in the lock."

Mallory snatched back the keys and closed them in a tight fist. "How many people would have these things?"

"Anyone who worked for Faustine might have one," said Charles. "And they're probably the originals. These days, it's wildly expensive to make new ones. A locksmith couldn't do it. You'd need a custom machinist, a real craftsman."

Mallory smiled. "So now I've got somebody in that circle of old men."

Riker threw up his hands in exasperation. "It's the *wrong* key. How can you look at the same evidence and—"

"You think Oliver didn't test the key? It took Charles three seconds to find the right master."

"Oliver might have been nervous," said Charles. "Stage fright. Accidents do—"

"He was in the restoration business," she said. "He understood metal fatigue. So what're the odds he'd use a fifty-year-old key extension that might get him killed? Somebody switched them. That's why it's the wrong key plug."

Riker was unconvinced, but not up for a fight. "It isn't enough to sell a jury on murder."

"Maybe not," she said. "But it's a damn good start. If the nephew had access to the old man's crossbows, he might know about this key. You have to interview him *today*."

"The reporters wanna talk to him, too," said Riker. "They'd like his point of view on the great balloon assassination. But they can't find him. Nobody can."

"Keep looking. And I want my .357 back."

"Oh, forget the damn gun," said Riker. "Why go out of your way to jerk Coffey around? Your .38 makes smaller holes, but it'll do."

Charles ducked out of this argument. He picked up a nine-foot post and climbed the steps to the top of the platform.

He was standing on a stepladder, holding the crossbeam over the two vertical posts, carefully fitting pegs into receiving holes, when Mallory called up to him. "That wasn't on Oliver's platform."

Charles nodded as he locked the pegs into place. "I know, but see this?" He pointed to a recessed lightbulb socket in the underside of the crossbeam. "It also holds up the curtains. There's a drapery rod running along the back—"

"Oliver didn't use curtains or a lamp."

"Mallory, let's put the whole thing together. Then you can eliminate the pieces you don't like."

Riker bent over an open crate and pulled out a crossbow. A thick band of strings dangled loose. The handle and trigger were shaped like a gun. Instead of a hammer to cock it, a long curving piece of metal extended out from the pistol grip. "Hey, Charles?" Riker pointed to the narrow box of wood on top of the shaft. "A magazine?"

"Yes, it's a repeater." Charles came down the steps, two at a time. "The magazine holds a load of three arrows." He took the weapon from Riker. "It needs a cleaning and some oil. A dry firing might wreck it." He carried it back to the platform and fitted the pistol grip into a receiving well at the top of the clockwork pedestal. Now it was aiming up toward the oval target. "Mallory, don't ever fool with this if you're down here alone. It's dangerous."

"Yeah, right."

"I told you, it killed someone."

Riker looked up from his perusal of another crate. "Someone besides Oliver Tree?"

"Yes, another casualty," said Charles. "Max was trying out the act in a small town. Two local boys snuck backstage after the performance. One of them claimed he could do the trick. A bet was made, and the boy died—only seventeen years old."

"So the trick was always dangerous." Riker looked at Mallory to say, *I told you so*. And then his eyes traveled over all the open crates and mechanisms. "Pretty big production for one lousy trick."

"Oh, no," said Charles. "This platform worked for quite a number of illusions. The crates have props for at least twelve different tricks. It's going to take a while to sort it out."

Mallory stood next to one of the pedestals of large brass circles with squared-off teeth. This one was not yet topped with a crossbow. A metal peg fell from a hole near the edge of the top gear.

"I'll fix that." Charles picked up the peg and slipped it back into place. "There should be a red flag on the peg. That's so the audience can follow it around the gear. When the peg gets to the top, it hits the trigger of the crossbow. Oliver missed that detail—no flags."

Riker nodded. "Makes you wonder what else the old guy missed."

Charles wound up a key in the side of the pedestal, then depressed a button near the top. The brass wheels began to move with a grinding noise. "Everything needs oil."

He bent down to the toolbox and picked up an aerosol can.

After a quick spray of machine oil, the gears revolved with the slow steady tick of a loud clock. Mallory watched the peg climb to the top of its orbit where the next crossbow would be installed. She looked at the remaining weapons in the crate at her feet. "They all fire?"

"Hopefully," said Charles. "No fakes if that's what you mean. But we can't shoot with them today. They need a good cleaning and new strings."

Riker sat on the bottom step of the platform and looked up at Mallory. "So you figure one of those old guys for a suspect?"

The clockwork gears were still moving. *Tick, tick, tick—*

"They were at the Central Park magic show, and the parade too."

"So was Charles," said Riker, smiling.

—tick, tick—

"Charles is excused." But Riker was not.

"Okay, Mallory." His tone was entirely too condescending. "Now what about the gunman in the crowd, the balloon killer?"

—tick—

Mallory turned on her partner. "What do you care, Riker? You and the lieutenant think I lied about that shooting. That's why Coffey won't let me do the interviews. And you don't even bother to tag the evidence."

—tick, tick, tick, tick—

For a large man, Charles Butler could move with surprising stealth. He was melting away, slipping back inside the platform, where the atmosphere was less disturbing and possibly safer.

"Hold on, Mallory." Riker rose to a stand. "You're *way* out of line."

—tick, tick, tick—

Her own voice was devoid of inflection. "I was a fool to tell you I shot that rat. You handed Coffey ammunition for his nutcase lecture. Did you guys practice that routine?" Her hands were rising, and his eyes got a little wider. Maybe he thought she meant to strike him.

—tick, tick—

Arms raised above her head in the prisoner's posture, she turned her body in a slow revolution to show him that she was not concealing a weapon. "When you report back to Lieutenant Coffey, tell him I'm not wearing a gun today. All the rats can rest easy." The implication was clear—she included him among the vermin.

—tick—

Riker was about to say something, but then thought better of it, closing his mouth in a thin tight line. He turned his back on her and rounded the dragon screen, heading for the way out.

She heard the sound of something being kicked out of the way in the darkness beyond the accordion wall. Judging by the crash, Riker's foot had sent its target a good distance. He rarely lost his temper. And his anger had never been directed at her, no matter how many tests she had devised for him during her childhood and in more recent times.

She had finally found Riker's trigger.

—tick, tick, tick, tick—

Five

THOUGH RABBI DAVID KAPLAN CUT A FIGURE OF LEAN ELE-
gance, he didn't look the part of a gambler, not by his turtle-
neck sweater or the loaf of bread in his hand. The
close-trimmed beard made him too distinguished, and the
sweet tranquillity in his eyes belied the fact that he could
hold his own in a round of cutthroat poker. In his first act as a
good host, the rabbi had confiscated Charles Butler's necktie,
arguing that a man could not concentrate on his game if he
did not breathe properly.

The tie was hung on the coatrack alongside Mallory's holstered revolver. How odd to see that deadly thing in David
Kaplan's house.

At the end of the foyer, Charles glanced into the living
room. Its sole occupant was an elderly stranger in a black
suit, who had been allowed to keep his necktie. A gray topcoat was folded on the visitor's lap, and a homburg hung on
the hook of one gnarled finger. As the old man rose from the
couch, his sad eyes focused on Charles, and he was clearly
disappointed, obviously expecting someone else. Slight and
frail, he seemed to hover over the carpet, delicate as a dry
dead leaf that had not quite settled to ground. His face had
the ashen cast of illness, and his eyes were the color of dust.

"That's Mr. Halpern," said the rabbi. "He wants a few
words with your friend when he arrives. It's very important
to him. I hope you don't mind?"

"Not at all." Because Mr. Halpern wore a necktie, Charles

had already deduced that he was not here to play poker. After the introductions were made, he lingered a moment to give the old man a polite nod. "You're sure you won't join us?"

Mr. Halpern made a slight bow with good manners from another age. "Thank you, but I prefer to wait here." He held up his hat and coat to show that he would be leaving shortly.

Charles followed the rabbi down the hall and into the den, where he was surrounded by the colors of leather-bound books shelved on every wall. Near the door, a tea cart was laid out with all the ingredients a sandwich maven could ask for. The usual crew had already assembled, and Charles was still overdressed among the sweaters and sweatshirts, jeans and khakis. He removed his suit jacket, unbuttoned his vest and rolled up the sleeves of his white shirt.

Dr. Slope was working at the cheese board, his serrated knife flying in the act of creation, slashing yellow slices and white ones. The medical examiner had a good face for poker, a stern composure that could not be cracked by a royal flush. His friends called him Edward. He was not a plausible Ed, not a man that one could comfortably abbreviate. The doctor inclined his head in a greeting to Charles as he piled the cheese on his plate.

"Hey, Charles!" Robin Duffy's eyes were full of delight, as if they had not seen one another for years, though last week's game had been at Robin's house. The retired lawyer was a small graying bulldog of a man, and a deceptive opponent, wearing the same agreeable expression for good cards and bad. Every laugh line in his face said, *I'm so happy to be here.*

Mallory stood behind Robin, pulling money from the pockets of her blue jeans and her cashmere blazer. She was putting in a rare appearance at the insistence of Rabbi Kaplan, valiant guardian of that place where her soul resided—though Edward Slope often argued that the rabbi was gatekeeper to an empty room.

And now Charles had his first unobstructed view of the new addition to the rabbi's den. The ancient folding card table had been retired, and in its place was a massive piece of furniture with thick legs tapering to lion's claws. "David, it's beautiful."

"A gift from my wife." The rabbi ran one loving hand along the curving mahogany edge, fingers gently grazing the green felt circle covering the surface.

In the simple act of pulling up a chair at the table, Mallory determined where everyone would sit. How predictable that she would position herself facing the door. She never left her back exposed. Dr. Slope sat down on her left side. He always liked to be within needling range of her, no matter what the setting or occasion. On her right was Robin Duffy, her adoring admirer. Rabbi Kaplan took the chair opposite the doctor and Mallory, so that he might act as referee.

Charles sat down in the single chair between Robin and the rabbi, for two guests had yet to arrive, and they would want to sit together.

All around the table, beer bottles were settling to coasters alongside plates of sandwiches and ashtrays. And now he noticed something else had been added to the game—real poker chips of red, white and blue instead of the usual mix of coins.

Mallory read his face. "Yeah, just like the *real* cardplayers." She turned to Edward Slope, not bothering to temper her sarcasm. "I'm guessing." She held up a white chip. "This is worth a nickel, right?"

Dr. Slope smiled as he leaned toward her with a return salvo. "Got any plans for your winnings? Why not have the giant puppy stuffed as a trophy?"

Robin Duffy glowered at the doctor. "You can't prove she shot that balloon."

"Spoken like a true lawyer, Robin. Hey, I was there when she blasted it out of the sky." Dr. Slope quickly stacked his poker chips in reckless little towers.

The doctor's stacking style and Charles's degrees in psychology told him that Edward Slope was not at all conservative in his game. The careless arrangement of his chips said, *I came to play.* But then, Edward said the same thing aloud each time he sat down at the table.

The rabbi was lining up his plastic tokens in neat columns, the hallmark of an inhibited bidder, yet he ran the best bluffs in every game.

In respect to cards, Charles's education had been a waste of time. His first game with these men had shattered his belief in an orderly universe governed by laws of cause and effect. Despite his extensive knowledge of body language, his high IQ and flawless logic, he never won. But he kept returning to the poker table, week after week, in the spirit of a whipped dog conducting a science experiment.

He had never played against Mallory before. Long before he met her, she had abandoned this game with her foster father's oldest friends. Charles stared at the perfect columns of her chips, so carefully aligned they might be solid shafts of plastic. If he were meeting her for the first time, if he did not know how many guns she owned, he would judge her an insecure player.

"I saw you on TV, Edward." Robin Duffy gathered his chips in loose piles of denominations. "The balloon autopsy wasn't too professional, but real funny."

"I know a bullet hole when I see one," said the medical examiner.

"My wife thinks *you* shot the big puppy, Edward—just to make the kid look bad." Robin's jowls gathered up in a wide bright smile for Mallory. Each time he looked at her, he seemed amazed, as though she were still growing up before his very eyes.

And now Charles understood why the rabbi had insisted on Mallory's attendance; it was for Robin's sake. Since the death of her foster father, she rarely made the trek to this Brooklyn neighborhood, and the old lawyer had missed her sorely.

Charles popped the cap off a bottle of beer, the standard beverage for every game. So it was odd to see the lone sherry glass set before one of the empty chairs. And wasn't the lighting a bit dimmer than usual?

Well, this smacks of collusion. A stage had been set.

When the doorbell rang, Rabbi Kaplan said, "Mr. Halpern will get it." Though the rabbi could see the front door if he only turned his head to one side, he kept custody of the eyes to allow the elderly man a private moment with the new arrival.

Not Mallory. She was looking straight down the hallway.

Charles had to lean over the table for a clear view.

Fragile Mr. Halpern opened the door to a tall figure in a long dark coat. A wide-brimmed black hat shadowed the visitor's face. With only this dark silhouette, anyone could tell that the new arrival was Mr. Halpern's opposite in every way, not the least bit delicate, conveying solid mass and strength even while standing in quiet repose. As he entered the foyer, light struck the strands of long white hair edging across his broad shoulders. The two men spoke in low tones that did not carry down the hall to the den. After a few minutes, they were shaking hands in farewell.

Charles believed the elderly Mr. Halpern was crying as he passed over the threshold and into the night, slowly, gently closing the door behind him.

Mallory was still watching the stranger as he removed his hat and coat, hanging them on the rack by the door. She was nodding almost imperceptibly, perhaps approving the superb tweed blazer and the blue silk shirt. The man's collar was open by two buttons, marking him as a subscriber to the rabbi's theory of poker and breath-restricting neckties.

Everyone at the table looked up as Malakhai appeared in the den. This man could never simply walk through a doorway, but always made a rather grand entrance. It was not affectation, but unavoidable, as he increased the energy level of a room to the tenth power. He smiled, and though his face bore deep lines of experience, something survived of the wild and handsome erstwhile boy. He had not yet given in to time, not bowed to it with a curved back nor any other sign of impairment. The long white lion's mane was aglow, a trap for lamplight. His eyes were quite the opposite, large and gunmetal blue, dark places where light could not exist.

Charles looked at the faces of the men seated around him. Just for a moment, he thought they might applaud this famed magician merely for showing up at the table.

Everyone but Mallory stood up as Charles made the intro-

ductions to this old friend of the family. After presenting
Kathleen Mallory, he winced as Malakhai asked, "May I call
you Kathy?"

"No," she said.

Charles rushed in, speaking quickly. "It's nothing personal. Everyone calls her Mallory, just Mallory."

"I don't," said the rabbi and Robin Duffy in unison.

Edward Slope resumed his seat and pushed the deck
toward Mallory, ready for the game to begin—on several levels. "You have to pick your moments, sir. Only call her Kathy
if you want to break her concentration. Otherwise it loses the
annoyance value. Right, Kathy?"

She ignored him and shuffled the deck.

And now Charles apologized for neglecting the rule of
ladies first. He introduced an empty space in the air beside
Malakhai, claiming there was a woman standing there. "And
her name is Louisa."

The rabbi inclined his head and smiled, speaking to the air.
"My pleasure, madam. You haven't changed at all." He
turned to Malakhai. "I saw your last performance."

"That was more than twenty years ago." Malakhai turned
his head to the space beside him and appeared to be listening.
He smiled at the rabbi. "Louisa thanks you for remembering
us." And now he spoke to the entire gathering. "My wife
plays a wicked game of poker. She'll sit in for a few hands—
if no one objects."

"Your *dead* wife? I don't think so," said Mallory.

"Kathy!" The rabbi's voice had the note of a warning bell.
"This man is a guest in my house."

"So?" She turned to Malakhai. "Nothing personal. It's bad
enough I got roped into playing with these amateurs. I draw
the line at dealing cards to spooks, okay?"

Though Rabbi Kaplan had suffered worse insults on his
poker prowess in silence, he was obviously about to upbraid
her again. His mouth was open, but nothing came out. Perhaps he was waffling between her offenses: the refusal to
acknowledge a woman who wasn't there, and her use of the
word *spook* as a possible slur. In a further convolution of

ethics, could he counsel her to avoid offending a guest by
sanctioning the lie that a dead woman could competently
play poker?

Charles leaned behind Robin's chair and whispered to
Mallory, "Did I mention that Malakhai helped my cousin
design the pedestals for the crossbow illusion?"

"Pull up a chair, Louisa." Mallory's ethics were miles
more flexible than the rabbi's. "Everybody, ante up."

While the white chips were being tossed into the center of
the table, Malakhai held out a chair for the phantom Louisa.
After taking his own seat, he purchased poker chips and set
them up for two players. Charles noticed the stacks were different patterns for husband and wife. Malakhai made a tidy
square of four columns, while Louisa's chips mirrored
Edward Slope's in recklessness.

After everyone had made a contribution to the pot, Mallory dealt out cards to each player, facedown, until she had
completed six hands for the living and one for the dead. "The
game is five-card draw. Deuces are not wild if it rains, and
jacks are not wild, whether the moon is full or not. *Real*
poker—got that?"

While the players were perusing their cards, Charles
noticed the smoke wafting up from the ashtray in front of
Louisa's chair.

"I'll open." Edward Slope tossed a blue chip in the center
of the table. And then he stared at Louisa's cigarette. The filter was stained with lipstick. And now the ashtray moved
slightly, as though someone had jostled it.

Very smooth, as always.

Charles nodded to Malakhai, who was folding his cards to
drop out of the hand. And now the other men were smiling at
the ashtray, almost shyly, as if this were a flirtation of sorts. If
Mallory noticed the diversion, she gave no indication.

It was Louisa's turn to bet, and two blue chips flew into the
center of the table of their own accord. Malakhai smiled at
Edward Slope. "Louisa will see your bet and raise you."

Charles admired the master's timing. Malakhai would
have to pick a moment when everyone was looking else-

where before he placed the chips at the edge of the table and shot them into the center. One mistake and a delicate illusion would be ruined.

When Louisa's bet had been matched, it was time for the draw. Edward Slope rapped on the table to announce that he would stay with his dealt hand, but Malakhai requested a card for Louisa. His wife's cast-off playing card slid across the table toward Mallory, slowly gliding along the green felt, as if pushed by an unseen hand.

Mallory stared at the felt surface, no doubt looking for the string that made the card move. It would be only a hair's width and as green as the tabletop, invisible in this low-key lighting. Charles knew there would be a hook at Mallory's end of the table so the card could slide toward her, but he didn't bother to look for the string's anchor. It was probably a thin wire painted to match the wood at the edge of the table. This was more evidence of collaboration between Malakhai and the rabbi, for such preparations were always done in advance.

Mallory picked up the card and examined it. Of course the dot of adhesive would have remained with the string when Malakhai snapped it back.

After a moment, the magician leaned forward. "My wife wonders if she could have her card soon. You'll forgive her impatience. She's accustomed to Las Vegas tables, where the action is a little faster."

There were grins all around the table. Only Mallory was not charmed with the dead woman. Her smile was forced when she looked up at Malakhai. "Nice work." She tossed a card toward the empty chair, and gave two cards to the rabbi.

"I'm out." Charles folded his exceptionally bad hand and stole a look at Mallory. Her face was masklike, impossible to read.

Her voice was dead calm when she spoke to Malakhai. "So how does the crossbow trick work?"

The magician smiled as if this were a great joke. "I'd never give up one of Max Candle's illusions."

She turned on Charles, and now he had no difficulty in

reading her. Her eyes were drilling into him, and her voice was decidedly testy. "What's the deal here?"

Charles opened his hands to show her that he was unarmed, and therefore not a fair kill. "I never promised he'd tell you anything."

Mallory stared at the white-haired magician, her opponent, her new enemy. It would be easy for her to suss out Malakhai's soft spot. It was sitting in the empty chair beside him.

In the next round of bets, Dr. Slope tossed two blue chips into the pot. Everyone turned to the empty chair. Louisa's cards sat on the lip of the table, tipping upward for a moment, as though a ghost were perusing them. A stack of four chips slowly moved to the center of the table as the phantom player raised the bet.

Slope put his cards down. "I'm out."

Mallory was staring at Louisa's sherry glass, now magically full and sporting a lipstick stain to match the one on the cigarette. The rabbi and Robin were folding their cards and staring at the sherry glass. It was rocking to communicate Louisa's impatience to get on with the game.

Casually, Mallory raised a beer bottle to her mouth, as if she were long accustomed to drinking with the dead. She met Louisa's raise, plunking four chips into the pot. "I'm calling."

Showdown.

Louisa's cards flipped over. No bluff—the ghost held a straight flush of diamonds, neatly beating her opponent's full house of three jacks and two treys.

Charles watched Mallory's green eyes flicker, and he knew she was computing Louisa's odds of drawing one card to make this remarkable hand in the first game. And the dead woman had raised the bet before the draw—how prescient. Mallory was probably considering how the cards of husband and wife might be combined.

Wordlessly, the deck was passed to Edward Slope. Over the next three rounds, Louisa folded every time, and Mallory won two of the pots. The deal had bypassed Louisa and fallen to Rabbi Kaplan. After the last show of cards, the rabbi stared at his dwindling chips as he handed the deck off to Charles.

They anted and made the first round of bets. Only Louisa drew cards in this game. "Two for Mrs. Malakhai," said Charles, dealing it toward the empty chair.

Malakhai smiled. "Louisa says you've known her long enough to call her by her first name."

"Of course," said Charles. "And what—"

"The sherry!" Robin was pointing at the glass.

Louisa's glass had been nearly full a few moments ago, but now it was half empty and a thin film of residue was sliding down the side of the crystal. On the napkin by her glass was half a sandwich marked by the delicate imprint of red lips on the rye bread. Robin Duffy stared at the empty chair, eyes focused on that space where a woman's face might be.

Mallory was far from enchanted.

Charles called a time-out and excused himself from the table. When he returned to the den with fresh beers from the kitchen, he saw the compact mirror lying open on Mallory's knee, positioned to catch a pair of hands straying under the table. Her conversation was in a civilized tone, no impending bloodshed, though Charles predicted that would change when Louisa won again.

"Only part of the secret is in the platform," Malakhai was saying. "You need the intellectual contribution. You have to know what Max was planning for an effect. Then you can work backward to figure out a way to do it."

"It's just a trick." Mallory set her own spread of cards on the edge of the table with the same amount of overlap as Louisa's. Her betting was so confident, the others dropped out of the game—except for the dead woman.

Edward Slope glared at Mallory, somewhat unkindly. "I even know it's a bluff." He threw down his cards anyway. "I hate this."

"There's more to illusion than props." Malakhai seemed uninterested in the game as he continued his discussion with Mallory. "If you only have the brushes and paints, can you describe the picture an artist created with those materials?"

"It was an escape routine," said Mallory. "Handcuffs, crossbow—not much to it."

"Fine, then why don't you work it out yourself?" Malakhai sat back and studied her with some amusement. He inclined his head toward the empty chair, as if Louisa had called for his attention. Turning back to Mallory, he said, "Louisa is calling your cards."

Two more chips shot from the empty seat at the table and stopped at the center of the green circle. The dead woman's cards flipped over, and this time, Louisa held a royal flush.

Mallory's expression was deadly. A half-bright child could guess the odds against this hand. Though Mallory was perfectly still, she managed to convey the image of a ticking bomb. Yet she gave nothing away in her voice. "Oliver Tree shouldn't have died. When I find out how the trick was sabotaged, I'll know who killed him."

"He probably botched the trick by himself," said Malakhai. "Or maybe it was bad reflexes. A man his age would've been excused for using breakaway cuffs, but he used the police cuffs—just like Max. Poor Oliver. What a stickler for detail." He leaned toward the empty chair, listening. "Louisa reminds you that you haven't turned up your cards." He smiled. "Of course, she doesn't want to embarrass you—if you'd rather not show your hand."

Mallory never heard this insult, never touched her cards, she was so intently focused. "Oliver did the trick right. It worked in all ten rehearsals."

Malakhai showed rare surprise. "How do you happen to know the exact number of tryouts? One of the other magicians—"

"No," she said. "They didn't know anything about the trick until they saw it done in the park. That was their *story*."

"So Oliver's nephew told you?"

She shook her head. "I can't find him. I was hoping you'd know where he was." This was close to an accusation.

"Can we finish this hand now?" Dr. Slope lightly slapped the table in front of Mallory. "I wanna see your damn cards."

"So you don't believe in accidents," said Malakhai. "They

do happen on stage. My wife's death was an accident during a magic act."

It was Charles's turn to be surprised. This was more information about Louisa's death than anyone else had. Why would Malakhai disclose this to people he hardly knew? The record contract for *Louisa's Concerto* prohibited any explanation of the death, and now a large financial penalty was riding on the discretion of strangers.

Slope drummed his fingers on the felt surface, prompting Mallory to turn up her cards.

She never took her eyes off the magician. "How does a woman die by accidental magic?"

"Louisa was shot with a single-fire crossbow at twenty paces," said Malakhai, in the same tone he would use to describe his wife's dress. "Fifteen minutes later, she was dead."

Now he had everyone's attention, even distracting Edward from Mallory's mystery hand. The doctor was looking at the empty chair. "Shot where?"

Malakhai pointed to the chair. His finger lightly touched down on an invisible shoulder.

"Here?" Mallory pointed to her own shoulder.

Malakhai nodded.

"What did the body look like—right after she died?"

The rabbi's cards settled to the table. He stared at Mallory, shaking his head, silently accusing her of blatant rudeness.

Malakhai was less shocked as he turned to the empty chair beside him to stare at the woman who wasn't there. "She has blood in her eyes, a bit of pink froth at her lips."

"In her eyes?" Mallory smiled somewhat inappropriately. "A blood splatter?"

"No, there's a lot of blood streaming from the wound." He pointed to the level of the phantom's shoulder. "But her eyes seem to be wounded from the inside looking out."

Charles studied the frowning face of Edward Slope. The doctor leaned back in his chair, as though he needed this additional support, suddenly realizing that he was sharing the table with a bloodied corpse, and not the charming ghost that a more traditional audience visualized.

Mallory was sitting at attention. "Are there any other marks on her body? Wounds, bruising, anything like that?"

"No," said Malakhai, still dryly delivering the description of a dead body. "Just a reddish cast to her face, as if she were blushing to be seen that way—embarrassed by her own death."

The effect on the medical examiner was deepening. Perhaps it disturbed Edward to have an animated cadaver intruding on the after hours of his workday. "And this was an accident?"

"As accidental as Oliver's death," said Malakhai. "The old boy might've had a sporting chance if he'd ever seen the real trick performed. He was just taking his best guess."

"Oliver's plan was pretty straightforward," said Mallory. "He wanted to get out of the way of all those arrows."

"If you believe it's that simple, then you don't need my help."

"I never said I *needed* help."

"You never would, Kathy," Edward Slope interjected. "Even if you *did*. All right, hotshot, maybe you can tell me how a dead woman beats you at poker."

She picked up the pack of cards and splayed them, inspecting their backs very carefully. Edward watched this for a moment, then lowered his reading glasses and leaned toward her. "What's the problem, Kathy? Did you forget how you marked the deck?"

Mallory looked up to glare at the magician. "I noticed that Louisa wins big when something moves on the table. Interesting distraction. I'm betting this deck is five cards light."

The rabbi's face went slack with surprise. David Kaplan was such a good poker player, Charles honestly couldn't tell if the man was innocent or acting as Malakhai's foil for a magic act. "You're not suggesting that anyone at this table would palm cards."

"I'm suggesting a bet—twenty dollars." Mallory laid a bill on the table. "Anybody want part of this?"

Malakhai's smile was generous. "So you don't believe in luck either?"

"It's nothing personal." Edward spoke to the magician in a

confidential tone. "She just really hates to be outdone at cheating."

Mallory was not indignant, but merely surprised. "I don't have to cheat to beat a pack of old ladies."

"You wouldn't talk that way if your father was here," said Rabbi Kaplan.

"Damn right she wouldn't," said Robin Duffy. "That was her old man's best line." He turned to smile at Mallory. "This is a friendly game, Kathy. For Christ's sake—sorry, Rabbi—we're playing for loose change here."

Rabbi Kaplan spoke in a Sunday school lecture mode. "Kathy, there's a reason we only play penny-ante poker. Do you know what that reason is?"

She nodded. "Because your wives won't let you play for folding money."

"Aside from that," said the rabbi.

"Less incentive to cheat?"

"Aside from that," said Edward Slope.

Robin put one arm around her shoulder for a brief hug. "Kathy honey, it's just a friendly game. The money doesn't matter."

"That's right," said Rabbi Kaplan. "It's only a—"

"Winning is the main thing," said Robin. And Rabbi Kaplan had to think about that for a moment.

Mallory rounded up all the folded hands and added her five cards to the deck.

David Kaplan reached across the table to put one hand over hers. "Kathy, I forbid you to count those cards." Among all her father's old friends, only the rabbi could forbid and get away with it.

Mallory was still holding on to the deck when she shook off his hand and rose from the table. "I'll be right back."

"Where is she going?" Robin stared at the door as it closed behind her.

Charles listened to the other door opening off the hall. "The kitchen, I think."

And now they could hear her riffling and slamming the drawers in the next room. "What is she—"

Edward lifted one hand to silence Robin so he could hear

the metallic shuffle of utensils. He turned to the rabbi. "Why didn't you lock up the silverware, David? You knew she was coming over tonight."

A motor started up, and then a grinding noise ensued. "That's the knife sharpener," said the rabbi. And now they all listened with increasing fascination.

The loud thwack on wood jolted David Kaplan. He tilted his head to one side. "The bread board?"

"Oh, fine," said Edward. "She's cutting up the deck. Selfish brat. If *she* can't palm all the aces, *nobody* can."

But when Mallory returned to the den, the deck was intact—more or less. It was impaled on a barbecue skewer with a very sharp point. She pulled the cards loose, sliding them down the metal pole, then set them on the table before Rabbi Kaplan.

"This is too much." The rabbi held up the deck and stared at her through the neat hole in its center.

She gave him a smile—well, half a smile. "I did *not* count those cards, okay?"

Charles looked at the hole, dead center. If Malakhai was holding any cards for Louisa, he would find it difficult to put them back into play.

The magician was laughing, unoffended. The rabbi sighed.

"I broke your bread board," said Mallory, taking her seat at the table. "I'll replace it."

Edward Slope picked up one of the damaged cards and held it to the light. "It would've been so much easier with a bullet. All right, Kathy, I *almost* believe you didn't shoot that balloon."

Only Charles was deeply disturbed as he picked up his hand and stared at the holes. This trick of hers should have been impossible. His good fleet brain was calculating the tensile strength of a deck of cards, estimating the force, the amount of tightly focused rage necessary to do what she had done.

They began the next round with the click of plastic chips falling into a pile at the center of the table. Perhaps, coincidentally, Louisa entered into a losing streak.

As Mallory would say, *Yeah, right.*

Three hands later, Mallory was sitting before the largest pile of chips, and Charles was still pondering the holes in the playing cards. He had only heard one thwack of the bread board. Maybe she was trying her own hand at illusion. She could have skewered them quietly, one by one, and then broken the board for effect. Perhaps this was her version of flexing muscles for an opponent. On the darker side, he now believed she could have done in the deck all at once—and in anger. Both possibilities worried him.

She was still pumping Malakhai for information. Everyone else was diverted by the movement of Louisa's sherry glass. It was levitating, floating in the air above the table and tipping back in the natural fashion of an unnatural person sipping her wine. The rigging for this trick was seamless. No illusion of Malakhai's had ever been destroyed by an obvious wire. The glass settled delicately to the wood.

Marvelous piece of work.

Yet the magician had failed to distract Mallory from her inquisition. Now he threw up his hands. "I don't see the problem. I'm sure you know Oliver died because his cuff key broke in the lock."

Her smile was so slight it was barely there. "But how did *you* know that?"

Indeed, how *did* Malakhai know? Charles remembered Riker saying that the press release would not be distributed until tomorrow. If the other magicians had known about the broken key, they would surely have mentioned it by now.

"Very simple," said Malakhai. "I asked the detective who made out the accident report. It *is* his case."

Apparently, she took that as a challenge to her authority. Her eyes narrowed, a sure sign of trouble. "It's my case now. And after I wrap it up, I might even have time left to find out who murdered your wife."

"She died by accident," said Malakhai. "An audience witnessed it."

"Oliver Tree had a million witnesses. So what? Let's start with the arrow in Louisa's shoulder. Here, you said." She pointed to her own shoulder and turned to the doctor. "Deltoid muscle, right? And you think I never pay attention during the autopsies." She faced Malakhai again. "The arrow had nothing to do with her death. The murder came later—in that fifteen-minute window."

"The arrow hit an artery," said Malakhai. "Louisa lost a lot of blood."

Mallory shook her head slowly and turned to Edward Slope. "Correct me if I'm wrong, *Doctor*. I could stick a hole in your aorta and you wouldn't bleed to death in fifteen minutes."

"Right," said Edward, studying his cards. "Shoulder wound like that one—simple pressure would've stopped the bleeding. Medical attention within the hour would've prevented the damage of shock." He looked up with a sudden afterthought. "But the timing is always off in an emergency. People panic and—"

Mallory shook her head. "Panicky civilians always estimate on the high side. If an ambulance shows in four minutes, the witnesses claim it took forty. So if Malakhai says fifteen minutes, it might've been only ten, or even five minutes."

The magician glanced at the empty chair. "I've never spoken about her death in public. It's—"

"Sensible," she said, nodding in approval. "Never talk without a lawyer present. Your wife knew her killer, and she was alone with him when she died. So I figure she was carried backstage. That's where the arrow was removed. Right?"

Malakhai nodded.

"And she was in a place with some cover, a door to close. Right again?" She didn't wait for his answer. "Of course. The perp needed privacy to kill her. So she's lying on the floor, and he takes a pillow, something soft that won't leave any marks or—"

"I've got a problem with the pillow," said Slope. "Not enough trauma for retinal damage and discoloration."

"Right," said Mallory. "The bleeding eyes, the red blush. And you forgot the pink froth at her mouth. We'll just put some pressure on her chest, okay?" She turned back to Malakhai. "So she's lying on the floor being smothered to death. But she's not dying fast enough to suit the man who's killing her. Louisa struggles, she's fighting to stay alive. That's where most of the blood is coming from. It's pumping out of the wound because she's using all her strength to push the pillow away so she can breathe. She's getting weaker—all that blood, not enough air. But she won't die. And the killer? He's frightened, panicked. People are gathering outside the door. One of them might come in at any moment. And she's *still* fighting him, still holding on, waiting for someone to help her. So he puts one knee on her chest to pin her to the floor. And then he puts all his weight on top of her—crushing the life out of her. She tries to scream, but all the while, he's pressing down with that pillow. She's in pain, but still fighting. Then she stops screaming. She knows no one can hear her. No one is coming. It's so quiet, she can hear the bones breaking in her chest. And finally, *finally* she—"

"Kathy, that's enough!" said the rabbi, breaking the spell she had cast over the room. "This is his wife's death you're discussing. It's—"

"Very rude," said Dr. Slope. "*And* presumptuous. I can think of three fast poisons that would've produced froth and retinal hemorrhage."

"Poison is unreliable," said Mallory, as if she were exchanging cookie recipes with the medical examiner. "Smothering is better—no obvious marks on the throat, no chemical residue in the body." She spoke to the empty seat at the table. "Who killed you, Louisa?"

Malakhai slowly turned his head toward the phantom. "She declines to answer."

Mallory smiled. "I thought she might. Did she tell you to call a lawyer?"

The rabbi slammed his hand flat on the table. "Kathy!"

Mallory feigned surprise, but not well. "I didn't accuse him."

Dr. Slope folded his arms across his chest, completely disengaged from the game. "What did the local coroner say?"

Malakhai shrugged. "There was no autopsy, no investigation."

Mallory nodded. "It was easier for the local police to write up the death as accidental, less paperwork—as long as no one protested the finding. And I'm betting you didn't. What a lucky break for the killer." She pushed her chair back from the table. "I think I've made my point on accidental death."

"But not proved it," said Malakhai. "If you can prove murder more than fifty years after the fact, I'll tell you how Max Candle did the Lost Illusion." The weight of personality was dipping back toward Malakhai's side of the table. He was calling her out.

All eyes were turned on Mallory.

"I told you, Malakhai—I don't need your help. And I don't need incentive either. Oliver dedicated his last trick to your wife. Maybe he was feeling guilty. Maybe *you* were angry. If I find out he's the one who killed Louisa, you're going to need a good criminal lawyer."

"The detective in charge said the matter was closed—accidental death. The key was an old one. He said it was clear—"

She raised one hand to cut him off. "Oliver did restoration work on old buildings. Not just the woodwork—old screws, pipes, rails. The old man had a lot of experience with metal fatigue. He didn't risk his life on a fifty-year-old cuff key."

"That's your opinion."

"That's a fact," said Mallory. "He ordered new keys from a machine shop he did business with. I checked that out three hours ago."

But if Charles recalled the events of the day—and he did—she was still eating pizza in his kitchen only *two* hours ago.

"The new keys were a better grade of steel—stronger," said Mallory.

Malakhai waved a hand to dismiss her argument—her lie. "So Oliver confused a new key with an old one."

"Sorry," said Mallory, not at all sorry. "The machinist still has the old one. He kept it for a reorder. Oliver wanted ten keys. According to the shop foreman, he used a new one for every rehearsal. Now that was a little extreme, wasn't it? Unnecessary, even with his life on the line. I suppose you could say he was paranoid about metal fatigue."

Had she gone too far that time? Charles remembered Oliver as a trusting soul who had done business contracts on a handshake, hardly a paranoid personality. But a great many years had passed since Oliver and Malakhai had met. And Mallory was such a confident deceiver, the magician appeared to believe her, electing not to argue the point. "Perhaps he had more than one old key?"

"Wrong again," said Mallory. "Oliver told the machinist to keep it safe. Said it was his *only* key, a souvenir from Faustine's Magic Theater. You performed there, too. I'd bet even money you had a key just like it. Still got yours?"

"You seriously—"

"I *know* you're part of this, Malakhai. You're just too damn helpful in showing me the error of my ways."

Malakhai smiled with just a trace of condescension.

"No," she said. "You only *think* I tipped my hand by accident. Wherever you go, keep looking over your shoulder. I'll be right behind you—and that should worry you. Just ask anyone at this table how *twisted* I really am."

Robin Duffy looked up with great surprise, as though she had shot him in the heart.

Mallory turned to the rabbi, who knew her better than all the rest of this company. Her face was an open challenge, defying David Kaplan to deny it—*waiting* for him to contradict her. And now she must realize that she would wait forever.

The rabbi turned away from her.

While Charles was casting about for words to say in her favor, it was Edward Slope who came gallantly riding to Mallory's defense.

The doctor put one arm around her shoulders and slowly shook his head in denial of her twistedness. Then he leaned toward Malakhai. "Watch your back. You've seen what she does to puppies."

Six

AT THE BACK OF CHARLES BUTLER'S BUILDING, THE PRIVATE office was sheltered from the noise and the tourist hustle of SoHo streets. It overlooked a city garden of monster weeds, trash cans and their attendant rats, but high-pitched squeals and the scrabbles of tiny nails did not penetrate the closed windows of the second floor. The room was furnished with cold metal and decorated with extreme order and death. Mallory never saw this as metaphor, but seriously believed that these environs gave no clue to her personality.

Three computer monitors were perfectly aligned on their separate workstations, soldiers in formation, and each machine had one glowing blue eye. They reported in silent scrolls of text rolling down their screens. One wall of shelves held peripheral electronics, boxes of disks, tools and manuals. The adjacent wall was clear of obstruction from the floorboards to the ceiling molding. Tonight it served as a giant video screen for the taped homicide in Central Park, and Oliver Tree was performing his final act. Mallory set the projection to loop endlessly, to murder the old man, then resurrect him and kill him again and again.

Charles Butler had offered her the warmth of wooden antiques to replace her steel file cabinets, desk and chairs. He had suggested drapes to kill the coldness of the institutional window blinds. And he thought a painting or two might break the monotony of the wall where Oliver Tree was bleeding from four sharp arrows, hanging dead in his chains.

But she preferred her own simple furnishings. They could be reassembled within any set of stark white walls, and she would feel instantly at home in familiar, albeit sterile, surroundings. The surface of the metal workstation was cold to the touch. In deference to her machines, she kept the room temperature several degrees below the range of human comfort.

In the next loop of the projected magic show, Oliver was alive again on the wall, screaming for help and only bleeding from the wound to his neck.

Her chair rolled back from a monitor. After a few quiet hours of research, some of it legal, she had found no trace of Louisa Malakhai. One after another, archivists had lamented that there were no portraits, no certificates of birth or death, no tangible proof that the young composer had ever existed—except for the music, opus number one and only, *Louisa's Concerto.*

Mallory reached into the pocket of her blazer and pulled out Louisa Malakhai's passport. She stared at the mutilated black-and-white photograph inside the cover. Around the scratched-out face were long waving tresses. The light shade must have been the color of bright fire, for Emile St. John had alluded to a red-haired woman.

The passport was Czechoslovakian, but the Interpol connection had turned up no record of Czech citizenship. She flipped through the pages to the last customs stamp. It dated Louisa's arrival in France to August of 1942. Mallory turned back to the previous stamps and examined them more closely. *Fake? Yes.*

Only the final mark was reliable. So Louisa must have used this passport to enter the country. But the letters and numbers of previous stamps were made by the pen of an artist, and not a civil servant with an ink pad. *Clever.* A new passport might have borne closer scrutiny in wartime Europe. Inside the cover, a circular embossing overlapped the photograph. This raised seal had very few imperfections.

She returned the passport to the pocket of her blazer, where it kept company with Louisa's French identity card, which had expired late in 1942.

On to Paris?

She looked at the clock on the wall. Just past midnight— too early to go traveling on the Internet. Her European connection would not be at his desk for hours.

Originally, she had cultivated the Interpol man to steal from him, to raid data from his foreign network. But now, she looked forward to his conversations printing across her screen. Because English was not his first language, he was precise in his phrasing, no idiomatic speech or slang. His text was economical, clean and cold. Like the coupling of machines, their intercourse never deviated from software and hardware.

The foreign policeman was her only friend—or the only one not passed down by her foster father, not inherited along with the old man's pocket watch.

One red fingernail touched the power switch, and the screen went dark. Mallory swiveled her chair toward the wall where Oliver Tree was taking another arrow into his flesh. She watched with detachment, her mind elsewhere, as the next arrow pierced the old man's heart, and blood streamed over the white breast of his shirt. She switched him off, giving Oliver a respite from his screaming agony, his repetitive dying.

Notebook and pen in hand, Mallory jotted down the data she would need from the platform that took up so much space in the basement. She planned to shrink it to numbers and graphics the size of a monitor screen.

Locking the office door behind her, Mallory treaded quietly past Charles's residence and on down the hall. Even before she cracked the stairwell door, she could hear the strains of music and a woman in deep pain. She recognized the voice at once—Billie Holiday.

Some blues fan was playing the old record albums on the turntable stored in the cellar.

Mallory leaned over the railing and looked down through the winding wrought-iron staircase. Harsh naked bulbs cast shadows of twisting metal all along two flights of the curved wall. Descending the spiraling stairs, she listened to the song recorded in the early years of a brief career.

Thanks to her foster father, Mallory's musical education was peerless. At twelve years of age, she could name every record cut by Billie Holiday. Markowitz had called her Lady Day. This song was from the thirties, the high time of the lady's short life, cutting loose, taking no prisoners, full-out song of songs.

Mallory pulled out her revolver.

The music ended abruptly when she reached the next landing, one flight away from the basement, as the next song began. The intruder had changed the record and the era. Now it was 1946, and the lady's voice had coarsened.

Mallory paused on the stairs. The high volume of the record player did not bode well for a covert burglary. She knew it wasn't Charles down there. He only cared for classical music. But he might have left the partition unlocked.

She slid her revolver back into the holster.

So which one of Charles's tenants might be in the cellar? The third-floor psychiatrist only played rock 'n' roll. And the top-floor minimalist artist didn't listen to anything but the white static between the stations on his radio.

She touched down on the bottom step. The old song ended in the middle of a lyric, and a more recent one began. It was 1955 and Billie Holiday was near the end of her career, three years away from her death at a jazz festival.

Mallory pushed open the stairwell door. Beyond the long field of black shadows, a tall crack of light split the accordion wall. She decided not to use the flashlight on top of the fuse box. If this turned out to be a learning-disabled burglar, she didn't want to be an obvious target in the dark.

The record had hardly begun when the cut changed again. Lady Day was singing in the fog of London Town as Mallory drew near the partition. She looked down at the large, old-fashioned padlock. It was closed, and the chain was still laced through holes in the joining sections of wood. There was room enough for a hand to fit through the divide, but why would the intruder close the lock behind him?

And what recording was he searching for? Another tune began in 1958, when Billie Holiday was close to death.

Mallory reached into the pocket of her jeans. Her fingers

closed on the rod of keys she had pocketed this morning. She held it up to the long crack of light in the partition, unscrewed the metal ball at the top of the shaft and selected the key post that Charles had called a Boer War master. The old padlock fell open, and she silently guided the chain out of the wooden holes. She used both hands to push against the slats of the folding wall, wincing at the unwelcome noise of unoiled hinges and the wheels of sliding panels moving across the metal tracks in the floor.

And now she was looking at the tall intruder's back as he bent over the record player and moved the needle to the next cut on the album, a Duke Ellington classic. Lady Day sang, *"If you hear a song in blue—"*

Apparently, this was the recording he had been searching for. He moved away from the old turntable and walked toward the open wardrobe trunk. His hands were busy at the drawers when she came up behind him.

Malakhai must realize that he was not alone anymore. Her presence had been announced by loud creaking wood and grinding metal, yet he seemed unconcerned, not even bothering to turn around.

This was insulting.

The magician shifted his attention to the garments hanging on the other side of the wardrobe trunk. The white suit was where she had left it this morning, spread across the other clothes on the rack. The satin gleamed as it flowed over his hand.

"I think this will fit you, Mallory." He slowly turned his head to show her his smiling profile. "A woman of your word. I look over my shoulder—and there you are." His hand brushed a lapel of the white suit. "You're Louisa's size. Do you want it?"

"It's not your property to give away."

"Oh, but it is. Ask Charles." The wave of his arm included all the surrounding stacks of cartons stamped with Faustine's name. "Max left me all the props, the wardrobe, everything from the theater in Paris. I just never bothered to collect it."

Malakhai opened a drawer and pulled out a black silk disk. With a quick turn of his wrist and a snap, the full crown of a top hat sprang from its center. He set it on his head. "Faustine bought this for me. I was her apprentice."

Mallory nodded to the trunk. "Did Faustine buy those clothes for Louisa?"

"No, she never met my wife. The Germans came to town one morning in 1940, and the old woman died that afternoon. Mere coincidence, of course. Faustine never met the German Army either."

Mallory looked up at the air-shaft window in the rear wall. The glass and the bars were intact. "How did you get in here? Did Charles let you in?"

One hand rose in a dismissive gesture. "Oh please. I was passing through locked doors before he was born."

Mallory folded her arms in the posture that said, *Yeah, right.* She was not impressed with his criminal potential. "So you turn on *all* the lights and crank up the music *way* too loud. Then you lock the door behind you—so no one will know you're here? Am I missing something?"

"I've confused you. Sorry."

Not confusing at all. He had probably relocked the door so he would not be interrupted while rifling the trunk. She held up the rod of master keys. "I guess you have one of these. Makes it a lot easier, doesn't it?"

The music ended. Billie Holiday was gone.

Good. She had had enough of dead women for one night.

Malakhai lit a cigarette and exhaled a stream of smoke as he sat down on a packing crate. A crowbar lay amid splinters of wood on the cement floor. A second plume of smoke rose from an ashtray atop a short stack of cardboard boxes. The filter bore the ruby imprint of a mouth.

Malakhai was staring at her, as he removed his tweed jacket and rolled back the blue silk shirtsleeves. His brows were rising, eyes widening in expectation, all but commanding Mallory to speak. But she saw this form of manipulation as her own job, not his, and she turned away from him to survey the surrounding crates. Half of the lids had been pried open.

He picked up the crowbar and set to work on another one. "What are you looking for?"

"A case of wine." He put his weight on the crowbar, and

the top of the crate lifted with the crack of breaking wood and tiny squeals of rusted nails. He looked down at the exposed contents, shaking his head. "Not here either."

Malakhai dropped the crowbar on the floor and sauntered back to the wardrobe trunk. He pulled out a suit of black sequins. It glittered with a million reflections of the lamplight, so dazzling, almost distracting her from Malakhai's covert search of the pockets.

"Now you must take this one. Louisa insists." He held it out to Mallory. "My wife says blondes look wonderful in black."

She let the garment shimmer in the air between them, dangling from the hanger in his outstretched hand.

Malakhai nodded his understanding. "As you like." He returned the suit to the rack. "But later, you'll come back for it." He glanced toward the space above the ashtray and its smoking cigarette, then smiled at Mallory. "Louisa says you won't be able to resist her clothes." He watched the plume of smoke for a moment, then nodded, as if in agreement. "The sequins will call out your name. They won't let you sleep until you give in."

Mallory suppressed a smile. She knew what he was looking for in the folds and pockets, while he played the part of his dead wife's Dictaphone.

His head tilted to one side, listening to the smoke again. He pointed to the fabrics at the end of the rack. "And these silks? They'll force you to take them to a party. They'll make you stay up all night long, dancing and drinking good wine. Louisa wants you to listen to these clothes. They know what's best for you."

"What's Louisa wearing now?"

"The dress she died in." He looked over his shoulder and focused on the smoke rising from the ashtray. "It's sky blue, almost as light as her eyes."

Mallory walked over to the trunk and stood close to him. He was wearing an expensive cologne, so discreet she hadn't noticed it during the poker game. And there was another scent on the air, a flower mingling with the dust of the cellar—a gardenia. She looked down at the open lingerie drawer. A sachet was tucked in with the garments. "All of your wife's clothes are here?"

"Well, those dancing shoes belonged to Faustine, but the rest are Louisa's. There was no armoire in our room. This was her closet. Yes, the clothes are all here, except for the dress. She was buried in that."

"Buried in a bloodstained dress?"

"It was a hasty funeral."

"Her *only* dress." Mallory ran her hand across the rack of hangers. "These clothes—suits, shirts, trousers—all made for a man and cut down to size. But she wore a dress the night she died. Why?"

"Women." He shrugged, as if this were an answer of sorts. Then he walked back to the crates from Faustine's and pulled another one from a stack. It was large, but he handled it as if it weighed only a few pounds and set it down on the floor. "Where is that wine? So much to drink, so little time."

Mallory drifted toward the ashtray where Louisa's cigarette was smoldering. Her eyes focused on the smoke. "Her hair—it's cut very short, isn't it?"

Apparently he didn't like it when she played his game with the invisible woman. He turned his back on her and bent over the crate. Now he paused, hands braced on his knees. His head turned slightly, only showing her the line of his cheek. "How did you know that?"

So she had guessed right. The long hair from the passport photo had been cut off in Paris.

He looked back over his shoulder. "The boys told you?"

Boys? He must mean the old magicians. She nodded toward the wardrobe trunk. "Short hair goes with the man-tailored clothes."

His head bowed as he put his weight into the crowbar. "She wore ties with the suits, just like the magicians. Louisa fascinated everyone who came to the theater. Halfway across the room, she could alter her sex with the change of her gait." He turned to consult the smoke from the ashtray, a last withering plume from a cigarette that had gone dark. "Her eyes are such a pale blue. There are moments when they seem solid white—eerie. She never needed makeup."

"But tonight she's wearing lipstick." Mallory circled the crate so she could see his face. "She wore makeup the night she was killed, right? And a dress, her *only* dress—all tricked out to die like a woman."

"Yes." His dark blue eyes were somber now and fixed on the crowbar as he worked it under the wooden lid. "She was very much a woman that night."

Mallory's hand pressed down on top of the crate to work against him. "Were you hiding her from the Germans or the French police?"

The crowbar fell from his hand and crashed to the cement. Mallory took her hand off the crate lid and stepped back. "I know a lot about Louisa."

He shook his head to say she was lying. "No, I don't think so. But you know a lot about death, I'll grant you that. Your lecture at the poker game was very instructive. I never imagined anything that brutal."

"No? Where were you when she was dying?"

"Elsewhere."

Mallory was distracted by the plume of a fresh cigarette. When did he light that one? "I've met your old friends from Faustine's."

"And they couldn't even tell you where Louisa was born." His hands were mauling the packing material. "I've never told anyone my wife's history."

"Right, the recording contract has a penalty clause."

He abandoned this crate and looked for a more likely one among the stacks. "Have you ever heard my wife's concerto? Louisa started writing it when she was only fourteen. She finished it in Paris."

"It's odd that your old friends wouldn't know anything about her background, unless you had something to hide *before* Louisa died. So I was right. She was wanted. Didn't you trust any of them?"

"You should play her concerto—she's in there, her entire personality. The music critics say the work is inhabited— haunted, if you like. Ah, but you don't believe in ghosts."

"And neither do you." She watched him pull up the loosened lid. "It takes a lot of effort to keep a dead woman walking and talking. You're the one who works the strings."

The crate's interior was exposed, and his face paled as he

looked down at the contents, a wooden crossbow. The pistol stock was cracked, and the bow was broken in two. He shook his head, as if this might clear his vision. Unlike the other crates, he took the trouble to replace the lid on this one.

"No wine here either." His composure was restored when he looked up at Mallory. "You know nothing about my wife."

"Her hair wasn't short in 1942." She watched his hands tighten around the crowbar. "Not in August—that's when she crossed the border into France. An eighteen-year-old bride."

"Only seventeen," he corrected her. "Louisa turned eighteen in Paris."

"You added an extra year. It was part of her disguise."

"Well, the boys didn't tell you that. They didn't know. You're fascinating, Mallory. I'll bet you frighten people."

"Her hair was long, wavy and light red. Then she cut it off." Mallory glanced at the wardrobe of trousers, suits and unfeminine shoes—except for the gold dancing slippers. "Louisa was passing for a boy, hiding out in Paris. She was murdered at Faustine's Magic Theater in the winter of 1942."

So far all the details were correct; she could see that much in his face. If Louisa's identity card was also a forgery, at least the late December expiration date was reliable.

"Why was she wearing her only dress the night she died? Were the Germans looking for a woman in men's clothing? Louisa was planning to leave Paris, wasn't she?" Mallory came up behind him and whispered in his ear, "Was she leaving without you?"

The wood creaked. The crate's lid crashed to the floor.

"I found the wine." He pulled out a case of bottles and set it on the floor. "You're not quite what I expected, Mallory. You're good at reading people—dead or alive. Charles gave me the impression that you preferred the company of computers."

She knew her name among the other detectives of NYPD—Mallory the Machine. She sat down on the overturned crate lid. It was the only space not coated with dust, the dreaded enemy of all machines. Malakhai lined up the bottles in front of her, and she read the labels of cabernet sauvignon, burgundy and port wine.

"Good old Max, sentimental bastard." He lifted a carved wooden box from the crate and shook it, frowning at the tinkle of broken glass. "What a pity. This was Faustine's best crystal." He opened the box and looked down at the set of twelve wineglasses, each pressed into a green velvet lining. Only half of them were intact. He set three glasses on the floor. More prowling in the crate produced a pearl-handled screw of tarnished silver. He stabbed its point into the cork of a bottle.

"That's a rare wine," said Mallory. "Too expensive to drink."

"You say that because it's old." He pulled on the screw, and it came out with crumbles of dry cork. "Damn." He sank the metal deeper, twisting it into the bottle's mouth. "I remember when this wine was young. And you're right, it was a rare good bottle even then."

The rest of the cork came out in pieces. The odor of vinegar poured from the glass neck, to tell them that the wine had gone over.

"Now that's criminal." He stared at the label, as if reading the obituary of a beloved friend. "This is why hoarding wine is not in my philosophy."

Mallory perused the other bottles. "Different wines, different vintners. Why are they all from 1941?"

"It was a wonderful year, a painless year. Louisa was still alive. The boys were all together then—Faustine's apprentices. That was before everything went sour." He stuffed the largest bit of the broken cork back into the bottleneck to kill the pungent odor. "You got the dates right, Mallory. By the end of 1942, Louisa was dead, and the boys were scattered." He wiped a wineglass with his handkerchief and placed it in her hand. "I'll find you a good bottle."

She set the goblet down on the cement and pushed it away.

"No wine for you?" He smiled. "Interesting." He turned to the space beside him. The ashtray was on the floor now, and Louisa had begun another cigarette. "My wife thinks you're afraid of losing control. She wants you to take more risks—have many lovers. Drink all the wine you can hold."

"Did Louisa have many lovers?"

He turned his eyes away from Mallory and began a search from bottle to bottle, looking for one that was not ruined.

✝   ✝   ✝

The rich bouquet of burgundy was tainted with the smell of machine oil. Mallory calmly watched her murder suspect reassemble a freshly cleaned lethal weapon, fitting the long curved section through a slot near the end of the arrow bed.

They had long since decamped from the wardrobe trunk, carrying unspoiled bottles around the dragon screen to settle near the platform. Mallory's internal clock had gone awry. Time was passing in increments of alcohol and repetitions of the blues. She was listening to the same record album for the fourth time. Or was it the fifth? Sitting cross-legged on the bare cement floor, she sipped from a crystal goblet, having forgotten her dread of dust and wine.

Billie Holiday sang, *"If you hear a song in blue—"*

"You're so young." He twisted a screw to realign the crossbow sight. "These lyrics don't mean anything to you, do they?"

"No," Mallory lied, not wanting to give him anything of herself, not her unique connection to Rilke's caged panther, nor T. S. Eliot's four-o'clock-in-the-morning thoughts—or a song in blue.

"—like a flower crying—"

Her glass was only half empty, but Malakhai was filling it again. At some point, the silk top hat had traveled from his head to hers, just when or how she could not say, and now the brim was falling over her eyes, and she pushed it back.

"Max should've been an engineer. He designed this bow." The veins and muscles of his forearm stood out in bold relief as he bent back the thick curve of metal to string the crossbow pistol. "This has a hundred-and-fifty-pound pull, but a child can work the lever to cock it. The arrow travels two hundred and thirty-five feet a second. Very deadly."

"—heart trying to compose—"

"I thought you'd be into classical music like your wife. Why Billie Holiday?"

"Well, we were all jazz babies in Paris, but I came late to the blues. I discovered Billie between World War II and Korea."

"Emile St. John said you found Louisa in Korea. After she'd been dead for—"

"More like she found me. Let's stay with the earlier war. I think you'd like that one better, Mallory. Lots of big guns."

"—a prelude that never dies—"

"A world at war." He picked up a narrow wooden box, a magazine to hold a load of three arrows. "I wish I could make you see the whole thing, the amazing scale of it. The bombs falling." He set the box in place over the arrow bed. "Parades and music, crowds cheering, whole cities falling down." He tightened the screws that bound it to the crossbow. "Goosestepping Nazis and Yanks in tanks. It was sublime."

"—my prelude to a kiss—"

Malakhai pushed up the curving metal rod extending out from the rear of the pistol section. "Charles was right. They all need new strings. But this should hold for a few shots." When he moved the rod down again, the string was pulled back to receive the first arrow.

The brim of the top hat fell over her eyes again. He reached out to her and tipped it back.

"In 1943, I saw a dogfight in the sky, a battle of fighter planes. The losing aircraft blew to bits, and the pilot was dropping through the clouds—still alive. The parachute never opened—just a white streamer of silk. His feet were pumping up and down like mad. Perhaps he thought, if he hit the ground running, he might get away with falling from an airplane. The ultimate optimist. He must have been an American."

Malakhai looked through the crossbow sight. She wondered if he realized that he was aiming at the ashtray, where Louisa's cigarette was burning. "Mallory, promise me you'll never walk in front of these things when they're loaded on the pedestals."

"Max Candle walked in front of four of them."

"Well, you're no Max Candle. And neither was Oliver."

Malakhai walked over to the platform and set the crossbow grip into a pedestal slot. He came back to her and picked up a half-empty wine bottle.

"A very good year." He refreshed the third glass by Louisa's ashtray. "Max ran away from boarding school early in '41. He used to be a Butler like Charles. When he followed me to Paris, he took the name Candle to hide from the Pinkerton men his parents hired. If you're not familiar with—"

"Private detectives, I know. So you met at school?"

"Yes. Max's father was in the diplomatic corps. His parents were about to take him home to the States when he ran away."

"What was your real name?"

"Malakhai. Disappointed?" He returned to the platform and climbed the stairs to the stage.

She watched him pick up the heavy target, easily lifting it from the slots in the flanking posts. "What's your first name?"

"Perhaps I'll tell you about that when I know you better." He moved the target behind the red drapes.

Mallory was becoming accustomed to this evasion. She never pressed him anymore, but only continued to collect the soft spots marked by unanswered questions.

Louisa was a chain-smoker. The ashtray was filled with red-stained cigarette butts, and Mallory had yet to catch the dead woman's husband in the act of lighting one. She had decided that all the cigarettes from Louisa's pack must be premarked with lipstick, but they were lighting up when Malakhai was nowhere near them.

A neat trick.

Mallory sipped her wine in the spirit of research. So this was the flavor of 1941, when Malakhai was a teenage boy with a war going on all around him. "How well did you get along with the Germans during the occupation?"

"Oh, the soldiers were our best customers. After Faustine died, we turned the place into a dinner theater. Couldn't make ends meet with admission for the magic show. So we ripped out all the theater seats and put in chairs and tables— one big dining room."

"You fed the enemy?"

"And poisoned them—the food was that bad." He disappeared around the dragon screen, and his voice carried back to her. "The wine was worse, so we never had any officers in the audience."

She could hear the splintering of wood as he pried open another crate.

"We were just a pack of children," he said. "When you're young and poor, you think about your stomach, not politics."

Malakhai returned to the platform, carrying a round café table in one hand and a chair in the other. "These are from Faustine's. Max must have bought up everything but the old lady's bidet." He set them down in front of the staircase.

"Was it a German soldier who killed Louisa?"

"Let's get off that, shall we?" His voice had only mild impatience. "Do you want to see this illusion or not?" He wiped down the chair with a cloth and held it out for her. "Sit down—please."

She took her seat at the small table as he acted the part of a waiter, setting out her glass and a wine bottle. His hands were steady. Maybe she would change that. "How did Faustine die?"

"In her sleep—no blood. I'm forever disappointing you, aren't I?" He had cleaned Louisa's ashtray, and now he put it on the table beside the wine bottle. "You probably won't like this trick. It's a small, unpretentious routine. We used it to open the show every night. Max created it. Louisa wasn't a magician, so he kept it very simple."

Malakhai gently lifted a violin from a dusty case and began to work the pegs where the long neck ended in a scroll of wood. "Don't expect too much." He plucked the strings, tightening and loosening them, tuning the instrument by ear. "Think of it as a little bit of poetry, a prelude to magic."

She was staring at the cigarette on the edge of the ashtray when the tip began to glow with a small flame, and now it smoked.

A chemical agent?

That would explain why she never caught him lighting one. Maybe it was something that would ignite when it was pulled from the pack and exposed to the air. She picked up the cigarette and sniffed at the smoke from the lit end, but there was no trace scent of chemicals. Now she put the filter to her lips and drew in the smoke to taste it.

Her throat burned, and she could not stop coughing. It was a fight to catch her breath.

"So that was your first cigarette." Malakhai was at her side, gently slapping her back. "How do I know these things?"

Her lungs were on fire, and her eyes were full of tears from the smoke. "There's something mixed in the tobacco. It burns—"

"Oh, it's always like that the first time you inhale. Makes you wonder why there's ever a second time." He handed her the wineglass, and she drank deeply—for medicinal purposes.

"Well, Mallory, now that we've sucked poison together, we're bonded, you and I." His hand rested on her shoulder until she stopped coughing. "So, you risked a dangerous cigarette—commendable. And you're well on your way to being drunk. That's even better."

She set down the wineglass and pushed it away.

Malakhai bent down to a crate and pulled out a burlap mannikin. He slung it over his shoulder and walked up the platform stairs. Other than the stitched-up wounds and patches, it was an exact copy of Oliver Tree's demonstration dummy.

Malakhai used twine instead of handcuffs to bind the cloth hands to the iron post rings, then turned on the lamp in the overhead crossbeam. "The dummy isn't part of the act. I need it to line up the shot." He descended the stairs and loaded an arrow into the magazine. When the weapon was armed and cocked, he glanced her way with a charming smile. "Tense moment?"

Not at all.

Under the cover of her blazer, Mallory felt the comfortable weight of a revolver, and she would bet the moon that a bullet could beat an arrow.

"Now, in the original trick," he said, "there was no magazine. It was a single-fire weapon with a wooden bow. And it was handheld—no pedestals. But since you're the audience, it would be rude if I asked you to shoot me." He flipped a switch on the pedestal. "So we'll improvise with automation."

The clockwork gears ticked as the teeth of the wheels meshed together.

He stood behind the pedestal and looked through the crossbow sight. "Max's inspiration came from the magic bullet trick. He'd never seen it performed, but he had a rough idea of the effect. In the original version, the weapon was a gun."

Malakhai walked toward her with an armload of crockery. "The shot broke a plate in the magician's hands, and he caught the bullet in his teeth." He bent low to set the small plates in a circle around the café table. "But during the occupation, the Germans frowned on civilians with guns." The pedestal continued to tick off its countdown. "And catching an arrow in the teeth would've been too dicey."

The ticking stopped. The bowstring twanged and the arrow fired too fast for Mallory to follow its flight from the pedestal to the heart of the mannikin, where sawdust was streaming from a hole in its burlap chest.

"Perfect," said Malakhai. "Now let's hope the string holds for one more shot." He placed an unlit cigarette in each of the plates on the floor around the table. "Atmosphere is half the effect."

She had been wrong about Louisa's lipstick stains being made in advance. All these filters were clean.

Malakhai tied a red scarf to the end of an arrow and loaded it into the magazine. When he had taken down the burlap dummy, he made a circuit of the platform, switching off the globe lamps and the standing lamps, diminishing her comfort level with the encroaching darkness. Only the platform bulb was left glowing between the posts at the top of the platform, and behind the stage was a wall of shadow.

Halfway up the stairs, he paused at the edge of the yellow pool of light and waved one hand, saying, "Ambiance."

On command, all the cigarettes in the saucers lit themselves, one by one, and she was surrounded by smoke on all sides, white wraiths swirling into the surrounding darkness.

She heard the tick of gears and turned toward the platform. Malakhai stood on the stage. The single lightbulb had a small circle of influence, thieving decades from his face. He was holding the violin and its bow. The ticking seemed louder in the dark.

"You're in Faustine's Magic Theater. It's 1942. If you look up, you can see small private balconies. And straight up—the ceiling is a mural of characters and scenes from famous plays. Oh, and the chandelier—a huge brilliant ball of crystal and light. Much too big for the space. Faustine's tastes were a bit gaudy. But it's wartime now. The old lady is dead, and we can't afford the lightbulbs. So the chandelier is dark, and the room is lit with candles. It's full of people, Parisians and refugees in street clothes. The soldiers are wearing gray uniforms. Guns are strapped to their thighs. All the waiters are young boys in top hats and tuxedos. Try to imagine that the wine is not so good."

The room was dead still, but for the tick of the gears and the movement of smoke. "You're not a cop anymore, Mallory. Not tonight. You live in occupied Paris. Everything that was familiar and comfortable—that's all gone now. You don't know how you'll feed yourself tomorrow. You don't even know how the night will end. Anything can happen."

The ticking—was it louder now?

"You can smell spilt wine rising up from the floor, cheap perfume on the women—and smoke." He raised the violin and positioned it between his cheek and one shoulder. "Now this is even more of a stretch. Instead of me, you see a lovely creature with fire-red hair. She's only eighteen years old. And you must imagine that her violin is in tune."

Mallory could hear the machinery's light grinding despite the recent oil. The pedestal gears were turning, ticking. The trigger peg was on the rise. Malakhai stood between the two posts. The violin's bow was suspended above the strings.

"While Louisa is playing, Max Candle enters stage left. There's a crossbow pistol in his hand. You see him take an arrow from his quiver. A long red scarf is tied to the shaft. He loads it into the crossbow. Louisa doesn't see him. She's so involved in her music." He closed his eyes. "Her body turns in slow revolutions, as if she doesn't realize that anyone is watching her. I can't play the concerto for you. This is a simple practice piece she taught me one rainy afternoon."

The music was sweet, light tripping notes. The gears of the pedestal were ticking in the rhythm of a metronome—or a bomb. Malakhai was turning round. One arm was in motion as he stroked the rosined bow across the strings. His other hand fingered the neck of the instrument to form the chords and pluck riffs of light running notes. She watched his back and the action of the bow arm working across the strings of the violin.

The weapon fired. She tracked the arrow by the flight of the red scarf streaming out behind it. Malakhai's foot kicked out. The trajectory stopped at his body, as if the arrow had pierced him. He recovered his balance, still turning round, still playing, completing his revolution until he faced his audience of one. And though the music had never ended, the violin's bow was gone, and he was drawing the deadly arrow across the strings for the final note. The red scarf hung from the shaft.

The overhead lamp went out. The whole world went black.

Without conscious guidance, Mallory's right hand was reaching for her gun. She heard his shoes on the steps, and listened to her target so she could shoot him in the dark.

A standing lamp switched on at the base of the platform. "Well?" Malakhai bent down to touch the globe lamp on the floor, and it pulsated with light. "Did you like it?" He walked around the base of the platform, turning on all the lamps.

And now she saw the more chilling illusion, a lithe shadow moving across the face of a distant packing crate. The slender silhouette was on the run, as if it had been left behind and was hurrying to catch up to the darkness at the back of the cellar. But between lamplight and shadow, there was no solid form.

Too much wine. She pushed the glass to the edge of the table. Cigarettes that lit themselves, and now this. "How did you do that? The shadow."

"Oh, that? I thought you'd be more interested in the trick that wounded Louisa."

"That was *it?*"

"Disappointed again?" He smiled. "But you liked the shadow, so it's not a total loss."

"I know you didn't snatch that arrow out of the air, not at two hundred and thirty-five feet a second. It can't be done. The arrow missed you, right? You hid the bow under the violin after you switched it for a second arrow."

"Wrong. There was only one arrow."

"You didn't catch that arrow." She walked over to the pedestal and looked into the empty magazine. "I saw you load it."

"But you didn't see me unload it. You were coughing, remember?"

"I saw it fly."

"You saw the scarf fly. It was tied to wire that fed from the crossbow to my hand. The arrow—the only arrow—was always under the violin."

"But you didn't pull on any wire. I would've seen that." It would have been a very long pull.

"The wire led through my fingers to wrap around a block of wood on the floor. When I kicked the block off the back of the platform, I sent it far enough for the wire to pull the scarf into my hand."

Now she tried to remember what had come first—the off-balance kick or the flight of the red scarf. All she knew for certain was that he had suckered her into behaving like a civilian witness, seeing things that were not there. "So that's all there is to it?"

"I knew you'd be irritated. It's all so simple—after someone tells you how it's done."

"Getting shot with a scarf isn't dangerous. You said—"

"Max was only a boy when he came up with this illusion. The dying finale came later in his career, a rather ingenious way of securing his tricks. No magician ever stole from him. He was the only one willing to take a genuine risk."

"A death wish?"

"Nothing that trite." Malakhai sat down on the bottom step

of the platform. "I think the war ended too soon for Max. He
saw it through the eyes of a Yank—a generational trial by
fire. His life was so much larger then. The postwar world was
an anticlimax. Nothing had color anymore. No taste, no texture."

"And he was married to a woman he didn't love," said
Mallory.

Malakhai nodded as he reached for a bottle, then held it up
to the light. "We're out of wine. I'll be right back." He
walked around the dragon screen and set the bottle down
beside the wardrobe trunk. Mallory came up behind him, but
not quietly enough. Her eyes caught his hand quickly with-
drawing from another pocket in Louisa's clothes.

He stroked the material of a green pantsuit. "Faustine's
gold dancing shoes would go well with this. I wonder what
they're doing in this trunk. I never saw Louisa wear them."

"Maybe she went dancing with someone else. I asked you
if Louisa had lovers. You never—" When the shadow moved
across the trunk, she pulled her gun and whirled around.
There was nothing there but smoke rising from an ashtray on
the floor.

"It's only Louisa," said Malakhai. "She won't hurt you,
Mallory. She likes you."

"How did you do that?"

"No one has ever figured that out. But you're welcome to
try." His hands moved on to a pair of plain cloth trousers.

"Maybe this is what you're looking for?" She handed him
the passport. It was opened to the inside page and its mutilated
photograph. "I thought Edith Candle might have done that."

He held up the ruined likeness of his wife. "This was the
only picture of Louisa. Yes, Edith probably did it. Poor
woman—jealous of a ghost."

"At first, I thought you married Louisa to give her a new
identity for a legal passport. But I underestimated you,
Malakhai. It's a professional forgery. I almost took it for the
genuine article."

He shook his head. "I can't take the credit. This passport
was Nick Prado's work. He had a small business forging
papers for refugees."

"He was in the Resistance?"

"Sorry, nothing that glamorous. Forgery was his day job. A local printer provided the clientele. Nick had a room at the back of the shop."

"So magic didn't pay very well?"

"Faustine's apprentices weren't on salary. We all had to earn a living on the outside. The old lady was only generous with her costume allowance. It didn't matter if we starved, as long as we made a good appearance."

"And after she died?"

"The profits were pretty meager. They wouldn't support all of us." He was still fixated on the ruined face in the passport. "I wish Edith hadn't done this."

Mallory took the passport from his hand. "Maybe you're the one who cut up Louisa's photograph. Did you go a little crazy?" She tapped the portrait. "Did you slash this face?"

He kept his silence.

She leaned closer. "You were angry, out of control." And now the gamble, the guess, the closing shot. "You knew your wife was cheating on you. Louisa was sleeping with Max Candle."

"Yes, I knew. But I forgave them."

Seven

THE ARMCHAIR'S SKIN WAS SOFT, AND THE DEEP CUSHION cupped around his backside in an intimacy he had never enjoyed with a woman. Yet Detective Sergeant Riker could not be entirely comfortable here, and it was nothing to do with the new tension between himself and his partner.

Mallory's living room had the cold look of a vacant apartment, though it was fully furnished in the high contrast of black leather and white carpet, sharp angles of costly woods, glass and chrome—appointments well beyond the means of a cop. The most striking feature was the panoramic window overlooking Central Park. Such views did not come cheap.

Riker didn't want to know where all her excess money came from. But he had dark suspicions that she might be up to something perfectly legal. She was too open about living higher and dressing better than cops who were known to be on the take. He coupled this with her catlike patience for the long setup to a vicious pratfall. So he never asked any blunt questions about money, lest he wind up falling on his face, the next victim of Mallory's unique tripping style.

Her back was turned to him as she stood before the open closet, holding his new coat in one hand and a hanger in the other. Her body stiffened slightly, and he knew she had found the stain on one sleeve, a small spot of spaghetti sauce.

Riker set a stack of videotapes on the glass coffee table. "These are more outtakes on the parade. The cameramen kept cutting to the dog balloon and the screaming kids. You won't see any action with the crossbow." When he turned back to the closet, Mallory was gone—probably off to the kitchen in search of spot remover; she had her priorities.

He took advantage of this private moment to inspect a florist's bouquet of long-stemmed red roses delivered in a tall crystal vase. He slipped the attached card out of the envelope and read the words: "Dinner at eight. I promise not to play the violin anymore." It was unsigned. The handwriting was an elegant script with the old-fashioned flourish of a much older man. On the other side of the card was the logo of a midtown hotel. This only told him that Mallory's admirer was filthy rich, but he had already guessed that by cost-estimating the vase.

He heard the noise behind him and feigned interest in the view as he worked the card back into its envelope. When he turned around, she put a cold bottle in his hand. Though it was not quite noon, he accepted this goodwill gesture and slugged back a taste of imported beer.

A peace offering? Or was it a bribe?

She sat on the couch and sorted through the tapes. "Did you find Oliver's nephew?" The subtext of her tone asked if he had even bothered to look.

"You mean Crossbow Man?" He flopped down in the arm-chair and tossed her a folded newspaper. Mallory opened it to read the comic strip name in large block letters across the front page, "CROSSBOW MAN MISSING."

"Your boy must've left town in a hurry," said Riker. "Nobody's seen him since the parade. If he stays lost, the city might squeeze out of a lawsuit. I think the kid skinned his knee when you brought him down."

She turned to the story on the inside page. "Suppose the crossbow routine was a diversion for attempted murder? Richard Tree could be a material witness. Maybe he's not lost. He could be dead."

In the spirit of détente, Riker refrained from telling her what he thought of that theory. While she scanned the story, he concentrated on not spilling his beer. God, how he hated this wall-to-wall white carpeting. The scatter rug in his own apartment was more adaptable to stains. Over the years, he had actually altered the pattern with colorful accents of sauces from deli containers.

He glanced at his watch, then picked up the remote control unit and touched the power button. The automated doors of a black lacquer cabinet swung open to display a television set. It was almost time for *Noonday New York.* "Mallory? Have you been watching the news? They're turning the balloon shooting into a damn miniseries."

"No." She was still preoccupied with the newspaper article.

Did she ever watch television? He tried to imagine her doing something purely recreational. And then he decided that she had only purchased the TV set to keep up the illusion that a normal human lived here.

He settled back with his beer, turned up the volume and fell in love with the image of a tarted-up newscaster sitting behind a long desk. She wore a tight sweater, and garish red lipstick outlined her prominent teeth.

Riker sighed. He had always been a sucker for hookers with overbites and electric-red hair that could only be described in the context of a bowling alley in Lodi, New Jersey.

Behind the news desk was a giant screen with a still picture of Mallory standing on the brim of the top-hat float. The electric redhead was saying, "—uncovered new evidence in the shooting of Goldy—" The image on the big screen dissolved, changing to a moving picture of the gargantuan deflating balloon. The camera closed in to focus on one elderly parade spectator. Riker remembered taking this woman's statement and praying that she would not die of old age before they were done. The camera froze this portrait as the newswoman crooned to Riker, "—witness died suddenly before she could offer testimony in the ongoing investigation of—"

"What investigation?" Mallory looked up from her reading. "This is official now?" Unmistakable was the implication that he had been holding out on her.

Riker shrugged. "I don't know where they get this stuff. There's no open case. The balloon's a dead issue, and so is Oliver Tree."

She continued to stare at him, waiting for him to confess to some crime of omission.

In his defense, he said, "Mallory, this is the *news* media." He pointed to the paper in her hand. "Did you get to the part where the one gunshot is now *three* shots?" He glanced back at the screen portrait of the parade spectator. "And that old lady is a mysteriously dead witness."

The screen image changed to show an elderly man emerging from a parked car on a residential street in suburbia. The ancient wrinkled face was fearful as his startled eyes took in the approaching mob, an onslaught of reporters with cameras and microphones, coming to crush him. Now the camera shot the old man's back as he hurried up the flagstone path toward the sanctuary of his little house. His walking canes slowed his flight, and every reporter was able to beat him to the door. He stopped and covered his face with both hands, yelling, "Yes, she's *dead!* My wife is dead! Are you happy now?"

A reporter was asking—shouting, "Was it a sudden death?"

"No," said the old man. "She was ninety-two years old. It took a long, long time."

In the background, a garage door flew open to reveal a young amazon in strapping good health. The girl ran into the front yard, armed with a baseball bat. She was heading for the reporters, swinging her weapon in blind fury and screaming, "My grandmother died of *pneumonia,* you freaking—" The camera crew dispersed quickly, and now their lenses recorded the jumpy, quirky images of many pairs of feet running across the lawn at top speed.

Riker turned to Mallory and raised his eyebrows to say, *I told you so.* "Who are you gonna believe? Me or those clowns?"

The large screen behind the news desk went dark as the redhead stood up to greet a slender young man with a concave chest and a failed goatee of straggling hairs. Riker noted elbow patches on the man's blazer and took this as a sign that the fop did no real work—probably a writer. But now the guest was being introduced as a weapons expert.

Go figure. In Riker's experience, weapons technicians were all actual men—even the women.

Beside the newswoman's desk, a large easel displayed the cartoon of a cartoon, a diagram of the Goldy balloon floating above the drawings of tiny spectators.

The weapons expert stood by the easel and pointed to bold blue lines drawn through the big puppy's body. "This is the trajectory of the bullet. These lines mark the entry of the bullet through the tip of the dog's tail, nicking the rear paw, passing through the hindquarters, exiting the dog collar and entering the jaw." He paused to catch his breath. "*Finally* exiting the top of the puppy's left ear." His pointing finger moved to a position on the pavement, and the camera lens zoomed in for the close-up of a cartoon blonde with a gun.

Riker glanced at Mallory, relieved to see her absorbed in the newspaper.

"And this line," said the expert, "shows the origin of the bullet as being consistent with the position of the policewoman who shot the balloon."

Mallory looked up as the newscaster turned to her television audience and flashed her glorious overbite. "So there we have it. Damning new evidence against the cop who shot Goldy. Expert testimony from the writer of best-selling technothrillers, Rolf Warner."

"That hack looks familiar." Riker leaned closer to the television. "Hey, isn't he the same expert they used to explain the war in Bosnia?"

The redhead was saying, "—to recap for viewers just tuning in. We have the sudden death of a witness to the shooting. And the mysterious disappearance of another witness, Crossbow Man." The woman smiled, momentarily dazzling Riker with her large buckteeth. "The police have made no progress in their search. Our sources at Number One Police Plaza tell us this has all the signs of an NYPD cover-up. Crossbow Man is still—"

Mallory grabbed the remote control from his hand and switched off the set. "I'll find that little bastard myself."

"No you don't," said Riker. "Coffey's right on this one. You don't go near Richard Tree. The lieutenant put two full-time men on the kid. They'll find him."

"So we *do* have an open homicide case." Suspicion was back in her voice.

"No, Mallory, we don't. But somebody leaked the kid's juvenile record to the press."

And now she glared at him to say, *So you were holding out on me.*

Riker knew when to make a timely exit. He grabbed up his hat and walked toward the closet to retrieve his coat. "We're following a directive from the mayor's publicist. He wants us to find Crossbow Man and deliver him to the reporters. This has nothing to do with police business."

He opened the door to the closet and looked down to see a cardboard package large enough to house a Shetland pony. "What's in the big box?"

"Rabbi Kaplan's bread board," she said.

Riker threw his hands up. "Okay, okay. Forget I asked."

✛   ✛   ✛

The young detective had left her gun hanging on the coatrack by the rabbi's front door, but she still seemed a bit dangerous as she leaned over the kitchen sink with her screwdriver and coaxed sparks from a jumble of wires in the wall.

Rabbi David Kaplan stood near the empty carton and nod-ded politely, as if he were actually following her plan to extend wireless electricity across the floor to the outlets of the new butcher-block island. But he knew nothing of electrical affairs. Only his wife understood overloaded circuits and knew the secret location of the fuse box. So the rabbi had no idea what Kathy Mallory was talking about.

While she replaced the cover of the wall outlet, he averted his eyes and stared at the grand piece of furniture she had assembled in the center of the room. The cart was well crafted, surfaced with strips of hardwoods in complementing grains.

The rabbi shook his head in silence. Kathy always went too far.

Or perhaps this was an atonement of sorts. But was it for past or future crimes? Should he regret arranging an interview with the old man?

Too late now.

Mr. Halpern was looking forward to seeing the "pretty child" he had met so briefly last night.

What was the worst thing that could come of their meeting again?

Well, Mr. Halpern was very fragile.

She had finished testing the outlets on the cart, and now she was frowning at Rabbi Kaplan, misunderstanding his expression. "You don't like it?"

"Oh, yes, Kathy. I like it very much. It's wonderful, but so—" *So extreme? So suspicious?* "You broke a five-dollar bread board, not an heirloom." She had also broken his heart and shaken his faith. It might be a bad idea to let her get away with that. But he must pick his words carefully; she was not very tolerant of criticism.

"Last night, you said anyone at the table could tell Malakhai how twisted you were. How could you say such a thing in—"

"You didn't rush in to contradict me, did you, Rabbi?"

Her face was turned away from him as she bent over to tighten a screw, but he had heard the cold accusation in her voice, the opening cut. The game was on.

"Kathy, under the circumstances, how could I contradict you? I would've stepped on your best line of the evening."

Good parry.

The rabbi smiled as he stepped up to the butcher block and pressed his advantage. "But now I want to know if you really believed that, or were you lying to a purpose?"

"*You* believed it."

He made note of her game point—a fast shot to a vital organ. His hand rested over his heart as he rallied with, "You think I believe you're twisted? I never did."

Was that entirely true? Well, no, but he had not intended to lie—not that time. Some of his counterpoints were pure acts of self-defense, words pulled quickly to fend her off. "I've known you since you were ten years old and—"

"Eleven."

"Ten. You lied a year onto your age. Don't deny it." Here he stopped to compliment himself on this maneuver, insisting upon honesty on the one hand, while the other hand was busy obfuscating the truth. "Helen Markowitz's judgment carries more weight with me than yours."

She was somewhat subdued by this. Invoking Helen's name still had some stopping power, but it would not last long. He needed a hook of words to hold his ground with her. "I remember the night when Louis brought you home to Helen." As if he might have forgotten a child felon in manacles, a tiny hellmouth of obscenities. "Do you remember your room, the way it looked that first time Helen put you to bed?"

She nodded. "It used to be the guest room."

"Yes, that's what they called it. They bought that house ten years before you came to live with them. And for all those years, Helen changed the sheets in the guest room once a week without fail. But whenever there was a houseguest, she always made up a bed on the fold-out couch downstairs. A little odd, don't you think?"

Yes, he could see that she thought so. "Ten years before you arrived, there was a baby's crib in that room. Louis disposed of it before Helen came home from the hospital—without the child."

Other than replacing the crib with a bed, over the ensuing decade, the bedroom had remained unchanged. The wallpaper stripes had never faded, but stayed true to the primary hues of a child's coloring book. A soft woven rug invited the soles of small bare feet, and the bed quilt was a cheerful patchwork of folk-art animals. The entire room had the look of a crafty trap that Helen Markowitz had set to catch a loose child on the fly. For ten years, that gentle woman had never uttered one soft word about her dead baby, lost before it was even born.

For ten years, the room screamed.

"Helen had been waiting for you such a long time. You completed her life, Kathy. She thought you were perfect in every way—not at all twisted."

And because of its blind spot, a giant gaping maw of a lacuna where heinous crimes were overlooked, motherlove was both imperfect and perfectly wonderful.

"Not by any word or act have I ever contradicted Helen—and you *know* that, Kathy."

And thus he completed a neat escape by the artful framing of words, but at what personal cost? He knew what she was—though her foster mother had vehemently denied it. Helen Markowitz had torn up the child's early psychiatric evaluation, putting great anger into the shredding of paper, strongly objecting to the word *sociopath* in connection to a little girl whose life had barely begun.

Rabbi Kaplan wanted to go on believing that Kathy Mallory did not know what she was. So long as she remained in ignorance of the truth, this ruthless, amoral child could exist in a state of innocent grace. Sometimes he believed that truth was not a shining thing, but a weapon of great destruction. At other times, he wondered if he had merely become a proficient deceiver, an uncommon liar.

In the moments of heavy silence between them, he scrutinized her face, looking there for signs of redemption—hers or his own? He could not say. Their wordplay was done, and he was bleeding only a little—as usual.

He ran his hand over the surface of the butcher block. "I didn't thank you for this. It's beautiful." He looked up, gratified to see the faint smile on her face. "Your meeting with Mr. Halpern is arranged for tomorrow. But it might be a waste of time. He wasn't in Paris during the occupation."

"I know those two have some history together." She picked up her tools and tossed them into her knapsack. "Last night, that old man was crying after he talked to Malakhai."

She had what she came for, and now she was turning to leave.

Not so fast.

"Kathy, you will *not* interrogate Mr. Halpern." This was the tone of the teacher. He was not yet finished with the

Promethean labor of Kathy Mallory's moral instruction. "Mr. Halpern is a good storyteller. You *will* listen to him without interruption. He'll tell you what he's willing to talk about. Whatever causes him pain will be left out. When he's done, you'll leave with whatever he gave you—and no more."

Eight

"I SEE YOU'VE BEEN BUSY THIS MORNING." CHARLES PUT THE useless key back in his pocket and trained the flashlight beam on a metal box bolted to the accordion walls. The chains were gone, and the partition had been closed to a thin crack of electric light from the other side. A number pad on the new lock required a code to open the door latch. "Were you planning to give me the combination?"

Mallory touched four buttons on the pad. A green light blinked at the top of the box, followed by a click of metal. "It's a good lock. Malakhai won't be able to open it."

Charles spread the wood sections apart. They moved silently on recently oiled tracks, and the hinges no longer creaked. "But I don't mind if Malakhai comes and goes when he likes. I think—"

"It's charming, right." And now she added trespassers to the list of decrepit furniture and malfunctioning electrical wiring that he found so endearing.

Charles walked around the dragon screen, pulling the new crossbow strings from a paper bag. He stopped to stare at the area in front of the platform. "Mallory, have you been cleaning?"

The debris of last night's drinking and magic was gone. Empty bottles and broken bowstrings had been thrown out with the trash, and she had swept the floor at the base of the platform. But even without dust tracks, she could see evidence of Malakhai's return visit. While she was busy with Riker and the rabbi, Malakhai's search had expanded to the boxes and trunks on the first row of shelves. So he had found no difficulty in getting past the new lock. And now she must rethink clichés about the generation that could not program VCRs.

Charles was hunched over the toolbox. "Have you been following the news today?" He pulled out a can of machine oil. "The reporters are taking another look at Oliver's death." Screwdriver in hand, he walked over to the crossbow he had mounted on the pedestal yesterday. "I didn't know his nephew had a juvenile arrest record. What did he do? Shoplifting? Something like that?"

"I'll ask Riker." Mallory smiled. Lieutenant Coffey would suspect her of the press leak, but he would never prove it. And the brass at Number One Police Plaza would stay on Coffey's back until he found the nephew—no matter how much it strained the budget. She had doubled the manpower on a homicide case that did not officially exist.

"I saw the mayor's press conference this afternoon." Charles pulled the crossbow pistol from its slot in the pedestal. "A reporter asked about the *murder* in the park, and the mayor was livid—*pounding* on the podium. He said Central Park is the safest precinct in New York City. Said it three times."

"He always does that," said Mallory. "Every time we find a dead body in the park."

Charles unscrewed the metal plate that covered the firing apparatus. "Then Central Park *isn't* the safest precinct in Manhattan?"

"Well, yeah, it is. The crime stats are lower. But the park is the only *uninhabited* precinct."

She stared at the opened cartons on the shelves. They were not part of the shipment from Faustine's Magic Theater. What was Malakhai searching for? And now she thought of another unanswered question, one that had hampered her background check. "What is Malakhai's first name?"

Charles appeared to physically duck under this question, kneeling down to examine the center gear of the pedestal. "If he has another name, I've never heard it." He held up one finger slicked with a dab of recent oil, evidence of last night's shooting party. "Have you been—"

"I searched the title on that upstate hospital. Nick Prado said Malakhai owned it."

"He does." Charles wiped the oil off on his jeans. "You didn't fire this—"

"According to the paper trail, a foreign trust fund owns that property."

"He's a very private man, Mallory." Charles pulled the crossbow off the pedestal and held it up to her. "I did mention that these were dangerous, right?" He bent the curve of metal as he pulled the new string across the horns of the bow, then turned his back on her to reinstall the pistol grip in the pedestal slot.

So he did not plan to discuss Malakhai anymore. *Fine.* A change of subject, a little detour—no problem. There were other avenues of investigation, other suspects. She could make use of his Ph.D. in psychology. "What can you tell me about a classic narcissist?"

"So Nick Prado made your short list. He'll be so pleased." Charles bent low to look through the sights of the crossbow. "A true narcissist would enjoy being the center of your investigation, whether he was guilty or not. Does that help?"

"Let's suppose he's guilty."

Charles shook his head in disbelief. "Nick had no reason to harm Oliver."

"Then help me eliminate him as a suspect." She put one hand on his arm. "If Prado didn't do it, I can't hurt him, can I? So *hypothetically,* let's say he did it."

"I'm not worried about you damaging Nick. His ego is indestructible." Charles loaded an arrow into the crossbow, cocked it and depressed the lever to set the pedestal gears in motion. He bent down to an open crate and pulled out another crossbow. Mallory sat down on the floor beside him as he dismantled it.

"All right," said Charles. "He *is* a classic narcissist. You probably guessed that when he flirted with you the other day. Most men would never approach a woman like you."

He looked up from his work of separating pieces of the crossbow. "You're beautiful." This had the sound of a guilty confession. Charles's face was comical even in serious moments. His were the eyes of a frog in love. "But Nick truly believes he's a good match for you. I know it sounds ludicrous, but he sees himself as young and virile."

Charles slotted the bow at the end of the shaft, then reached into his bag of strings. "I wasn't joking when I said he'd be pleased to be a murder suspect—even if he *was* guilty. The true narcissist believes he can outwit everyone in the immediate world."

"So if he planned a murder, he might get sloppy with the details?"

"No, I wouldn't put it that way. The plan would be very carefully thought out, but perhaps too complex. The more intricate the plan, the greater the possibility of error. That's the blind spot of the narcissist. And it wouldn't fit your theory of a key switch. That's much too simple for Nick."

The pedestal stopped ticking. She heard the twang of the string, and in the same instant, the arrow was wobbling in the center of the target on the stage.

"But the simple murder is the smartest one," said Mallory. "This one was damn near perfect."

"And that's the problem with it." Charles laid the crossbow aside and picked up another. "It doesn't fit the profile of a narcissist. Switching the keys is hardly a challenge. Simple sleight of hand. No, if Nick was planning a crime as large as a murder, he'd do something more convoluted. So he's probably your worst suspect." Charles held up a screw with obvious rust, then reached for a can of oil. "You know, Malakhai was right. This apparatus won't help you work out the Lost Illusion."

"What's to work out?" She looked up at the target. "He was supposed to get the cuffs off before the arrows hit him."

"A cut-and-dried escape routine?" Charles shook his head. "Oliver was trying to re-create a Max Candle illusion. An accident was built into the act—Max's trademark. Oliver explained that to the policemen and the reporter. He didn't want them to rescue him when he started screaming. When the first arrow drew blood, they wouldn't let me up on the stage. I guess they thought I was acting, too."

Charles stood up and dusted off his jeans. "Unlocking manacles and dodging arrows." He threw his hands up.

"Where's the magic? If you'd ever seen one of Max's illusions, you'd understand."

"Okay, show me."

"Well, that's a snag. I don't know how the major illusions were done."

But Charles's intelligence scores went right off the charts. Was he holding out on her? No, that would show on his face. "Do you know how *any* of them work?"

"I could show you a trick Max designed for a children's party. The illusion is called matter through matter." He climbed to the top of the platform. After pulling the target from the slots between the two posts, he laid it on the floor at the edge of the stage. "This illusion uses the lazy tongs. Remember when Oliver spread out his cape, and it fell to the floor—empty?"

"That metal thing that comes up through the trapdoor?"

"Right." Charles descended the stairs. "At least you'll see how that works." He bent over an open crate and lifted out a large flat object covered in quilted material. After propping it against the wall of the platform, he pulled the wrapping away to expose a mirror in a thick frame of maple. It was the size and oval shape of the target, with the same black support pegs at the sides. The glass surface wildly distorted every object in its field. It reminded her of a carnival mirror that alternately made giants and midgets from the reflections of ordinary people.

"I learned this trick when I was nine years old. I'm going to pass through this glass." He carried the mirror up the stairs and fitted the frame into the slots of the standing poles, suspending it three feet above the floorboards. "Max created this illusion for a children's Halloween party, so it's a bit of a departure from the regular routine." He pulled on the red velvet drapes, drawing them closer to the mirror, almost touching the support posts. "He didn't die in this act."

"Why not? Kids love stuff like that." She walked to the foot of the staircase. "Halloween is supposed to be scary."

"No, he wouldn't die for an audience of children." Satisfied with the setup, Charles came down the stairs again and moved slowly through the mass of cartons, reading all the labels. "I was accustomed to watching Max die onstage. The other kids weren't." He opened a box and pulled out four brass pipes and disks. "You still don't understand. Realism was his priority. An adult audience really believed he died in the finale of every act."

"Lots of blood and gore?" She sat down on the bottom step.

"Nothing that crude." He quickly assembled the parts into freestanding poles, then screwed metal loops into the heads of each one. "The audience never saw any actual blood, but the mind's eye supplied it—lots of it."

"Didn't he ever worry that somebody in the audience would try to save him and ruin the act?"

"No, never. I think Houdini had that problem in the thirties. I guess the world changed." Charles set out the brass poles to form the four corners of a square near the foot of the staircase. He connected the poles with lengths of red velvet rope hooked onto the brass loops. "Max could always count on a few Good Samaritans rushing the stage. They added some drama to the act. But they were always too slow, too late. Most people just sat and watched him die."

Charles was looking at the café table and the chair that Malakhai had used last night. "Max had no degrees in psychology, but he understood the darkest things about his audience." Charles picked up the chair and set it in the center of the velvet-roped square. He dipped one hand into another carton and retrieved a long cape of scarlet silk, an exact copy of the one Oliver Tree had worn.

"You think it's like herd instinct? Is that what keeps them in their seats?"

"Yes, but there's more to it." He examined the material and draped it on a pedestal. "I understood the phenomenon better when I was at school. I did a paper on crowd behavior. My best case study was a small town in New Jersey. A clothing store caught fire. A schoolgirl was trapped in a room fronted by a plate-glass window."

His face was somber as he unchained one of the velvet ropes and entered the square. This was not a pleasant memory. "Her name was Mary Kent. She was fifteen years old." Standing behind the chair, he glanced up at the platform. "There were broken bones in Mary's hands. That's how hard she beat on the window, but the plate glass was too thick. She was a tiny little thing, not strong enough to break it. This was a Saturday afternoon, and there were lots of pedestrians passing by on the street. They gathered in front of the window, completely mesmerized by the fire—and the girl who was screaming and beating on the glass. I suppose the window was a lot like a giant television screen. They formed an audience and watched her die."

"Where was the fire department?"

"No one called them. Eventually, a fireman saw the smoke from the other side of town. But they were too late for Mary. Not their fault."

He stepped outside the square and walked up the platform staircase. "I interviewed all the witnesses—the audience. They blamed the firemen for Mary Kent's death—actually ragged them for being too slow with the fire truck. They all believed that someone else had called in the fire—or that's what they told me. I asked why no one had thought to pick up a rock and break the glass so Mary could escape. 'Never thought of it,' they said. Just never occurred to any of them."

"Did you believe the witnesses?"

"No, I didn't." He pointed down to the roped-off square. "You're going to sit there. Remember, this illusion was staged for an intimate audience and a narrow field. That's because of the mirror. So don't move outside the ropes."

Charles checked the reflection of the chair in the mirror. "Max arranged the Halloween party for me." He touched a switch on the side of the left post. A lightbulb glowed from its submerged socket in the crossbeam. "The other guests were children of magicians—a very tough audience."

Mallory took her seat inside the ropes as Charles ran down the stairs, two at a time, and retrieved the scarlet cape. She glanced at the nearby carton filled with the same material. "Why so many?"

"Real silk." He turned off the floor lamp near the base of the platform. "Sometimes the material ripped when the metal tongs came up through the floor. So Max needed a large supply."

He disappeared around the dragon screen. And now the

lights were going out all over the basement. The bulb in the crossbeam made a dull halo around the mirror.

"Ready?" Charles returned, wearing the scarlet cape. A monk's hood covered his hair and shadowed his face as he walked toward the platform.

The mirror reflected only the black shadows of the space behind her chair. When Charles neared the top of the staircase, she could see his face climbing in the wavy distortion of the glass, elongating and compressing in grotesque caricatures. He stood center stage and spread his arms wide. The material of the cape concealed the entire mirror and touched the curtains on either side of the posts. After a few moments, the silk collapsed. Charles had vanished, but the red material was not falling to the floor. It was slipping through the center of the mirror in a thinning stream of scarlet silk.

And now the cape had disappeared into the looking glass, and Charles's disembodied head was floating inside the oval frame. The light shone all around the mirror, no feet, no physical man to make that image. His nose elongated in the carnival glass, turning to a snout, and his eyes widened to saucers. When he bared his teeth, they grew longer in the distortion of the mirror, turning into fangs as he mouthed a silent howl.

Two white hands appeared beside the floating monster head. He snapped his fingers, and the mirror revolved on its pivots, spinning end over end between the posts. When the oval frame stopped revolving and righted itself again, Charles was no longer trapped inside the glass. The mirror was empty and black.

A finger tapped Mallory's shoulder, and she jumped, startled.

Charles stood behind her.

And that must be the scary part.

He was grinning, utterly pleased with himself. "What did you think of it?"

"Good trick." She glanced back at the platform. "So tell me if I've got this right. The cape was tied to a wire that fed through a hinged opening in the mirror. That's why he used a carnival mirror, right? So the distortion would hide the imperfection?"

Charles nodded, not smiling anymore. He was turning on the lamps.

"The drapes are lined in black," said Mallory. "I know you can't move the support posts. But the mirror frame is thick enough to reposition the glass inside it. When the lazy tongs spread the cape, you pushed the glass out of alignment and stepped behind the curtain. And then you were reflected in the mirror from a different angle."

"Well, yes." He turned to her with a face full of disappointment. "But what about the effect? The illusion—"

"I got the mechanics right?"

Charles didn't answer her. He walked back to the platform and climbed the steps, moving slowly, as if suddenly very tired. When he stood before the oval frame, he pressed on one side of the glass to reposition it. And now he found her face in the wavy distortion. Their eyes met, and he stared at her with his unhappy reflection. In this new angle, the carnival mirror shortened Charles's nose and contracted his bulbous eyes to more normal proportions.

Mallory sipped in a breath and held it.

In the distortion of the mirror, Charles was reborn as an incarnation of his famous cousin. Mallory's eyes were riveted to the beautiful man inside the glass—alive and a hundred times more compelling than any of the old photographs. The man in the mirror was touching her insides with chemistry and flooding her face with heat. It was a fight to remain still, to keep the fragile illusion in place. One move would destroy it, but she had the sense of levitating with a lightness of head and body, almost hollow now, rising slowly.

So beautiful.

This was what Louisa saw the day she met Max Candle. In that first second, Malakhai was doomed to lose his young wife. This man was so—

And then Max was gone, vanished in the moment when the mirror was lifted from the post slots. Charles turned to her with his more familiar face, his large nose and the eyes of a sad but charming frog, unaware that he had resurrected the dead.

"Magic is wasted on you," he said.

✝ ✝ ✝

After Charles had left the basement, Mallory continued to prowl through the boxes until she found the missing leg irons for the Lost Illusion.

All four crossbows were fixed on their pedestals and angling up toward the target. She cocked the weapon nearest the staircase. Very smooth operation, no problems. No need to run the pedestal gears again. Every weapon had fired in good working order. Now she only needed to work out the rest of the mechanics.

With a cape slung over one shoulder, she climbed to the top of the platform and stood before the target. She had watched the crossbows work from every angle on the ground below. Now she planned to see the trick from Oliver Tree's point of view on the stage.

She knelt on the floor and attached a leg iron to the ring at the base of each post. The shackles had no locks, only catches to keep them closed. In her mind, she was replaying the tape she had watched a hundred times. These irons were exactly like the ones Oliver had worn on his ankles when he hung spread-eagle across the face of the target.

Mallory reached down to unhook a pair of NYPD hand-cuffs from her belt. Oliver had used two pairs, but there had been only one key. She had blown up segments of his film performance and found the piece of the broken key extension falling against the gray backdrop of the band shell. There had been no sign of a second key when the fingers of his left hand splayed wide with sudden pain.

Out of habit, she pulled out her own cuff key. Of course, it would never work. When her hand was bound to the posts and stretched out, this one would be too short to undo the lock. She set her key ring down on the floor and reached into the back pocket of her jeans for the relic from Faustine's Magic Theater. She unscrewed the bulb at the top of the extension rod and selected a post with teeth to match her own cuff key.

Mallory stood up and closed one of the bracelets around the iron ring on the right-hand post. The handcuff chain dangled the open bracelet within easy reach—easier for her than Oliver. His corpse was five inches short of her own height of five ten.

And now she was confronted with her first problem. This platform was made for Max Candle, a man seven inches taller than Oliver. Yet there was no difference in the post-ring positions. On Oliver's replica, the iron loops appeared to be the same distance from the top of the posts.

Mallory shook the dust off the silk cape and draped it across her shoulders, then pulled the hood over her hair. The long hem trailed on the stage behind her. She looked down at the outline of the trapdoor. The foot pedal was in plain view, and when she stepped on it, a square of wood dropped open behind the heels of her running shoes.

The mechanical framework rose out of the floor, slowly coming up beneath the trailing material, silently spreading its metal bones to fill out the cape in the form of raised arms. A curved metal dish imitated the top of a human skull beneath the hood. She stepped away from the cape, and spread her legs to attach the floor shackles to her ankles. Reaching up, she slipped her right wrist into the handcuff dangling from the iron ring. It took a bit of fiddling to close the bracelet with one hand while holding on to the skeleton key. Oliver Tree had done this much faster with two sets of handcuffs.

It was the first tick of the pedestal that made her drop the key.

Her mouth went dry as she watched the piece of metal clatter to the floorboards, landing beside her own discarded key ring.

The spread cape blocked her view of the crossbows. Mallory stretched one foot the length of the leg-iron chain, but she could not reach the floor pedal to drop the cape and give her a clear view of the weapons. How had Oliver Tree done this?

Bound by both legs and one hand, she listened to the ticking, the gears grinding. The noise was coming from her left side. She imagined the peg rising, moving closer to the crossbow trigger.

What is the crossbow aiming at?

She had seen Oliver die so many times, and she knew each trajectory by heart. The test firing of Max's crossbows had agreed with the tapes of the park death.

The pedestal was ticking, ticking.

Think! Where is the arrow going to strike?

She saw Oliver clearly now. The left-hand bows fired arrows into his thighs. There was only time to frame this thought, to shift one leg. The ticking stopped. The arrow ripped through the spread silk and pinned her to the target.

No pain.

Mallory looked down at the arrow that had torn through the blue jeans and missed her skin by a hair's breadth. Her breathing was slow and shallow, the better to listen for the movements of company in the basement, sounds of a would-be assassin. She had so little faith in accidents these days.

The gun was in her free left hand, but Mallory had no memory of pulling it from the holster. She had been that intent on the sound of footsteps on the staircase.

The red material was pulled to one side.

Malakhai.

He was looking down at the arrow pinning her leg to the target. He glanced at the open trapdoor and stepped on the floor pedal in front of it. "The lazy tongs work in slow gear. They'll go down in another minute." He ignored the gun in her hand and pointed at the floor pedal. "You're supposed to step on that *before* you put on the cuffs and leg irons. Timing is everything, Mallory." He was mildly distracted by the rising muzzle of her gun. It was harder to miss, now that she was aiming at his face.

"Point taken," he said. "I'm forgetting my manners. Good evening. You're looking well."

"You missed me by an inch."

He glanced down at the arrow in the denim material. "I'd say it was closer than that. You probably jarred the pedestal gears when you cocked the crossbow." He reached into the breast pocket of his coat and extracted a pack of cigarettes, acting as if this were perfectly normal, holding a casual conversation with a chained woman. "You *did* cock the bow. Am I right, Mallory?"

"Am I supposed to believe this was another accident?"

His slow smile implied that this might be the more charitable view—an accident instead of a stupid mistake. "I told you not to walk in front of a loaded crossbow."

Had the weapon been loaded when she cocked it? She could not recall checking the magazine for an unfired arrow from her test round. Was she going to own up to an oversight like that?

Well, no.

She pulled on the handcuff bracelet that bound her wrist—a not too subtle suggestion for him to unlock it, and right now.

Malakhai lit a cigarette. "The pedestals are as delicate as Swiss timepieces. In fact, the gears *are* Swiss." He exhaled a slow stream of smoke—portrait of a man at leisure. "It takes some finesse to do this illusion."

She yanked the chain, but he did not get the hint.

Malakhai looked down at the revolver as she extended it toward his chest. "I gather you dislike criticism." Ignoring the gun, he reached down and pulled the arrow from the target. "You remind me of an old proverb. The girl who can't dance always blames it on the band."

And now he was holding a sharp arrow in one hand and standing much too close. Her finger rested lightly on the trigger.

There were so many fractured parts to her emotions. Malakhai showed no fear of the gun. That was enough to make her angry. And she wanted this to be his fault, not hers. But now he was looking down at the keys lying on the floor. This was more evidence of her own errors, and she hated him for that. She stared at the arrow in his hand. Did he mean to do some damage? Or was this a sick game he was playing?

Her body went rigid. Every muscle flooded with adrenaline for the fight, as if it would take any force to squeeze a trigger. And darker chemicals were released into her brain as a response to rage, magnifying it to obliterate reason.

In the last untainted part of her mind, she heard herself speaking calm, icy words, "Let go of the arrow. Let it fall and step back."

A drop of sweat rolled down the side of her face. The trembling in her gun hand was nearly imperceptible. It was a muscle spasm of tight control—to prevent her revolver from firing into his chest.

Mallory pulled down on the manacle until the metal bit into her wrist. Pain was a focus, a trick of her own to clear her mind of violence. But she could still feel the anger massing, building toward a single convulsive act. If she could not stop it, she was going to kill him. She strained at the bracelet, pulling it down harder to bring on more pain, but it was not enough.

"Drop it!" she yelled.

At the moment Malakhai turned away from her to send the arrow flying off the stage, her manacled hand shot straight out with more force than she possessed in a normal state of mind.

The crack was loud, and for an instant, she believed her gun had gone off.

Malakhai turned around, surprised to see her metal bracelet freed from the post. Dangling from the other end of her handcuff chain, the iron ring was attached to a splintered piece of wood.

"Are you bleeding?"

"No." She bowed her head over the red abrasion on her wrist, not wanting him to see that she had also been startled. The breakage was unintentional. She had only wanted the pain. "So you just happened to be passing by? Is that your story?"

He took her metal bracelet in both his hands. She never saw him work a key. The handcuff simply opened and released her wrist. He held up the manacles and the splintered section of wood. "I can fix this. But don't break anything else, all right? Perhaps if you kept your hands in your pockets?"

He knelt down to open the leg irons, and Mallory pushed him away. Then she reluctantly holstered her gun and undid the catches that bound her ankles. The anger was not receding, but it was under control as she stepped to one side of the target.

"Nasty tear in those jeans, Mallory. Lucky it wasn't your skin. Maybe next time it'll be a vital organ—like poor Oliver."

"Is that a threat?"

"That's a fact. I guess you'll have to wear something else to dinner. We have reservations for eight o'clock. No time for you to go home and change. Did you like the roses?"

"How did you know my address?"

He pointed down toward the wardrobe trunk, just visible over the top of the dragon screen. "I suggest the green silk."

✛   ✛   ✛

Mallory was dressed for a different season in 1942. Walking away from the cab, she felt the wind whistle around her feet. The gold dancing shoes were not made for the month of November. Though they fit well, she felt crippled by the slender straps and delicate heels. Near the front door of the restaurant, they paused by a mirror, and Malakhai drew her attention to the gleaming material of the suit. "Louisa says the silk has faded a bit. Once it was green enough to match your eyes."

The Greenwich Village restaurant catered to Europeans. The single long room was filled with accents of other languages. Near a window overlooking West Fourth Street, a small table was laid with three place settings. Three people sat down—if one counted Louisa, and Mallory did. As Dr. Slope would say at every poker game, *I came to play.*

Malakhai pulled out a package of cigarettes.

"They won't let you smoke in here," said Mallory. "That's the law."

"Ah, the new draconian regime." Malakhai took a cigarette from the pack. "But you can't possibly believe this restaurant enforces the mayor's petty little fits?" He pointed to the name of the café emblazoned on the menu. "These people are French, are they not? What were you thinking?"

Mallory no longer wanted to kill him.

Other women in the restaurant were looking their way—his way. And the men were also stealing glances at him. Though the table was next to the street window, Malakhai was the gravitational center of this room.

His eyes were dark attracters. She was alternately leaning toward him and pulling back. "Did you plan to search the basement? Or did you just show up to scare me?"

"Does anything scare you?" There was no sarcasm in his voice. "The pedestal mechanism is old. Who knows what else is broken—besides the post."

"Your ashtray, sir." A young waiter in a red dinner jacket had materialized by the table. It was not an ashtray he set before Malakhai, but a plain saucer. "If anyone should make a scene—"

"I know, Jean. You'll be shocked to see me smoking in your establishment—and very loud when you tell me to put out my cigarette. I promise to be contrite." After the waiter had left them to consult their menus, Malakhai rolled the unlit cigarette between his fingers. "You see that woman over there? The indignant one in the purple dress?"

Mallory turned around to look at a party of three patrons near the door. They were pulling on their coats and gesturing to the woman in purple. But she ignored them to blatantly stare at Malakhai and his cigarette, a red flag to a militant antismoker.

He smiled at this woman as he spoke to Mallory. "She and her friends are ready to leave. And yet, how can she go without exercising this bit of power over a stranger?" He pulled out a silver cigarette lighter. "Here I am, about to indulge in a simple pleasure, something *she* can deny me."

The woman's eyebrows shot together. She was waving down their waiter, as if the boy were a passing taxi. Jean cruised on by, pretending not to see her. The three dinner companions were standing by the door and hailing her. The woman in purple joined her friends with obvious reluctance. Out on the sidewalk, she was still not finished with Malakhai. She paused by the window to glare at him, to be sure he was not getting away with anything.

He made the unlit cigarette disappear into his closed fist. When he uncurled his fingers very close to the window glass, his hand was empty. The three companions applauded the trick as the purple woman stalked off down the sidewalk. Malakhai closed his hand again. This time he opened it with a lit cigarette resting between his fingers.

Mallory looked down at the saucer, where a second cigarette was smoking. There was lipstick on the filter. He must have put it there while she was distracted by the little magic show at the window. She stared at it for a moment, watching the smoke curl upward. "Where did Louisa come from?"

"If you knew that, you'd be an instant celebrity in the music world. There's no record of Louisa anywhere. Some frustrated historian even started the rumor that I made her up."

"Any rumors about murder?"

"Quite a few. Nick Prado started most of them to boost record sales in the early fifties. This was fifteen years before he quit the stage to start his public relations firm. But even then, he had all the instincts of a first-rate publicist."

"Prado knows the real story."

"Does he? He's never said so—not to you, Mallory."

"You never believed her death was an accident. You knew Louisa was murdered. You knew it long before the poker game."

She had expected him to deny that. But he didn't. There was nothing in his face to tell her whether she had guessed right or wrong.

"Why are you so preoccupied with Louisa?"

"Oliver's will left everything to charity, so I don't have a money motive. I think he frightened the man who killed your wife."

Their conversation stopped when Jean the waiter returned with a bottle of burgundy. He poured a small amount into a wineglass and hovered by the table, waiting for Malakhai's approval. Then the young man filled all three glasses and left.

"Oliver *did* botch the trick," said Malakhai. "I could tell that much from the television coverage."

"What was his mistake?"

"Oh, I'd be the last one to spoil your fun. I'm sure you'll work it out."

"What about that boy who died when Max Candle did the act? Was that another one of Nick Prado's stories? A publicist's pipe dream?"

"No, that really happened, but the story isn't widely known. Max was devastated. He was hardly going to use the boy's death for publicity."

"That accident should have made the national news."

"Why? Max Candle died on stage and magically came back to life. The boy stayed dead—less magical, only an accident report on a police blotter. Nothing more."

"Maybe you were in the audience the night Max did that trick."

"In fact, I was."

"So you would've known how to sabotage Oliver's trick in Central Park."

"Not necessarily. He didn't do it the same way Max did. So I'd have to know Oliver's version."

Hours later, she was no closer to a solution for the Lost Illusion. Her magical wineglass was never more than half empty, though she had never seen Malakhai refill it. And toward the end of a long evening, she had learned to be more careful in the pronunciation of every word, lest she slur her speech or drop any more syllables.

✛   ✛   ✛

All the way home in the cab, Mallory sat up straight, but the rest of the world would not. It leaned, it spun. *It* was out of control.

Her Upper West Side apartment building slid into view alongside the passenger window. The rear door opened and Malakhai stepped onto the sidewalk. He extended one hand to assist Mallory out of the car, as if he feared her feet might miss the ground attempting this maneuver on her own. As they crossed the building's marble threshold, she nodded toward a blur of green uniform, which must have been Frank the doorman.

In silence, they rode the elevator upward, not straight up but tilting off to one side. When they reached her floor, Malakhai escorted her down the hall, politely and firmly holding her right arm. This was a bygone courtesy she recognized from another era's black-and-white movies. Canny Mallory made use of his archaic good manners to keep herself from tripping on the unruly roiling carpet.

They stopped in front of her door, and he waited patiently while she tried three times to work the lock. Twice, she lied and blamed the problem on a new key. Finally, the door opened. Malakhai stood close beside her, yet his voice seemed distant as he said, "Good night."

At last, Mallory was inside her apartment, leaning against one stationary wall and willing the rest of the room to stand still. And now she remembered the question she had wanted to ask at the top of the evening.

She pulled open the door on her second try at turning the knob in the right direction—around. And then she was running down the hall. The elevator was engaged. She pushed through the door to the stairwell and accomplished a remarkable ballet of footwork to keep her balance on the concrete that shifted out from under her in a staircase conspiracy to break her neck.

She crossed the lobby, running uphill much of the way, and thanks to the quick efforts of Frank the doorman, there was no steel-framed glass impediment between herself and the street. Mallory was out on the sidewalk, breathless, and weaving only a little—or so she imagined.

Malakhai had just climbed into the backseat of a yellow taxi. He was instructing the driver when she appeared beside the passenger door.

"Whose side were you on in World War II?"

The car was rolling away from the curb as he leaned out the window and called back to her, "I was wearing a German uniform the night I shot Louisa."

Nine

THERE WAS NO HARMLESS WAY TO HOLD HER HEAD. TWO DEGREES of tilt in either direction brought on more painful throbbing. Mallory sat on the sofa, facing away from Charles Butler's front windows. Her sensitivity to sunlight was another unfamiliar symptom.

Riker, the wise man of hangovers, looked deep into her reddened eyes, then turned back to Charles. "Naw, she's not sick. This is fixable."

The two men walked off toward the kitchen and left her in merciful silence. She bowed her head over the thick text of legalese in her lap.

On the street just outside the window, a cat's sudden scream elongated into a howl of agony, and Mallory's fragile nerve endings thrummed in a sympathetic vibration—not to be confused with sympathy. She even took some satisfaction in the animal's obvious pain as she wished it a quick and violent death, then resumed reading Oliver Tree's last will and testament.

Riker's voice carried down the hall from the kitchen. "I need a raw egg, club soda and Tabasco sauce."

She barely heard Charles's response. "You're sure this won't kill her?"

When Riker returned to the living room, he was carrying a glass of suspicious dark slime topped with frothy bubbles. "Charles is making you a cappuccino chaser."

"I'm not drinking that," said Mallory.

"Yeah, you will." He handed her the glass. "Drink it down in one gulp. It'll put you out of your misery. Then we won't have to shoot you."

She tipped back the glass and all but inhaled the contents to get this over with quickly. The taste and the mucous texture were equally vile. This was gross betrayal. She glared at Riker, her poisoner.

"Okay, kid." He sloughed off his coat and tossed it on a chair near the door. "The next time you tie one on, take an aspirin before you go to bed. Drink lots of water too. Half the pain is dehydration."

Her wounded eyes were riveted to the brown spot on the lapel of his coat—fresh aggravation. How long had that coffee stain been setting in?

She held up the pages of the will. "How did you get this away from the lawyer?"

"I thought that might cheer you up." Riker sat down beside her and rummaged through his suit pockets. "I dropped by the executor's office. Man, that place even *smells* like money. So I asked the secretary for the name of her boss's cruise ship. I was gonna cable some questions on the will."

He pulled out a mess of cards and crumpled sheets of paper. "Then the secretary, what's her name—" He held out a business card at arm's length, rather than put on his reading glasses. "Gina. She tells me she's on a waiting list for the police academy. Nice kid—*loves* cops. Well, Gina asks me what I think of her chances for acceptance. So I say the odds get better if I write her a recommendation. Then she tells me her boss was never on a cruise ship."

"He's been hiding from the police?"

"More like he's hiding the platform and the crossbows. After the archery stunt at the parade, he thought we might take another look at Oliver's death—maybe impound the props before the auction." He pointed to the paperwork in her lap. "Cut to page thirty-two."

Mallory flipped through the sheets until she found the list of items to be auctioned for charity. All the magic props were listed by category. She ran one finger down the first column of the inventory.

"Let me save you some time," said Riker. "The platform isn't on that list. But Gina says it's the big-ticket item for the auction. The bidding starts at one o'clock this afternoon. The lawyer wants to unload all the magic props before the media hype dies down."

He handed her the business card, and she read the address line penciled on the back. It was more than thirty blocks from her next appointment in Times Square. "What's the going rate for a magic trick that bombed?"

"Quite a bundle," said Riker. "And the lawyer gets a cut of the action. The heavyweight bidder is a Hollywood producer. He wants to make a movie out of Oliver Tree's fatal flop."

"Who else was invited?"

"A lot of magicians in town for the festival. That's why nobody gets to look inside the platform till they lay down the cash. The lawyer's afraid they'll rip him off."

Mallory checked her pocket watch. It was close to the time of her meeting with Mr. Halpern. She wondered how long it would take to work through Rabbi Kaplan's instructions for dealing with an elderly Holocaust survivor. Since she didn't intend to miss the auction, she also computed the penalties for hurrying the old man's interview along.

What was the worst thing the rabbi could do to her?

"Riker, did the secretary say anything about Oliver's nephew? He's not on the list of bequests." And neither was the platform mentioned in this section.

"Yeah, she did." He looked down at an open notebook. "Richard Tree is a grandnephew, the grandson of Oliver's half brother. He's the old man's only living relative."

"But the chief beneficiary is a local hospital."

"Yeah, Gina says Oliver spent all his Sundays there. He did magic shows for sick kids. So the nephew doesn't inherit squat, but he has a huge trust fund."

"So he *does* benefit."

"By the death? Not a dime. His trust was activated years ago. The kid has to take a drug test to get his allotment checks. Hasn't passed one yet. That's why he took the cross-bow job for a hundred bucks. There's a pile of money in the trust, but he can't stay clean long enough to collect."

"With the old man dead, it's easier to break the trust."

"Wrong again," said Riker. "Oliver didn't have much use for his nephew, but he didn't want the kid to die from an overdose of money. So the old man hired the best lawyer in Manhattan to make an unbreakable trust. Oliver's attorney is the mother of all sharks. Remember that when you meet him. You can't bullshit this bastard."

Mallory held up a crisp twenty-dollar bill. Riker nodded, and the bet was made.

"Okay, next interview." Riker turned back pages in his notebook. "I talked to the guy who managed Oliver's company after the old man retired. He says Oliver still did some work on the side. He owned an old theater uptown. The renovation was kind of a hobby. That's where he built the platform a couple of years ago."

She drummed her fingers on the ream of paper. "This will is dated eight months ago. So why isn't the platform mentioned?"

Riker shrugged. "Old guy, bad memory."

"Maybe he gave it away before he died. Remember the dinner party, Riker? Those gifts to his old friends? One of them got the platform and Oliver's plans for the Lost Illusion. That man knew how to sabotage the trick."

"It's a good theory, but—"

"It gets better. I went over Max Candle's platform last night. The loops for the handcuffs are set high on the posts. Same position for both platforms."

"So?"

"The trick was originally designed for a taller man. Max Candle was six feet tall. Oliver was seven inches shorter. Prado and Futura are both about the same—"

Charles returned with a tray of coffee mugs. He set it down on the low table in front of her, and the aroma of cappuccino did not make her nauseous. Riker's hangover remedy had actually worked. "Thanks, Charles. How bad is the damage on the post? Do I need a carpenter to—"

"The post isn't broken," said Charles, and he appeared to be sorry about that.

"Of course it is," she said—she *insisted.* "I broke it last night."

"Are you quite sure you broke it?"

"What the hell is that supposed to mean?" Did he think that she imagined it?

Riker was squinting at Charles. "Would I want to know what this is about? Did I miss a good party?" He turned to Mallory. "You never take me anywhere."

"That's enough," said Mallory. "I *did* shoot the rat, I did *not* shoot the balloon, I *did* break the post." She hoped they both understood that it would be a big mistake to challenge any of this. "Malakhai must've fixed it." He had obviously been visiting the cellar while she was sleeping through the alarm this morning.

So it was not the passport he wanted. Malakhai was still searching for something.

✛   ✛   ✛

The young messenger's bicycle basket was loaded with packages as he rushed down the mighty artery of Broadway, ignoring the traffic light and aiming his front wheel at a crowd of pedestrians in the crosswalk at 42nd Street. He screamed out a warning to those who were foolish enough to block his way: "No insurance! No insurance!"

Mallory pulled Mr. Halpern back, and the rest of the crowd divided to clear a path for the bicycle. The messenger whizzed through the crush of bodies on either side of him. Jeers and raised fingers suggested that the rider should commit an unnatural sex act upon himself at the first opportunity.

Mr. Halpern shook his head and smiled as he stared at the back of the departing bicyclist. "That's New York." He said this as if it might be a good explanation for a near-death experience. And it probably was.

The night of the poker game, the old man had carried a homburg. Today he wore a deerstalker with fur flaps to protect his ears from the cold. "On my lunch hour, I always take a stroll around Times Square, no matter what the weather. Anything to get out of the office."

Mallory strained to hear his weak voice. The nervous streets of flashing electronic signs, fast-walking pedestrians and vehicles converged on them from all directions. Broadway merged its cars and tour buses with Seventh Avenue traffic, and all the cross streets contributed more hustle to the flow.

"It's changed so much," said Mr. Halpern. "It's like watching a child grow." He pointed to the Disney store. Flights of cheerful cartoon characters had displaced hookers, peepshows and adult bookstores. Mickey Mouse reigned over Times Square. "My great-grandchildren love the—" And now he stopped, perhaps recalling newspaper headlines to the effect that Detective Mallory was not a friend of the cartoon world.

A car honked to break a city ordinance against unnecessary noise. And now the warm scent of roasted chestnuts turned Mallory's head. A sidewalk vendor had illegally set up his cart, despite the fact that the mayor had recently driven small entrepreneurs from the square. In the absence of a police presence, there were a lot of violations going down today. And that was odd—not a single uniformed officer in sight.

She focused on the old man again, walking alongside him, taking his measurements. According to the rabbi, Mr. Halpern was Malakhai's age, but he seemed decades older. Was he ill, or only tired?

"I can read your mind, Detective Mallory. Why do I still work? It's almost indecent, isn't it? I should yield to the young—my replacements."

"Not if you don't want to." She was following the rabbi's protocol to the letter. This was the warm-up, the casual conversation, an utter waste of her time.

"Oh, but I wanted to retire," said Mr. Halpern. "When my son took over the family business, I wanted to make an art studio in my garage. At last, I would have the time to work on my drawings. I'd waited so many years for the chance. But my boy had other plans. Now he keeps an office for me. I sit there every day and do work of no importance. He pretends

I'm needed. I pretend not to notice that I'm in his way. Such loving lies we tell each other."

"Why don't you tell him what *you* want?" At best, this old man would only have a few years left to draw his pictures.

"I *did* tell him. I said I wanted to retire. But my son knows I love him very much. He was sure I must be lying to him." Mr. Halpern shrugged. "So to prove his love is greater, he told the bigger lie. He said he couldn't run the business without me. Well, he's my son. How can I accuse him of lying?" He raised his eyebrows to ask if she saw the humor in this.

Yes, she did. And thanks to Rabbi Kaplan, who had invented the concept of irony, Mallory had even predicted the punch line.

She pulled out her pocket watch and frowned at the time. Well, this little warm-up chat was definitely over. "The rabbi said you had a story about Malakhai?"

"Oh, yes." He looked at the watch in her hand, nodding his understanding that she had more important business elsewhere.

"You spoke to him at the rabbi's house the other night." She kept the watch open in her hand, a visual prompt to make him talk faster.

"Yes, I was surprised by how well he looked—how young. Only his hair had grown old."

"How old was he the first time you met him?"

"In the camp? He was about my age, maybe seventeen. I was unloading mailbags from the train. That was my—"

"This was a concentration camp?"

"Yes, but there were no ovens, no gas chambers in this place. It was a transit camp, a limbo station on the way to worse places. It was prison, but there was food enough. And that day there was music. There was always music when we had visitors from the outside. That was the day the Red Cross inspection team arrived. While they were touring the camp, the train came in with new prisoners to be processed. Later, the list of names would be called out for boarding. When the train pulled out again—"

He winced at some old memory and looked down at the pavement. "Well, you never wanted to be on the outward-bound trains. My parents, my whole family had gone down that track to Auschwitz. Not one of them ever came back. Not one cousin, an aunt or an uncle. And I knew my name would be on that list one day." He paused again. "But I'm rambling—sorry." He leaned down, the better to see the face of her pocket watch.

Mallory snapped it shut and put it away. "I have time," she said. "All the time you need."

The old man nodded and took a package of cigarettes from his coat pocket. He held them up to ask if she objected. She didn't.

"Louisa had been in the camp for about a month. I didn't know her name then. I never spoke to her. But I saw her every day when she was led to the commandant's office. Her eyes were always in a faraway trance—a walking dreamer. I thought she had lost her mind."

He stabbed the air with one finger as if marking a moment in time. "But *that* day was different. Louisa stood on the bandstand and played her violin to entertain the visitors. The Red Cross team had come to inspect the camp. The commandant was anxious to show them how well treated we were. The camps down the track—what went on there . . . It was the worst-kept secret on earth. The prisoners all knew about the death camps. And the Red Cross people—they knew. Yet they came to photograph the *transit* camp, to show *this* to the outside world."

He held an unlit cigarette as he dug into another pocket for his matches. "I was standing by the train with my cart, waiting for the mail car to open. Malakhai just appeared by my side—a young boy, straight and tall. His eyes were the same dark blue. Odd that his eyes never changed. His long hair was the color of lions. Such a handsome boy, but so strange and out of place. It was a warm day, but his shirt collar was buttoned up and his sleeves were pulled down. I knew he hadn't gotten off the train with the others. Not a prisoner, not a soldier either. Later, I decided he must have come in with the people from the Red Cross."

Mr. Halpern's wooden match made a false strike on the side of a small box. "After the mail was unloaded, the boy walked along with me and helped to push the cart. No guard ever looked his way. They only recognized fear and covert acts. Nothing else got their attention. As the cart rolled along, Malakhai never took his eyes off the bandstand. It was maybe ten feet high, a stage on four thick legs, and guards were posted at the foot of the stairs. The lines of prisoners from the train moved around it like a living river."

Mallory was aware of someone standing close to them. She turned to see a small bearded man wearing a ski cap and pretending sudden interest in a shop window. Was he hiding something?

She turned her attention back to Mr. Halpern's story.

"There were three musicians on the bandstand. The cellist and the oboe player were middle-aged women. Louisa was only a schoolgirl. Long red hair and light blue eyes. She had milk-white skin like yours. I can still see her face in every detail. But her expression is what I will remember till I die. I don't think she knew what was happening. She seemed so lost in her music, dreaming or insane."

The old man was seeing it all over again in that middle ground of vision, looking back at time. "The prisoners marched past the bandstand. A soldier called out names for the death train. And the music was Mozart." He waved the wooden match in the air, a tiny baton conducting a memory.

"I was distracted, listening for my name on the list. I wasn't called that day. When I turned to the young stranger, he was gone. I looked up at the bandstand, and Louisa had also vanished. The two older women were still playing their instruments. The guards stationed at the foot of the stairs didn't seem to notice that one musician was missing. No one was aware of the escape, though it happened in front of hundreds of people. No one saw it."

"Do you remember anything else going on?"

"You mean a diversion?" He put the unlit cigarette in his mouth. "Yes, I figured that out afterward. I remember a commotion somewhere beyond the lines of prisoners. I didn't see what it was—I was so intent on the list of names. Louisa must've jumped into his arms while the guards were distracted."

Mallory nodded. "If the diversion was on the ground, the guards wouldn't have any reason to look up." Most people went through their days without ever looking any higher than their own heads.

The cigarette dangled between his dry lips. "The train was loaded, ready to pull out. The last time I saw the boy and girl, they were hiding in the brush by the side of the tracks—too close. I wanted to warn them that the soldiers would see them when they secured the train. And then I realized that Louisa and Malakhai meant to climb aboard."

Mallory was watching the other man, the smaller figure with the ski cap. He was hovering closer now, holding a valise in his arms, cradling it like a baby, as he skated back and forth on his sneakers. A pickpocket looking for a likely mark? No, that didn't fit with the valise. She looked around the square. Why were there no cops?

"I wanted to stop them, to warn them," said Mr. Halpern. "It was insanity to board the death train. When they climbed into the mail car, I was so frightened for them. Then I looked away. I didn't want to draw attention to them with my own fear. The search of the mail car only took a few minutes. Not a big security problem. Who would willingly get on board? That way down the rail was death and worse things."

He struck another match absently. It failed to light. "The soldiers checked inside the mail car, but they never found the boy and girl. The train rolled out."

"So Louisa and Malakhai hid in the mail sacks?"

"That's what I thought when I made my own escape. There were always ten or twelve mailbags on that car. Only one was unloaded at the transit camp. All the sacks were large enough to hide a body, and most of them were never full. I figured the train would make a number of stops before it entered Germany. Until that moment, I never thought of escaping death that way—on a train to an extermination camp."

Mallory was distracted again. The bearded man with the ski cap slid back into her field of vision, still clutching his valise. He was waiting for something or someone.

Mr. Halpern pulled another match from the box. The unlit cigarette moved in the corner of his mouth as he spoke.

"Twenty years later, I saw them again on the stage—right here in New York. Louisa was long dead by then, and her ghost was part of a magic act. I could hear Malakhai speaking to her, but I couldn't see her—only the objects she carried. And then he sent her out into the audience, this poor dead girl. I felt a rush of air near my chair. I could smell a woman's perfume—the scent of a flower."

"A gardenia?"

"Yes, perhaps a gardenia. And then, I swear Louisa brushed my cheek with her hand. After the performance, I wanted to go backstage, to ask him then—how did they make their escape? But I was in tears. I couldn't speak."

Mallory had lost track of the odd little man in the ski cap. He had melded back into the crowd. "But didn't you say *you* escaped?"

"Not the way they did, though I thought so at the time. I made the run myself on the next train. Once the guards knew Louisa was gone, the camp would lock down. I'd never get the chance again. I walked along the rails with my cart. I paid no attention to the guards, and so I was invisible to them— just as Malakhai had been. I waited for the steam of the engine to cover me, and then I boarded the mail car. There were no names on the sacks, only numbers. There was no way to tell when or where the next mail drop would be. They searched the car before the train pulled out. The butt of a rifle missed my head by an inch when a soldier jammed it into my sack. You begin to see the problem? How did they miss two people in different mailbags?"

He struck the match; it flamed in the wind and died. He pulled out another. "I hid in there for hours and hours. I was afraid the train would never stop before we entered Germany. When it finally did stop, the mail car wouldn't open from the inside—there was no latch. Can you imagine that moment? I gave myself up for dead and crawled back into that canvas bag, my shroud.

"Then the door was pulled open. Only one sack was unloaded, and I was in it. A stroke of luck, one chance in a pile of ten mailbags to escape from the train. I was thrown onto the back end of a supply truck. Once it was on the road, I crawled out of the sack and jumped off. I was free."

He struck another match, and Mallory cupped her hands around it to shelter the flame from the wind.

"But you see, don't you? That couldn't have been the way Malakhai and Louisa escaped. You can see the odds against it." He bowed to the glow of the match and lit his cigarette. "But I think I've figured it out—the only way it could've happened."

He turned to exhale the smoke away from her, and a look of extreme horror flooded his eyes. Mallory stepped to the side and saw the gun rising in the hand of the little man with the ski cap. The spray gun was firing a black stream of paint at Mr. Halpern. And now there was also surprise on the face of the smaller man. He was trying to stuff his spray gun into the valise as he ran.

Mallory didn't have to chase him far. He was laughing when she brought him down, unafraid, even proud—until the pain set in.

"You're breaking my arm," he screamed, as she ungently pulled it back to handcuff him.

A group of people gathered around them, some for the show, and others were probably hoping to catch her in an act of police brutality. Never a willing crowd pleaser, Mallory elected not to break the little man's bones.

"Thanks," said a woman in street clothes, kneeling on the ground beside her. A man joined them, flashing his identification and badge for Mallory as he crouched over the prisoner. "We'll take over now."

She looked past these two to see the others approach, at least ten cops in plainclothes, coming out from under cover, pinning badges to their coats as they ran. Turning around, she saw more of them coming from across the square.

So this had been a stakeout. That would explain the lack of uniforms. All of them had known what the little freak was planning. They had probably been watching him while he shot the old man with the spray gun—and they let it happen. An attempted assault was no substitute for the real thing.

She walked away from the cluster of spectators and plain-clothes cops. Mr. Halpern was alone, standing apart from the crowd. His face was splattered, and his coat dripped black paint on the ground. Taking the old man's arm, she led him along the sidewalk. Mallory saw every approaching pedestrian as a potential criminal who might jostle him, and she held Mr. Halpern's arm a little tighter.

✛   ✛   ✛

The small room was at the end of the hall, far from the traffic of office workers in this firm which bore the Halpern name. The walls were decorated with a collection of drawings by Paul Klee and Max Ernst. The desktop was clear of paper-work, and the *Times* crossword puzzle had already been completed and discarded in the wastepaper basket.

"I'm sorry this happened." Mallory set a cup of tea on the desk blotter in front of Mr. Halpern. His face was still spotted with red blotches from scrubbing off the paint splatters. His coat had taken the worst of the assault, and only a few spots were visible on his pale gray suit.

Again, she said, "I'm sorry," knowing there were not sorries enough to cover this kind of damage. She could not forget the look in his eyes when the spray gun fired. She should have been able to protect him.

Another screwup.

He reached over and rested his hand on hers. "Not your fault." His skin was cool and dry, and his thin hand was like a delicate covering of wrapping paper. She wondered how much time he would have left to draw his pictures.

In the hall outside the office door, Mr. Halpern's son was speaking with a uniformed officer.

"Detective Mallory, tell me about this little fellow with the paint gun," said the elder Mr. Halpern. "Was it my fur hat that made him angry? One of the animal-rights people spat on me a few months back."

"No, he was one of the antismoking people." And now Mallory was envisioning tomorrow's headline: "Puppy-shooting Cop Assaults Political Activist." "Your cigarette set him off. His father died of a heart attack, and he blames it on secondhand smoke."

"But—out of doors?"

"The freak always works on the street. Easier to hit and run. He's done this to a lot of people, usually women. He's never splattered anyone big enough to put a fist through his face. Detective Rodriguez said you must have turned around at the wrong time. He usually gets his victims in the back. Then he lectures them on smoking and runs away before they find out they've been hit."

"So the other officers knew who he was before—"

"Times Square is his favorite spot." And now she confirmed the old man's suspicion. "The arresting officers were waiting for him this time."

Fifteen cops had been assigned to one vandal. God forbid the spray gun should splatter an out-of-towner and upset the mayor's tourism promotion. Meanwhile, she had to cheat and lie to get a fraction of that manpower on a homicide case.

She turned to look at the officer waiting in the hallway. "When you're ready, that cop will drive you home to Scarsdale."

"No, Detective Mallory. I'm fine, thank you. My son wouldn't understand if I—"

"He will when I get through with him." Did the old man's face tense up slightly? In a softer voice, more reassuring, she said, "Any kind of assault leaves people a little shaky, even if it's just a shouting match on the street. I'll explain that to your son. He'll understand."

"Is there time for the rest of the story? I want to tell you my theory—how Louisa and Malakhai got away."

"Sure." She had given up the idea of getting to the auction in time for the opening bids. So far, this had not been a profitable day.

"I told you, the first time I saw Malakhai, his shirt was buttoned up and the sleeves rolled down. I think the clothes covered up—"

"A German uniform?"

"Yes, yes." He smiled and slapped his hand on the desk. "Malakhai's clothes were hiding a *uniform.*" He seemed so pleased with her, as if she were his promising student. Or perhaps he was only gratified that she had been paying attention. That would be a rare event on any day spent in this office, this nicely decorated holding cell.

"That was the surest way to evade the soldiers checking the cars and jamming the sacks with their rifle butts," said Mr. Halpern. "Malakhai must have been the soldier who searched the mail car before the train pulled out."

"Good idea," said Mallory. "So you think Malakhai was in the German Army?"

"Oh, no. It was definitely a disguise. He only said a few words to me that day. He had a child's grasp of the language, and the accent was no good at all. I'm German-born. I promise you, he was not." He leaned toward her in the spirit of collaboration. "I believe he knew what was going to happen when the train made the next stop to drop off mail."

Mallory nodded. "He probably cased the whole route."

"So the train stopped. The car door opened for the mail drop, and Malakhai was standing there in a German uniform. He was the soldier who unloaded the mail sack with Louisa inside. As I said, he had a poor command of the German language. Yet there he was, a young boy carrying an escaped prisoner in his arms—surrounded by all those soldiers. It's always been much more than a puzzle to me. This was a love story."

Mr. Halpern sat back in his chair, frowning now. "Ah, but I'll never know if I got it right."

"You didn't ask him? That night at Rabbi Kaplan's house—"

"Malakhai didn't remember how he stole Louisa from the camp. He said I had waited too long to ask. He has strokes, small ones that destroy his memories. It's been going on for about a year. He said they happen all the time. Bits and pieces of his life are missing every other morning. So I'll never know how he did his best trick—if I got it right or not."

"It works for me." Mallory turned to the door, where the uniformed officer was waiting to carry Mr. Halpern home.

"Will I have to testify against the little man with the paint gun?"

"No, I don't think so," she said. "The arresting officers have more than enough complaints to nail the freak. He's criminally nuts."

"That's your perception today, Detective. Things change—and so quickly. A few years from now, when you think back on this business with the paint gun—you'll remember *me* as the criminal who smoked a cigarette." He smiled as he patted her hand. "Not your fault. Things change."

She motioned for the officer to come in. "He'll take you home now. Maybe you should stay there? Just draw your pictures and forget about this place. You don't want to be here anyway."

"Ah, but my son." His sweet smile reminded her that there were loving lies to be maintained. Every day he would return to do work of no consequence. Father and son would go on pretending that he was needed here.

And now the younger Mr. Halpern was entering the old man's office.

"Things change," said Mallory.

Ten

DETECTIVE RIKER'S HEAD LOLLED ON THE BACK OF THE VELVET theater seat. He was staring up at the chandelier. A million sharp crystal shards dangled from a giant ball of light, and he had the sense that it might fall on him at any moment.

The fear of falling objects was common in the hazard zone of Manhattan, where pedestrians were routinely flattened by crumbling gargoyles and cornices. This lottery of city life brought out the sporting nature of New Yorkers, who kept score on direct hits—disparaging near misses and nonfatal glancing blows.

This chandelier was on much too grand a scale for a theater with only three hundred seats. *Piss-elegant* was the term he was looking for. Though, according to Nick Prado's press release, it was an exact replica of the original fixture from Faustine's.

Oliver Tree had spent a fortune re-creating his grandmother's theater. The grand opening was three days away, and the construction work was not yet complete. The air had the smell of fresh plaster and paint.

Riker looked at his watch.

Where is she?

If Mallory didn't arrive soon, she would miss the main event, the bidding on the platform.

He looked up at the stage, where men and women were inspecting long tables decked with magic props. During the intermission, the auctioneer had left his podium on top of the platform. The man from Hollywood was favored to make the high bid, and then Mallory's precious evidence would be on its way to the West Coast. He wondered if the auctioneer had been nervous standing in Oliver Tree's place and looking down at the crossbows.

Nick Prado gave Riker a friendly wave as he walked down a short flight of steps at the side of the stage. For the past hour, this man had been exuding professional charm and warmth, presuming the role of a dear and close friend. But Riker preferred the distance of a suspicious acquaintance. He disliked Prado's wide smile that said to everyone he met, *Love me. Ah, but then how could you not?*

Now the man was coming toward him, swaggering up the long green carpet. And green was the color of the theater seats, the walls and their high balconies, and the long drapes gathered in golden ropes at the sides of the stage.

Prado hunkered down by Riker's aisle seat. "Well, what do you think of the place?"

"So this is what the inside of an avocado looks like."

"You can blame the decor on Oliver's grandmother. Actually, it's Federal green, the color of American money. Faustine loved tourists. That's why she spelled out the name in English. She wasn't sure Americans were bright enough to work out Théâtre de Magie."

Emile St. John stood at the edge of the stage, hailing his friend. Prado excused himself and walked back toward the auction crowd.

When Riker had gotten past his fear of the chandelier, he admired the ceiling fresco of characters from famous plays. None of the actors' roles were detailed in Prado's handout sheet, and the only one Riker could identify was the long-nosed figure of Cyrano de Bergerac. This was an obvious departure from the original painting, circa 1900. But was it a joke or a tribute? Apparently, decades had passed since the old man and the younger one had met, for Cyrano was portrayed as a teenage Charles Butler.

Riker left his chair and turned to face the lobby door.

Where is she?

Though Mallory carried a pocket watch, he knew she only

consulted it for show, a prop of normalcy. She was guided by an interior clock wired directly into her brain, and she was never, *never* late.

He walked down the center aisle and climbed the steps leading up to the stage. When he was past the lengths of heavy green curtains, he looked up again.

Oh, *more* things to fall on him.

Space expanded upward for twenty feet beyond the curtain valance. A narrow suspension bridge spanned the length of the stage. This catwalk of wooden planks was none too stable, swaying high in the air as a workman stood at its center, testing the rigging that held massive backdrop screens in place over Riker's head.

He turned his eyes down to the less hazardous display tables and made a rough head count of thirty bidders examining the remaining auction items. A small group was clustered around the base of the platform, and a lone magician stood behind the auctioneer's podium. Franny Futura was the new target of the crossbow pistols.

For the second time this afternoon, Riker stopped by each of the pedestals and checked the weapon magazines to be sure they were empty of arrows. And still it made him edgy to see the old man standing in the crosshairs of four pistol sights.

The white-haired magician walked to the edge of the platform and caught the eye of Nick Prado on the stage below. Futura made a rolling motion with his hand. "Nick, come up here. Come up and look at this."

Prado shook his head and turned away.

"Still afraid of heights?" Futura said this with great glee, as if scoring a point. "It's only nine feet. Not that much of a—" His words faltered as Prado's body went rigid, then slowly turned back toward the platform.

"Franny, may I remind you that I live in a penthouse—a very *high* penthouse?"

Riker counted a double-point score in Prado's favor. A fear of heights did not square with an apartment in the sky. And Futura did not have the means to live as high as Prado did, not according to Riker's credit reports on both men. Futura's face took on the humble aspect of a timid man, the poorer man, a mere ground-dweller. He moved back from the edge with some fear of his own. Perhaps he was seeing the cross-bows for the first time and feeling vulnerable. Cautiously, he made his way down the platform staircase.

Prado was staring at the lobby doors and smiling.

Riker looked over his shoulder to see his partner walking down the aisle. Mallory's eyes took in the chandelier and the painted ceiling, then traveled over the green walls and the balconies. She had the look of—what? Recognition? Had she been here before? No, that was not quite it, for she was obviously surprised by her surroundings.

As she climbed the short flight of stairs stage left, Riker made an exaggerated point of looking at his wristwatch, relishing this rare opportunity to rag her about punctuality, to inform her that she was tardy by a full forty minutes. This chance might never come again.

But now a familiar giant in a three-piece suit was running down the center aisle toward the stage, and Mallory called out to him, "You're *late,* Charles."

Riker ceased to look at his watch.

"Sorry." Charles Butler paused by the front row to catch his breath. "I was down in the basement and lost track of the time. Thought I'd have another look at the posts on the platform. You know, there *is* a fracture line—"

"So *now* you believe me." Mallory turned away from him. "Riker, who bid on the platform?"

"Nobody yet. The auctioneer called a time-out."

Charles was staring at the ceiling. He had found himself in the painting of Cyrano. Yet he was smiling, playing the good sport, as he walked up the stairs toward Mallory. "You want me to have a look inside the platform now?"

"You can't. It's sealed." Riker pointed to the security guard posted by the platform staircase. "The door stays shut till the lawyer has the cash in his fat little hand. I talked to the movie producer. He's a sure thing for the high bid. After the auction, he'll let us have a quick look inside before he ships it out to the Coast."

"Not good enough," said Mallory. "That platform's not going anywhere till I have time to—"

"Hold it." Riker put on his let's-be-reasonable face. "You can't impound it, and there's no search warrant. We don't even have an open homicide case. The new owner can ship it to the moon if he wants to."

Charles was distracted by a table of magic props. He read one of the authentication tags, then held up a round silver object that Riker had taken for a covered cake plate. "This dove load is over a hundred years old."

Mallory drifted toward another table, finding the firearms more interesting. She glanced at each tag as she made her way down the length of the table.

Shopping?

As if she didn't own enough weapons. But none of these should appeal to her. What good was a gun that could not fire bullets? Riker had already checked them against the auction list in the will and read the tags identifying their different functions. The old muskets only fired smoke. One Luger could be loaded with lines and darts, and several revolvers looked as deadly as anything Mallory carried, but these starter pistols were just for noise.

Franny Futura was standing at the foot of the platform staircase when Mallory approached him from behind. "I had dinner with Malakhai last night," she said. "I know what happened at Faustine's."

Futura turned around to face her, his hands opening and closing in nervous fidgets. "I don't—"

"It's all right, Franny." Nick Prado appeared at the foot of the staircase and smiled at Mallory. "Emile and I had brunch with Malakhai this morning. I wonder why he didn't mention that conversation."

"Well, his memory isn't what it used to be." There was an unmistakable subtext in Mallory's voice, but Riker could not follow its meaning. She was clearly disappointed in Prado's response when the man shrugged it off.

As she moved closer to Futura, the man's head was backing away, comically attenuating his skinny neck, while his feet remained rooted to the floor.

"Malakhai didn't tell me how you got rid of the body," said Mallory. "What did you do with her?"

Riker felt sorry for Mallory's target, but he knew she was onto something. Futura's mouth hung open—stunned speechless.

Nick Prado answered for him. "We buried her in the cellar."

Futura nodded with a sickly smile. "It's not as if we killed the old lady."

It was Mallory's turn to be surprised. "*Old* lady?"

Prado grinned to show her every tooth he owned. "Oliver's grandmother, Faustine. I can assure you she died of natural causes."

"And that's why you hid the body in the cellar?" Mallory waved one hand in the air. "Of course."

"Well, we did neglect to inform the authorities when she died." Prado's tone was casual, as if covert burials were an everyday thing with him. "We needed her pension money to pay rent on the theater. She was Oliver's grandmother. If he didn't mind, why should you?"

"Fine, I don't care if you had the old woman stuffed and mounted. Let's talk about Louisa." She was speaking only to Futura, and now the man got control of his feet and stepped back. Mallory moved a step closer. "I'm betting you were the informer, the one who turned her in."

Riker shook his head. This bluff was miles too obvious, not Mallory's style at all.

"I wouldn't give odds on that bet." Nick Prado stepped between Mallory and Futura. His smile was easy and affable. "You'd have a fifty-fifty chance of being right. At least half of Paris was collaborating with the Germans."

Riker repressed a smile. Nick Prado had just confirmed Louisa Malakhai's status in the scheme of war. Mallory had pegged this man right, the ultimate egoist. He would never miss a chance to play a fast round of one-upmanship.

"That's right," she said. "But the Germans didn't kill her." Mallory was still looking at Futura, or what she could see of him behind Prado's back.

Then Futura straightened his spine and held his head a bit

higher, braver now that another man had joined them. The larger, more placid Emile St. John rested one massive hand on Futura's slight shoulder, playing the role of protector.

Riker felt an odd affinity for St. John, who walked about in a portable atmosphere of tranquillity, affecting everyone in his sphere—except Mallory.

Of course. St. John shared this trait with her late foster father. Did Mallory see it, too?

"Louisa's death was an accident," said St. John. "It wasn't—"

"You mean the magic-bullet trick?" Mallory shifted her position to one side of Nick Prado. And now she had a clear bead on Futura again. "The gun trick adapted for the crossbow? No, an arrow didn't kill Louisa."

Futura was slightly off balance, not cocking his head in his habitual startled-bird fashion, but leaning his whole body to one side, and even St. John had been caught off guard. But not Prado, whose smile never wavered.

Mallory skirted around Prado to get to Futura. "Did Louisa know she was going to be shot for real? Did she know Malakhai was using a loaded crossbow?"

Futura took this as a physical jolt. His head moved somewhere between a wobble and a shake of denial. "If she knew, she was a wonderful actress." He looked up at St. John. "Remember her face, Emile? She was stunned."

Riker decided this might be a bad time to remind Mallory that she had been forbidden to conduct interviews. A loud squeal of electronic feedback called his attention up to the smaller stage on top of the platform.

Oliver Tree's attorney was standing behind the microphone on the auctioneer's podium. "May I have your attention?" The bald head was shining with reflections from a bank of overhead lights. Though he must weigh three hundred pounds, no one would call him a fat man; money had cured that glaring flaw. An expanse of dark suit material elegantly draped his wide girth with the genius lines of Armani. "We'll end the intermission in a few minutes. If you would all take your seats?"

Mallory walked to the foot of the platform staircase and

held up her gold shield. "First I want a look at the room inside this box. Are you the executor? Atkins?"

"Ye-e-es." Only a man with a Park Avenue address could put that many syllables into a three-letter word. And by his attitude, it was clear that she should address him as *Mr.* Atkins. The attorney walked down the short flight of stairs on tiny mincing patent-leather feet so incongruous with his mass. Waving her identification away with one white hand of glittering jewels, he made a point of not meeting her eyes. He addressed the air above her head: "I know who you are. You're the balloon shooter. I've already spoken with the other detective—*Riker*, was it?"

The lawyer's tone was clear—Riker should substitute the word *riffraff* for his own name.

Atkins wagged one finger at Mallory in the gesture of admonishing a child. "No one but the buyer may inspect the platform's interior room."

"This is police business," said Mallory—substitute the words, *You prick.*

"Do you have a warrant? No? I didn't think so." The lawyer turned around, and in the manner of a large dark ship leaving the harbor, he grandly sailed across the stage.

She called after him, "Atkins? This platform ties into a homicide."

And now she had everyone's attention. Thirty heads were turning in her direction.

The attorney was smiling when he turned around. "But *no* warrant?" He sailed back across the stage and docked in front of her, this time deigning to look into her eyes. "However, I'm sure your little comment did raise the bidding considerably. You want to make a scene? Go ahead. Rant and rave about murder, and I might cut you in for a small percentage."

"Sounds like a bribe to me, Counselor."

Atkins snorted and covered his mouth with one hand. His fingers sparkled with the large gemstones of four rings. "You'll have to do better than that, Detective." His tone implied that this was obscene wealth and power speaking, so she would have to do a *lot* better.

Mallory pointed at the crossbows. "Do you have a license

to sell firearms?" She smiled. "No? Then I'll have to stop the auction."

The attorney only raised one eyebrow. "Don't even repeat that threat. Oliver Tree had a special permit signed by the mayor. Executor's privilege extends that license to the disposal of his effects."

Riker thought that had the sound of a lawyer's bluff, but Mallory, a consummate card shark, showed no signs of calling him on it. She seemed distracted by the table display of prop weapons. "I've seen the permit, Atkins. I know it doesn't cover the sale of guns."

"These are all harmless props, and you know it."

"Maybe not. I know Oliver Tree's nephew had access to this collection. One of these guns could be a murder weapon. If you can't produce the license—"

"Oliver Tree was killed by arrows. Odd that I should have to point out this simple fact to a police officer."

"Wrong investigation, Atkins." Her voice was so low, Riker had to crane his neck to hear the words. "I have a dead drug dealer in the East Village."

What? Well, actually, that was a safe lie. There was always a dead dealer somewhere downtown. But now that the Dominican drug gangs had completely finished murdering the American gangs, she would be lucky to get a fresh corpse.

"The nephew is also your client, Atkins. I know you bailed the kid out on his last drug arrest." Now she spoke loud enough for everyone to hear. "When a cop wants to see your gun seller's license, you don't get to argue the point. Are there any other simple laws I can explain to you—before I shut down this auction?"

Riker smiled. He knew the big money in this room was returning to Hollywood on the morning plane. Atkins's cut would be smaller if the auction was delayed. Mallory had scored a blow to the lawyer's wallet, the equivalent of a groin shot on a human being.

"Let's read the tags, shall we?" The attorney lifted a revolver from the table, brandishing it in a careless manner. Apparently, he had never handled a gun before—or perhaps he had, for he was pointing the muzzle at Mallory's face as he checked the tag. "All harmless props. See here?" He held up the tag. "This one only fires smoke. Not the least bit deadly."

"He's right, Mallory." Nick Prado was looking over the attorney's shoulder. "Lots of smoke and bang, but no bullets. That one won't even hold ammunition. The mechanism runs through the barrel and—"

His words ended abruptly when he met Mallory's eyes. In that moment, they formed an odd alliance. Taking his cue from her, Prado stepped back and bestowed an evil grin on the attorney.

Mallory looked down at another revolver on the table, bending low to examine it closely. It was tagged as a starter's pistol. "This one looks real to me, but I'm only a cop. What do I know? I think I'll just stop the auction until I get a decision from the DA's office. It shouldn't take more than a few days." As an afterthought, she said, "Or I could have a look inside the platform."

"I'm not buying it, Detective." The lawyer had lost his patronizing smile. "Look around you. I have a room full of magicians, *experts*. They can tell you these guns are props. Look at the damn tags." Now a hint of menace came stealing into the man's voice as he lowered his volume. "But you were right about Oliver's nephew. The boy *is* my client." He advanced on her, perhaps believing that she would retreat. She did not. And now he was in the awkward position of stepping back a pace and yielding ground to Mallory.

He sighed and gave her a long and pitying look. "Considering what you did to Richard—hurtling him to the pavement with utter disregard for his person." He sighed. "Well, I think the boy might sue for false arrest and police brutality. When the district attorney finds out how easily that lawsuit could've been avoided, you'll lose your job, won't you, Detective?"

The crowd of bidders gathered close around them in the spirit of spectators at a street fight.

"Sounds like a threat," said Mallory. "And in front of witnesses, too."

"Oh, run along, Detective—before you become a laughingstock *again*. Go shoot another balloon." The lawyer turned to the crowd for their support, but he met with disapproval on every face. Apparently, they liked Mallory best, perhaps in the false assumption that she was the underdog in this exchange.

"There's a faster way to check out the guns." She picked up a revolver from one table and reached for a deck of cards from another display.

Riker stood behind Atkins's back, shaking his head and mouthing the word *no*. She turned away from him. He moved quickly around the attorney and reached out to her.

Too late.

She threw the deck high in the air and fired the gun into the falling shower of playing cards. The shot banged out in an explosion.

The attorney's face was pale. His abstract world of law books and contracts was far removed from the extreme violence of gunshots.

Mallory leaned down and picked up a card from the floor. She turned to the lawyer and looked at him through the round hole in its center. "*Real* bullets."

And at this vulnerable moment, when the lawyer was still slack-jawed with shock—no, call it horror—she barked the order. "Get me the damn paperwork on this gun! I want to see your license! I want—"

Her voice was drowned out by loud applause and whistles from the gallery of bidders. They cheered her as the clear winner. But Riker noticed the lawyer was rallying and staring at Mallory with solid hatred.

"Maybe we can forgive paperwork on both sides?" The attorney smiled somewhat insincerely. "Feel free to look around inside the platform. Just get it over with." He walked back through the crowd of onlookers. "Gentlemen, ladies, if you'll just take your seats and wait a few more minutes."

Most of the gathering retreated to the theater seats in the front row. Charles Butler remained on the stage close to Mallory, and his voice had an unfamiliar icy quality. "May I see that gun for a moment?" Not waiting for her to surrender the weapon, Charles took it away from her—winning new respect from Riker.

She was about to protest when Riker pulled her off to one side of the stage, and he did not handle her gently. "Mallory, are you *nuts*?" He held her by one arm, gripping it tight enough to leave bruises; he was that angry. "How could you fire a gun in a place like this? That bullet could've ricocheted off a—"

"Are you going to rat me out to Lieutenant Coffey?"

"What? *Listen* to me! You can't—"

"I can't be trusted with guns?" She shook his hand off with a jerk of her arm. "Go on—report back to Coffey. Tell him all about my little card trick—and then he'll fire me. That's what you want, isn't it? You figure it's better I lose my job than get killed for a psycho cop." She poked a long red fingernail into his chest and put some force behind it. "Right?"

He turned his face upward and stared at the workman on the catwalk high above them. *Oh, sweet Jesus.* The man in coveralls had been directly in the path of her bullet. Riker came all undone as Mallory looked up at the man and smiled. This innocent bystander had not been planned on, but she clearly regarded him as an unexpected bonus.

Riker raked one hand through his graying hair. He wanted a drink so badly. "If it was only the balloon. But first you pulled that stupid stunt with the rat, and now—"

"I never waste a bullet, Riker."

"Don't lie—not to me. Four cops saw you shoot that rat off the candy machine."

"Riker, if I'm such a sick puppy, how come it's so easy for me to read all you nice, normal people? You think I'm a gun-happy nutcase? Fine. Go to Coffey. Go *now*. Run!" She stood back and regarded him as if he were a stranger, and not a man who had watched her grow up. "Don't you get it, Riker? You're the one *I* can't trust. How do you like that feeling? I'm your partner, and I can't trust you."

"I don't deserve that."

"You're not working this case with me. You're only around to watch me. And I know why. Good housekeeping? Isn't that what you call it when a nutcase cop goes down? I'll just have to hope I'm never in a bad spot where I need you for backup."

She stalked away from him, heading for the platform, but Charles Butler blocked her path. He was holding out his hand. Finally, reluctantly, she crossed his palm with the mutilated playing card.

Charles held up the gun he had taken from Mallory. "It really is a prop, Riker. Lots of noise, but no bullets."

"She put a hole in the—"

"Not a bullet hole." Charles looked down at the mutilated playing card in his hand. "This one was made by a shaft of metal. Stainless steel, to be precise. Let's narrow it down further, shall we?" He held the card closer to his eyes as if divining more information from it, saying dryly, "Obviously a barbecue skewer from the kitchen drawer of Rabbi Kaplan." He flipped the card over. "And this pattern on the back? It doesn't match the cards on the floor."

Charles turned on Mallory and pointed an accusing finger at the cashmere showing through her open trench coat. "You were wearing that blazer the night of the poker game. That's how you just happened to have a card in your pocket—a card with a *hole* in it. You *palmed* it during the game."

Mallory was not the least bit contrite. "Well, the spook was cheating, wasn't she? Just open the platform and check it out, okay, Charles?"

"But to palm a card? Mallory, I'm shocked."

And so was Riker. He stood with both hands jammed into his pockets so his partner would not see them balling into fists.

Charles lightly touched the wood at the center of the platform wall, and the compartment door opened. He looked inside and quickly pulled back from the stench.

A human arm extended slowly and hit the floor of the stage with a soft thud of dead white flesh on wood. A sleeve was rolled to the elbow. And now the upper torso unfolded and tumbled out the door. There was an arrow in the ruffled breast of a formal dress shirt, but no blood at the wound site. This might have been a staged illusion—if not for the very real hole in the chest. Riker had never seen the crossbow shooter without his top hat. The carrot-red hair was wild with a boy's cowlicks. The white face was contorted and conflicted between pain and the astonishment of dying.

The gallery of bidders was stealing back to the stage, all but tiptoeing toward the platform.

"That's Richard—Oliver's nephew," said Nick Prado. His face was composed, and his voice was calm.

Riker decided that Prado must be familiar with the smell of dead bodies, standing his ground while the rest of the civilians were visibly shaken and driven backward by nausea. The corpse had emptied its bowels in the postmortem relaxation of muscles. The containment of the odor spoke well for the seal on the platform door.

Franny Futura had retreated to the edge of the stage. His formerly ruddy cheeks had lost all their color. Emile St. John showed no emotion whatever, and Riker wondered what it would take to unhinge that man.

Mallory knelt down beside the corpse and touched it. The limp body moved easily under her probing hand. The rigidity of rigor mortis had run its course and passed off.

"Couple of days dead." She wore a faint smile when she looked up at Riker. "And now I've got a real live game."

✛   ✛   ✛

Jack Coffey looked down at the paperwork on his desk, a police report on the death of Crossbow Man, a.k.a. Richard Tree. "So when do we get the medical examiner's report?"

"First thing tomorrow," said Riker. "Dr. Slope's doing it himself. And she got Heller to do the forensic workup on the platform. Looks like the kid had a good instinct."

Coffey pushed Riker's report to one side of his desk. "Slope's doing a full autopsy?"

"Yeah, all the trimmings," said Riker. "Mallory got real lucky with that arrow sticking out of the body. It's enough to impound the platform. And now she has an open homicide case. Damn good police work."

"I never had any problem with her work," said Coffey. "It's her state of mind that worries me. Are you keeping an eye on her?"

Riker shook his head. "No, I don't do midget duty anymore. She's a grown-up now."

"She's dangerous."

"Is she?" Riker lit a cigarette, despite the absence of an ashtray. "Maybe you're just buying into your own lecture, Lieutenant. Incidentally, that didn't scare her one bit. But it was a good try."

"It scared you, Riker. You *know* what she is."

"Yeah, she's my partner, and she's good. You never saw that much talent in a cop—except maybe her old man. But, you know something? I think she's gonna be better than Markowitz in his prime. Well, you took your best shot, and it didn't work." He stood up and buttoned his coat. "Fun's over, Lieutenant. Give me Mallory's revolver. I'll see that she gets it. Now that the kid's back on the job—"

"She has enough guns to play with. She can make do with her .38. I'm keeping the cannon for a while." He smiled. "Tell her I'm waiting on a recovered bullet from the dead balloon puppy, so we can match—"

"Bullshit," said Riker. "Nobody's looking for that bullet. You got no call to keep her gun. You *want* her to think you don't trust her?"

Coffey was incredulous. "I *never* trusted her. That's news to Mallory? And the balloon isn't a dead issue. There's more fallout." He flicked a remote control at the small television in the corner of the office. The VCR played a repeat performance of Officer Henderson falling off his rearing horse as the giant balloon descended from the sky. "This tape is Henderson's evidence in a lawsuit against the city."

"Lawsuit? The idiot fell off his horse. Who knew he was such a lousy rider?"

"He's claiming the horse wouldn't have dumped him if Mallory hadn't created a dangerous, life-threatening situation. It's a ten-million-dollar lawsuit, Riker. And it all hangs on whether or not Henderson can prove she shot the big puppy."

"Well, screw the job. I'm gonna get me a horse and a lawyer," said Riker.

"It gets worse. Henderson claims the city knowingly hired a dangerous psychopath. Now his terminology is a little off—but real close." Coffey rewound the tape and played it again. "I *do* like watching that little bastard fall on his ass. He broke his tailbone."

"I hope it hurts like hell."

Coffey switched off the set. "Mallory can go on working the case, but she's not officially on the job. Maybe in a week or two, the city will settle the lawsuit to make it go away. But Mallory has to learn—"

"Oh, screw the balloon. She says she didn't pull her gun in that crowd. I—"

"Yeah, right. She didn't do it. I'd say that was a good joke, Riker. But I know Mallory has no sense of humor. And she didn't deny shooting off her gun in the station house, did she? A stupid cowboy shot, and for what? A damn rat. Burns me up every time I think about it."

"I don't think—"

"It's not up to you, Riker. It doesn't actually matter what you think."

"Well, yeah, it does. But I'm sorry you feel that way, Lieutenant." Riker put his gold shield on the corner of the desk. "Give me the kid's gun, or I leave my badge behind when I walk out the door."

"Riker, don't take that personally. It's the perception of the thing that matters. I have to worry about what those cops were thinking when she shot the—"

"Those uniforms are all big boys. They've all lost pet hamsters. I'm sure they'll get over the rat." Riker pushed his gold shield across the desk. "Lieutenant, I never bluff. I never will. It's a religion with me."

✝   ✝   ✝

As the weary detective emerged from the stairwell, carrying a paper sack heavy with the weight of Mallory's largest gun, the desk sergeant called out, "Hey, Riker. You got a minute?"

"Yeah, sure."

Riker ambled over and leaned one crooked elbow on the edge of the raised desk. It was more like a grandiose pulpit, and that fit well with the desk sergeant's job of meting out rare blessings and more common penance to his patrolmen.

"What's the problem, Harry?"

Sergeant Harry Bell was a beefy, red-nosed man in uniform. He and Riker had gone gray together over the past thirty-five years on the job. "You gonna see your partner before she gets back from vacation?"

"Yeah."

"Well, you tell her she called it right on Oscar the Wonder Rat." Sergeant Bell leaned over the desk and handed down a fistful of currency in tens, fives and singles. "That's four cops, ten apiece. We're all square with Mallory."

"What?" Riker stared at the money in his hand. "You guys made bets on a freaking rat?"

"Riker, I told you about the rat. When you—"

"No, Harry. You only said she shot it."

"Well, she said the rat was sick. That was the bet."

"Talk to me, Harry. 'Cause Mallory never talks to me anymore, and I get real lonely. What's all this crap about a sick rat?"

"You've seen him. Fastest thing on four feet, right?" Harry Bell made a quick darting motion with his hand. "But the other night, Oscar was movin' real slow, tame as a stoned kitten. He was just sittin' there on top of the candy machine watchin' the world go by. So Pete Hong—"

"The new recruit?"

"Yeah. The kid's real young. Comes from a nice quiet town upstate. I don't think he ever saw a rat before. So he waves his nightstick at Oscar. No reaction. He gets closer, like he's gonna pet that dirty little sacka fur. But before I can say anything, Mallory pulls rank and orders Pete to back away from the rat."

That's my little diplomat.

"So, Harry, how'd your boy take it?"

"Not real well. Then Mallory says the rat's sick, and even a rookie should know better than to touch it. Well, that

stopped Pete cold for a second. I felt kinda bad for the kid—
first week on the job, and your partner makes him feel like a
fuckin' idiot in front of two other cops."

"So then you had to back up your guy, right?" Riker was
nodding. He could guess the rest of it.

"Damn right, I backed him up," said Sergeant Bell. "I can't
have one of my men look stupid in front of a damn homicide
dick—no offense, Riker. So, I figure she's right, but I say the
rat's just overfed, bloated—and *that's* why he's slow. Old
Oscar's been raidin' our lunch bags for years, and he *was* a
fat little sucker. So now the other two guys are goin' along
with my bloated-rat theory." The desk sergeant shrugged.
"They know a sick rat when they see one, but—"

"But backing up their guy is the main thing," said Riker,
smiling.

"Damn right. So your partner says, 'Put up or shut up.' "

"Mallory knows a good sucker bet when she sees one."

"Yeah, she does. So we all put money on it."

"Let me get this straight," said Riker. "You and the other
two cops—you *knew* she was right, but you still made the
bet? *All* of you?"

"Yeah, it'd gone too far. And Pete Hong was the first one to
lay his money down. Hey, what could we do? Ten bucks—
not a big wad to save the kid's face. Well, now we all got cash
riding on the little hairball. So Pete doesn't want Oscar to get
away, but Mallory still won't let him touch the rat."

" 'Cause the rat's sick, maybe dangerous."

"Yeah, you never know with rats. So Oscar's just about to
take a slow dive behind the candy machine. That's how he
was gettin' in. Damn hole in the wall, big as your fist. Just as
the rat's going into a roll, Mallory picks him off with one
round. Nice clean shot."

The desk sergeant held a sheaf of paperwork out to Riker.
"This is the lab report from the Board of Health. Came in this
morning. Mallory was right—that damn rat was diseased.
Now the city docs are comin' in to do blood tests on everybody."

Riker scanned the sheets. They included a copy of the
watch commander's report. Less colorful than Sergeant

Bell's telling, it briefly described the lawful and necessary dispatch of a potentially dangerous animal.

"Harry, I want you to send all this paperwork up to Special Crimes. Make sure Coffey sees it." Riker lightly slapped the desk. "Right now, okay?"

"Sure thing. Did the lieutenant have something riding on the rat?"

"Yeah, he did." Riker was grinning as he strolled toward the front door.

Jack Coffey had been wrong about Mallory. She had a sense of humor. And he had been right about her, too. The kid truly was a monster. She had let the lieutenant run his mouth on deadly payback for gun-happy cops. And all the while, she had been patiently awaiting this official delivery of a world-class punch line from the Board of Health.

What a setup.

When the report hit Coffey's desk, the lieutenant was going to implode or put his screaming head through a wall.

Riker left the station house with one fist raised high in triumph.

Mallory rules.

Eleven

IN A BID TO OUTFOX THE LAW, THE RESTAURANT HAD SECTIONED off one quarter of the room. Enclosed by glass from floor to ceiling, people relaxed at their tables, lighting cigarettes and cigars. Their smoke plumed upward into the slow swirling blades of a ceiling fan.

Lest any illicit smoke escape the enclosure, an air-purification system was hard at work in the main dining room, vacuuming the atmosphere, suctioning out the aromas of wines and sauces, meats and pasta. In this odor-free section, nonsmokers observed the diners caged in glass as historical exhibits from the days before the sterilization of New York City.

The maître d' stood behind a lectern, turning pages in his reservation book and pretending not to notice the people queuing up in front of him.

A smiling waiter in a white dinner jacket walked toward the woman at the end of the line. "Detective Mallory? I recognized you from television."

The celebrity alert had been sounded, and now she also had the attention of the maître d', who was admiring her black leather trench coat, the wildly expensive running shoes and a slightly less pricey handbag from Cartier. In the waiting line, more heads were turning, flashing movie-star-hunting eyes in her direction.

When she removed her coat, the black cashmere blazer and satin-trimmed jeans also passed inspection. The maître d' mouthed the words, *Oh, yes.* The people in his waiting line wore more formal attire, but Mallory was dressed in money.

The waiter took her coat and draped it over his arm. "They've been expecting you."

"They?"

"Mr. and Mrs. Malakhai." He waved one hand toward the glass smoking section.

"Right, the invisible woman."

Puzzled, the waiter looked toward the table where only Malakhai was seated. "His wife must be in the ladies' room."

"You've *seen* her?"

"Yes, of course."

This man was reinforcing every bad thing she believed about civilian testimony to gunshots never fired, events that never happened—and now ghosts. She followed him to the smoking section. "Wait," she said, to stop him from opening the glass door. "What color is this woman's hair?"

"It's red. A bright fiery red."

Mallory pointed toward the table. "He told you the color of her hair?"

"Well, no." The waiter seemed confused. "You mean it's not real? But it looks so natural."

As Mallory entered the glass room, she noted three place settings at the small round table, and a glass of wine had been poured for the corpse in the bloody blue dress.

Malakhai stood up as she set her new black handbag on the table beside the only clean wineglass. If her host had known her better, he would have been suspicious. She never carried a purse.

"Good evening." He dismissed the waiter before the man could pull out her chair. Now Malakhai performed this service himself. "You're right on time." As Mallory sat down, he glanced at his watch. "And I mean to the second."

In lieu of hello, she said, "You got a lot of mileage out of that German uniform. You wore it the day you took Louisa out of the transit camp—and again the night you shot her."

Malakhai calmly took his seat and moved the wine bottle to one side of the table, the better to see his dinner companion—the living one. "I missed you all day. I kept looking over my shoulder, but you weren't there."

Back to that old game, simply ignoring what he did not want to deal with and diverting her to other things. Even his conversation was a magic act of misdirection. But tonight she had come prepared.

"You're sure I wasn't there? I know you had breakfast with Prado and St. John. In the afternoon, you worked on your act." According to the stage manager at Carnegie Hall, Malakhai had spent hours rigging strings and small anchor loops of metal.

"I gather *you* spent part of the day with Mr. Halpern." He blew smoke into the air. "And of course, your visit to the auction was on the evening news. Did you like Oliver's version of the magic theater?"

"No." It had not lived up to the vision Malakhai had created for her in the basement. Oliver's theater was only a pale copy that lacked the drama of wartime, smoke and wine, perfume and soldiers with guns. Even the corpse in Oliver's platform had suffered a bloodless wound, more like an imitation of violence.

"About that uniform," she prompted him. "You were never in the German Army."

He signaled to the waiter and pointed to the empty bottle, then turned back to Mallory. "I remember it well—superb tailoring. It belonged to an SS officer."

"Did you kill that officer?"

"No. Sorry to disappoint you, Mallory." He blew a smoke ring and watched it rise into the blades of the fan. "I stole the man's bag at a railway station. A mistake—I meant to steal his orderly's clothes, a private's uniform. I wasn't old enough to pass for an officer. But then I realized that no one ever looked at the faces of the Gestapo. They only saw the SS insignia."

She reached across the table and delicately plucked a hair from the sleeve of his dark suit. So this was the waiter's evidence of a redhead. There was no root follicle for a DNA match. Even so, she made a show of folding it into a tissue and placing it in her purse. He followed this action with mild curiosity.

"You're getting careless, Malakhai. I guess there wasn't time to change clothes—after you stuffed that body into Oliver's platform."

"So his nephew had red hair. There were no pictures of him on the news." He set his cigarette in the ashtray next to one marked with Louisa's lipstick. "I never met the boy. I can't say I'm sorry he's dead."

"You don't remember hiding the body? Not surprising. I know about the strokes."

"Courtesy of Mr. Halpern? He was so upset when I couldn't remember how—"

The waiter appeared with a tray balanced at shoulder level. After unfolding a stand with his free hand, he set his burden down, then rearranged all the items on a tabletop barely large enough to accommodate three plates and silverware, glasses, a bottle, an ashtray and a purse. Mallory and Malakhai watched in silent fascination as the waiter altered the laws of physics to expand space, creating more room for a basket of bread, a candle, another wine bottle and a large plate of hors d'oeuvres.

"I couldn't have done that," said Malakhai.

When the three glasses had been filled with red wine, and the waiter had departed with their dinner orders, Mallory slipped one hand into the open purse by her plate. Malakhai took no notice. He was staring at her face, not expecting anything out of the ordinary tonight, certainly no magic—not from her.

"It's an interesting problem," she said. "You have to get even for Louisa's death before you forget who she was." Her blind fingers found the anchor loop inside the purse. The string was still in place. "What about the day Oliver died in Central Park? Do you remember where you were?"

"At home, hundreds of miles from here. I watched it on television."

She teased a length of string from her handbag. "What time was that?"

"There are no clocks in my parlor. I believe it was a live

performance—whatever time the show went on that night."

"Night?" said Mallory. "You didn't notice the sun shining on the bandstand and the crowd?"

"Not bright camera lights?" He smiled to say that this was an honest mistake. *Sorry.*

Yeah, right.

"Oliver Tree was pronounced dead at three thirty-one in the afternoon." She liked to be precise about death. "But you watched the show at night." Under the cover of her napkin, she moved the string toward Louisa's place setting as she leaned forward. "Can you explain that?"

"After a stroke, sometimes it's all I can do to find the right decade. Mistaking night for day is one of my lesser errors in time."

"Or you watched Oliver's show on a VCR. Maybe you taped it because you knew you wouldn't be home that afternoon."

"I remember an alarm clock going off. It might have been ringing for hours. Perhaps I did tape the show—as a precaution against a stroke."

She left the napkin by Louisa's glass. "So you have no alibi for that afternoon?"

"No, I'm something of a hermit. Days can go by without my seeing another soul, and it's been years since I asked anyone for the time of day."

"What's your first name?"

"Malakhai is the only name I have. My father abandoned my mother and never acknowledged me as his bastard. So Mother put his surname on the birth certificate. It drove his family wild. My mother had an interesting sense of humor." He was staring at the bulge of her blazer where it covered the shoulder holster. "The gun ruins the line of the jacket. Does that upset your tailor?"

Other detectives had solved this problem by wearing the gun lower, but she liked the intimidation value.

"Louisa had a better tailor," said Mallory. "Very expensive alterations. How much loot did you get after you buried Oliver's grandmother in the cellar?"

He laughed. That was not the reaction she wanted.

"My compliments. I won't ask how you pried that story loose. The only profit was Faustine's pension. It was barely enough to cover rent on the theater. Louisa's clothes belonged to a boy who left the troupe. She remade all the costumes herself."

Mallory shook her head. "I know expert tailoring when I see it. And I know what it costs."

"My wife was a tailor's daughter." When he turned to the dead woman's chair, he was suddenly unsettled. Louisa's plate held oysters and shrimp speared with bright-colored toothpicks, but he had not placed them there.

"Why was Louisa in that transit camp?"

When he turned his eyes to Mallory again, he was still disconcerted. "Oh, lots of people wound up there. Refugees were always being rounded up on the street in mass arrests, twenty at a time. They were sorted out later at the transit camp. Most of them were let go."

"There's more to it," said Mallory. "I know the camp commandant questioned Louisa every day. She was more than a tailor's daughter."

"She wasn't a spy, if that's what you mean. But her father was more than a tailor. He had a list of names that interested the Germans. They thought Louisa might know where he was."

"So you were working with the Polish underground."

"No, I was only a runaway schoolboy in love with Louisa. I've loved her since we were children." His head turned as Louisa's wineglass moved, but not by *his* hand, not *his* strings. There was a grave disquiet in his eyes. But he showed no suspicion that Mallory was working his dead wife like a puppet.

"So you risked your life for her, and then she cheated on you."

"Louisa didn't ask me to get her out of that camp." Malakhai mashed his stub in the ashtray and stared at Louisa's cigarette, burned down by half, dark and smokeless. "In Central Park, there's a wide pedestrian boulevard. It leads away from the band shell. Very dramatic space, lined with statues and benches. Do you know it?"

Mallory nodded. She had recently spent some time there, pacing between the long rows of trees that formed a canopy of overgrown branches.

"It's not Paris," he said. "But it'll do. Our last night in France, Louisa and Max met with me in a place like that. It was a few hours before show time at Faustine's. Accordion music was coming from some bistro across the park. I remember the tune was bright, and the rain was falling. I held an umbrella over Louisa. She was very upset—frightened. Wanted posters had been delivered to the local police station. The next day, the whole city was going to be papered with Louisa's photograph and the offer of a bounty. Emile St. John had warned her that morning."

"What kind of connections did St. John have?"

"Emile was a policeman. I told you we all had day jobs. Louisa was desperate. She wanted to make a run for the Spanish frontier. Well, that was suicide. No exit visas were being issued, and security was tight all along the border. Spain had closed like a door. If we tried to use Nick's forgeries, we'd be arrested. Louisa said she'd rather die than go back to the camp, the interrogations. She was determined to leave France that night—without me. Said she didn't want me to take one more risk, not for her sake."

He poured another glass of wine. "I think I laughed at that. I told her I would always take care of her." He poured a glass for his wife. "And then Louisa said she was in love with my best friend. I remember Max's face—all that pain. And tears? I'm not sure now. That might've been the rain." He exhaled a cloud of smoke and watched it swirling upward. "I *hope* Max was crying."

"You hated him."

He shook his head. "What *was* I feeling? It was like the three of us had been in a terrible road accident. I was shocked by the sudden damage, the impact. And then this odd hollowness. I always imagined death that way, the soul floating out, weightless, nothing solid to hold it to the earth anymore.

"Then Louisa sent Max away—so we could have a private moment, my wife and I. You know what I remember best? The smell of her wet wool coat. That was the last time Louisa put her arms around me. She asked me to forgive her—and Max."

"You were angry."

"No, I don't think so—not then. After she'd gone, I put a cigarette in my mouth. I remember standing there like a fool, striking matches in the rain."

"And that was the night you changed Louisa's plans to make a run for the border. You shot her with the crossbow during the opening act. But you weren't in the theater when she was being killed. You ran away."

Everything in his face was asking how she could possibly know that.

"You were too young to pass for an officer. And Mr. Halpern said you couldn't speak the language well enough to pass for a German. But there were always German soldiers in the theater. So after you shot Louisa, you *had* to run."

He nodded.

She pressed on. "It looked like a magic trick gone wrong. Does that sound familiar? Poor old Oliver. But let's stick with Louisa's murder. What were the odds the French cops would want to find you? An SS officer who shot an unarmed woman and ran away? No, the local police wouldn't look too hard. Much easier to report the death as an accident—less embarrassing for everyone. And while you were running away, your wife was being murdered backstage."

When Malakhai turned to the ashtray, it contained a fresh cigarette stained with lipstick in Louisa's shade. He looked at his wife's glass. It was half empty.

Mallory closed the purse on the wet sponge soaked with wine. "So you left your wife lying there on the stage, bleeding. Now you're out on the street. You peeled off the German uniform and stashed it in an alley. You wore street clothes underneath. None of this took more than a few minutes. But Louisa was dead when you got back to the theater."

He flicked his lighter. The flame trembled so slightly, Mallory might have missed it if she had not been watching for every sign of weakness. He was staring at the ashtray again—and Louisa's cigarette. Now it was only a mashed-out stub fetched from Mallory's purse. He must be wondering if he was missing time, whole minutes, the length of a smoke.

The waiter had returned to the table. He was asking permission to remove Louisa's remnants. Malakhai glanced at the cast-off shrimp tails on his wife's plate. But he had not tampered with the food. How, then? His choices were three: madness, loss of memory—or Mallory.

The waiter left them with a clean ashtray, removing the evidence of the cigarette stub. Mallory had not yet touched her wine. Malakhai drank deeply.

"You risked your life for Louisa, and then she slept with your best friend. But you did get even with her. That must be a comfort."

No reaction. He had gone elsewhere, traveling in his thoughts.

"You know what was going through your wife's mind when you actually shot her—when you drew real blood?"

He was back again, more alert now, watching her—waiting.

"She wasn't expecting that," said Mallory. "Louisa thought she was going to be shot with a long red scarf—the way she opened every performance. I can see the look on her face when she saw you in that German uniform. It must have blown her mind away. So she was already stunned like some poor dumb animal in a slaughterhouse. What an easy target. And then you shot her—*you* of all people. That's what she was thinking about while she was dying in that back room. You shot her and ran away. That's all she knew in the last minute of her life—while that bastard was working on her, murdering her."

Louisa's wineglass moved again as Mallory drew the string through the anchor loop inside her purse. A quick tug, a flick of the wrist under the cover of the table, and the end of the string was hidden inside the handbag again.

Malakhai would not look at the glass anymore.

She leaned forward. "What did you do in the war?"

"In Paris? I ran a shell game on the street." He looked up at the waiter, who had suddenly appeared at the table to replenish his wineglass. "Milo, do you have any walnuts in the kitchen?"

"Yes, sir."

"Bring me three empty shells." He turned back to Mallory. "I believe the only murder you really care about is Oliver's."

She nodded. Diversion was his predictable fallback to avoid any more pain. And now she would get what she came for. "Everyone keeps telling me the old man did the trick wrong."

"Oliver's platform isn't an exact replica."

"I know that. I've seen his improvements. Give me something I can work with." *Distract me from Louisa, so I won't hurt you anymore.*

"Only the fourth arrow was fatal. If he hadn't been so frightened, he could've avoided the first three. Fear can paralyze a man. Oliver stopped struggling when he realized his key was jammed. That wouldn't have mattered to Max."

"You're saying Max used fake arrows?"

"No, he didn't. Police officers always checked Max's props. The arrows were identical. No fakes. All the crossbow magazines held three of them."

"Then it was a blocking device in the arrow bed?"

"No. Remember, the dummy gets hit by all the crossbows. And whatever blocks the arrow bed would block the bowstring too. But all the strings release with every shot. And the policemen cocked the crossbows. Oliver got that part right."

The waiter reappeared with three walnut shells.

"Thank you, Milo." Malakhai lined up the shells on the empty dinner plate. "This is an easier trick. I used to do it with peas. May I borrow your gun?"

"You're kidding, right?" As a rule, cops did not loan out their weapons. The rules became more stringent when the would-be borrower was a madman who dined with his dead wife.

"Are you afraid I'm going to shoot you in front of all these people?"

"You shot your wife in front of a bigger audience."

"But you don't really believe I'm planning to kill you."

"No, of course not." Mallory smiled pleasantly. "But given your history, there's a good chance I might have an accident."

"But you watched me load a crossbow and cock it. I know it's not fear. Prudence?" He picked up his napkin and unfolded it. "Perhaps you think someone might object to the sight of a gun in the dining room. We don't want to start a stampede for the door." He handed her the square of linen large enough to hide three guns. "Here, we'll be discreet. Wrap it in this. Go on, risk it. I know you want to. You like life on the edge, don't you, Mallory? I think you'd give it to me, fully loaded, just to see what happens next."

It was an exhilarating moment, a replay of her favorite nightmare, flying through the air at great speed—in total darkness.

He smiled. "But I only need the bullets. If you like, you can leave the gun on the table—just to make it more interesting."

She took the napkin from his hand and covered the gun as she slid it out of her holster. In the shelter of her lap, she released the cylinder and emptied six bullets from the chambers.

Now she handed him the ammo and set the linen-wrapped revolver in the empty space where Louisa's plate had been. The hidden muzzle was pointed toward Malakhai.

"You really don't want to touch that gun." Elbows on the table, her hands formed a steeple, fingertips barely touching in the fashion of a tense prayer. "If you want to test your reflexes against mine, it'll cost you an eye—maybe two."

"Understood, but I wasn't planning a duel." Malakhai dropped five bullets among the rolls in the bread basket. "I only need one." He placed the bullet under a walnut shell, then moved all three shells in slow circles, interchanging one with another. "You can't always trust your senses, Mallory. That's the only warning you get." The shells moved faster and faster. Then the action stopped abruptly, and he removed his hands from the table. "Where is the bullet?"

"Here." She picked up the center shell, and there it was.

"But are you sure it's the same one?" He picked up the remaining shells to show her two more bullets that should have been in the bread basket.

"Cute trick. How does this help me?" There was an edge to her voice. She lightly touched the rim of Louisa's wineglass, a small deliberate gesture to threaten him with fresh pain.

"You believe your eyes, Mallory. That's a mistake. Magic is what you don't see. And every good illusion is designed to defy logic." He held up a single bullet and pushed the other two aside. "This time I'll play fair. We'll only use one."

He set the bullet beneath a shell and began the little table dance of circling decoys. When the shells were once again lined up in a row, he put one finger lightly on the top of the first one. "Say I killed Oliver to avenge my wife." He touched the second shell. "Or maybe his killer fired that wild gunshot during the parade." His finger moved on to the last shell. "Or Oliver screwed up the illusion and killed himself. You don't want it to be this shell, but it's a possibility. Now where is the bullet?"

"It's none of those things, and the bullet is in your hand."

"Very good, Mallory. You're getting there. However—" He opened both hands and the bullet was not there.

One by one, she picked up the shells—no bullet.

"You still have a ways to go." He reached for the napkin concealing the gun.

Mallory was faster. Not taking her eyes from him, she clutched the mass of rumpled material. It was empty—no gun. She turned to see a single bullet drop from the cloth and roll across the table. The napkin fell in a crumpled heap, and in the next moment, she held Malakhai's face between her hands—so gently, the other diners must take them for lovers. None of them could see how close her thumbs were to his eyes, long red nails brushing his eyelashes, almost touching his dark blue irises, threatening to blind him. "Very slowly, put both hands flat on the table."

His hands appeared on the large dinner plate, the only clear space. He was much too calm.

"Where is my gun?"

"Inside the napkin. Have another look."

"I'm not playing with you, Malakhai. I'm going to put your eyes out."

"All right, *now* it's inside the napkin. Look again."

Without taking her eyes from his, she reached out one hand for the napkin, and her fingers closed on the solid mass of her revolver.

Angry, she ripped away the linen and held the naked weapon in her hand. Six bullets silently rolled toward her in single file between the wine bottle and the bread basket. She reloaded them into the chambers of her revolver, not caring that the waiter was standing only a few yards away, watching her and perhaps taking this for a comment on the service.

Malakhai was smiling. "You must learn to think beyond standard parameters, or you'll never work it out."

Mallory did not see herself in the role of his student; she cared nothing for his instruction. "You haven't spoken to Louisa tonight. Forget the routine? Did you have another stroke?"

Disappointed in his silence, she continued in hopes of causing real damage. "You're losing more memories every day."

She caught the unconscious nod of his head. He put his cigarette in the ashtray, and now he noticed Louisa's fresh one. It was stained with lipstick. Mallory had added no chemicals for smoke; its mere appearance in the ashtray was enough. He stared at it, suddenly wary, as if it might be dangerous to him.

"It'll be over soon," she said. "You'll forget your own name."

"Less baggage to carry."

"Your wife is slipping away from you."

"Less heartache." He turned his eyes to Mallory, to show her a bit of pain as a gift, an offering he knew would please her.

"You lost the first Louisa. All you've got now is pieces of the monster you made—maybe half a woman left." She slipped her gun into the holster. "Let's keep this simple. I don't see Oliver killing your wife. But he knew who the murderer was."

"Wrong." Malakhai shook his head slowly. "Poor Oliver never had a clue. He believed her death was an accident. Louisa was the only corpse he ever saw during the war. The army gave him a desk job, and that embarrassed him. He wanted to fight so badly. Such a brave little man—standing up to all those arrows."

Mallory watched his hand close into a fist. Oliver's death made him angry. This was no act. She had never caught him at that particular kind of deceit and did not see it as his style.

"No," said Malakhai. "I doubt that murder ever crossed his mind. Oliver was a rare good man and very loyal. He would never believe that one of his friends was capable of that."

"If Oliver didn't kill your wife, then he wasn't murdered for revenge. And he left his fortune to charity, so I don't have a money motive either. That's how I know he frightened somebody. That's all I've got left."

"You call him by his first name," said Malakhai. "You never met him, but he's always Oliver to you."

She ignored this. "The gunshot that went wild and hit the balloon—that was an attempted murder. So I know the killing isn't over yet. I can't find you or Nick Prado on the parade tapes. Everyone else was in plain sight when that gun went off."

"You take Oliver's death personally, don't you?" Malakhai's faint smile was wistful. He was oddly affected by this small habit, the use of the dead man's first name.

"Maybe Prado was shooting at you. He's a logical choice," said Mallory. "Wasn't his old stage routine built around trick shots? But he probably wouldn't have missed what he was aiming at. I think you're the one who fired that bullet into the balloon. Before the shot went wild, you were targeting the man who killed Oliver. Was it someone on the float? Or did you see Nick Prado in the crowd?"

"Oliver would've adored you—his very own champion, his paladin."

"Maybe you blew the shot because you stroked out with the gun in your hand. Or maybe you just don't have what it takes to kill. What did you do in the war—*after* Louisa died? Was it a desk job like Oliver's? Whose army were you in?"

"I started my basic training with the British. Then, before I was finished, they transferred me to an American unit."

"Where you did *what?*"

"Mass murder." His hand was steady as he sipped his wine. His voice was even, almost mechanical. "I tore human beings to shreds with explosives. And then I did my usual meticulous body count. I walked among the dismembered corpses—and the living too. But survivors never lingered very long. I always tallied them up with the dead, even when I could hear them screaming. I counted the broken bloody heads. That was the easiest way to figure out how many people there would've been—if all the parts of them had been all together."

Twelve

THIS FACILITY WAS HIGHLY RATED BY THE STATE OF CONNECTI-cut—and Mallory. The doors of every room stood open for her inspection, and cold white interior walls carried on the institutional theme of the corridor. There was no personal clutter of family photographs, no stale odor of sedentary patients, no hint of cologne or perfume. Every sign of the residents had been erased. A strong scent of disinfectant further killed any idea of a human habitat; only a fanatical cleaning woman or Detective Mallory could comfortably breathe in this atmosphere. She also approved of the tall nurse who walked beside her. The fragrance of laundry starch hung about his crisp white uniform.

The nurse was all too familiar with Mr. Roland. "The old man turned eighty-seven last month. Outlived his wife and son. The grandchildren could hardly wait to dump him here. Keep your distance, and forget everything you've heard about officers and gentlemen. He spits when he talks, and sometimes he aims it."

"He's gone senile?"

"Well, he does ramble some. But just between you and me, I think General Roland was always—" One of his fingers made a spinning motion beside his head, as an illustration for toys in the attic.

"He told you he was a general?"

"Yes, ma'am, a five-star general. You'd think the war was still on, the way he barks orders to the staff."

But according to Mr. Roland's service record, obtained by midnight requisition from a military computer, the old man had never been promoted past the rank of lieutenant, and he had been dishonorably discharged before the end of World War II.

Mallory and the nurse walked down a hallway of tall windows. The glass sparkled with a recent cleaning and gave them a clear view of the dead garden. This long gallery was lined with chairs of wicker and chairs on wheels, each one only marginally occupied by an elderly person in a green robe and paper slippers. Their faces were devoid of expression, not enjoying the vista of bare trees and brown grass, their only activity, for they seemed to have been parked here and abandoned.

And now Mallory better understood the old man she had yet to meet. "You humor Mr. Roland, don't you?"

"Oh, yeah, everybody does," said the nurse. "My grandfather was in World War II. He'd flay me alive if I didn't show the old man some respect. So I call him 'General,' and sometimes I even salute. He likes that."

Perhaps Mr. Roland was not deluded, but merely cagey. She turned back to look at the chair-bound people in a holding pattern at the windows, disengaged from life and unattended. Yes, Mr. Roland had been wise to elevate his rank in the world.

"You'll be two minutes late for your appointment, ma'am. My fault—sorry. He might make you pay for that." The nurse stopped by a door at the end of the corridor and opened it for her. "He's all yours."

When she entered the private room, she found a withered little man with stray wisps of white hair sprouting in soft horns on either side of his balding head. He seemed lost in the network of technology. A plastic bag hung on the arm of a metal pole and dripped liquid into his veins. She could see the bruises on his arms from many other needles. A cable from his bedside monitor wove between the buttons of his red pajamas and stood out in a bold line to his heart. More tubes carried oxygen from the wall unit to the plastic device under his nostrils.

"So you're Detective Mallory." Mr. Roland's voice was the last remnant of strength, and it carried the authority of his falsely escalated rank. He looked her up and down, as if he were indeed a general reviewing his troops. His eyes came to rest on a bulge in the line of her blazer. He pointed to it with one gnarly finger. "Is that a gun? Now who'd give a gun to a little girl like you? Show me your identification." This was an order.

Mallory reached into the back pocket of her jeans and pulled out her shield and ID. She held it up to him, and he squinted to read her name and rank.

"Thank you for seeing me on such short notice," she said, stepping back out of range from any spittle that might come her way.

"The police are all children now." The old man shook his head. "But *girls* with guns. If that ain't the limit."

Mallory settled into a chair beside the bed. "I need information about a man under your command in World War II."

"Oh, the *real* war. Now that was a time and a half. I was career army, you know. In my first command—mostly sabotage details—damn few came back alive, and that's a fact. That's how much action my battalion saw."

By Mallory's count, it was hardly a battalion, and only two men out of twenty had come back alive. The U.S. Army had been less than satisfied with Roland's explanation for this carelessness. "You could save me some time, sir. You know how long it takes to get anything out of the military."

Actually, it had taken very little time. Hacking into the Pentagon computer was a rite of passage for the high-technology generation. A child could do it, and many children did. The military system suffered thousands of hits every year. But her time inside the files was limited by the bells and whistles of electronic watchdogs. "The soldier was Private Malakhai. Do you—"

"Do I remember him? Hell yes, I do. I did my level best to kill that son of a bitch." He paused to gauge the effect on her, and he was clearly disappointed that she was neither shocked nor impressed. "On his last mission, I made him jump from a plane in a daylight run. Damn fluke. The German gunners on the ground must've been napping when the boy's parachute opened."

"You wanted him dead—one of your own men."

"Oh, yeah." He seemed more pleased with himself now that she had recognized his godhood. "The corporal—Edwards was his name. Damn kid, younger than you are. Well, that pissant tried to keep Malakhai in the plane. I had to pistol-whip the little bastard to keep him from blocking the door. Then I ordered Malakhai out of the plane. I should've pushed Edwards out too. But he wasn't wearing a chute. I like to give a man a sporting chance."

Mallory nodded. Edwards was the one who had chased down the lost medals belonging to his unit. Among the decorations he had secured for Private Malakhai, there were too many Purple Hearts, each one standing for a wound. She could not get them out of her mind.

"Oh, yeah," said the old man. "I saw it as my responsibility to make sure Malakhai never went home from the war. That boy wasn't something you could turn loose on a peacetime population—not in good conscience."

"He won a lot of medals." Her voice was soft but obstinate.

"Mostly shrapnel." The old man waved his hand in the air to say this was of no consequence. "It was a mistake to give him medals. He didn't assassinate his targets one at a time, you know. He blew up troops by the dozen, by the damn truckload. And sometimes he forgot to make distinctions between soldiers and civilians. That kind of butchery never makes it into the permanent record."

Covert missions. That would explain the lack of detail on Malakhai's records and the alarms going off each time she had peeled back another layer of security codes.

The old man raised one clenched fist. "We took all the risks and got damn little glory."

We? "So Malakhai did a lot of high-risk missions."

"Mostly suicide runs. But he kept finding his way home again, turning up at field camp, torn up like a damn alley cat. And all the time, his eyes were getting colder and colder." Roland smiled, warming to his subject. "Hollow Boy—that's what I named him. After a while, he even answered to it.

Toward the end, he wasn't human anymore. I should have done it right—just taken out my gun and shot him the way you'd put down a dog. I had the sweetest little pistol, a gift from General Patton."

Yeah, right.

"Did you know his wife died two days before he enlisted?"

"That's what the British said. Malakhai did basic training with their boys. Damn doctors wanted to sedate the shit out of him and put him in a hospital. In 1942, they were taking kids and old men, but they didn't want any part of Malakhai. Said he was out of touch with reality. They didn't think he'd stand the chance of a child in battle. Yeah, he was sick all right, but such a useful kind of crazy—no sense of fear. You could fire a rifle right next to that kid's head—no reaction. So I figured, why waste him? I had a clerk fiddle his papers for repatriation and reassignment. He was born a Polish bastard, so we gave him an American father. Pulled him out of basic training before the Brits could ship him off to the funny farm. Now that was a neat piece of work."

"You fiddled a lot of paperwork for your unit. Weren't you supposed to send your men home after they'd been shot to pieces? Wasn't anyone counting Malakhai's Hearts? He was wounded seven times, *seven* Purple Hearts."

"The paperwork was delayed. Wartime bureaucracy."

"And there were other medals for valor. They caught up to Malakhai five years after the war. You never wanted him to have them, did you?"

"Not while he was still useful. If I'd reported every little piece of metal in his hide, they would've shipped him Stateside."

"And you wanted him dead."

"Well, I couldn't ship him home, could I? Private Malakhai was a damn murder machine. And it's not like he was a *real* American."

"He wore the uniform."

The old man was clearly exasperated. "You still don't get it, little girl. You know why Hitler used gas chambers? He wasn't being efficient. He mechanized death to lessen the shock on the troops. That bastard knew what hands-on mass murder would do to them. They'd all be like Malakhai. It would gut their souls. A whole generation of hollow boys would never be able to go home again. It would poison the seed of a whole damn country. And Hitler would be the king of nothing."

"All those medals." She was taking more pride in Malakhai as an opponent. "Medals for wounds, medals for valor."

"The boy was *insane*!" The old man made a weak fist, frustrated that she could not grasp this simple fact. "And pathetic. Sometimes tears would roll down his face at the damnedest times. He wasn't crying—no emotion in that one. It was a mechanical thing. The tears would just come and go with no reason—like the machine was broken. Even then, his eyes were so cold, so—"

"Were you jealous of him?"

That made the faux general angry. He turned away, and now she was sure of it. She leaned closer to his bed. "Were you afraid of Private Malakhai? Is that why you wanted him dead?"

"I was never afraid of anyone. And I'm sure as hell not afraid of you, girlie." He raised his head and aimed the spittle well.

Mallory started. A glob of mucus was sliding down her cheek. In stone-cold anger, she moved her hand toward him. He cringed, eyes rounding with surprise and fear. The little tyrant of the nursing home was not accustomed to reprisal. Her hand slowly dropped to pick up the corner of the bed-sheet. She used it to wipe the slime from her face.

Braver now, assured that she didn't intend to harm him, he shook his head in mock disappointment. "You've got the same cold, empty eyes, little girl. But you're not in Malakhai's class." More spittle flew from his mouth with the sputter of words. "I bet you'd like to take a turn at me." One hand rose in a defiant claw. "You wanna pull out all my tubes and wires, bring down the old general, right? Well, you just—"

"Wrong," she whispered, leaning close to his ear as she reached into the breast pocket of her blazer. He was staring at her hand, his face full of dread. Did he think she was going for her gun? Now that truly was a delusion of grandeur.

"One more question." She pulled out a computer printout and unfolded it. "I have your service record here—from the telephone company." She held it up for him to see. "In 1950, when you were repairing a phone line, you were bitten by a dog—a little dog. Did they give you a medal for that?" She rose from the chair and looked down at him. "No?"

Whatever Roland had been about to say, it was forgotten. She had finally shut his mouth. Getting the last word was her art, and getting even was wonderfully satisfying—but not today.

Mallory watched the old man shrink back from her, burrowing in the bedsheets, growing smaller in every way. Was he frightened? Yes. Perhaps he believed she would rat him out to the hospital staff—that his days as an esteemed general were over.

He was terrified.

And yet she took no joy in this. There was only a vague feeling that she could not readily identify as pity, for she had little experience with that emotion; it did not fit into her philosophy. She had less personal experience with guilt, and felt none as she turned her back on the soft weeping from the old man's bed. Roland was forgotten by the time she passed through the front door and walked toward the parking lot.

Well, it had not been a total waste of her time. She understood Malakhai a little better. According to Emile St. John, Louisa's violin concerto had become part of the magic act after World War II. But that was only a prelude to the real insanity. The fully formed delusion of Louisa had been created in the next war.

And now she knew why he had signed up for the North Korean conflict of the fifties. It was yet another opportunity for an interesting death. But instead, he had been taken prisoner. His war records for that period had been more complete, detailing the year of solitary confinement in a cell—no, a box—five feet wide by five tall. After his release, he had passed the following six months in a veterans hospital, recovering from the trauma of torture—and playing cards with a woman who wasn't there.

✛   ✛   ✛

Detective Sergeant Riker stood by the wall of steel drawers, where corpses were tagged by toes and filed away. He watched Mallory slip the .357 revolver into her holster. The less satisfying weight of her police issue .38 was now resting in the knapsack at her feet. It had not occurred to her to thank him for retrieving her favorite gun from Lieutenant Coffey— along with her winnings from the suckered cops in uniform.

Well, she was smiling. That was something. And she had not counted the bet money, which might imply some measure of renewed trust.

Chief Medical Examiner Slope put on his reading glasses and consulted a clipboard as he moved down the length of the steel wall in company with a morgue attendant. They stopped in front of a locker, and the attendant opened a door to roll out the body Mallory liked best.

Riker buttoned his coat as he walked toward the corpse on the locker bed. The cold air lessened the odor of dead meat and chlorine. And now he was looking down at all the signs of a full autopsy. Cruel cuts ran the length of the gutted torso. Each organ had been probed and weighed. The chemistry of fluid and tissue had been checked. Even the skull had been violated to get at the brain, and every orifice had been savaged—royal treatment for a dead junkie. It had been this corpse's great good luck to belong to Detective Mallory.

The unflayed sections of skin mapped out a small, mean life. Riker could count all the ribs of this addict who had loved heroin more than food. The hands were marked with crude drawings of snakes made with ink and pinpricks. This self-mutilation spoke of extended time in a lockup, perhaps one of the many drug treatment centers his uncle had paid for. The face was frozen in the interrupted whine of a pulled-back upper lip. A more professional tattoo emblazoned the dead boy's complaint on one shoulder in capital letters, LIFE SUCKS.

Dr. Slope dismissed the morgue technician with a curt nod. Lowering his glasses, he turned to Mallory. "Back from your little vacation?"

Mallory shook her head. "If the reporters ask, you never saw me."

Riker looked down at the late Richard Tree, better known in broadcasting and print as Crossbow Man. He had been misnamed, for he was closer to a boy. Though his age was listed at twenty-two, the face had failed to grow a beard, only stray hairs here and there, and the pug nose made him more childlike. "So the kid OD'd, right?"

Dr. Slope nodded. "The test results won't be in for a while. But I don't think there'll be any surprises."

"The arrow wound was made after death," said Mallory.

"If you're going to do your own autopsies, why bother me?" Dr. Slope handed her the clipboard. "Cause of death— overdose of a longtime user. But you knew that too, didn't you?" He turned the corpse's arm to show her the needle marks inside the elbows. "I found older tracks on the soles of his feet and behind his knees. He was probably hiding the addiction until those veins gave out. I'd say he's been a needle away from dying for a long time."

"So there's no way this could be murder." Riker pulled out his notebook.

"Definitely not." Slope was somewhat irritated, perhaps because this was also something that Mallory already knew. "No sign of a struggle, no bruising or defensive wounds. And his last needle puncture is consistent with injection by his own hand. He's probably the only one who could've found a good vein in that arm."

"What about AIDS?" Riker's pen hovered over a clean page, though he doubted there would be anything worth writing down. "Maybe a suicidal overdose?"

"No," said Slope. "I'm guessing he came into money recently. The heroin was a good grade. He was probably accustomed to cut-down drugs laced with crap. Help me roll him."

Riker pocketed his useless pen and notebook, then pulled on a pair of plastic gloves, not wanting to touch the dead flesh. He had levels of squeamishness that depended on the freshness of a corpse, and this one was way past ripe. Why couldn't Mallory do this? It was *her* damn junkie.

When the corpse lay facedown, the marking on the upper back was exposed. It was a uniform pattern of crisscrossing lines within the hard edge of a rectangle.

"Now these marks are postmortem," said Slope. "But made close to the time of death and before the body was moved. Might be a metal grate for a floor vent. You match that pattern and you'll know where he died. I figure the body was moved at least twenty-four hours after death."

"So the only criminal charge would be mutilation of a corpse," said Riker. "That's it?"

"That's the one odd note." Slope handed Mallory the arrow, bagged and tagged as evidence. "The chest was punctured days after the boy died. An accidental death staged as a murder—I call that interesting."

"I call it misdirection," said Mallory. "Why don't we sit on the autopsy findings for a few days?"

"Fine. You get me some paperwork to make that legal, and we'll talk about it."

"It might take a few days to get the paperwork."

"Right." Slope threw up his hands. "So, is this at all helpful? Or was I wasting my time here?"

"Nothing I can really use," said Mallory. "But you might help me with something else. What can you tell me about cluster strokes?"

"Save me some time," said Slope. "What don't you already know?"

"It's Malakhai."

And now she had the doctor's attention. He was as startled as Riker.

"It's been going on for a year," she said. "Every time he has a stroke, a little piece of his brain dies, memories are destroyed. I know they're happening faster now. I need to know how much time I've got before he dies or his brain is wiped."

"I'm sorry to hear that." The doctor pushed the steel bed back into the wall and closed the door. "If he's on medication, he might last awhile without dramatic impairment. I can't tell you the date when any man is going to die. Could be tomorrow or next year. But one day, there'll be a massive stroke. What he's going through now probably isn't that debilitating—missing time, minutes or hours. Dexterity and motor skills won't be affected. Not his intellect either—no dementia. Dates and specific memories are most susceptible to loss."

"And people?"

"He might not recognize certain people from his past. It depends on the severity of the strokes."

Riker looked at his shoes, hoping to hide his surprise from Slope—and the humiliation. What else might Mallory be holding out on him?

"Right now, he's only having small strokes," said Mallory. "Could he have committed a recent murder and then forgotten it?"

"It's possible," said Slope. "But unlikely at this stage. It's not like Alzheimer's. Usually the present remains intact, and the distant memories go first. But you were the one who told Malakhai how his wife was murdered. Doesn't that preclude a revenge motive *before* the poker game?"

Riker was angry, for he had not been privy to this information either. He tried to catch her eye.

Mallory pointedly ignored her partner, turning her face away, speaking only to Slope. "Malakhai already knew how his wife died. Maybe he didn't have all the details, but he knew she didn't bleed to death from a shoulder wound. He's seen more corpses than you have. And he's had worse wounds than Louisa's."

Dr. Slope shook his head. "Why would he wait more than fifty years for revenge?"

She didn't notice that Riker was edging away from her. "I don't know." Mallory was staring at the locker that housed her junkie. "But that body was a prime piece of misdirection." She held up a small green velvet bag. Riker recognized it as the one Charles had given her when he showed her the key rod from Faustine's Magic Theater.

She handed it to the doctor. "Look familiar?"

Slope examined the embroidered *F.* "It's just like the one we found on Oliver Tree's body."

"We?" asked Riker, hoping that Slope was referring to his assistants. "Did I miss something here? There was an autopsy for an accident victim?"

Slope lowered his glasses. "A *violent* accident, and very high-profile. Sure we had a look at the body. No cutting. Nothing fancy. Mallory was the only cop who bothered to show up for it. She didn't tell you?"

"Must've slipped her mind." Riker slumped against a locker, feeling suddenly wasted.

Mallory took the velvet bag from Slope's hand and turned to her partner. "I told you Oliver's killer only had to substitute the keys—exchange the new one for the old one with a little sleight of hand. The key bag made it easier. Any garden-variety pickpocket could've done it."

Riker would not look at her as he put on his hat and buttoned his coat. She did not seem to notice that he was angry. More likely, she did not care. He left Mallory talking to the air as he pushed through the swinging doors. He had walked half the length of the corridor before he heard the slap of her running shoes on the floor.

"Riker, wait!"

He kept on moving, only wanting the fresh air of the sidewalk and some solitude. She caught up and walked alongside him. He would not look at her—he could not.

"Where are you going, Riker?"

"To the theater." He checked his watch. He would be late for his appointment with Franny Futura. "I'm pulling the crime scene tapes so the magicians can—"

"Not so fast. I need some specs from the room inside Oliver's platform. I'll meet you there. We'll have lunch, okay?"

"I'm not hungry, kid." He was almost to the end of the hall, the end of his patience with her. "We'll do lunch some other time—when you're a grown-up."

He felt her hand on his sleeve, and now he stopped dead and turned on her. Was that surprise in her eyes? Yes. She was reading his face, probably wondering how he could be angry with her. Empathy was not her strong point.

"You never changed, Mallory. As I recall, you never did learn to share your toys with the other kids."

"The other kids wouldn't have anything to do with me, and you know it." She had delivered this line without complaint, as a dry fact of life. It was a good shot, well placed.

In all the years of watching Kathy Mallory grow, he had never known her to have one playmate her own age. She had made do with the cops of Special Crimes, and computers had replaced the playground jump rope. She had frightened children from more traditional homes than cold streets and cast-off refrigerator cartons.

His voice softened, as if he were speaking to Kathy the child. "You know this is no way to treat your own partner. I gave you every piece of information I had. But you—"

"And every time I gave you evidence, you picked it apart. *Every time,* Riker. You couldn't just be on my side."

Now she was the one who was angry. He had blinked once, and their roles had reversed—but how?

She squared off, hands on hips. "What if I *had* mentioned Oliver's autopsy? That day on the parade float—wouldn't you have laughed at me anyway? Then you double-teamed me with Coffey."

No, wait. This was not going to work on him—not today. She was in the wrong, and this was not going to wind up as his fault.

"Fine," he said, undoing his coat buttons. "You want your damn present back? You got it."

"No, stop." She reached out and put her hands over his. "You earned the coat." The storm was over. She wore a vague smile as she carefully redid his buttons. And then she brushed the shoulders and inspected him for other debris. She was Kathy when she smiled, ten years old again.

This was not a fair fight.

"The coat is payback," she said. "For the day you nailed the dentist."

"What?"

Mallory turned around and walked back toward the morgue, leaving him in confusion and nursing a small heartache. That was her style, hit and run—unchanged in fifteen years.

The dentist?

He had not thought of that incident in years. How old had she been that day—eleven? He had volunteered to take her to an appointment after school. In the reception room, the dentist had greeted him with a smirk. "So where's Inspector Markowitz?" He had pointed to the little girl at Riker's side. "Did she kill him?"

Young Kathy had not seen the humor in this. She had been moving her foot toward a clean shot at the man's shinbone, but Riker's tight grip on her coat collar had restrained her youthful enthusiasm for violence.

In love with his own wit, the dentist had said, "Can we handcuff the little monster to the chair this time?"

After Riker had shoved the dentist against the wall and pinned him there, he further terrified the man by asking if any other little girls had been manacled to his chair. And did the little bastard think that was *normal?*

There had been one excited, gleeful moment in Kathy's eyes, when she thought the dentist would lose all his teeth, but Riker had disappointed her and released the man.

Then he had taken the child by the hand and led her outside to a quiet hour of feeding squirrels in Washington Square Park. He had talked about life and warned her that it could be unfair, unkind. *What an idiot.* As if the former street kid had needed that reminder, she who had dined out of garbage cans on days when she could not steal her dinner. When he asked if the dentist had hurt her with words, the little girl had shaken her head in the silent but emphatic lie, *No, of course not, fool.*

In that brief moment, he had gotten to know her better; it

was something about the lower lip tucked under her front teeth—stoic Kathy. If she had only cried or made some complaint—just once—she would never have this hold over him today.

Now he looked down at his new topcoat. *Payback?* That was the last time she could remember him being on her side?

Thirteen

MALLORY'S HAND BLOCKED OUT THE LOW-RIDING AFTERNOON sun, as she stared up at the man on the ladder. He was working on an old-style marquee lined with yellow lightbulbs and topped with a row of elegant gold type. The workman bolted down the last letter to spell out "Faustine's Magic Theater." Less permanent text appeared in the white areas on three sides of the square overhang. Among the magicians listed for the upcoming performance, Franny Futura was the headliner and the only name she recognized.

The building was twenty-five blocks north of the theater district, but it *was* Broadway. Not a bad address for the man Charles had described as a tired museum of magic.

Mallory turned to the glass doors trimmed with thin wheels of steel. Riker had removed the yellow crime scene tapes. Was he still here? Still angry? Her birthday gift should have covered a multitude of sins, payback for crimes she had not yet thought of committing. Actually, she had bought the coat because his old one was too threadbare to keep him warm in winter. But this simple explanation would have cost her too much.

She paused by the entrance to inspect a recently installed display case of chrome and glass. Photographs of Oliver's grandmother were arranged in a circle around her memorial plaque. In a clockwise history of snapshots and publicity photos, Faustine aged from a slight dark-haired girl to a portly diva sporting an obvious wig. In the most recent portrait, hard black lines rimmed her eyes, and the mouth was made wider with dark lipstick. Among the traits that had remained constant throughout Faustine's long life was a look of hunger, a prominent determined chin and heartless eyes. Mallory wondered if anyone had ever crossed this woman. She thought not.

Pushing through the doors, she stepped into a small lobby. More alterations had been made since the auction. This intimate space was decorated with a dark green couch. The smell of new leather mingled with the odor of fresh plaster. A tarnished brass spittoon sat on the floor beside a standing ashtray. The walls and carpeting were paler shades of green. Faustine had obviously had a penchant for this color—and for attractive young boys.

The old woman's apprentices were ganged together on a giant theater poster framed in ornate gold. Mallory read the small brass plaque on the wall to her right.

So this photograph had been rescued from 1940, while Faustine was still alive; before the theater seats had been ripped out to accommodate dining tables; before the war had marched into the city in the gray uniforms of occupation forces. It would be two years before Louisa arrived in Paris. Oliver Tree was not listed in this company of boy performers in tuxedos and top hats. Evidently his own grandmother had not considered him a magician.

Young Max Candle stood in the background, barely contained inside the borders of the frame. There was a boy's explosion of energy in his body language. He was set to fly, to escape the camera and rush into real life. In his eyes was an expectation of things to come—wonderful things.

But there was so much more to Malakhai, though he could only have been fifteen that year. He was the dynamic center of the photograph, enthroned in a high-backed chair, a boy king with long hair spread across his broad shoulders. In a sense, Mr. Halpern had been correct—only Malakhai's hair had grown old. Something of the boy and his beauty had stayed with the man.

The others had followed the more natural course of time,

morphing into entirely different faces and forms. The young version of Emile St. John was glorious, with thick curling hair and the body of a god—a remote god, for his eyes were focused on some interior landscape. Franny Futura had been delicate, almost girlish with his full pouting lips and long eyelashes. But Mallory could barely recognize the teenage Nick Prado, sleek and saturnine. Standing a bit apart from the others, he was a dark figure with liquid Spanish eyes and a wicked grin that said, *Yes, I am beautiful, aren't I?* There was not enough resemblance to make Prado the father of this graceful boy. All that survived was the love affair with himself.

Mallory turned toward the sound of laughter. She peered through a glass circle in the lobby door. Three of Faustine's apprentices were on the stage. Emile St. John stood against the backdrop of a green curtain. Nick Prado and Franny Futura sat on wooden crates, passing a wine bottle between them. The auction tables were gone, and so was Oliver's platform. The movie people must have taken it.

Damn you, Riker.

He knew she wanted another look at the interior room, yet he had allowed the new owner to ship the platform out to the West Coast. Angry now, she pushed open the swinging door and marched down the wide center aisle.

"What are you people doing here?" Three heads turned her way. "I'm guessing this isn't a wake for Oliver's nephew."

"Well, hello." Nick Prado smiled and sucked in his paunch. "Just collecting the spoils of the auction." He held up a set of keys. "Sergeant Riker let us in." He looked down at the champagne bottle in his hand. "And of course, we had to properly christen Oliver's theater."

Squinting to see her better, Franny Futura walked perilously close to the edge of the stage. Normally a clean and tidy man, his tie was awry, and so was his mouth; it wobbled in a foolish smile. He was holding a plastic wineglass and weaving in an intoxicated line when he tangled his feet and tripped, landing on his backside. Eyes round and innocent as a startled gray-haired baby, Futura sat bolt upright on the floor of the stage, legs splayed out. He stared at his glass and the miracle of unspilt wine, mumbling something incoherent, which might have been, "There *is* a God."

Mallory climbed the stairs to the stage. "Where's the platform?" If it had been collected recently, it might be in the city and still within reach.

"Not to worry." Emile St. John parted the backdrop curtain to give her a glimpse of the large wooden structure behind it. All the crossbows were in position and pointing up toward the wooden posts at the top of the staircase. "Riker told the Hollywood people they couldn't ship it for a few more days."

"Oliver's lawyer adores you." Prado was at her side and standing too close, exhaling fumes of wine with every word. "That corpse probably doubled the opening bid on the platform. And of course, Franny loves you, too. His performance is sold out for the entire festival." He looked down at Futura, who sat on the floor calmly sipping his champagne.

"And you thought this place was too far from the theater district to pull in a crowd." Prado bent down to clap Futura on the back. The man's torso slumped forward, then slowly toppled the other way. Now he lay flat on the stage, and the wine was still unspilled.

Emile St. John left off the chore of uncorking another champagne bottle. He wrapped one massive hand around Futura's arm to lift the smaller man from the floor. "Enough wine, Franny?"

Prado's smile was all for Mallory as he flicked his wrist to snap a disk of black silk, popping out the crown of the top hat. "You'll excuse Franny? He's not himself."

Too bad.

Futura was leaning on the arm of St. John, grinning at her and utterly impervious to fear—but that would change. Tomorrow morning when he was sober, she would officially own this case. Just for the fear value, she would order two uniformed cops to haul Futura downtown. She didn't think much of his chances for holding out more than five minutes into the interview.

Nick Prado straightened Futura's tie. "He's not much to look at now, is he? I wish you could have met Franny when he was young and beautiful. Faustine only hired the most alluring boys in Paris. Ah, what time can do to the human body."

Apparently, Prado did not include himself in the aging process. What an odd mirror this egoist must have, a looking glass that blinded him to time, perhaps something like Max Candle's carnival mirror. Oliver Tree's replica of that prop had been laid across a wooden crate. The distorted glass surface served as a makeshift tabletop for champagne bottles and an assortment of delicatessen containers.

She followed St. John's shifting form in the mirror, alternately thinning and expanding. His aging had been less dramatic. The serenity of the boy in the poster was still in evidence, and he carried his excess pounds as ballast in the world. This man would not be shattered easily. As an interrogation subject, he posed the most interesting problem.

Mallory surveyed the leftovers of their impromptu picnic. The carnival glass was littered with remains of gourmet items on paper plates. She stared at Futura until she caught his wandering glazed eye. "You didn't invite Malakhai to the party?"

"I'm sure he'll be along in a while," said Futura, unruffled and entirely too happy. "He's prowling around Charles's basement."

St. John pulled a plastic wineglass from a paper bag. "Now where is the other champagne—"

"I'm on it, Emile." Prado was working the cork off a fresh bottle. It popped like a gunshot. A moment later, Franny Futura jumped in a delayed reaction.

St. John handed Mallory a wineglass and poured from a vintage bottle that must have cost the moon. He lit a cigar, also very expensive.

"Cuban," said Mallory, staring at the discarded wrapper. And he nodded, apparently not caring that he was flaunting contraband in front of the police. She addressed her remarks to the wineglass in her hand, hoping to make them seem casual. "So Malakhai didn't find what he was looking for in the basement?"

St. John only shrugged to say that he had no idea. "Charles

might know. We were running low on food, so he's making a deli run with Detective Riker. They'll be back soon."

"You think Malakhai might be looking for a photograph of his wife?" She set the wineglass down on the mirror. "I understand pictures of Louisa are scarce." She turned to Futura. He smiled and slowly put up both his hands to show her that he had nothing she wanted. Mallory moved a step closer. "Do you remember what she looked like? How long was her hair the first time you saw her?"

Futura gestured to a point just past his shoulder. "About so long."

"As I recall, her hair was very short." Prado poured wine into the moving target of the drunken man's glass.

"But that was later," said Futura. "The first time I saw her—"

He lost the thread of this thought as Prado raised a wineglass to propose a toast.

"To more glamorous days at Faustine's."

St. John clinked glasses with him. "Glamorous? Oh, Nick, you liar." One hand made a wide gesture that encompassed the surroundings. "Oliver made a few improvements. The original Faustine's was wonderfully seedy. After the old lady died, we turned it into a dinner theater. The air was always full of smoke. The floor reeked of whiskey and wine."

"And the food was very bad." Mallory faced St. John, squaring off in a pugilist stance. "German soldiers were your best customers. No officers, though. Unless you count the night Malakhai wore that Gestapo uniform on stage." How was she faring under St. John's appraising eyes? She could tell nothing from his placid face. What would it take to unnerve this man?

"Still, we did a good business." Nick Prado stepped into the awkward silence between Mallory and St. John, and he filled their glasses. "There were just too many free drinks for the Germans. So there was never enough money to go around." He picked up Mallory's discarded glass and put it into her hand. "But it was a grand party. It went on for years."

"But no profits." Mallory kept her eyes on St. John. "You all had day jobs to pick up the slack. What was yours?"

"I had a flair for picking pockets." The large man bowed from the waist as he held out a bright gold object swinging from a watch fob. "I believe this is yours."

Mallory was now holding unwanted wine in one hand and her pocket watch in the other. Her source at Interpol had confirmed St. John's history, and she was trying to reconcile his law enforcement career with this talent for theft. It never occurred to her to look in the mirror for clarity as she set down her glass. "How did Louisa make money?"

Emile St. John spoke first. He would always be the lead in this company. The others deferred to him. "Louisa played her violin on the street."

Futura slugged back his wine, saying, "But she made more money playing poker in a back room of the theater."

"The same back room where she was murdered?"

A moment of sobriety stole over Futura's face. Then Prado slapped him between the shoulder blades, as if this would knock the man back into a happy drunk—and it did.

"Louisa's death was a tragedy," said St. John. "An accident."

She turned around to face him. "Like Oliver's accident?"

"Exactly." He smiled, pleased that she understood—finally.

"I can prove Oliver was murdered." She looked from face to face. Only Futura was showing some wear, losing the glow of the wine once again.

Prado gave her a stage leer. "So pretty to have such a morbid interest in murder. Is there anything else in your life—besides death?"

"It's a professional interest, Prado." She watched him in peripheral vision, not bothering to look his way, only tossing this remark in the air. "I know what you did in the war. You threw in with the British. You were an expert marksman."

"A bit more to it than that." His smile was gracious, making allowances for her oversight, her failure to fully appreciate him. "On the stage, I was a master of the trick shot."

"You were a sniper." She said this as if it were an insult, glancing at him, as if she had just noticed him standing three feet away and found him inconsequential. "You never got this close to your victims. They were the size of insects when you killed them. And that works nicely with the murder attempt at the parade. I just happen to be looking for a long-distance killer—the man who fired that gun."

He laughed out loud, disappointing her. She had been aiming for a display of temper.

"Is that what this is all about? Who shot the big puppy?" Prado pointed to her untouched glass. "Drink your wine, Mallory. Lighten up."

St. John was more serious. "If this is a police interrogation, perhaps I should call my attorney."

"But you couldn't have shot the balloon." Futura spread his lips in a silly grin. He tottered over to Emile St. John and squeezed the larger man's arm in a reassuring gesture. "When that gun went off, you were on the float with me."

"The next time," said Mallory, "the sniper won't mess up the shot. One of you is going to be seriously dead. If you like your skins, you'll talk to me. It all ties back to Louisa's murder. Why don't we start there?"

"When Louisa died," said Prado, "we didn't have any experience in killing. None of us were in the war yet."

"Not true." Futura stood up, a little wobbly for the wine. "Emile was in the war. He worked for the Resistance."

St. John was taken by surprise for the first time. "You knew that, Franny? But how?"

"Let me guess." Mallory turned on Futura. "Because it takes one to know one?"

"Guilty," he said.

Mallory moved closer to Futura. "And there's one other way you could've known—if you worked for the Germans."

Prado draped one protective arm around the shoulders of the drunken man. "I told you, Mallory. Half of Paris worked for the Germans. I had some dealings with them myself. I loved American cigarettes, but the Germans had the best French wines. What's a boy to do?"

Mallory ignored him and spoke to Futura. "Resistance fighters? That's another way of saying *terrorists.* You and Emile tossed your bombs and ran away before they hit the ground. So between you two—" She glanced at Prado. "And this sniper—I now have *three* long-distance killers."

"You make it sound so cold," said Prado. "Not like a police officer's job, is it? You run toward the enemy. You want to embrace him, to bring him down. It's very sexual, isn't it? Is there an absence of *normal* sex in your life, Detective Mallory?"

"Nick," was all St. John had to say. He was the voice of censure here, and the other man reluctantly retired to one side of the stage.

Mallory followed Prado across the boards. She was not done with him yet. "In 1942, you had a nice little business going. I saw some of your handiwork on Louisa's passport." She turned back to St. John and Futura. "All of you had something to lose if she was captured by the Germans. Their prisoners always talked, didn't they?"

"Vichy French were just as vicious," said Prado. "And what would the Germans want with Louisa? She was a schoolgirl when she came to Paris."

Mallory turned back to him and shook her head, to tell this man she had caught him in a lie. "You knew Louisa wasn't just another refugee. When Malakhai brought her to Paris, he cut off her hair and dressed her as a boy. Then he hid her in the one place no one would think to look for her—under a spotlight on a stage surrounded by German soldiers. Even if he never told you she was an escaped prisoner, you *knew* she was wanted. You *all* knew."

She focused her attention on Futura, the one most likely to fold, drunk or sober. "Malakhai shot his wife with a crossbow. But he's not the one who killed her. The murder went down after he ran out of the theater."

Futura turned to Nick Prado, perhaps believing that he spoke in a whisper. "Malakhai broke the—"

Prado put one arm around the man, stared into his drunken face and willed him to be silent.

St. John refilled their glasses. "Less talking, more drinking, Franny." He turned to Mallory. "So this *is* an official police interrogation?"

"Not at all," she said. "More like I'm doing you a favor. One of you murdered Louisa." Mallory was staring at Futura, pleased to see him spill his wine this time. She leaned close to his ear. "Better I get you before Malakhai does. You *know* what he did in the war. All his kills were ripped to pieces."

Prado was not smiling anymore as he replenished Futura's lost wine. "We all agreed to keep quiet about Louisa—for Malakhai's sake. It's old business, Mallory. Let it go."

"Oliver's death was pretty damn recent."

"But what has *that* got to do with Louisa?" Prado seemed genuinely annoyed.

"Oliver helped Max Candle and Malakhai work on the platform, but he didn't see the rest of you between 1942 and the day he died in Central Park." She turned from face to face, watching for the giveaway look to tell her she might be wrong about this, that they might have lied in their police statements. "So fifty years go by. And then he comes up with this cryptic invitation. One of you thought he was going to talk about Louisa's death. A murder charge never goes away. But it gets really scary if you know her husband's war record. Who would want Malakhai for an enemy?" Who besides herself?

Futura put his hand to his mouth, a signal of impending vomit. Nick Prado nodded and led the man down the steps toward the lobby, saying, "I guess the party's over, Franny."

St. John followed after them. When the lobby door had closed behind the trio, Mallory drew the curtain aside to expose the replica of Max Candle's platform. This time she checked the crossbow magazines for arrows before she climbed the thirteen steps to the top.

She spent a few quiet minutes on her hands and knees, making measurements and inspecting the floor levers. Their positions were an exact match to Max Candle's original platform. The only difference was in the hinges of the trapdoors. These were better, sturdier. There was no wide crack in the floorboards where the hinges joined with the stage.

When she was done with the exterior, she touched the pressure latch on the wall near the center panel, and the door swung open. She stared at the dim interior. In her younger days, she would never have entered this room, for there was only one exit, and Kathy the street-smart child had always avoided every enclosure with the makings of a trap. Even now, she was not comfortable with the idea of going inside.

What made her look back she could not say. Emile St. John had made no noise stealing up behind her. He was holding out her pocket watch—again.

"Sorry, force of habit." He returned it to her, then walked back through the opening in the curtain, heading for the makeshift table. He picked up the full wineglass she had left on the mirror. "There's something we should discuss. Perhaps over a drink."

Mallory accepted the plastic goblet from his outstretched hand. "You want me to stop scaring Franny Futura."

"Well, that would be nice." He smiled as he poured more wine for himself. "Franny was always a timid soul. But I'm sure you guessed that within a minute of meeting him."

She nodded. "So how did he wind up in the Resistance? It doesn't square with—"

"Molotov cocktails and tommy guns?" He laughed as if this were a great joke. "In Paris, Franny's day job was clerking in the post office. Never tossed a bomb in his life, never held a gun. His Resistance work was intercepting denouncement letters. Do you—"

"Letters from snitches." Personally, she was in favor of snitches. The police department could not run without them.

"Yes, it was a nasty wartime habit, people turning on one another." He walked back behind the curtain and sat down on the bottom step of the platform. "But the real offenses were rarely mentioned. Is your neighbor's dog peeing on your azaleas? Is the postman diddling your wife? Well then, denounce him as a subversive. Do it in a secret letter. No need to sign your name."

St. John leaned one arm on the step behind him and regarded her glass with suspicion.

Because she was not drinking with him?

She tipped back the wineglass—a sip to keep him talking.

"It still goes on," he said. "Reporters and their secret sources—cockroaches who won't come out in the light. We haven't learned a damn thing from the war."

When he paused, she took another sip. Riker had always maintained that he did not trust anyone who refused to lift a glass with him. She had never gone drinking with Riker, and that might explain a lot.

"Franny saved a lot of lives with his interceptions," said St. John. "But he existed in a permanent state of fear—waiting for the knock on the door, the arrest in the middle of the night. Do you have any idea what monstrous things were done to people like him? A bullet in the head would've been a kindness. And here you are, Mallory, young and strong, carrying a gun and knocking on Franny's door."

She considered this new role he had cast her in—the monster. "Can I ask you something—cop to cop?"

He only smiled at this. Perhaps Malakhai had told him about dropping that bit of information into the dinner conversation.

She sat down beside him on the step. "You quit magic in the fifties. So I have to wonder about your assets, *large* assets. You didn't amass that capital on the salary of an Interpol bureau chief."

That got no rise out of him either. And that was odd. The long tour of duty with Interpol was not information from Malakhai, but gleaned from her computer connection at the foreign bureau. Had St. John been expecting this? Yes, that was in his smile, which said, *At last.*

So her Internet pen pal in Europe had ratted her out.
That weasel, that miserable little—

"You're right." St. John sipped his wine, savoring it, taking his own time. "My stage career was a short one compared to all the years at Interpol. But I did inherit sizeable investments from my family. I wasn't in the black market, if that's what you—"

"Let's back up. In 1942, you were a rookie policeman in Paris. I know Louisa's death certificate was faked. You were on the crime scene the night she died. What did—"

"Now you're only guessing." St. John put up one hand, in

the manner of a traffic cop, to stop Mallory's lie of protest before it was fully formed in her mind. He produced a cigar from a platinum case, then gestured to her wineglass. "You drink, I'll talk."

She watched him go through the stalling machinations of taking a small clipper from his breast pocket, then cutting the tip off the end of his cigar. He pocketed the clipper and slowly searched his suit for the lighter. Mallory liked his style; she was taking mental notes on torture-by-delay as she tapped her foot—waiting for him to get on with this.

"Mallory, I know you made inquiries about me. I spoke to the Interpol agent—your Internet playmate." He feigned sadness with a slow shake of the head. "You really should pick your friends better. Philippe Breton was not discreet. I've been retired for fifteen years, so he must have gone through a great deal of trouble to track me down at my New York hotel. He called to ask if I had actually met you. Wanted to know what his mysterious American cop looked like."

St. John flicked his gold lighter and puffed on the cigar, exhaling a cloud of smoke. "He's a shallow young man. You're much too good for him. So I told Philippe that you had thick glasses and thicker ankles. Forgive me, Mallory, but I also gave you a rather bad skin condition. I hope you don't mind my taking an avuncular interest."

They spent a quiet moment of companionable silence, watching the smoke escape to the catwalk high above them. She sipped her champagne, and he continued.

"Of course, Philippe won't be chatting with you anymore. He's doing fieldwork now—no more computers. You see, I gave his superiors quite a different description. I told them about your golden hair, your lovely green eyes—your insatiable quest for knowledge. They thought it best to remove the young man from temptation. You wouldn't expect that attitude from the French, now would you?"

"Nice work." And she meant that. She was not angry that he had killed off her Interpol connection. Emile St. John had been a good cop in his day. If it turned out that he had murdered Oliver, she would not hesitate to put him in line for the death penalty, but there would be some regret. "You know

I'm going to interrogate Futura. So you're planning to get him a lawyer, right?"

"Absolutely." He exhaled a smoke ring and watched it rise in a halo until it disappeared. "My lawyers are quite good. I'm afraid they won't allow you to terrorize poor Franny on some fishing expedition for evidence. But it's these unofficial interviews that bother me. That will have to stop. I don't want to bludgeon you with money and influence—so crude. But I will if you force me."

This threat was more than she had hoped for. He would not go to this trouble if Futura were not a gold mine of information. But she was suspicious of everything that came to her too easily. There might be another motive: Perhaps St. John was simply a decent man who would not stand by while she tortured his pet rabbit.

"What did *you* do for the Resistance?" And per their established ritual, she sipped her wine to lead him on.

"Some men like to talk about the war. I don't." St. John studied her face for a moment. Whatever he saw in her eyes, it disturbed him. "And now I must go." He lifted the bottle from the floor and set it on the stair beside her. "I'll trust you to finish this. It would be a crime to waste vintage champagne."

"I suppose some people have good reason to hide what they did in the war."

He paused by the front curtain. "I don't expect you to understand, Mallory. You weren't there."

"You knew Futura was in the Resistance. They asked you to keep an eye on him, right? You were his watcher."

He turned to face her. "Very good, Mallory. Yes, some people were concerned about Franny's timid nature. But that's what made him a personal hero to me."

"How many people knew about your connection to the Resistance?"

"Four men. Three of them are dead."

"And Futura wasn't one of them. That's why you were surprised that he would know. Who would trust him with a secret like that? You didn't. That was pretty obvious." Still his face gave up nothing useful. "I don't think you and Prado traveled in the same circles with Futura. Neither one of you has seen him since the war. Am I right?"

St. John nodded. "The theater closed down after Louisa died. That was the end of everything. We were all—"

"When Futura said you were in the Resistance, Prado wasn't surprised."

"Well, Nick always knew. I made good use of his forgeries."

"You missed my point. I was watching Prado's face. He wasn't surprised that *Futura* knew. Your old friend was the one who told him. And now you're asking yourself—*when* did Prado give you up? Was it last week? Or during the occupation? When did he give your secret away to that frightened little man?"

Yes, she could see a tiny fault line in the wall of magicians. Emile St. John would have to wonder about that betrayal, and wondering was all he would ever do. She knew he would never ask Prado any questions. He would simply live with the doubts—the damage. That was the man's style.

There was a deep sadness about him; it went to the bone in the way of damp weather—and chilled him, though the shudder was very slight. "You're better than I ever was. You were born to the job."

This was not entirely a compliment—Mallory understood that. Emile St. John had already explained it to her: She was the cop of all cops, the monster knocking at the door of Franny Futura's nightmares.

Mallory stood at the opening in the back curtain and watched him walk away from her. When he had traveled up the center aisle and the door swung shut behind him, she set her glass down on the carnival mirror. Her eye caught the movement of her reflection in the glass, a face distorted in a smeary elongation. The image grew more grotesque as she moved, contracting her features in an aspect of cruelty. She bobbed her head, looking for another way to see herself, but there was no normal woman in this mirror.

A light rush of cold air moved through her hair, as if someone had passed behind her. She turned to look at the backstage window. Its frames of glass were missing, and a sheet of plastic covered the opening. Thin streams of wind whistled around the edges between tenpenny nails.

Mallory reached inside the platform to pull the chain for a lightbulb dangling from the low ceiling. Like Max Candle's version, a round tin shade made a bright pool of light on the floor and left the ceiling in shadow. Along the walls, the platforms did not differ in the design of grooves and pegs.

She looked up at the trapdoors, barely able to distinguish the shadowed edges. The levers and latches were all on the top of the stage—just like Max Candle's original. She finished collecting statistics on the room, needing no drawings, only numbers she could feed to her computer.

At her back, she felt the inrushing air of the closing door. She turned too late.

No!

It was shut tight. Also like Max's platform, this one had no interior doorknob. She pushed on the wood, but the center panel would not give. Her fists beat on the door to the rhythm of *Stupid, stupid mistake!*

Even as a child, she had known better than to turn her back on a door. By the age of eight, she had learned to avoid any room without a second exit to escape the baby-flesh pimps and the lunatics on the street. The child had suffered beatings to earn this hard lesson, and then she had crawled off to lick wounds and review what she had learned from experience and pain—trust no one—never turn your back.

Never! Never! She pounded on the wood again.

How could this have happened to her? She should have propped the door open.

Stupid mistake.

Now she beat on the wood with one fist, just hard enough to hurt her, but not to break her hand. Pain was good. It cleared her mind. Mallory pulled a cell phone from her blazer pocket, but there was no dial tone. She was standing in a dead zone.

St. John had said that Charles and Riker would return soon. But would they stay if they thought the theater was empty, if the party was obviously over? This room had a tight enough seal to prevent the stink of Richard Tree's body from escaping. Was it airtight? Was it soundproof too?

Mallory heard the spit of electricity above her head. The lightbulb died, the room went black, and she had to remember to breathe.

Though she knew every inch of this room, she could not conquer the idea that one misstep would plunge her into an abyss. There was no up or down in absolute darkness, no marker for the solid world. Her arms hung useless at her sides. And her lungs were also failing her, taking air in shallower sips. A sensation of fluttering insect wings brushed the walls inside her chest.

But she would not call it panic; she called it remembrance.

This was every vacant building where she had made herself into a tight ball of a child, holding her breath and waiting for dangerous feet to pass her by in the dark. Then came a little girl's life-and-death decisions about staying too long or leaving too soon. The magic men were right—timing was everything.

Was the platform airtight? If she stayed too long—

One hand rose by force of will, and not her own. Kathy the street child was taking over, forming one tiny hand into the hammer of a fist and pounding on the wall. Mallory stood off to one side of her mind and listened to the outraged little girl. Young Kathy was screaming, "Let me out, you bastards! Let me out!"

The platform was not soundproof. Mallory could hear noise on the other side of the wood. Running feet were coming toward her. The child was hollering at the top of her tiny lungs, a torrent of anger and obscenity; but the woman, absent all emotion, coolly pulled out her revolver and aimed it at the place where the door would open.

The light was a wide painful crack in the wood.

Riker's startled eyes were fixed on the muzzle of her gun. "Well, it can't be something I said. I just got here."

Fourteen

CHARLES BUTLER WONDERED IF IT WAS JUST THE DUBIOUS PERK of a very large nose, for he was the only one who seemed to be put off by the faint odor, that stale souvenir of yesterday's dead man emanating from the platform room. Riker was unaffected. The detective chewed on his pastrami sandwich as he stood by the open door.

Charles forced a smile, knowing full well that every happy expression made him look like a circus clown on medication. He hoped it might assuage the cold anger in Mallory's face. "Locked yourself in?"

Oh, wait. That was the wrong thing to say. It implied an error on her part.

"No, I didn't!" She turned away, dismissing him as she spoke to Riker. "Someone locked me in and cut the electricity."

Riker stopped chewing, his eyes clearly saying, *What?*

Charles looked up at the rack of burning spotlights overhead. And beyond the opening of the back curtain, he could see the glow of footlights and the brilliant chandelier, all clear indications of uninterrupted energy. But he was not inclined to point this out to Mallory. "Well, you know the wiring is new. There might be a problem with—"

"It wasn't faulty wiring," she said. "The timing was too damn perfect."

There was only one way to take the tone in her voice. She was obviously counting him among her enemies. The enemy team was everyone who was not in complete agreement with her.

Charles braved the odor as he entered the platform room and reached up to the lamp suspended from the ceiling. He unscrewed the lightbulb and shook it. "You're right, it wasn't the wiring." He emerged from the room, shaking it again so she could hear the sound of the metal filament against the glass. This was the time-honored test of a burnt-out bulb. Now that should reassure her.

Too late, he saw his second error of the afternoon. He looked down at the dead bulb in his hand and shrugged his apology for this indisputable evidence against her own theory.

Riker made a game effort to distract her from Charles, saying, "If Nick Prado hadn't mentioned that you were—"

"Where is Prado now?" She was not in a pleasant mood.

"Here I am."

Charles looked toward the end of the stage behind the backdrop curtain and beyond the reach of the overhead lights. In this shadowy silhouette that didn't show his paunch, Nick Prado might pass for his own delusion of never-ending youth.

"Someone locked me inside the platform." Mallory was glaring at Nick, not exactly aiming for ambiguity in that accusation.

Feeling a draft at the back of his neck, Charles turned to the square hole in the wall where the window glass had not yet been installed. A sheet of plastic had come loose at one corner, allowing a steady breeze in his direction. So the wind had blown the door shut. He hesitated to mention this. First, there was the rudeness of pointing out the obvious. And then, she so disliked being corrected, particularly when she was wrong.

Riker, wise man, jammed his hands in his pockets and kept silent.

"Only the wind," said Nick Prado. "You get a lot of things wrong, don't you, Mallory?" He was aging badly with every step toward the lights. "Take Louisa's death. It looked accidental to me. I was there, and you weren't."

Mallory was cooler now. Her words had only the barest trace of malice. "It might've been staged as an accident, but she wasn't mortally wounded."

Nick seemed to be considering this as he walked beyond the backdrop curtain to look over the new bags from the deli. "She could've died from shock. That happens."

"In fifteen minutes? Not enough time," said Mallory, walking away to inspect the plastic over the window.

Charles noticed that Nick was slightly irritated, disliking her insult of the turned back.

"Right, I keep forgetting. You know everything." Nick looked down at the fun-house mirror that served as a tabletop. It was littered with paper bags and a half-empty bottle of champagne. He lifted the bottle and held it out to Riker in an obvious invitation.

In a rare exception to habit, Riker shook his head, declining to drink with the man, and Charles had to wonder about that. A half hour ago, the detective had no problem lifting a glass with this man. And who could eat a pastrami sandwich without something to wash it down?

Nick poured wine for himself. "You know, it could've been shock. During the war, textbook rules for death were broken all the time."

Mallory was busy collecting tenpenny nails from the floor beneath the plastic window covering. "The medical examiner said—"

"Do you ever *listen*?" Prado raised his voice. "To *anyone*?"

Charles was staring into his wineglass, as if it might offer him sanctuary, and Riker was looking at his scuffed shoes. But Mallory did no bloodletting. She only dropped her collection of nails into a zippered compartment of her knapsack.

Nick continued, expanding his voice in a stage projection, as if he had a larger audience. "One morning toward the end of the war, a plane went down near my field camp. It was in flames seconds after it smashed into the ground."

He paused for dramatic effect, and Mallory squashed the moment, saying, "I don't have time for war stories."

"Shut up!" said Prado, in a rare display of anger—in fact, the only show of temper Charles had ever witnessed.

Oddly enough, Mallory did shut up, ignoring the man as she opened a notebook to a page of numbers, which she seemed to find more interesting.

Nick went on in a louder voice. "One wing was sheared off in the crash, and the nose section was crushed. A dozen of us ran across the field toward the fire. And then—ten yards from the wreck, I couldn't believe what I was looking at."

He turned to Mallory—a mistake. She did not care what he was looking at, past or present. Only slightly daunted, Nick played to Riker now. "The plane's three crewmen were walking away from the crash—unharmed. Well, this was impossible. Everyone aboard should've died. But the crew walked away—all of them. They sat down in the shade of a farmhouse, and *there* they died. It was over in minutes. *Minutes.* Not a mark on them, not one injury in the lot."

"Shock?" said Riker, in an effort to be a polite audience.

Mallory, clearly unimpressed, ran her pencil down a column of numbers. "Shock doesn't work for me."

"Me either," said Nick. "I had a different idea. All three men had seen the ground coming up to kill them. People believe their senses, and this was an indisputable fact—there was no way they could've survived that crash. I think those three boys bowed to the logic of their situation. It was absurd to be alive, and so they closed their eyes and died."

Charles thought the man might take a bow, but he only retired to sit on the steps of the platform and sip from his wineglass.

Mallory's attitude changed to mere annoyance on the level reserved for flies. "For the last time, Louisa was not mortally wounded. She had no idea she was going to die until that bastard put a pillow over her face."

"Mallory, you don't know that," said Charles. "What went on at the poker game—it was all speculation. You can't expect Edward to do an autopsy secondhand and half a century late."

"Thank you, Charles," she said, not at all thankful, and

making the strong suggestion that he should close his mouth—*now*. She folded up her notebook of numbers. "Oliver's death was no accident, either."

"Poor Oliver," said Nick. "The Quixotic aura of the hapless failure. But in reality, it was a rather pedestrian death. He screwed up the trick. Life can be so simple, Mallory, if you will only let it."

Nick was entirely too smug. Apparently, Mallory was about to adjust his expression. All the signals were there. She was rising off the balls of her feet, all but levitating in anticipation of a strike. If she had a tail, it would be switching. Charles adored her feline grace—but some of the things cats did just turned his stomach.

In the spirit of throwing himself in the path of raking claws aimed at the older man, he said, "Nick's right, Mallory. Oliver did mess up the trick. He obviously didn't know the effect—"

"You've been talking to Malakhai." Her implication was clear. Charles stood accused of consorting with her enemy, his lifelong friend.

"Just a series of accidents?" Her eyebrows arched. "All right." Her hands moved to her hips. There would not be another warning sign. "I've seen the error of my ways." She said this too gently. "But what about that nasty little corpse I found inside the platform? Oliver's nephew? Remember him?"

Nick slugged back the rest of his champagne. "The boy died of a drug overdose. Everyone knew Richard was an addict. There was a spot of blood on his shirtsleeve. That came from the needle, right? But no blood from the arrow. The dead don't bleed—so there was no murder." He waved his hand. "Lessons of war."

And now Charles could tell that Riker was listening between the words. The detective exchanged glances with his partner. In silent understanding, Mallory retreated to the side of the platform as he drifted closer to Nick.

"You said *everyone* knew the kid was a junkie." Riker fished through his pockets. "But how? The kid went to a lot of trouble to hide his habit—needle tracks in the soles of his feet, behind his knees." He pulled out a worn notebook and sat down on the steps with Nick. "Oliver Tree knew about his nephew's habit. He paid for the kid's treatment. But it's not something the uncle would've bragged about, is it?"

The detective flipped through the pages, scanning the penciled lines. "Oh, here we go." He had found the page he was looking for. "You and your friends, St. John and Futura, you all got into town the day Oliver Tree died. That was your statement to the police. None of you spent any time with the old guy since the war."

"That's true," said Nick. "We got to know Oliver's nephew after the accident. The boy was always hitting us up for money, just a few dollars here and there, but it was obvious he needed cash. That's why I gave him the crossbow job in the parade."

Riker's pen was working across the page. His tone was dry. "And the kid told you he needed money for drugs?" Unspoken were the words *Fat chance*.

"It was a simple observation."

Riker nodded. "From a spot of blood on his shirtsleeve. Not bad. More lessons of war?"

"You could say that," said Nick. "I spent some time in an army hospital. I had my own flirtation with morphine."

Charles avoided looking directly at Mallory. "So it *was* a drug overdose. Well, let's say Richard crawled into his uncle's platform for privacy. Workmen were coming and going all the time. He didn't want anyone to see him shoot up, did he? Say he got locked in the platform, the same way—"

In peripheral vision, Charles detected a sudden rigidity in Mallory's body language, and he altered his thought in mid-sentence. "Maybe Richard couldn't find the light chain. He might have panicked in the dark. Now if the crossbows had been stored in there—"

"Right," said Mallory, nearly congenial. "He tripped in the dark and fell on the arrow—after he'd been dead for a few days. Oh, Nick didn't tell you that part." She turned to the magician and inclined her head, all but taking a bow. "Lessons of war, Prado."

Her war, of course.

"And Forensics didn't find a syringe inside the platform room," said Riker.

Mallory nodded. "A tidy dead man. I like that. And talented too. I know the corpse was still moving around after death. The marks on his back matched up with the pattern of the floor grate in his apartment. That's where he died. But we won't let the facts get in the way of a good story."

She turned to the door of the platform. "So the dead man picks himself up off the floor of his apartment, and—*still dead,* he takes the subway. I'm guessing the corpse traveled cheap. You see, *after* he died, he left his wallet back in the apartment. No cash for a cab, but he did have a transit card in his pocket. So then the dead man walks into the theater and locks himself inside the platform—*accidentally.* See? I'm a good sport. I'm looking for the flaws in my logic. And sticking the arrow into his own dead body—*days* after death? Well, that was a trick and a half."

Charles could see where she was going with this monologue. Nick Prado's condescending smile was telegraphing the news that he had caught her in an error or a lie.

Arms folded, she stood over Nick, looking down at him and smiling, "So, tell me what part I *didn't* get right."

And the trap snapped shut.

Nick's eyes widened only a little—just enough to indicate that he might know the details better than she did. Or, he might only be surprised by the implied accusation.

Charles stepped between them, smiling, as if that would save his own hide. "But Richard wasn't actually murdered if the arrow—"

"But *Oliver* was." She shot Charles a look to ask why he would step on her best line. Was he trying to deflect damage away from Nick?

Well, yes, of course. And it was going to cost him.

She walked away from him, pausing by the curtain. There was reproach in that turned back and in her voice. "You knew that old man, Charles."

"Actually, I hadn't seen him in a long—"

"You *knew* him, and you liked him." Mallory turned around to show him how shocked she was, though her expression was somewhat contrived. "Oliver died all alone on that platform, scared out of his mind while he was being murdered."

Now Charles was in the odd position of being lectured on his lack of sensitivity, but—by *Mallory*? How to explain that unlikely event? Perhaps she did possess genuine human compassion.

No, that's not it.

But he knew she had some agenda beyond correcting his imagined attitude problem, his lack of outraged indignation for an accidental death.

She stalked off toward the steps leading down from the stage. "Oliver *was* murdered. So don't talk to me about accidents, Charles. Don't talk to me at all."

That sounded final—false, but final.

The lines were drawn, and she had left him standing on the other side with Nick Prado. Riker was following his partner up the center aisle, distancing himself from the enemy camp.

✛   ✛   ✛

Only four hours had passed since they had parted company on the sidewalk outside the theater. Riker looked around the den of Mallory's Upper West Side condo and wondered how she had pulled this off. It took most New Yorkers ten days to have a couch transported from a downtown furniture store to an uptown address. She had moved the contents of an entire room more than eighty blocks north of Charles Butler's SoHo building.

Mallory sat at a computer keyboard, fingers flying, tapping, typing. "Was I wrong about the grate?"

"Yeah, I didn't find any floor grates in the stiff's apartment. But the marks on his back match up to a heat register in the theater. I found it after I pulled the crime scene tapes."

"Heller's team missed that?"

"They weren't looking for it, Mallory. They didn't undress the corpse at the crime scene. There was no—"

"Right, nothing fancy for a dead junkie. Just another damn accident."

But the platform had been examined in great detail. Heller had come to the crime scene and personally supervised the crew. And this made Riker wonder what kind of dirt Mallory might have on the head of Forensics.

He looked down at his notes. "The heat register was in a little room backstage. That's probably where Richard was shooting up. There's a lock on that door."

"A locked room wouldn't be a problem for anybody on my short list," said Mallory. "Is that where Heller's techs found the wallet?"

"Yeah, but you were right about the money—no cab fare. He must have spent his wad on the heroin." Riker folded his notebook back into his breast pocket.

There had been one bad moment upon walking into Mallory's den. It went beyond déjà vu. But for the view of Central Park, he might have been standing in her private office back at Charles's place in SoHo. She had even re-created the alignment of the computer terminals at perfect right angles to the windows. The one bare wall was a moving projection of larger than life-size spectators at the Thanksgiving Day parade.

"That's film from the six o'clock news," she said. "Some tourist sold his videotape to the network."

Why couldn't Mallory just watch the news on television like a normal person? He stood before the wall, looking up at the projected image. The camera was focused on a rocky knoll in Central Park. The outcrop loomed behind the low wall along the sidewalk. The volume was turned down, but he could still hear the broadcaster's interview with the amateur cameraman, a sixty-year-old tourist from Rhode Island.

Eyes on the knoll, Riker waited to see what would happen next. And now there was a white puff of smoke among the shadows of trees and rocks.

A gunshot?

Yes, the broadcaster was confirming that the timing of the white smoke was in perfect sync with the sound of a gun. And now the television voice was lamenting that the network's weapons expert, a writer of technothrillers, could not be reached for comment. The shot from the rocky knoll would kill the novelist's carefully diagrammed trajectory. Mallory could not have fired the bullet that brought down the balloon.

"So, you're off the hook for shooting the big puppy."

"Not yet." She depressed a button on the projector's remote control. The tape ran backward until the white puff of smoke had uncreated itself and sipped back into the shadows of rocks and trees. "They still claim there were three shots. So now I'm part of a conspiracy. I'm also a suspect in the death of Crossbow Man and Oliver Tree."

"Well, let Slope release the autopsy findings. Why sit on it now? We already gave it away to Prado."

Mallory reran the tape and froze the image on the wall. She was staring at the still shot of a cloud of smoke. She pointed to the rocky knoll. "Guess who that is."

Riker walked closer to the wall. "Too grainy. I can't make out a thing." He looked around the room one more time. "When did you have time to move all this stuff out of SoHo?"

"I hired a crew of art handlers. They're very careful with sensitive equipment."

And they probably would not recognize its illicit uses and applications. The most delicate electronic lock picks were in the carton Riker had carried up from the trunk of her car.

He settled into a cold metal chair. "How did Charles take it when you told him you were moving all your stuff out?"

"There's only one way to take it. The partnership is over. He's too careless with the locks."

Or perhaps Charles had not been careful enough in picking his friends. One of these crimes had been the deciding factor. "So you didn't tell Charles you were leaving."

No, of course not. She had left the poor bastard to walk innocently into an empty room and figure it out for himself. "I guess you don't need Max Candle's platform anymore?"

Mallory pointed to the small screen of a computer. It scrolled columns of numbers and symbols glowing white on a field of blue. "It's all in there—the whole apparatus."

He picked up the green velvet bag from the edge of her

steel desk and slipped out the rod of dangling key plugs. "I can see why the old guys kept these things."

"Now do you believe the keys were switched?"

"Yeah, but I still got a few problems with your theory. What about that line you handed me at the parade? 'My perp loves spectacle.' That's what you said."

"And you figured I was just spinning a story? No, I only lied to Coffey." It was clear that she considered that an honorable lie, only doing what was expected of her. "I know what you're thinking. It's a matter of style. Oliver died screaming, lots of noise and flash. But the gunshot at the parade was real straightforward, wasn't it? Quick and to the point. The shooter only wanted to get it over with. The victim would never know what happened to him." Mallory turned to the image on the wall, the puff of smoke. "That's Malakhai up there on the rocks." She switched it off.

"And the Central Park murder?"

"I like Nick Prado for that one. A public relations man makes spectacles for a living. But I'm keeping my options open." Now she revolved on her chair, turning to study his face. "Someone locked me in that platform. Do you believe me?"

Riker knew that she was really asking if he was on her side. "Yeah. If it was just the locked door or the bulb by itself—but I'm not a big believer in coincidence. I figure one of those things had to be deliberate."

"The door was deliberate." She pulled a clear bag from her knapsack and tossed it on the desk. Inside were five shiny nails. "Those came from the plastic sheet over that backstage window. They didn't fall out by themselves. He wanted to make it look accidental, like the wind blew the door shut. And the dead bulb was deliberate, too."

"Mallory, Charles showed you the bulb. You heard—"

"Charles knows as much about electricity as you do." She turned on her desk lamp. "Keep your eye on that lightbulb." She bent down toward the socket.

Riker was watching the lamp when he saw the spark and heard the noise, and then the bulb went dead. Mallory removed it from the socket. When she shook it, he could hear the filament against the glass.

"I shorted it out with this." She held up a metal nail file. "The cable for the platform lamps was on an independent fuse. That's why only one light went out. If Faustine's Magic Theater had been an exact replica, I could've shown you a burnt-out fuse, but Oliver upgraded to switches."

Riker sat down on the edge of her desk and folded his arms. "So you like Nick Prado for that setup?"

"Maybe. I'm guessing Futura was in the men's room throwing up when you and Charles got back to the theater. But that could've been an act."

"I didn't see him around. But I don't think Futura could do anything that—"

"Because he's a rabbit? He's more interesting than you know. He was in the Resistance during the war. That doesn't fit either, does it? He stays on the list. So where were the other two when you walked in?"

"Prado and St. John were in the lobby. We kibitzed for a few minutes before me and Charles went inside the theater."

"Could've been any one of them. Somebody wanted to restore my faith in accidents. Or maybe he just wanted to make me look hysterical. That worked on Charles, didn't it? He bought the whole thing."

Poor Charles. But she had a good point. In the early days as a beat cop handling domestic disputes, Riker had noticed that men relied heavily on the hysterical-woman defense: Who could take the word of a bloodied woman who could not stop crying?

So someone had come up with a novel variation on a bad old game, and Charles had fallen for it. Riker could think of a few more reasons for the breakup of Mallory's business relationship—Charles Butler's big brain, his giveaway face and proximity to all the suspects. She had been wise to distance herself, but she should have done it the right way.

"I almost forgot." He pulled a CD from the pocket of his suit coat and set it on the corner of her desk. "A present. *Louisa's Concerto.* Emile St. John wanted you to have it."

She opened the case and slipped the disk into a computer slot. A full orchestra poured out of amplifiers in every wall. He was surrounded by musical instruments, a wall of sound. It was classical, not his taste, and he listened with the confusion of trying to sort out an alien language.

"Pretty, I guess. But you know what your old man would say? What good is it if you can't dance to it?"

That had been his old friend's criterion for all the music in an extensive collection of blues, jazz and rock 'n' roll. Even the slow, sad tunes did something to the human body. But now the dead woman's music was touching him in other ways. Suddenly, it had his complete attention, as if the strings and horns were speaking to him in a more familiar language. This passage had a sad, lonely feeling.

The phone rang. Riker's hand hovered over the receiver while he read the printed line on the caller-ID machine. "It's Charles."

"Don't answer it."

"You're gonna let him sit around staring at the walls in your empty office till he figures out where things went wrong? Is that the plan?"

"Yeah, so?"

"He's a friend of yours, remember? And your old man liked him, too."

Louisa's Concerto was plaintive now, lending melancholy to the ring of the telephone, backing it up with the low octaves of a sad, sorry horn. And now Riker was surprised. While the concerto affected Mallory not at all, the telephone made her inexplicably sad. Her head moved slowly from side to side, as if she could shake off the blues this way.

Riker's solution was to turn up the volume of the music and avert his eyes from the phone. "So if Charles isn't on your side all the way down the line—"

"Riker, save it, okay?"

When the phone ceased to ring, he looked at it, as if a conversation had ended abruptly, with no satisfying resolution.

Mallory switched on the answering machine so the ringing would not disturb her again.

"Did you leave the guy a note?"

"No!" Mallory's eyes were fixed on the computer screen. Her face was masklike as she merged with her machine.

Realizing that he did not exist anymore, not for her, Riker quietly let himself out.

✦   ✦   ✦

An hour had passed before Mallory looked up from the computer screen. Where she had been all that time, she did not know. Her internal clock had failed her again. This was happening more often. Perhaps it was only an effect of Emile St. John's wine.

She had finished cannibalizing files from a computer game of sudden death by joystick. It contained all the lines of programming to fire the on-screen crossbows.

The phone rang twice, and then she listened to Charles's voice on the answering machine. "Mallory? Are you there?"

Not really. She was intent on the screen where her creation came alive, numbers and symbols translating into an image that revolved in space like a three-dimensional object, showing her all its sides, then upending itself to expose the base. She switched on the projector at the other end of a flat feed cable. Now the image was cast on the wall. The platform continued to turn in slow revolutions.

"Mallory, please pick up if you're there," said the disembodied voice on the phone.

She tapped the keys to make the staircase wall transparent, disclosing the interior mechanisms of the lazy tongs and the levers.

"I'll change all the locks," said Charles.

She diddled the keys again and again. One trapdoor dropped down into the platform. The lazy tongs slowly emerged, opening the metal arms, spreading them wide to support the cape.

"Will you call me back?" There was not much hope in Charles's request. "You *are* planning to explain this, right?"

Wrong. Mallory fired off four animated crossbows. One by one, they hit the target. And now she extended the time between the shots.

"We should talk." Charles was showing some wear in his voice. "This is—well, it's cold."

You think I'm a monster.

"No, I didn't mean it that way," said Charles, as if he could hear her thoughts. "When I walked into that empty office—I was so surprised."

She set off another round of graphic arrows.

"Goodbye, Mallory."

The high-tech toy was boring her. Charles had been right about one thing. A simple escape routine was too simplistic for a Max Candle illusion. Where was the *magic*? The collapsing cape was only a taste, a teaser.

"Of course, I didn't mean goodbye in any permanent sense," said the persistent voice on her machine.

Where *was* the magic?

"I only meant goodbye for now." Charles paused. "So—"

There must be more to it. She killed the platform animation and cued up the tape of Oliver's murder. The old man was back on the wall, dying again.

"So, you'll call?"

Yeah, sure.

Max Candle always died. He was not supposed to escape all the arrows.

"Goodbye," said Charles.

But all the crossbows had fired, and there was not a fake arrow in the pack.

"For now," Charles amended himself.

She stared at the wall where Oliver was being shot to death. If the trick was incomplete, how could Malakhai know it was botched?

Another hour had been lost inside the machine, perfecting her own illusion. The door buzzer called her out of a trance of codes and numbers.

Charles? It had to be. Frank the doorman liked him. On her last birthday, he had allowed Charles into the building unannounced, so she could be surprised with flowers. And of course there had been a generous tip. Had she punished the doorman for that? No, it must have slipped her mind.

Five minutes later, the incessant buzz was getting on her

nerves, and she really wanted to hurt Frank for failing to announce a visitor. She left the den and walked down the hallway, irate and laying plans to verbally gut the doorman so this would never happen again. But right this minute, she was going to cut Charles dead with a few terse remarks so she could get back to work.

When Mallory opened the door, Rabbi Kaplan was standing in the corridor. *Oh, fine.* Now what would she do with all this excess adrenaline?

"It's late," said the rabbi. "I won't come in. This shouldn't take very long."

His face was not committed to any particular expression, and she had no idea how much trouble she might be in.

"It's about what happened yesterday," he said. "Mr. Halpern tells me you took time out of your busy day to yell at his only son."

The rabbi's hand went up to silence her before she could interrupt. "I understand you accused the poor man of parental abuse. When the son came home that night, Mr. Halpern spent hours reassuring him, telling him he was not really a— what did you call him? A heartless little bastard."

"I didn't—"

"Excuse me, Kathy. Was I finished talking? I don't think so."

He smiled, and now Mallory was on guard.

"Well, the son *fired* his own father." Rabbi Kaplan undid the latches on his briefcase. "Mr. Halpern wanted you to know that he had finally retired. That's all, Kathy."

No way.

The rabbi was only lulling her into a false idea of escape. He would follow up with a killer punch line. Once, he had been wickedly good at this game. Now he was becoming predictable.

"I'm not buying it, Rabbi. You could've phoned in that lecture."

"But not this." He extracted a small, flat package from his briefcase and looked down at it for a moment. "It seems that no one ever apologized to Mr. Halpern for the inconvenience of being put in a concentration camp—for the murders of his parents, his entire family. He was charmed by your apology for the paint gun man." Rabbi Kaplan held out the package. "This is a gift for you. He worked on it all day."

She unwrapped the package and held up a framed portrait in colored pencil. A schoolgirl's face floated in loose waves of long red hair. Faraway blue eyes were deep in thought, as if the girl were working on a great problem—how to survive in hell.

Mallory looked up at the rabbi. "Louisa Malakhai?"

Rabbi Kaplan nodded. "Good, isn't it?" He strolled back to the elevator, and she walked alongside him. "That was copied from old journal sketches he made when he was young—when he had plans to be an artist. Mr. Halpern is a talented man, and a very happy one. Now he has all the time in the world to draw his pictures. So you got him fired." The rabbi shrugged. "By his own son." He pressed the button to call the elevator. "So? All in all, you did well."

His smile was entirely too sweet, and she braced herself for the coming shot.

"If it matters to you, Kathy, I still agree with Helen." The elevator opened, and he stepped inside the humming box. "I find you quite perfect—*twisted* as you are." The metal doors closed on his great pleasure in her annoyance.

The rabbi's timing was flawless, as always. Once again, he had gotten the last word. She had yet to beat him at this game. But he was getting older, slowing down—his day would come.

Fifteen

MALAKHAI AWAKENED, FULLY CLOTHED, ON THE BED IN HIS
New York hotel room. He was not running through his
dreams anymore, but neither had he shaken off the confusion
of things unreal.

And the ringing had not stopped.

He switched on the bedside lamp and looked at his watch.
It was two o'clock in the morning. He picked up the telephone receiver, intending to slam it down again, when he
heard a woman's voice.

"Malakhai?"

"Yes?"

"When you were a prisoner of war in Korea, was your cell
completely dark? Or did it have a light?"

"Mallory." Odd child—and rude. Malakhai glanced
toward his wife's side of the bed. He stared at the glint of
gold foil and his hand tightened around the telephone
receiver. So it had happened again. He had fallen asleep
before removing the hotel mint from Louisa's pillow. No—
he had *forgotten*. "I'm so sorry."

"That prison cell," said Mallory's voice at his ear, no doubt
believing that he had spoken this apology to her. "Was there a
light? A window?"

The sense of shame was overwhelming him—all for a bit
of chocolate wrapped in gold foil. He kept the tears out of his
voice when he spoke to Mallory. "There was light during the
day, but not much."

This old history was an event with large gaps in it, but the physical surroundings were clear. "My cell had a small window facing a stone wall. I could see the light, but not the sky, not the sun. Shadows moved from one side of the wall to the other. That's how I kept track of the time."

"What did you do with all that time?"

"I spent it with Louisa."

"And that was the beginning of—"

"My madness? That's what the army psychiatrists said." But he had always thought of it as a discipline, a religion with a requisite of absolute faith and a complement of sins and atonements—even a litany of guilt. He took the mint off Louisa's pillow and crushed it in his hand. *I'm so sorry.*

What would he forget tomorrow?

"It wasn't war you loved—the killing," said Mallory. "That's not why you signed up for Korea."

"It was Louisa I loved." He sat up and unbuttoned his shirt, averting his eyes from the other side of the bed. "But there's an interesting parallel. I once saw a poster in Warsaw, a bit of political art. It was the portrait of a young woman. The top of her head was obscured in a wash of bloodred, as if it had been blown away. Beneath the poster were the words—how shall I translate them? 'War, what a woman you are.' I think that sums it up."

The line went dead. Apparently, Mallory had been satisfied with the short answer. Would she have understood the music? No, it was pointless to attempt that explanation. It would only try her patience.

He had given Louisa form and substance in a Korean cell, but she had come back for him years before that, in the chaos of World War II, when Roland had aptly named him Hollow Boy.

Malakhai lay back on the pillow. The ceiling became low clouds over the plains of a European winter. His arms wrapped tight around his shoulders, for it was bitter cold. Not night anymore, but morning—first light.

He could have spared the child if he had called out from the safe cover of the rock wall, but he didn't. He watched a five-year-old boy walk into the field. It was perfect, really.

Instead of waiting another hour for one of the Germans to trigger an explosion, the curious child was heading toward a land mine.

Young Private Malakhai had been rubbing his frozen hands through the succession of annoying miracles that had kept the German boys alive. They had nearly finished dismantling the heavy tree, clearing it from the road, section by section. He didn't know or care what all the soldiers in the troop truck were laughing at. One of them was pointing at the child who would be dead in minutes. The soldier beckoned to the little boy, and the small figure moved closer, stepping quickly now.

Good.

Malakhai's fingertips were going the blue-gray color of frostbite, and he wished the child would hurry even faster to his dismemberment and death.

A smiling, yellow-haired soldier was holding out a sausage. The little boy moved forward, shy eyes round as brown cookies, his tiny hand extending to the promised treat.

The first mine blew under the child's foot, and the rest followed. There was hardly a second in the chain of explosions for the soldiers to register the shock of what was happening to them as the parts of their bodies bid torsos farewell and flew elsewhere. And it rained blood for a time; a fine mist crystallized death into frozen red drops.

The truck was on fire. The air was filled with the acrid stew of odors, sulfur and smoke, burnt tires and burnt boys. Malakhai had not yet felt the pain of the head injury made by a fragment of metal. He moved out from behind the cover of rocks and began the death count of the thirty-four soldiers for his report. He didn't count the child, who was not a military statistic.

When he was done, he stood over the smallest corpse. The little body at his feet was mutilated, but not divided. The boy had been at the center of the first explosion, yet the tiny, perfect face was unspoiled, and his limbs still clung to him by red tendons and bones.

Malakhai felt the hardening of an erection. And this was also curious. He could not explain it away, but as Louisa's face filled his mind, he found it natural to be thinking of her, coupling her with all things sexual. He could feel the heat in his crotch, more intense now—live fire in winter. And inexplicably, it had all begun with this little corpse at his feet. The child must belong to that farmhouse in the distance.

Malakhai's body stiffened and froze in the attitude of attention—listening. Across the snowy plain, he heard the music of a violin.

Impossible. The head wound?

Auditory hallucination? Of course, and it was not his first. He was learning all the medical jargon, wound by wound. But this was not the familiar ringing, the pain of hellish bells and bombshells. This was music, and violins were not in his repertoire of injuries to body and brain.

He looked down on the face of the child. Snowflakes settled upon the rounded glass of brown staring eyes, and they melted there. Malakhai felt nothing but the sex warming his crotch in a spill of cum.

He turned his head in the direction of the farmhouse, the better to hear the music. A wind was rising, and the faint notes were drifting away from him. And now there was another sensation of wetness. His hand moved up to his face.

Tears?

For Louisa.

Thoughts of her had conjured up no companion emotions of pain or loss. He was only tasting the salt of tears— Louisa's gift. The hollow boy was weeping by conditioned reflex to an imagined violin. He credited Louisa with this trick, creating false tears for a dead child, trappings of sorrow, an illusion of regret.

But why?

Two indistinct figures were emerging from the distant farmhouse. The parents? Perhaps they had just discovered that their child was not sleeping in his bed. He knew their frightened eyes would be turning toward the fire of the burning troop truck. And yet, Malakhai was feeling no empathy or sympathy, nothing but the throbbing of his head wound.

What would Louisa have him do now?

Oh, of course.

Private Malakhai picked up the small body, which weighed nothing, and turned his back on the dark smoke and twisted metal, the charred uniforms and dead boys. He made his way across the white field newly dusted with snow, following the small tracks of the littlest boy.

The young soldier walked with uncommon grace upon frostbit feet, moving slowly toward the farmhouse where the child's footprints had begun.

✦   ✦   ✦

Mallory was bored with the wall where Oliver Tree was being murdered again in a larger-than-life projection.

She ejected *Louisa's Concerto* from her computer. A portable CD player lay on the desk. The old batteries had been tossed out long ago, and now she hunted through all the drawers, searching for the new ones. Where were they? The movers could not have lost them. She had packed the contents of this desk herself and carried the box in her own car.

No batteries—no matter. She connected the CD player to an adapter for the wall socket, then draped a bulky audiophile's headset around her neck. Tethered by a wire, she passed in front of the projector's lens. The moving pictures wrapped around her body, and flying arrows moved silently through her hair.

She opened the closet door and pulled out all the neatly folded cartons. One corner of the den had been cleared for use as two of the walls in a Korean prison cell. She reconstructed the packing boxes into large cardboard building blocks for two more walls only five feet high. When she was done, strips of masking tape ran from the top of one cardboard wall to the opposite wall of plaster—a reminder that there was no room to stand upright. The tape roughly effected bars across her view of the ceiling.

Pulling the last of the boxes into position, she sealed herself off from the rest of the den and sat cross-legged on the floor of her cell, five feet square. After a few minutes she was aware of small noises never noticed before, the tick of the wall clock and rain pelting the window glass. Tinny music from a strolling boom box wafted up from the street. But the enclosing walls were at least devoid of Oliver's flying arrows and his death. Mallory looked up at the faux bars of paper tape covering her new minimalist world. She put on the form-fitted headset, and its cushion blocked out every sound beyond the cell.

Perfect peace.

This was not what she had anticipated. There was no discomfort, though she could not see the door or the windows. Perhaps it was her absolute trust in the alarm system.

No, it was more than that, something familiar. An old memory was surfacing.

My little house.

Mallory had re-created a piece of her childhood, a refrigerator carton that had once been home to a ten-year-old fugitive. Her cardboard house had been a peaceful sanctuary from the insanity of city streets, the roller coaster of emotions from flight to fight.

She felt safe here.

And Malakhai had done this for a year of solitary confinement. She would almost welcome such a sentence. But what had Malakhai done with his time, besides listening to interior music in his memory and reconstructing a dead woman?

Mallory picked up the CD and set *Louisa's Concerto* on replay so it would repeat endlessly. The stereo headset created the illusion that the orchestra played in the center of her skull. But there was nothing for her in this music, no ghosts from 1942, only notes chaining into one another, strings blending with horns.

Malakhai, what did you do with all the days?

Well, he had retained every detail of Louisa's corpse, the blue dress, the blood behind her eyes and the pink froth at her lips. He must have replayed her death a thousand times inside his head.

Mallory ceased to pay any attention to the music. She concentrated on an image of Faustine's Magic Theater—Malakhai's version, not Oliver's. She decorated it with café tables and wine bottles, peopled it with civilians and soldiers, then filled the air with smoke. The chandelier dimmed and the stage was lit with a row of candles. Standing on the stage beside her was a red-haired girl, who held a violin. Mallory stepped into the girl's skin and turned Louisa's head toward young Malakhai. The boy stood in the wings, hidden from the audience by the edge of the curtain and awaiting his musical cue.

Mallory's hand was rising, lifting the violin to cradle it between her shoulder and her chin. Then Louisa stroked the strings with a bow that smelled of rosin. Hidden beneath the instrument was the arrow meant to replace the bow at the end of the act. Mallory turned her eyes back to Malakhai.

Do you see him yet, Louisa? Do you see the uniform?

No, not yet. And only Mallory could see the arrow loaded in his crossbow. Louisa's eyes were closed. She was so involved in her music.

This illusion was Max Candle's routine. But tonight, Malakhai holds the weapon on her—on them.

He's so young. Eighteen years old, all new again. The pistol grip of the crossbow was in his right hand, and his eyes were shaded by the brim of an officer's cap. The crossbow pistol was rising.

The uniform's material was gray, the buttons were silver— and the collar was red. No detail should be lost. She looked at young Malakhai through Louisa's eyes. The handsome boy wore fine black boots. His crossbow pistol was aiming at her now.

What was Louisa thinking? It was easier to creep inside the mind of a killer—so difficult to be a victim in the crosshairs of a weapon sight. First she saw the uniform, and then she saw the SS insignia. *Malakhai?*

Yes, she knows him now. She was moving past her fear of the uniform. Louisa looked at her old love. His finger was on the trigger. Was she wondering why Malakhai was doing Max's routine? Yes.

Why isn't Max here?

Max can't shoot you, Louisa. Only Malakhai could do that—because he had loved this girl since they were children.

Mallory waited for the boy to deliver the missile. Did Louisa still believe that a silk scarf would fly—harmless silk

on a wire that she could wind round the hidden arrow?
Franny Futura had spoken of her surprise. No, Louisa had no
idea what was coming. She turned away from the audience,
revolving as she played, to hide the switch of the violin bow
for an arrow. She was going through with the act that had
opened every show.

Why do you trust him, Louisa?
I've known Malakhai all my life.

Mallory, less trustful, looked at the boy. His dark blue eyes
were on Louisa's face, probing, touching—the last caress of
a distance. His finger pulled the trigger.

Foolish, Louisa.

There was no time for her to cry out with surprise. The
shaft from the crossbow was buried in her shoulder, so deep,
such pain. The violin and its bow fell to the stage. The hidden
arrow dropped from Mallory's hand. How could this be happening? Louisa stared at him as he turned to run. *Why? Why
did you hurt me?*

He was running away from her. Louisa was falling, and
Mallory's cheek was pressing to the cool wood of the stage.
His boots made a pounding sensation that Louisa could feel
through her skin as she lay on the floorboards.

Over the next hour, Mallory played the scene over and
over again. In one scenario, she left Louisa falling to the
stage and ran away with Malakhai, weaving across the room,
upsetting tables and startling patrons. Then they were outside
the theater and breathing deeply, Malakhai and Mallory. It
had rained that night. The air was damp and cold. Malakhai
looked up the street and down, but Mallory saw no one on the
sidewalk. In the cover of rain, the cover of night, he tore off
the outer layer of his uniform. Beneath it, he wore street
clothes. He ran back into the theater. Only a few minutes had
passed by, not the fifteen he had estimated, not even ten. He
was so young, time would crawl and drag for him, but only a
few minutes were passing by.

Louisa is dying. Is that what you wanted, Malakhai?

The next time Louisa was wounded, Mallory lay down
upon the stage with her and bled from the same arrow, from
many arrows, betrayed time after time, left ripped and

bloody, listening to the sound of Malakhai's pounding boots hitting the wood, running away, leaving her behind to bleed and die.

Now Louisa was deep in shock. Someone lifted her from the floor and carried her to a room backstage. Strong arms laid her body down. Mallory could hear the door closing on the noise of the crowd, the sliding chairs and tables, the clink of glasses and babbling voices.

A pillow was covering her mouth.

No air. Panic was rising. The primal instinct to breathe was overriding all her senses. Her hands pushed the pillow away. Mallory fought with more strength than she had, adrenaline gorging every muscle, lungs burning, bursting, dying for a sip of air. He pressed the pillow down harder. Louisa writhed and pushed. Her legs kicked out. Blood poured from the wound, greasing the floor, making it all slick and red.

Where is Malakhai?

He's gone, Louisa. He ran away. You know that.

No help was coming, not ever. Her assassin was on top of her with his full weight, pressing down on the pillow. Mallory could hear voices on the other side of the door, speaking in foreign tongues.

Why don't you scream, Louisa?

I can't. There are German soldiers at the door.

So soon? Only minutes had passed by since the shot. Soldiers from the audience?

Her killer was so desperate now. She wasn't dying fast enough. His knee pressed down hard on her chest with all the weight of his body. She could hear her breastbone breaking, snapping. Pain was layered over with shock. She could feel her heart being crushed under the weight of him, torn by shards of broken bone.

No, no!

And then her body ceased to thrash. Blood welled up behind her eyes. What Malakhai had begun was being finished now—nearly done. And then Louisa lay still, eyes wide and staring. A pink froth spilled past her lips, and tiny delicate bubbles burst, one by one.

Mallory curled into a ball within the dimensions of

Malakhai's prison cell. There were no sounds or images anymore, no life of the sleeping mind, for the dead do not dream.

When she opened her eyes again, morning light was splashed across the ceiling beyond the masking tape bars, and every muscle ached. She felt the stiffness in her neck and limbs. The concerto was still looping on the CD player, flooding her brain with music that meant nothing to her. So much for the myth that Louisa inhabited her composition.

She had never considered musical metaphors before. Her foster father's swing music and his rock 'n' roll had moved her body without conscious effort or thought. Louisa's music was too difficult.

Mallory forced a meaning on the composition. Between the strings of violins, the cornets were firing high notes. Perhaps they stood for guns. And now all the pieces of the orchestra loomed up in a great wall of sound. It exploded into shards of clarinets and flutes—bombs bursting in air, bright shrapnel falling like stars. And then music cascaded into liquid valleys of rich low octaves. When the lull came round again, that hollow place in the music, Mallory nodded unconsciously. She had a long-standing acquaintance with emptiness.

How much had Malakhai figured out during his year in the box?

The killer was marked by Louisa's blood. The others might be dabbed with it, but the assassin would be splashed with it. Malakhai had always known who the man was. Not one small detail of that night had been lost to him. And yet he had waited all this time for revenge.

She picked up the CD player to turn off the music. The cord was no longer taut, but loose. She pulled on it, and the black wire slipped easily through the crack between the boxes until the plug jammed in the narrow cardboard crevice. The machine was not connected to the wall anymore. It had come loose while she slept. The battery bay was empty—she knew that. She had thrown away the old batteries long ago. Yet she could still hear the music inside her head.

No! That was not possible!

She kicked out at the enclosing cartons, then screamed in

sudden pain. The tendons in her legs were on fire. A shoulder muscle spasmed. Panic was rising in a swirl of music, spiraling up and up. It was a fight to be still, to lie back and let the muscles uncramp. The music gathered speed. Beads of sweat slicked over her face. Her heart was beating faster, harder, hammering to the music. She pushed the cartons out of the way to make an opening, and pain stabbed her arms.

The music was welling up again, about to crash down on her in a crescendo. Her hands went up in a defensive posture. And then the music softened, like a living entity deciding not to bludgeon her with a heavy falling wall of sound. Mallory slowly rolled her body, and on her hands and knees, she crawled out of Malakhai's box, dragging the CD player by the wires of her headset. And the music crept after her.

This isn't real!

The score was climbing again, rising. In a rage, Mallory smashed her fist down on the music machine. A small rectangle of plastic broke away to expose the battery bay. Not an empty compartment.

She had believed that the old cadmium batteries had been thrown away, but there they lay, side by side—*alive,* recharged in the night.

Idiot.

Mallory touched the power switch. The music ended. She breathed deeply. So nothing was what it seemed. Even insanity was only a cheap trick.

✛   ✛   ✛

Lieutenant Coffey opened the window blinds spanning the upper half of the wall. In the squad room beyond the glass, all his detectives were gathered around a small television set, and cash was being laid down. He guessed it was still an even-money bet, for no one but the mayor's publicist knew how the TV script would play out this morning. He turned back to the larger television screen in the corner of his office.

Detective Sergeant Riker slouched in a chair, showing no enthusiasm for the coming event—perhaps because he had no money riding on it. He had been hustled through the office door before he could even make conversation with the gamblers in the next room.

Jack Coffey ran one hand through his hair, stopping short of the bald spot, which he attributed to stress and blamed on Mallory. In silence, he and Riker watched the weather segment of the morning talk show. Jack Coffey resented the smug weatherman, a happy idiot with luxurious, unmerited hair and a huge paycheck for presiding over a gang of cartoons. Smiling suns and frowning raindrops decorated the map in the background. A single large snowflake was menacing the entire state of Connecticut.

The lieutenant leaned forward and browsed through a fresh stack of paperwork on his desk.

What the hell?

He ripped off the top sheet and waved it at Detective Riker. "How did she get Heller's crew to go along with this? I signed off on the platform inspection, *not* the parade float."

Riker shrugged, and Coffey decided that his sergeant might be genuinely in the dark. Mallory had probably covered her partner with deniability for this less than legitimate work order.

Coffey looked back through the glass. Last-minute bets were going down while the weatherman laughed at the cartoon raindrop converging on New York State with incoming storms.

The screen image changed to a tourist's home movie of the Thanksgiving Day parade. The camera was focused on Mr. Zimmermann's wife and children. The little family was gamely smiling as Mrs. Zimmermann's hair stood straight up in the wind. The children waved as they stood beside the giant snowman float. For no good reason at all, the video camera panned to a clear shot of the rocky knoll overlooking the rear end of the parade route. Mrs. Zimmermann and the children jostled one another as they hurriedly regrouped in front of the camera's new position. Now they all moved backward toward the park, while every other camera in New York City was pointing at the spectacle of giant balloons flying in the opposite direction.

The image dissolved and was replaced by the stage set of

the mayor's favorite morning talk show. A man and woman were sitting on a couch. The ma-and-pa duo of broadcast journalism had not changed dramatically since Jack Coffey was a schoolboy. The anchorman had always worn a bad toupee, but the dark color no longer agreed with the facial crags and the triple chin of middle age. His female cohost was spookier. She had not aged at all, and she never stopped smiling. Her perpetual grin was rumored to be an accident of plastic surgery.

Riker leaned toward the set and turned up the volume as Heller walked out on stage. The head of Forensics appeared to be shaking hands with the TV people against his will. Perhaps Heller was only uncomfortable in the public eye. Or maybe Mallory was holding his family hostage in a remote location.

The large bear of a man sat down on the couch between his television hosts. Heller had great composure, hardly blinking as they mangled the list of his formidable credentials and previous triumphs in law enforcement. His slow-roving brown eyes turned to the monitor beside the couch. A split screen enlarged the same image for the television audience. It was a frozen shot of the rocky knoll above the head of the tourist's smiling wife.

"Now watch the knoll," the anchorman instructed his viewing audience. The still shot moved into the slow-motion action of Mrs. Zimmermann's hair waving in the wind. The television host carefully pronounced each word. "See the dark shadow on the rocks? See it? See the puff of white smoke?"

Riker picked up the television guide and ran his finger down the column for morning programs, perhaps to reassure himself that the mayor's publicist had not booked NYPD's forensic expert on some kiddie program.

"Now that puff of smoke. That's a gunshot, right?" The anchorman turned to Heller. "Clear evidence that the police-woman didn't act alone. Is that right, sir?"

"Detective Mallory didn't act at all," said Heller. "The smoke is in sync with the sound track on the news films. The movement of shadows was also matched to the tourist shots.

The smoke came from a rifle. We recovered the cartridge from two kids who were playing in the park that morning."

The grinning woman touched Heller's sleeve. "But are you sure it was the rifle shot that hit Goldy? I mean, the balloon was so big." She faced the camera as her hands made a wide arc to express *big* for the learning-disabled audience. "It could've been the gun, right? You couldn't miss a thing like that with *any* weapon."

"The balloon wasn't the target," said Heller. "It was hit on a ricochet. My team examined the evidence on Detective Mallory's suspicion that the float was the primary target. We found two holes in the material of the giant top hat. There's an entry hole for the shot and an exit hole for the ricochet. I found corresponding marks on the metal armature underneath the hat material."

The anchorman raised one eyebrow and held this pose. "You're saying it was an assassination attempt on one of the magicians?"

"No," said Heller. "I'm saying a bullet ricocheted off a parade float. Beyond that, you might only have a gun-happy drunk."

"Well, at least we've accounted for *one* of the bullets," said the grinning woman. "Now the shots—"

"One shot," said Heller, holding up his index finger, making no mistake about whom he was dealing with. They obviously needed this visual aid to count a single bullet. And this lent credence to Riker's theory that they might indeed be watching a children's program.

The male host countered with three fingers. "We have witnesses who heard *three* shots."

There were two electronic bleeps to censor words in Heller's response. Coffey suspected they were uncomplimentary adjectives for civilian testimony. Heller went on to reiterate this in more polite language. "You've run those tapes a hundred times. Did you hear three shots? No." His index finger was rising again. "*One* shot. Detective Mallory never fired her gun."

Coffey turned to the wide window on the squad room. There were loud cheers and whistles behind the glass. Money was being grabbed up and jammed into pants pockets. A few wadded bills were flying through the air, propelled by unhappy losers.

Riker leaned over and switched off the set. "Like it or not, boss, the kid's in the clear. You want me to dust off her desk?"

Coffey nodded with a rueful smile.

"Lieutenant, I know what you're thinking," said Riker. "How's Mallory ever gonna learn the rules if you can't catch her breaking them?" He smiled. It was not the wide grin of an ungracious winner. Riker was merely content to be on the opposite side of the loser—his commanding officer.

In peripheral vision, Coffey was tracking a man in uniform. Sergeant Harry Bell had cleared the stairwell, and now he was crossing the squad room. When the desk sergeant was only a few steps from the office door, Coffey slowly stretched out one arm and turned his palm up. As if on cue, Sergeant Bell came through the door and deposited four ten-dollar bills into the lieutenant's hand—his winnings.

Harry Bell's face was deep in disappointment as he turned on the startled Detective Riker. "You never made a bet on your own partner? Jesus, Riker, even if you thought Mallory was guilty, you could've put down *something* just for show."

✦   ✦   ✦

Mallory knelt down on the cellar floor and shined the flashlight across the cement. The talcum powder was undisturbed. It was a wide field of dusting. There were no marks for a makeshift scaffolding of boards to get him past the powder trap, and he didn't fly over it. Yet Billie Holiday was singing on the other side of the accordion wall, and she knew he was in there. She could smell the smoke from their cigarettes, Malakhai's and Louisa's.

At one end of the partition, she studied the long row of bolts securely holding the edge of the wood to the basement wall. No common crowbar could pry them loose. Judging by the size of the metal heads, their shanks would sink deep into double rows of brick. Yet she pulled on the end panel, and the bolt-lined strip of metal came away from the wall, sliding easily, silently, to accordion the rest of the panels backward along the track and away from the brick. And by this new door, she entered the storage area.

She crept along a row of shelves and bent low as she circled stacks of cartons. It was a pleasure to see the surprise on Malakhai's face when he looked up from the open box at his feet.

He smiled. "I wondered how long it would take you to work that out. Even Charles thinks the center panels are the only way in. I suppose it helps if you know Max's sense of humor."

"Did you find what you were looking for?"

He held up the charred leather spine of a book. The carton at his feet was filled with ashes and blackened pieces of book covers. "They used to be Max's journals. I suppose Edith found them after he died." He held a smoking cigarette. Louisa's had gone out.

"Why did you want them?"

He dropped the book spine into the carton and wiped his hands on a cloth. "My wife was in there. Max told me about his diaries one night when we were out on the town. He was very drunk and feeling guilty."

"He kept diaries in Paris?"

"No, he started them much later—after I came back from Korea with my resurrected Louisa. Putting my late wife in the magic act affected Max more than I realized. His diaries were love letters to a dead woman. That's why Edith burned them—jealous of a ghost." He made a halfhearted kick at the box.

"Was Max Candle as crazy as you are?"

Malakhai smiled as he lifted a bottle of wine from the case and examined the label. "I always know where I stand with you, Mallory." He poured out a glass of wine and handed it to her. "I know it's obscene to drink before noon."

She accepted the glass.

"Good," he said. "I hope you never become too well behaved." He looked down at the carton. "The wives always know, don't they? A dead rival must've sent her right over the edge. Poor Edith—poor Max."

He took a drag on his cigarette and tilted his head back to watch the plume of blue smoke rising to the high ceiling. "I can tell you my life story by the cigarettes. Like the night we ran from Paris, Max and I. He saved my life, dragged me through the streets and pushed me onto trains. We made the crossing at the Spanish frontier."

"You told me the border was shut down tight. You said you couldn't get Louisa out of Paris—not that way."

"It *was* closed. Oh, sometimes it would open for an hour or a day, but that night the border was closed down tight as a coffin lid. What did I care? I was in a bad way. Max had a better chance to make the crossing alone, but he wouldn't leave me. There was really no way out, you see. However, Max always listened to an inner voice that said, *Jump or die.* Even then, he took such absurd chances."

He closed the box of ashes.

"We got off the train at Cerbère. The frontier police were lining up all the passengers and checking their travel documents. We had some of Nick's forgeries in our pockets, exit visas to leave France, letters of transit to get us out of Lisbon. They were useless of course. No one could get a legitimate exit visa that month, so all the papers were suspect. We had no baggage—that was suspicious, too. And Max was still wearing his tuxedo. The frontier police were Frenchmen, a fashion-conscious race, but still they must've found that odd, particularly the silk top hat.

"Max went off to chat with a policeman guarding the station door. When he came back to me, all his money was gone, but he had directions for circumventing French checkpoints. The guard told him all the papers were being cross-checked by telephone and cables, so we couldn't get back on the train. We left the station with the passengers who were stopping in Cerbère. Then we climbed a steep hill. I remember passing low stone walls and olive trees. There were a million stars in the sky. We stopped at a Spanish sentry house.

"Max spoke to the border guards. I sat in that hut and cried through the whole interview. They asked him why his friend was so upset. He told them my wife had died that night. Then they asked Max why *he* was crying. Tears were streaming down his face when he told them he was the lover of his friend's wife. Then he *really* startled the guards. Told them he only had a few francs in his pocket and half a pack of cigarettes. He had not come prepared for a bribe. Oh, and the paperwork was forged. He mentioned that too. Well, now the guards were on the floor laughing. I didn't get the joke, so my weeping went on. They let us through, I don't know why. It was a fluke that we weren't arrested that night. German soldiers were waiting all along the border, like cats at a mousehole.

"There was another joke waiting for us when we finally arrived in Lisbon. The letter of transit was proved a forgery. Of course, I knew it would be, but I didn't much care what happened next. We were sitting on a bench in the anteroom of an official. This fool in a fine suit stood over us, waving the evidence in his hand. The man was so angry. Max stood up in his dusty tuxedo and bowed. He was so charming. Said he hoped the official hadn't been offended by a *bad* forgery, because it was never our intention to insult him.

"Oh, no, said the official. The papers were really first-rate. He was *consoling* Max. Then the two of them disappeared into the man's office. From time to time, I could hear laughter through the door. An hour later, we were on a plane out of Lisbon. I don't know why. It was absurd. The whole war was like that." He tapped the end of his cigarette in the ashtray. Louisa's lay dead and dark.

"I remember having a cigarette on the plane. There was smoke all over the world that night. Boy soldiers puffing in foxholes, generals having cigars with their whiskey—hookers lighting up on street corners, glowing in the dark. Between the gunfire and the cigarettes, I wondered that any of us could see with all that smoke. Later it turned out that none of us could."

He looked at the slender white shaft between his fingers. "It's medicinal, you know. My wife was dead. I took a few small puffs of nicotine and consolation. I believed I had killed Louisa with my arrow. More pain set in. Another cigarette, more consolation." He tilted his head to one side.

"And after she died," said Mallory, "when you used her in the act, how do you know Max was still—"

"Still crazy about Louisa? When I brought her ghost back from Korea, I took her to dinner at Max's house. He fell in love with her all over again. Never mind that she was dead. He was an American. All things were possible to Max."

He pushed the ashtray to one side. "But that's another story and another cigarette." He walked over to the wardrobe trunk. "Oliver's memorial service is tonight. I recommend the white satin tuxedo."

"That's customary for the death of a magician, isn't it? But everybody keeps telling me Oliver wasn't one."

"And they're right about that. Hopeless bungler. There won't be an elaborate service, not like the one we held for Max Candle. That was quite an event. Magicians came from all over the planet to give him a proper send-off. I haven't heard of anything on that scale since he died. Anyway, Oliver's already been buried. We're just having a wake at a little place in your neighborhood."

"Futura said Oliver loved Louisa, too."

"He was devoted to her. Oliver never married, you know. Never cheated on her memory."

"And you've never loved anyone but Louisa?"

He knelt down beside Mallory. "You're still wondering— am I crazy, or is Louisa just part of the act? Do I carry her around for guilt or profit?"

"I think you might've been legitimately crazy once. But now it's just a routine. It's getting harder to work the wires, isn't it?" Mallory pointed to the ashtray. "Her cigarettes keep going out. It's almost over now." She smiled, and he took that as a warning, backing away from her.

"This is my second trip to the basement this morning," she said. "I thought I found what you were looking for—an old letter stuffed in the toe of a shoe." That was where Mallory's foster mother had hidden valuables to keep them safe from burglars—as if there had been a black market for bad poetry written by Helen's middle-aged husband.

Malakhai was hovering over her. "Was it a letter from Max?"

"From Louisa. It was addressed to you. She probably thought you'd keep her personal effects if she didn't make it through the night." Mallory glanced at the wardrobe trunk. "I always wondered why you didn't." She looked down to inspect her fingernails, as if this transaction meant nothing to her. "I'll trade you for the letter. When you fired that gun on Thanksgiving Day, which one of them were you aiming at?"

He shook his head slowly to say, *No deal.*

"I've got rules, Malakhai. Nothing is free. Tell me which one you were aiming at—or I destroy Louisa's letter."

"So be it." There was no hesitation. He was not bluffing.

Mallory stood up and walked over to the wardrobe trunk. "I know she wrote it the night she died." She pulled out the white tuxedo and draped it over one arm. "Louisa mentioned the confession in the park." She turned back to him. "Last chance. Was it Nick Prado? Was he standing near the float when you fired that rifle?"

He looked down at the case of wine, head shaking from side to side. *No deal.*

Mallory reached into the pocket of her blazer and drew out the single page. It was a fragile thing, yellowed and creased—such delicate paper. The ink was a faint flourish of violet lines, almost illegible. She walked back to him and put it in his hand as an offering—for free.

He looked down at the aged paper, not quite believing in it yet.

She turned toward the partition. Malakhai's head was bowed as he read the faded lines of his letter. It was written by a woman who did not know how the night would end, if she would escape or be captured—live or die. "Dear Malakhai," it began, and the long goodbye followed after.

Mallory had received a similar letter from her prescient foster father, written before his own violent death and delivered on the day of his funeral. Three generations of Marko-witzes, all police officers, had written these letters to their families. The cop's daughter understood the importance of the farewell.

Walking close to the accordion wall, she headed for the side exit, never turning back for the chance to catch him crying.

She had rules.

Sixteen

FRANNY FUTURA LISTENED FOR A NOISE TO TELL HIM THAT HE
was not alone. At last, he was satisfied that all the chorus
boys and stagehands had left for their lunch break.

He laughed out loud and did a little dance across the floorboards, tapping his feet and whirling in his own arms, hug-
ging himself tightly, as if this might contain his joy. It did
not. His grin was wide as he paused and bowed to the empty
theater seats.

"Broadway." He spoke this name, holy of holies, as he was
rising on his toes. Then, soft as a prayer, "Thank you, Oliver."

True, this patch of the road was far uptown, but he had
never expected to come so close to an old dream, the Great
White Way. Franny knew his place among magicians. They
had dubbed him a living museum, a compendium of tired old
tricks that amazed no one. However, come Friday night, he
would perform a Max Candle illusion to a sold-out crowd. In
this theater, he would be the headliner. On the marquee outside, his name was writ larger than all the other magic men
on the bill.

He walked over to the long black table supporting his glass
coffin. The transparent panels were edged in dark lines of
lead. And lead molding marked the midsection where the two
halves of the coffin joined together. Holding on to the pewter
handles, he separated these independent boxes, and they slid
back easily along metal tracks embedded in the table. He pat-

ted the large pumpkin at the center of the bed. It was held in place by a metal brace so the razor would not knock it to the floor with the first swing. He had chosen this seasonal fruit over Max's burlap dummy because it would bleed. Though the juice was pale in comparison to blood, it was miles better than sawdust.

Four feet behind the table, a narrow rectangle of black wood rose from the floorboards to the catwalk. It was decorated with functional springs and toothy wheels that resembled bright clockworks strung out along a giant velvet jeweler's box. At the top of this mechanical base, two metal arms reached out to support the pendulum, a thin stalk of steel ending in a crescent razor.

He tap-danced toward the wings with a soft-shoe shuffle and climbed the ladder to the catwalk. When he walked across the narrow wood planks of the suspension bridge, it even swayed the same way Faustine's had done. He gripped the rails and smiled.

Just like the old days.

This theater was no mere re-creation; it was Faustine's revisited. He had come full circle—home again.

Franny looked down and imagined Max Candle lying in the glass coffin, bound hand and foot, screaming well-rehearsed lines to tell the audience that something had gone wrong with the pendulum, that the machine was going to kill him—night after night.

From the dark of the wings stage right, smoke was curling forward into the footlights. "Emile?"

The only reply was a knock on wood, and now he knew his visitor. How many years must he put behind him before that sound would cease to make him afraid?

Nick Prado said, in a badly disguised sotto voce, "Suddenly there came a tapping."

Franny's hands tightened on the rail as the man walked into the light of center stage. Nick stood beneath the catwalk and looked up as he slaughtered the poet's line. "Who's that rapping at my door? Franny, you must try to work something of Poe into the act." Nick's gaze traveled down the long stalk of the pendulum to the razor-sharp crescent. "I heard a rumor that you hired six chorus boys." He looked up again. "Say it isn't so."

Franny leaned over the rail. He could hear a shrill note in his voice, too high, too loud. "It's a slow buildup. I didn't think the act would hold the attention of a modern audience. The dance routine is really very good."

Nick made a stagy shiver of distaste. "Are you coming down? Or must I keep shouting?"

It was an effort for Franny to loosen his grip on the rails. He felt safe on the catwalk, but what reason could he give for remaining here?

None.

He dragged his feet to the end of the suspension bridge and slowly descended the ladder. Perhaps there were no safe places. He had not found one yet, not in all the years of a life-long quest.

Nick ran his hand along the top of the coffin. "A pity you can't do it Max Candle's way. You're competing with big spectacles downtown. Lots of high-tech acts. Now if the public thought there was a chance to see you die—" He walked over to the base and pressed the lever to set the pendulum in motion. "It was such a beautiful illusion."

Now the men stood side by side and watched the gears mesh, wheels spinning wheels, setting springs in motion, ticking, ticking. Nick flashed him an evil grin. "I hope this isn't the apparatus Oliver made."

"No," said Franny. "I was afraid he might've botched that one too. Charles loaned me Max's old props."

Nick watched the pendulum swing in a small arc. "Any problems calibrating the mechanism? It would be a crime to shatter the original coffin. It belongs in a museum."

"No, Emile helped me. Well, he did it all, really. It swings between the boxes, very precise. Never varies more than half an inch."

Nick looked up again as the pendulum gathered momentum and its razor described a wider arc. "Lovely machine. All Swiss gears and balance, you know. Only millionaires like

Max and Oliver could've built them. I can't persuade you to do it Max's way?"

Franny said nothing. He only watched the pendulum. It was dropping lower, swinging over the divided glass coffin.

Nick clapped him on the back. "Forget I mentioned it, old man. The original machinery would make it too chancy. It's so old. Do you really trust it?"

"Emile says it's in perfect condition." Franny watched the razor drop a little lower to slice through the partitions of the box. "What on earth is that doing there?" Nick pointed to the bright orange fruit inside the coffin.

"The pumpkin? It's a variation on Max's dummy. I want the audience to see that it really does cut into— Oh, no!" Franny's head moved in sync with the pendulum swing. Seeds and slop were stuck to the crescent razor. Pale yellow pumpkin blood was dripping on the floor and spreading over the interior of the coffin. More drops of liquid flew out over the footlights with the widening of the arc.

"Brilliant." Nick took out his glasses and put them on to survey the mess. "Shot in the dark—is this your first rehearsal with the pumpkin?"

Franny ran to the backstage room where the cleaning supplies kept company with his sound equipment. When he returned to the stage, Nick was standing at one end of the coffin, staring at the interior. He looked up at Franny. "No pumpkin guts on the microphone, but you probably should test it again. If it's ruined, the audience won't hear the screams from the box. That is what you're planning, right?"

Nick walked around the back of the coffin and shook his head as he examined the somewhat clumsy cable outlet leading under the hinged side. "There'll be critics in the audience on opening night. I went to a lot of trouble to make that happen, Franny. You don't want to screw it up, do you?" He glanced at the cloth squares neatly folded on the floor beside the coffin. "So you're going to cover the boxes while you make your exit."

"Of course. There's no other way."

"Well, there's Max's way. He stayed in the coffin, screaming for help, watching the pendulum drop lower and lower. I could tell you how he pulled it off."

Franny shook his head slowly as he mopped the inside of the coffin with a towel.

Nick smiled. "You're using breakaway cuffs, right? We can adjust the pendulum so the lowest part of the arc swings in front of the coffin." He gestured to the panel of gears. "That's why the table and the base are painted black. You couldn't see where Max's tuxedo cummerbund left off and the backdrop began. Of course there's a risk with every mechanical thing. But you could perform the best trick of the festival."

After cleaning the seeds and juice on the coffin bed, Franny looked at the microphone, dry as a bone. "I don't think so, Nick."

"They'd talk about it for years and years if you risked your life—just a little."

Franny looked at the seeds on the floor. The cleaning crew would take care of the rest of this mess. He wadded up the towel and threw it into the wings.

"I'd give my eyes," said Nick, "for the chance to see it done right, just one more time. It was so hypnotic—and terrifying." He walked all around the coffin, inspecting the lead-rimmed holes at both ends. "I can improve on your version. Nothing risky. We could put a mechanism in the box where your legs are supposed to be. Something to break the glass so it looks like you're in there trying to kick your way out. Max kicked out a pane in every performance. Just a touch of violence to startle the audience. That's all you need. I'll take care of the preparations for you."

"No—sorry. I mean—thank you, but Emile is giving me a hand. He's coming back. In fact, he'll be here any minute." Why had he said that?

"We have to go now, Franny. We'll leave Emile a polite note at the front office."

"Where? Go where?"

Nick rapped on the wooden table. "Maybe—just before you go on stage—we could have a raven fly out. He could perch on the platform. And the knocking." He rapped on the wood again. "Oh, definitely. We must have knocking. New York has a literate theater crowd. I know they'd get it."

Franny shook his head.

Nick shrugged. "Overkill? I suppose it would be a bit much. But we should definitely have a talk about those chorus boys. You need help with this act."

"Emile will—"

"Emile can't help you now, Franny. He's doing Max's hanged man illusion downtown, remember? I hope Oliver didn't botch that one too. When I left Emile, he was still testing his props. I don't think he'll make it up this way for quite a while."

Franny pressed the lever to raise the pendulum again. "My assistants are coming back soon. I should—"

Nick shook his head slowly. "We had an agreement, Franny."

"I never told Mallory anything."

"Because I had Faustine's death to give her." He looked up at the razor hanging in the air. "My sources tell me Mallory's in charge of the case now. It's an official inquiry into Oliver's death." He stopped a moment to listen to the ticking of the gears.

Franny turned his eyes toward the catwalk where he had been safe.

"Maybe we can amplify that sound with a small microphone," said Nick. "Tick, tick, tick. More suspense, don't you think?" He turned around to look at the lobby door, then glanced at his watch. "Mallory will come for you soon, Franny. Relentless child. She'll drag you into the police station. You know what happens in those places. You won't get out again until you fold and tell her everything."

Would she come at night?

"Ah, what a creature," said Nick. "She has the coldest eyes I've ever seen—on a *living* woman."

"Did you really think Oliver was—"

"Oliver is dead. He's not the problem, Franny. Now what shall we do with you? Can't leave you here." He stood up and waved toward the exit light. "Shall we?"

"What about Malakhai? He's already talked to her."

"What of it? He's the best documented lunatic on the planet."

Though there was no gun, no raised fist, not even the hint of force, Franny walked toward the exit sign. He was not a willing companion, yet he offered no resistance. In his own private world, the storm troopers had never left. Shadow soldiers marched behind him as he passed through the stage door and into the street. He could almost hear marching footsteps traveling along with them as he and Nick walked down Broadway. Franny squinted in the noonday sunlight. There were pedestrians on the sidewalk. Two policemen rolled by in a patrol car. There were many people he might have cried out to. But he went quietly, crying only a little—afraid to make a scene in public.

✝   ✝   ✝

Every old thing was new again.

The walls echoed that theme with murals depicting the Prohibition era of speakeasy flappers and bathtub gin. On the low stage, musicians were playing vintage jazz. And best of all, there were ashtrays on the tables. Detective Riker sat in his own cloud of smoke and stared at the gardenia on the windowsill. He could swear it had not been there a moment ago.

The bar crowd was very young, except for the few gray heads of magicians he recognized. He had avoided them for the past half hour, not wanting to begin the interviews until Mallory arrived. She was late again, and this worried him. There was a time when he could have set a watch by her appearance.

Charles Butler was rushing the door, and this was Riker's first clue that Mallory had arrived, for he could only see her blond curls and bits of white satin between the bodies of other patrons.

Wait. Satin?

And now he caught the flash of golden strappy heels where running shoes should be. His only good view of her was the reflection in the window. A white tuxedo floated in the night-dark glass. Elegant lines of material flowed over her body and threw off sparks of reflected light. She was carrying a purse instead of her knapsack.

He had been robbed; this was not *his* Mallory. She was late, the way a woman is late, and she was even dressed like a woman. There was no blouse worn beneath her jacket, and he had a vague feeling that it would be wrong to stare at that reckless neckline—almost incest. He had never mistaken NYPD for real family, but Mallory had always been a source of confusion. And now the kid was changing her rigid patterns and her style.

He hated change.

Riker put the blame on her new habit of sharing wine with suspects. Well, that would have to stop. This was what happened when amateur drinkers were set loose in bars and liquor stores.

She draped her leather trench coat over Charles's arm, as though he were a living coat tree—not that he appeared to mind. His face was so happy and hopeful. Now Charles raised his empty hands, perhaps as a prelude to peacemaking, assurance that he came to her unarmed. Suddenly, a gardenia appeared in his right hand.

Mallory's smile was strained, and Riker guessed that she was damn sick of tricks.

She slipped the flower stem through the boutonniere slit in her lapel. And now the black leather coat was flying Riker's way. He caught it in midair and watched Charles lead Mallory toward the musicians. He held her in a slow dance to an old blues tune from the forties.

Mallory was humoring Charles, dropping the pretense that she could have any reason to be angry with the poor bastard. So she was on best behavior tonight, and this also worried Riker. His only consolation was the familiar bulge that the gun made in the line of her white satin suit.

Nick Prado was standing at the bar, lifting a glass with Emile St. John. Malakhai had not arrived yet, but both men had assured him that he would know when this man walked into the room.

The band abruptly ended their set to have a few words with

the harried-looking manager. Charles and Mallory walked back toward the table. Prado intercepted them and touched the flower in her lapel, pretending interest in it, as if there were not fifty identical blooms appearing all around the room. "The gardenia was Louisa's favorite. Oliver's too. He left funeral instructions for a carload to be—"

Prado was distracted by the entrance of two uniformed police officers. Every head was turning toward the door. "Oh, good! It's a raid."

Riker recognized one of the uniforms, a man his own age who had not yet been forced out in NYPD's rush to replace all the gray men with kids fresh from school. Officer Estrada was standing with the manager when Riker joined them. "What's the problem?"

Estrada pointed to a young couple sitting at a table a few yards away. "Those two called in a complaint about the smoke."

The manager chimed in, "Right. But smoking is legal here. This is a bar, not a restaurant. We only serve hors d'oeuvres. So now they're changing their complaint to dancing."

"What?" Nick Prado had joined them. "No dancing?"

The manager rolled his eyes back, showing all the classic symptoms of a New York mugging victim. "We don't have a cabaret license, sir. The mayor says no—"

"Right." Riker never had the patience to listen to the back story. "No smoking in the restaurants, no dancing in the bars."

Officer Estrada grinned. "It gets worse, Riker. The mayor shut down your favorite strip joint today."

Riker winced as he amended his list. "And no more sex in New York City." He looked down at the gun belts of Estrada and his young partner. Both were sprouting gardenias. "Okay, you guys are with me."

As the three policemen walked toward the complaining couple, Riker noticed a flower growing from his breast pocket. He swatted it to the floor, as if this might be a visitation of the delirium tremens that had once covered him with crawling spiders.

"Good evening, sir, ma'am," said Riker. "You wanna press charges, right?"

The couple said, "Yes," in unison, as if this were a response at a prayer meeting. And Riker supposed it was. He was becoming accustomed to the religious fervor in a taxpayer's exercise of power.

"We need a written statement, folks. These two officers are gonna run you down to the South Bronx. Shouldn't take more than a few hours."

"You're kidding!" The man looked up at Riker with an expression of shock. The woman was shaking her head, saying, "Not the *Bronx*." But her tone of voice said, *Not the thumbscrews.*

Riker pegged them as Manhattanites, and he could even roughly guess their address on the Upper East Side. They would regard the outer boroughs of New York City as remote satellites, faraway planets requiring visas and vaccinations.

The woman pulled a gardenia from her hair and held it up to her startled eyes, truly mystified in the absence of an identifying price tag.

"Sorry, folks," Riker was saying. "That's the law. All the dancing statements go to the South Bronx. But I really appreciate you screwing up your whole evening to do the right thing."

The uniformed cops were looking elsewhere, hiding smiles, as the couple gathered up their coats, heads shaking in deep denial. And now they were marching toward the door.

Riker pursued them. "Hey, where are you going? If you won't do the paperwork, how're we gonna shut this place down?"

As the door swung shut behind them, Riker turned to the silent assembly and shouted, "Resume dancing!"

The band and the crowd obeyed.

In the middle of cheers for the hero of the evening, Riker's thunder was suddenly stolen. As promised by Prado and St. John, he recognized Malakhai the moment the magician walked into the room.

Every pair of eyes was on him, this genetic celebrity of

natural grace and form, unconsciously moving in time to the music as he crossed the floor. Or perhaps the band was playing to the tempo of the man.

Though he had never used the word *beauty* to describe another male, it was in his mind. Malakhai's dark blue eyes were young and incongruous with the long mane of white hair. Riker had seen this phenomenon before in the faces of ballplayers from another era, boys of eternal summer, and he called it magic.

✛   ✛   ✛

Mallory's eyes were drawn to the bar, where Malakhai was drinking alone. He had not looked her way since his arrival, but she was constantly aware of him. And so were other women. She was not the only predator in this room.

Emile St. John stood alone on the bandstand, his hands waving to conduct a floating black silk scarf across the small stage. The material was rounded out in the shape of a globe. When he pulled away the silk, the audience gasped to see a dove flapping its wings against the interior wall of a clear balloon. St. John lit a cigar and touched it to the rubber. The balloon popped with a bang, and the dove vanished.

Charles leaned across the table so Riker could hear him above the sound of applause. "My cousin Max got a thousand doves for his funeral."

"Well," said Prado, "Oliver botched the trick, so he only gets one. And if he hadn't died in the act, he wouldn't have gotten that much."

"So that was good timing on Oliver's part?" Riker's smile was wry.

"Timing is everything," said Prado, missing the sarcasm. "Oliver bailed out before life went sour. Now me—I plan to die when the world has exactly six minutes of joy left. And that can't be far off." He raised his glass in a toast. "Many die too late and some die too early. Still the doctrine sounds strange—"

"Die at the right time," said Riker, completing the line. "Nietzsche, right?"

Three heads turned to stare at the shaggy detective. Startled, Charles looked up through the wide front window, craning his neck to catch the moon over Columbus Avenue, perhaps to reassure himself that it remained in orbit and at least one aspect of the universe was in normal working order.

Nick Prado smiled over the rim of his wineglass. "So, Riker, what brings you out tonight?"

"Police business." Riker nodded to Emile St. John as the man pulled up a chair to sit beside Prado.

"What's happened now?" asked St. John.

"Oliver Tree's death was reopened as a homicide case." Riker turned to Nick Prado. "But you already knew that, sir. The mayor's publicist told you this afternoon."

Judging by Emile St. John's expression, this was obviously news to him. And now St. John's wary eyes settled on Prado, who was grinning in an attitude of *touché*.

"Oh, call me Nick. So you're investigating Oliver's death."

"Mallory's the primary on this case." Riker lifted his glass, not a stickler for police regulations against drinking on duty. "But you knew that too, sir—Nick." Riker was searching the faces lined up at the bar. "I thought Franny Futura might be here tonight. He left his hotel in a big hurry. A gypsy cabdriver settled the bill, and a bellhop loaded the bags into the trunk of an empty junker."

Prado sighed. "Ah, poor Franny. Not a stylish exit."

"Well, his credit rating wouldn't support a stretch limo," said Riker. "Any idea where he went?"

Mallory watched the magicians trade looks. St. John was hearing this story for the first time, but Nick Prado was not.

"No? Okay, next question. That name of his." Riker bent over his notebook and flipped through the pages. "Franny Futura. It doesn't go with the French accent. He made it up, right?"

"No, Oliver made it up," said St. John. "Franny was just sixteen years old when Oliver rechristened him."

"What's the guy's real name?" Riker's pencil hovered over the page.

"François something," said St. John. "Nick, his last name was close to Futura, wasn't it?"

Prado shook his head. "I only remember that Futura was the worst possible way to mangle the original pronunciation. Oliver renamed him in a stage introduction. It was a joke, a little revenge. Franny was always correcting Oliver's bad French. But then, Franny got a nice write-up in the morning paper and decided to keep his new name—so as not to waste the review."

Riker turned to a clean page in his notebook. "So those two didn't like each other much?"

"Oh, but they did," said Emile St. John. "They were best friends. I'm not sure they kept in touch after the war. Franny never played New York. He's been waiting for this chance all his life. Don't worry. He'll turn up for the performance." St. John spoke to Riker but he was looking at Nick Prado, and the message was clear: Franny Futura *would* appear on opening night. And as if a silent bargain had been struck, the other man made a barely perceptible nod.

Riker caught that. He was also staring at Prado. "Is this a publicity stunt? I don't like to waste my time."

"No," said Prado. "But I might be able to do something with it. Another witness to the balloon assassination disappears under mysterious circumstances. You're a genius, Riker."

Mallory turned toward the bar. Malakhai was gone, and a row of gardenias grew in a straight line along the mahogany surface. She spotted him at a table on the other side of the bandstand. He was in conversation with a young brunette one third his age, and she was clearly the aggressor in this flirtation. Mallory watched the woman go through stages of the mating dance, leaning forward as she played with a strand of her hair, then lightly touching his arm as she laughed.

Malakhai turned to catch Mallory's eyes on them. He smiled and rose from the table. As he walked across the dance floor, Prado was rising from his chair and moving away, quickly crossing the room.

Mallory reached up to her hair and pulled out another unwanted flower as she kept track of the magician. In his wake, all the women he passed on the dance floor sprouted flowers. When he was standing by her chair, Charles introduced him to Riker, then excused himself to fetch another glass and a fresh bottle of wine from the bar.

Emile St. John was out on the dance floor, twirling a partner close to his own age. They were moving to a swing tune from the forties with dance steps half a century old. Malakhai sat down at the table and nodded toward the dancers. "I could teach you how to do that."

"My father taught me how to dance," said Mallory. "It seems I have less and less to learn from you. And I'm tired of all the lies."

"I never lied to you—not outright." Malakhai rested one hand on her arm. She looked down at it. He took her point, and his hand pulled back. "I think the best lies are told with the truth, and maybe a bit of distortion and misdirection."

Across the table, Riker was unconsciously nodding, recognizing his partner's own style of deception.

"Right," said Mallory. "A conventional liar needs a good memory. You don't have that anymore."

Now she was aware of the young brunette closing in on their table. The woman bent down to show Malakhai all the cleavage of a low-cut blouse. Her voice was breathy as she invited him to dance. The moment Malakhai left the table, Nick Prado came running back.

Mallory exchanged glances with Riker, and he nodded. There was another weakness in the ranks of the magic men.

When the music ended, Emile St. John pulled up a chair and sat down. "I still can't get over the dancing laws. What's happened to this town?"

Prado tilted his head to one side, considering this. "I think I like it better this way. More laws to break." He smiled at Mallory, who was the law. "Did the mounted policeman cancel his litigation? I understand you were cleared of the balloon shooting."

"Naw," said Riker, speaking for his partner. "The lawsuit is still on, but the wording keeps changing. Now Henderson blames the mayor for letting dangerous cartoons run loose in the streets. So the mayor ordered Macy's to retire all the big balloons. If they don't, he's gonna cancel their parade permit." He lifted his glass. "And then the city will be safe for Henderson—idiot-proof."

Emile St. John clinked glasses with Riker. "To the last parade." And now he held up Mallory's gold watch, but her hand was still attached to the fob at the end of the chain.

Her face was icy as she put her pocket watch away.

Prado sighed. "You're getting slow, Emile. Time to call it an evening. I'll pick up this round. I think your wallet is getting a bit light."

"Nonsense," said the Frenchman, reaching into his breast pocket. When he opened his wallet, there was nothing inside but bits of paper.

Nick was nodding in approval. "Nicely done, my dear."

Mallory held up a handful of folding money and credit cards. Grudgingly, she laid them on the table.

St. John seemed a bit subdued as he settled the tab with a waiter, but Prado was laughing. The two men said their good nights and walked toward the door, which was now framed in garlands of flowers.

Riker turned to Mallory. "And what else have you got, kid? That little item from Nick's side pocket? Were you gonna share that?"

She pulled another flower from her hair and tossed it over one shoulder. Next she drew out a folded prescription sheet and spread it on the table. "I'll run it by Slope in the morning. Probably harmless, but you never know what can kill in the right dosage. What do you bet the doctor's signature is a forgery?"

"Ah, bless him," said Riker, watching Nick Prado's back as the door swung shut. "I hope I'm up to bumping people off when I'm his age. But poison's too tame. No bet—I won't take your money, kid. Or is it St. John's money?"

The band was playing the opening bars of a tune for slow dancing. Malakhai appeared at the table and took her by the hand. She didn't resist as he led her onto the floor.

"I'm going to teach you one remarkable trick." When they stood in the center of the dancing crowd, he released her.

Other partners swirled around them. "I've never done this illusion with a live woman before."

He held up his right hand in the posture of a dancing partner. As her hand was rising to meet his, he said, "Now don't touch me. Keep your palm flat and in front of mine. Hold your left hand about an inch above my shoulder. Don't let it drop. Don't ever forget to keep your distance." He smiled. "As if you could."

His arm reached around her, and she sensed a hand at the small of her back, though there was no physical contact. Her own left hand rode in the air above the material of his suit, her fingers curling to the shape of his shoulder.

"Close your eyes, Mallory, or you won't sense the next move. This thing can only be done in the dark."

The scent of flowers was stronger when her eyes were shut. She felt the warmth of his raised hand pressing the air. Mallory stepped back, and his heat followed with her.

"Very good," he said, moving toward her again as she retreated to keep the distance between them. He moved to the right and she with him, not following his lead this time, but moving in anticipation. A clarinet was melding into the velvet saxophone.

They turned in a circle, revolving to the music, never touching flesh to flesh. One tune blended into another with a faster tempo. She felt lighter as the music speeded up. The trumpet was rippling. Quick notes ran round and round in the dark to the heartbeat of drums. Mallory's face was suddenly warm with a rush of blood beneath her skin. The music was zooming. And then it slowed, swaying her body with mirror movements to the partner she could not see or touch. Downy hairs at the nape of her neck were standing out and away.

She was turning and turning, eyes closed, blindly chasing the tease of heat. The music mellowed into a luscious basso, sweet and thick, notes dripping like slow honey. There was a sensuous rhythm in the strings of the bass, endlessly drawing out this prelude, this thrumming expectation of bodies not yet meeting. It was close to pain as they moved nearer to one another. The music was slowing, so soft now.

Whispers of reeds.

A sigh.

In the last sweet extended notes of the horns, Malakhai's left arm was warm and solid against her back. Her right hand was folded into his. She had not yet opened her eyes. The sweet scent of flowers mingled with wine and smoke. His hand lightly touched her hair, and Mallory's head tilted back. Eyes shut, stone blind, she was staring into the blue eyes of a boy's unlined face. The large spread hand at the small of her back pressed her body close to his. Closer still. The saxophone moaned in the thrall of sex at the peak, at the top of the act, warm and liquid. It was 1942—it was Paris.

Mallory had made an error in timing and distance.

She stepped back quickly, one hand rising, as if she meant to ward off an arrow. Malakhai stared at her with a boy's blue eyes—so cold now that their dance was done.

He turned around and walked away.

She had not expected that.

Suddenly absent the guidance of heat and music, Mallory stood alone at the center of the floor, not knowing whether to move right or left. She looked down at the white satin tuxedo—inspecting it for what? Blood?

Seventeen

MALLORY STOOD BY THE DRAGON SCREEN AND NODDED AT SOME-
thing Charles Butler had said, keeping up the pretense that
she was paying attention to his words.

It was his clothing that made her suspicious.

For the third time in a week, Charles was wearing blue
jeans, though he had been raised to wear formal attire. She
had sometimes envisioned him as a toddler going off to a
dress-code nursery school in a tiny suit and tie.

And why was he still working on the platform?

"I'll put security cameras on every floor." Charles came
down the stairs of the platform, two steps at a time. "And I'll
ask Malakhai to ring the bell, instead of finessing the locks.
How's that?"

He was so happy this morning. Encountering her in the
basement had been unexpected—for both of them. He must
assume that she had dropped by to explain her disaffection
from the upstairs office.

"It's not just Malakhai's lock-picking." Mallory stared past
him, focusing on the platform, the unsolved riddle.

Charles sat on the floor and opened the toolbox. Mallory
hunkered down beside him. "Emile St. John is doing a routine with a hangman's noose. Did Max use the platform for
that one too?"

"Yes," said Charles, "but Emile is doing the early version.
Max created that illusion long before the platform was built.

I hope you don't want to see the original gallows. It would take all day to—"

"Just tell me what it looks like."

"It's a cliché of every cowboy movie you've ever seen. Very narrow and maybe ten or eleven feet high. And it's got a rickety look to it—that's deliberate. It increases the visual tension." He turned around to look at the platform. "You know, this one looks a bit like a gallows. Maybe that's why Max built thirteen steps—tradition."

Mallory walked over to the platform door. The room was lit and she could see the gleaming brass of new cogs and chains for the mechanisms. So Charles was overhauling the entire apparatus. "You're trying to work it out?"

Charles looked up from the toolbox. "The Lost Illusion? Yes, but Malakhai doesn't think much of my chances. He promised to leave me the solution in his will."

She sat on the edge of a packing crate full of red capes. "I can't wait that long." One weapon lay on the floor, the same crossbow that had misfired and ripped her jeans. Its empty pedestal was stripped down to the gears of inner wheels and springs. "So the pedestal *was* broken."

"One of the springs snapped." Charles searched through the tiers of toolbox shelves, then lifted out a length of chain. "Malakhai took it to a repair shop. He thinks he can match it up to a new one."

And that would explain the ashtray on the floor by the toolbox, though none of the cigarette stubs were marked by lipstick.

The carnival mirror was propped against the side of a wooden crate. She found Charles's reflection in the wavy glass, but no matter how she moved her head, she could not make his features flow into the image of Max Candle. She was never going to see that trick again.

He met her eyes in the reflection. "So it's just a temporary thing, right? When this is over, you'll move your computers back upstairs?" Charles had such a ridiculous smile, and he seemed to understand this, always appearing to apologize for sudden happiness with the lift of one shoulder. Even now he was trying to tuck his smile back in before she could take him for a fool.

She looked for some easy way to put him off again. "You don't have any clients right now. We'll talk about it when the case is wrapped." Perhaps she would come back when her erstwhile business associate was no longer consorting with the enemy, greeting Malakhai with that tell-all face that betrayed every secret. If she did not come back, she would miss that face.

"How well do you know Franny Futura?"

"Before Thanksgiving? I only knew him by reputation." Charles stood up and carried the chain to the door in the platform wall. "If I ever met him as a child, I've forgotten."

"You never forget anything."

"Eidetic memory is imperfect." He entered the small room, and his voice carried back. "I've managed to block out every boring church sermon from my childhood."

She stood in the open doorway. "So what's the man's reputation?"

"Tired magic." Charles replaced the chain for a trapdoor. "Franny was a headliner in London, but that was in his younger days—late forties, I think. All his tricks are from the first half of the century. Even before the high-tech illusions and the laser shows, he was getting left behind. But he never gave up. I like him for that. Franny's the only one in the pack who still makes his living with magic."

She watched him work the chain into the gear teeth. "Futura is still missing. He's not staying with you, is he? Or maybe he called?"

"No, sorry."

"Thanksgiving Day at your house—Futura said he staged that crossbow stunt with Oliver's nephew. But he's not the type to get in the path of a live arrow. What about a fake? Rubber, something like that?"

"No, I saw the arrow after Franny pulled it out of the float. It was just like Max's set. Simple metal shaft—quite deadly." He emerged from the room and walked around to the platform staircase. "But the arrow wasn't actually loaded into the crossbow. Franny probably hid it under his cape, then jammed it into the float. The crown of the top hat was only papier-mâché on an iron frame."

"But that wouldn't look real."

"Of course it would." He bent over a crate of equipment and pulled out a broken crossbow. It was different from the others. The cracked bow was made of wood and had no magazine.

"This one is single-fire." He handed it to her. "Like the one Richard Tree used for the parade stunt. The arrow bed is lined with steel, same color as the arrows. And there's a reason for that. There's no magazine covering the shaft. But from any distance, no one would notice if the crossbow was loaded or not. An audience only sees the weapon and the release of the bowstring."

"This one doesn't have a bowstring."

"Right. But if you like, you can still shoot me with it."

"The bow is broken, Charles."

"Doesn't matter." He bent over the box filled with scarlet capes and plucked one out of the jumble. He draped the material across his shoulders and knelt on the floor, moving into a crouch as Futura had on Thanksgiving morning. "Ready? Shoot me."

She pointed the stringless broken crossbow at him and said, "Bang."

Charles doubled over, and when he lifted his head again, she could see an arrow planted in his chest. His fingers covered the tip where a wound should be, and the shaft vibrated, as if it had struck him with great force. It looked too much like the real thing.

"Not bad, Charles." So that was all there was to it. Another cheap trick. "But that wasn't what Oliver had in mind for the Central Park show. All those weapons were loaded by cops, three arrows in every magazine." And she still had a problem with that. "Only two rounds were fired in the act, right? One for the test dummy and one for Oliver. So why *three* arrows in every magazine?"

"Well, Max always used three arrows."

"But Oliver never saw the Lost Illusion."

"No, but he might've seen an earlier crossbow act. Only two crossbows in that one."

"You never mentioned another crossbow illusion."

"Emile told me about it. It's an old routine, but no one ever did it Max's way." Charles cocked the long lever at the back of a crossbow pistol and pulled the bowstring taut. Then he tied a length of ribbon to an arrow and loaded it into the magazine.

Mallory replayed Oliver's death. On the tape, this was the crossbow that sent an arrow into Oliver's neck.

"This illusion was an early prototype." Charles walked to the pedestal on the other side of the platform step and cocked a second crossbow. "Max used three arrows, but I only need one in each magazine." He put another ribbon-tied arrow in the magazine. This weapon would aim for the heart. "There's no demonstration dummy in this routine."

Mallory looked into the tilted magazine of the near crossbow. This time, there was no sleight of hand, no deceit. Charles was playing with real arrows—and Emile St. John's instructions.

"I don't need to see it," she said. "Just tell me how it works."

"Now where's the fun in that?" He waved her to the chair in front of the platform. "I was planning to try it out anyway. It's all set up. Now sit down. Don't leave your seat, or you'll ruin it." He smiled. "You're only the audience, all right? There are no manacles, so I don't need a cop in this act."

He touched the button to start the gears on the first pedestal. The ticking began, the wheels moved slowly, and a red-flagged peg was rising toward the crossbow trigger.

Charles pulled the monk's hood over his head and walked over to the second crossbow to start its gears. Two pegs were rising, ticking, as he walked up the stairs. At the top of the platform, he faced the target. His arms spread wide, and the scarlet material covered the target and grazed the curtains.

The first crossbow fired and the arrow pierced the cape. Predictably, Charles was not wearing it. The material collapsed to the floor, and a long red ribbon trailed from a hole in the crumpled material to the end of the metal shaft in the target. Charles was probably standing behind the drapes. The second pedestal continued to tick.

Mallory's head snapped right with the sound of something

hitting a cardboard box. *A diversion?* She turned back to the platform. The cape was slowly rising off the floor, filling out, as if reinhabited. The lazy tongs spread the material in the convincing illusion of a man taking shape beneath the cape, spreading arms that were not there.

Over the loud tick of the pedestal gears, she heard the noise again, but her eyes never left the stage this time. She followed the sound as it moved behind her. Her hand was reaching for the gun; her eyes were on the red peg in the rising gear that would pull the trigger on the second crossbow.

The next crossbow fired, and she followed the flight of ribbon as it penetrated the back of the cape. But this time, Charles was inside. She saw his head go back. He cried out as he turned to face her and sank to his knees. A section of bloody ribbon extended from a spreading red stain on his chest to the arrow vibrating in the target. His hands were not covering this wound, not holding the ribbon in place. He collapsed on the stage, falling backward, his head lolled over the top step, eyes wide with the stare of the recently dead.

She left her chair and walked up the staircase, taking her own time. When she reached the top step, she sat down beside his still body, careful not to allow any spots of blood on her clothing.

"Charles? The next time you die—don't smile as you're going down. Real stiffs almost never do that." She dipped one finger into the red liquid. "And you made the blood too thin."

He rolled his eyes toward her. "Well, it's old blood. It was part of my Halloween costume when I was a little boy." He sat up with a face full of disappointment. "But other than that—"

She pulled out her revolver.

"You're a tough audience, Mallory."

"We're not alone down here. Be quiet." She was looking into the darkness of the cavernous space all around them—a hundred hiding places. Then she heard the noise again.

"Stay here." She descended the stairs. The cellar was full of shadows, but none of them moved. There was no more noise until a rat darted out from the stacks of crates.

Another cheap trick.

She glanced back at Charles, planning to remind him of the rat traps. That was the last project he had foiled, contending that breaking the backs of vermin was inhumane. She aimed the barrel of the revolver in the direction of the fleeing rodent, only meaning to point out the rat was a—

"Mallory, don't!"

"I know." She holstered the gun. "You think rats are charming." *And faulty electrical wiring and housebreakers and—*

"Not at all," he said. "But if you shoot a rodent in the back, how will you ever explain that to Lieutenant Coffey?" He sat down on the top step with a rare deadpan expression, his best attempt yet at a poker face. "So other than my smile and the watery blood, how did you like the illusion?"

"Not bad. I couldn't see the other crossbow magazine. There was no arrow in it, right?"

"Right, I faked the loading. But you assumed it was loaded when you saw the string release, and you saw the first crossbow shoot a real arrow."

"You hid the second arrow under your cape."

"Right. The ribbon wire loops from the crossbow through this." He removed the torn cape and opened his shirt to show her a thick metal tube wrapping around to the back of his body. "I didn't know what the tube was for until Emile told me."

Mallory nodded. "And you used the weight again, right? The ribbon wire was attached to it when you kicked the weight off the edge of the stage. That's how you made the ribbon fly through the body tube. Then you caught the ribbon when it came through the tube. You disconnected the wire, wrapped it around the hidden arrow and jammed it in the target."

"Sorry, was I boring you?"

Perhaps he wasn't being deadpan this time. No, he was mildly pissed off.

"You took a risk with the first shot, Charles. Suppose it went wrong? Maybe another broken pedestal spring? You could've been killed."

This worked rather well. Now he seemed pleased that he had impressed her with *something*.

"But the cops did the loading for Oliver," she said. "And they cocked the bows. All the strings released—no jam-up, no dry firing."

"You're right. A dry firing wouldn't figure in that routine." He turned back to look at the target. "Now for this one, the wires and loops are an advance setup for bad light on a deep stage. You couldn't do this sort of thing in broad daylight."

Another wasted morning. "So Oliver just borrowed from other illusions."

"But I know he got a lot of things right. Max used police officers for every manacle act. Otherwise the audience wouldn't believe the handcuffs were real. Since the police were there, they had to inspect the crossbows too. Would've seemed odd if they didn't. And Max—"

"He liked authenticity. Right." Mallory climbed the staircase and sat down on the top step beside Charles. "What kind of an act did Emile St. John do?"

"Birds were the focal point. It was a wonderful pickpocket routine. He'd take your wallet and make a parakeet fly out of your pants. Of course, they all did pickpocket routines. In the old days, that kind of skill was a staple of magic."

"No weapons in St. John's routine?"

"Never. I told you, the trick shot was Nick's act. I remember my cousin saying that Emile hated the sight of firearms."

But St. John had racked up many years with the French police and Interpol; weapons went with the trade. "Charles, that doesn't make sense, not with his history. He never told you what he did?"

"You mean during the war? You knew about that?" There was more to Charles's expression than mere surprise; there were traces of guilt. "He actually told you?"

She nodded in a silent lie. "I've been listening to a lot of war stories." At least that part was true.

He turned his face down to look at the crumpled cape and the fake blood splatters. "I always had the impression that it was a secret thing. But I was only a child when I heard the story. Such a long time ago. It gave me nightmares for months. You shouldn't think badly of Emile—for what he did." He gathered up the red material. "Considering the context of war."

Mallory kept very still, not wanting to spook him with an obvious prompt. She simply left the opening in the air between them and waited for him to fill it with secret things.

"I only heard it mentioned once," said Charles. "Emile probably thought I was asleep when he told the story to Max." He wadded the cape into a tight ball. "After the liberation of Paris, Emile *was* on a Maquis firing squad. But you must understand, there were lots of trials in that period— hasty justice for collaborators."

"Emile St. John was an *executioner?*"

✛   ✛   ✛

Mallory stepped out of the cab on 56th Street, near the less glamorous back door to Carnegie Hall. The arched windows were grated with iron, and the overhang with its gold lettering was only a small seedy reminder of the grandeur on the other side of the block. She passed between parked delivery trucks and walked around the Dumpster on the sidewalk.

The tan doors of the stage entrance were open. Nick Prado was leading an entourage to a place on the sidewalk just beyond the shadow of the overhang, and there he stopped to pose for photographs.

"Hey, Mallory!" Shorty Ross was the last one out the door. He rolled toward her in his wheelchair.

This reporter was strictly cophouse press—not here for publicity blurbs on the magic festival. Ross must smell blood.

"I hear you're back on the job, Mallory."

"Yeah, Shorty, that's today's rumor." As a twelve-year-old girl, she had first met him on a rainy day at Special Crimes. He had done a brief tour of midget duty as a favor to Inspector Markowitz, passing the hour by telling Kathy war stories of Vietnam. And then he had rolled up his pants in response to a child's rude curiosity about his missing limbs and the prostheses strapped on below his knees. The fake legs had

been interesting, though not entirely satisfying, not quite—
enough. But he had refused to remove his stump socks,
claiming that he never got naked on a first date.

"We can't find Franny Futura," said Shorty. "And somebody else checked the guy out of his hotel."

"Really? Mr. Prado might know where he is."

"You wouldn't hold out on me, would you, kid?"

Mallory smiled. They knew each other too well. Now she
waited on Shorty's habitual offer to play the whore and show
her his naked stumps in exchange for information.

The photographers abandoned Nick Prado to snap pictures
of the famous cop who did not actually shoot a giant
puppy—but what the hell. And now the reporters joined the
jam, and Shorty Ross's wheelchair was locked out of the
fray. Prado appeared by her side and draped one arm across
her shoulders. She spoke only with her eyes, explaining that
he should move his arm, and *right now,* or she would hurt
him.

The arm fell away.

"You don't mind posing for a few publicity shots, do
you?" Prado faced the cameras. "It's so hard to get people to
turn out for the older acts, anything low-tech. But sex sells."

Flashing strobes were in her eyes. Prado was smiling. Mallory was not. She leaned closer, so the reporters wouldn't
hear her. "Where's Franny Futura? Is he dead yet?"

He never stopped smiling, nor did he move his lips when
he said, "Have you looked under the bed in his hotel room?
That would be my guess."

The mob was pressing up against them, shouting questions
and aiming microphones like gun barrels. A woman in the
back yelled out in pain, and Mallory heard Shorty Ross saying, "Oh, I'm sorry. Was that your foot?" Other reporters near
the front of the crowd had already earned their wheelchair
scars, and now they stepped aside, allowing him to roll up to
Mallory's legs. "Detective, what do you know about the disappearance of Franny Futura?"

"No comment." She glanced at Prado—her turn to smile.
She could also speak without moving her lips. "Is this
another sleazy publicity stunt?"

"You recognized my style. I'm flattered."

"Maybe you frightened him, Prado." Her voice was louder now. "Maybe hiding out was Futura's idea."

Shorty had heard that. "The guy's in hiding?" And this set off another barrage of shouted questions.

Mallory leaned toward Prado, keeping her voice below the level of the noise. "Smart move. You knew I'd break him in five minutes."

Prado's smile lapsed for a moment. "You just have to nail somebody for that balloon shooting, don't you? Well, Franny was on the float, in plain view when the big puppy went down."

"But he had a good view of the rocky knoll."

The reporters had fallen silent. They were straining their eyes in the art of lipreading.

"*You* weren't there, Prado. No alibi for the time." Now she was speaking loud enough for all to hear, and Shorty Ross gave her a thumbs-up gesture of thanks.

"Richard Tree didn't fire that arrow at Futura," said Mallory—and that much was true. "Maybe it came from another bow." In peripheral vision, she could see pens and pencils writing down this lie verbatim. Other reporters held out tape recorders as she said, "And you don't have an alibi for the rifle shot either."

In a bid for Mallory's attention, Shorty Ross nudged her legs with his chair. Then he wheeled back quickly, knowing that she was not above swatting a legless war veteran. "Detective? Is there a new conspiracy angle here?"

Prado planted himself in front of the reporter's wheelchair. "Ladies and gentlemen—a few moments, please?" He drew Mallory back to the wall, saying, "This is great stuff, but I think you're making it too complex." The wave of his hand took in the whole crowd of reporters. "They need something short—headline material."

"Futura knows who killed Louisa, doesn't he?"

A woman had crept close to their conversation, and now she was thrusting her microphone in Mallory's face. "Louisa? Is that what you said? Is that *killed* as in *murdered?* You mean the dead woman in Malakhai's act?"

Prado bowed to Mallory. "Excellent. Your work is done." He walked on down the street, followed by the throng of cameramen and reporters.

Assuming Futura was still alive, he would stay that way for the rest of the day. The press corps would be on Prado's back for hours—almost as good as a police tail. If she only had a bigger share of the Special Crimes budget, she would not have to improvise this way.

"That *was* rather good," said a familiar voice behind her.

Malakhai was leaning against the frame of an open door. In the daylight, she could see a few strands of light brown, reminders of a time when his hair was the color of lions. His blue shirtsleeves were rolled back, and the khaki pants bore traces of a morning's work in the dusty knees.

"You handle the press better than Nick does." His dark blue eyes were smiling, drawing her closer. And for a moment, she felt inexplicably lighter, made of less solid stuff. She was casting about for something to say, when he dropped his cigarette and smashed it under his heel. "I don't mean to sound ungrateful, but my show is already sold out. I didn't need the boost." He rubbed the gooseflesh on his arms. "It's cold. Come inside."

She followed him into the building and up the stairs to a storage area, where chairs were racked against one wall. Beside a lighting panel of monitors and switches, two large drawing room doors stood open to an expanse of polished blond wood. A tall metal scaffolding dominated the stage. It had not been here the day she interviewed the stage manager. Cables hung down and trailed across the floorboards to the lighting panel.

"I thought you finished rigging your props."

"I've made a few changes."

Mallory followed him through the doors and onto the stage of white-paneled walls, columns and cornices trimmed in gold. She had never seen the main hall from this side of the footlights. Rows of empty red velvet seats stretched back across vast space. She looked up at the balconies stacked to the height of a seven-story building. Their four tiers were

fronted by bold curving lines. And at the top of the hall was a
halo of light with an outer ring of satellite stars.

On Saturday night, three thousand people would fill this
hall, and curiously, she felt their absence. The room was lit
for the show and awaiting its audience. There was tension in
the silent emptiness, like the moment before a dam burst, as
if the crowd were only held back by the lobby doors. This
void wanted to be filled.

Malakhai was halfway up the metal ladder at the back of
the scaffolding. "You don't mind if I work while we talk?
The lighting takes a lot of preparation."

She was looking at the top balcony near the ceiling. "How
will they see you from the cheap seats?"

"They're going to mount a giant screen on the wall to project the more intricate illusions. That's why the lighting is
critical. One mistake and the whole act is ruined. But I think
most of the audience is coming to hear *Louisa's Concerto*. I
never used the music to accompany the act. It was always the
other way around."

She followed him up the metal ladder to the top of the
scaffolding. "Did you hear the news about Futura?"

He stood before a board of switches and lights on a metal
folding stand. "You found him?"

"Not yet," she said. "He's hiding or dead."

Malakhai smiled at this. "Probably just another one of
Nick's publicity scams." He flipped a series of switches, and
the overhead light hit the back wall in bright circles of primary colors. "I'm sure he'll turn up again."

"He knows who killed Oliver, and so do you."

"So I'm not a suspect in Oliver's death anymore?"

"Well, I like to keep all my options open." She watched
him flip a switch on his extension lightboard. The houselights
dimmed. He flipped another switch, and she watched two
spotlights chase one another across the floor. "A programmed
routine?" She looked up to see the bank of lights hanging
from the top of the stage alcove. "I didn't know you were so
high-tech."

"I'm not. Fortunately, I can afford to hire people who are."

"You don't trust the lighting director?"

"It isn't a matter of trust."

"It's about control," said Mallory. "Like Max Candle and his fully automated platform."

"I was about to say that I only use the board for rehearsals. But I suppose I am a bit like Max. We were very close."

A shadow slipped along a back wall and disappeared through a side door. She turned on Malakhai. "How do you make the shadow?"

"I'll never tell. That's my gift to you, Mallory. At three o'clock some morning, you'll be lying awake, and it'll cross your mind that the shadow might've been Louisa."

"You don't believe in her any more than I do."

"Oh, but I do. Creating absolute faith is a magician's game—always has been." He pulled a black scarf from his pocket and held it up to her. Slowly, he lifted it to expose five floating cards. "And behold a miracle—a royal flush. Oh, I forgot." The cards fell to the floor, and he kicked them aside. "You've already seen that one, and you didn't like it."

Mallory stared at the rod of lights suspended above her head. He might be doing a projection with spotlights and silhouettes, but she could see no evidence of it. There were other racks of lights, at both ends of the third-tier balcony, but neither of them was lit. She looked down at the extension board. Perhaps the answer was here. A dedicated unbeliever, she hunted for Louisa's shadow in a bank of lights and switches.

Malakhai folded his arms and watched her for a moment. "When Picasso paid a visit, he always warned a man that he came to steal."

"Did you know Picasso?"

"No, and now you've ruined a perfectly good story. I'll have to tell you another one. How about the liberation of Paris?"

"I'd rather hear about the night Louisa died. You didn't stick around very long, so what happened to the body?"

"Emile took care of her. He was anxious to get me out of the city, and quickly. I was half crazy and dangerous to everyone. Louisa was buried in the St. John family plot."

Mallory looked up from the board. "So St. John had possession of the body—all the evidence of a murder. After the war, did he tell you how she really died? Or did he cover it up? The day of the parade—was he the man you wanted to shoot?"

"May I?" He motioned her to move aside, then resumed his work at the board. "You're getting ahead of the story. When we got to London, Max and I were split up. We didn't meet again until the liberation of Paris."

"The battalions converged on Paris the same day. I already know that."

"Then why don't you tell the rest of it, Mallory?" He hit a switch and a silver orb rose from the stage and floated toward her head. She was backing up to the edge of the scaffold when it veered upward and popped against the heat of a spotlight—only a balloon.

The houselights went dark, but for the tiny lamps that trimmed the balconies, stars in close formation.

"When the Allies liberated Paris, I left my unit to hunt for Max. I ran through the streets all day. The war was still going on all around me. The Commander of Paris had surrendered, but the occupation forces were still firing on us. And there was an absurd party in the streets. People were screaming for joy, and then dying from shells and bullets. Girls were kissing every man in a uniform. And a small crowd gathered to watch the duel of two tanks on the place de l'Opéra. I wish you could've seen it—a battle of dinosaurs."

The stage turned red. More switches added bursts of yellow light.

"All around us, the city was wired to explode. While the dynamite was being dismantled, we were all existing inside a giant bomb. People came out on the balconies with their children and waved little flags. Then they ran for cover when the bullets started flying. The whole day was like that—an emotional slingshot.

"I looked for Max's face on every troop truck, every marching column. Finally I went to Faustine's to wait for him there. If he was still alive, I knew he'd come. The theater was boarded up. I waited by the door until dark."

The color of the walls changed to indigo, and tiny stars of silver confetti fell from the bank of dark lights in the false sky.

"I came back to Faustine's the next day and the next. I remember crying when I realized that my best friend must be dead."

"He forgot you."

Malakhai only looked at her to say, *Whose story is this?* "I went on a—the Germans would call it the *Wanderjahre*. A time of wandering." He worked over his board. And now the walls were bathed in a purple glow. "When I came back to Faustine's again, the theater was empty. A rich American had bought out the entire stock."

"Max Candle."

"Yes. When we met in New York, he told me he was waiting at the theater while I was searching for him in the streets. Emile also showed up for that reunion. He found Max banging on the padlocked door, shouting my name over and over. Emile used his police sources to get a list of casualties for my unit, and my name was at the top. I was reported dead quite a few times."

Mallory turned to the sound of running footsteps on the stage below. The stage was empty, but the feet ran round and round the platform, faster and faster. *A recording?* Was the lighting board a soundboard too? The amplifiers must be set into the base of the scaffold.

The footsteps ended.

"Max had saved Louisa's music," said Malakhai. "He had the presence of mind to hide the manuscript before we left Paris. That's why he bought up all the stock from the theater. There were so many old trunks, he had to be sure they'd ship the right one. We used his family connections to get the concerto published. That was my stake for a magic act and a new life."

"When you went to Korea, was that another tour of mass murder? Or just an interesting form of suicide?"

"I never killed anyone in that war. I was captured a few weeks after I enlisted."

Mallory nodded. This agreed with his war record. She had

yet to catch him in a lie. "So you came back from Korea and put your dead wife in the act. You didn't want to die anymore?"

At the edge of the stage, gray scarves were whirling, barely detectable against the shadowed theater except where the silk threw back the light. A spotlight came on and the scarves changed to blue in the illusion of a whirling dress.

"And now?" Mallory looked at him, refusing to be distracted anymore. "How do you feel about dying now?"

The spotlight died, and the scarves fell to the floor in a heap of crushed silk as he turned his face to hers. "You think I'm baiting one of them to kill me? An elaborate suicide?"

"Why not? I know what's waiting for you. You're losing your brains a bit at a time. But sticking a gun in your mouth never was your style. You went into two wars looking for a more interesting way out."

"You'd make a terrible magician. Your logic is too complex. The solution is always going to be something simple."

"Revenge is pretty simple," said Mallory. "You always knew which one of them killed Louisa. It was the man covered with her blood. You were fifty years late, but that's the simple solution you were going for when you fired on the parade float. Or were you aiming at someone nearby? Nick Prado?"

"Do you still think I put that body in Oliver's platform? The red hair you pocketed at the restaurant—"

"It came from a wig—very good quality, but not human." She looked around at the mass of props on the stage. "Charles says you don't use a wig in the act. So what do you do with it—besides fooling waiters? Do you leave hairs around the hotel room for the maids to find?"

He seemed to understand the look in her eyes. She was asking, *How crazy are you?*

"Well, at least I'm off the hook for Oliver's nephew. That's promising."

"No," said Mallory. "You might have planted the body if you wanted to rattle someone. Futura's an easy target for something like that."

"Hysteria *is* my best trick. You just can't admit that Oliver bungled the illusion, that everything has a logical explanation."

"You stayed friends with Max Candle until he died. Where's the logic in that? The bastard was going to run off with your wife. And you still carry that dead woman around with you. After what she did—"

The scarves were rising off the floor, and moving toward her in a swirling storm of silk.

"Louisa didn't have to confess the affair." The scarves stopped their forward movement and hung limp in the dead air. "In a normal world, she would've kept the secret. You don't understand, do you? She had to tell me. Louisa couldn't allow me to risk my life that night—not after what they'd—"

"That must have killed you. Max was your best friend."

"I owed everything to Max. He saved my life. And he saved Louisa's music." Malakhai looked past her to the houselights rising all over the theater. "The stage lighting is always difficult."

"Hard to hide the wires?"

"More to it than that. I have to make the audience believe in Louisa. I spare them the details of death, except for the blood on her dress. The concerto does all the real work." He looked down at his electronic board. "This machine also plays music. I only use it for staging. Tomorrow I rehearse with a live orchestra."

He touched a key at the top of the panel and the concerto poured out of speakers on both sides of the stage. "I told you my wife was in the concerto. Hear the beat in the bass notes? It's very subtle. It takes an oboe, a soft drum stroke and a cello to make a believable human heartbeat." His hands moved over the switches, masking every other instrument until all that remained was the rhythm of a beating heart, a mighty muscle contracting and pumping blood.

"There she is—Louisa." And now he turned a knob to amplify the sound. "There's a strange lull in the concerto, and the audience finds it disquieting. They want to fill the emptiness with something. It drags out to an exquisite pain of anticipation, and all you can hear is the heartbeat." He turned down the volume. "So low, it's almost subliminal."

He waved an arm, and a thin stream of pale blue feathers poured from his hand and moved into the audience, dispersing in a cloud that gently settled to the velvet chairs. "And then I send her out into the crowd. Now, Mallory. Do you feel the air moving in Louisa's wake? Can you smell the gardenias?"

Mallory nodded, listening to a woman's beating heart. The breeze was almost imperceptible; she felt it in the rise of downy hairs on the back of her neck. The scent of a flower was faint and sweet.

Malakhai leaned close to her face. "But I never use perfume in the act."

The odor instantly changed its character to the spice scent of his aftershave lotion—another cheap trick.

His eyes were laughing at her. "And that slight movement of air as she passed you? All in your mind, Mallory. No wires. The sensation is strongest in a full theater. It's like orchestrating mass hysteria. As I said, I'm good at that."

A black silhouette was looming on the wall. It disappeared when he cut off the heartbeat.

"Is that what you did to Futura? Did you scare him with shadows? Did you make him hysterical?"

"Are you sure the shadows are even there, Mallory? Can you believe any of your senses? What is truth?"

Unbalancing people was her job, not his. "When Louisa told you the truth, it ate you alive."

"Yes, you're right about that. I can never forget the pictures in my brain—my wife in bed with another man."

"And then you shot her. An interesting way to solve the fidelity problem."

Not rising to the bait, he moved to the center of the small elevated stage and turned to look out over the empty theater. The overhead lights washed away the fine lines of his flesh. They made his eyes a more brilliant blue and turned his mane of hair to gold.

"Even after her death, I was never sure of Louisa—not

while Max was still alive." He was speaking to the vacant rows of velvet chairs, darkest red toward the shadow end of the great hall.

"Whenever I played New York, he came to every single performance. Max always entered the theater late, after the houselights had gone down. He'd take a seat in the back rows, as far from me and the stage as he could get." Malakhai stepped to the edge of the scaffold and hovered there in accidental elegance, eyes distant and bright. "It wasn't me he came to see. Max only wanted to be near Louisa—secretly, covertly. And each time I sent my dead wife into the audience, I always wondered if she met him out there in the dark."

✛   ✛   ✛

The maître d' hovered at a discreet distance, subtly suggesting that it was closing time.

The only patron, Emile St. John, sat in a far corner of the hotel dining room, though wealth should have gotten him a better table. Mallory decided that he didn't care to be the center of attention, preferring this exile on the sidelines of restaurant traffic and real life.

She shared the sensibility.

The white tablecloth was laid with good silver and crystal. A waiter was removing the remnants of a meal for one.

And dining alone was also a similar trait.

As Mallory walked toward him, St. John smiled and lifted his wineglass in greeting. He said a few words to the waiter, who left his tray behind to hurry off toward the kitchen.

St. John rose from the table to hold out her chair. "What a lovely surprise. What can I do for you, Mallory?"

"Oh, just a few questions." She sat down at the table, and a clean glass appeared in front of her. The waiter collected his tray, and when he was out of earshot, she said, "Seems like everyone was in love with Louisa. Max Candle and Malakhai—even Oliver."

"Yes, Oliver was devoted to her." He poured out a glass of

red wine for Mallory. "When music paper was impossible to get, he spent hours ruling lines on wrapping paper and the backs of posters, making all the bars for her notes. She was endlessly rewriting the concerto. You know, if she'd been born in another era, I don't think she could've done it. I don't mean to take anything away from her genius, but the concerto was such an ambitious piece. And she was so driven to complete her single opus. Sometimes I wonder if Louisa knew she would die so young."

Mallory had resisted the urge to cut him short, but enough was enough. "And Futura? Did he have a thing for Malakhai's wife?"

St. John shook his head. "Franny had no chance with her. I'm sure he realized that from the day they met. Louisa was a man's woman, if you understand that term."

"She pegged Franny for a wimp."

"Succinct. I like it."

"And what about you?"

"I had my work to obsess about. Ah, but I forgot. You have such a dim view of the French Resistance. How did you put it? Toss the bombs and run away before they hit the ground. The whole city was full of paranoia, and—"

"And spies. I went to school. I know what happened to people when they got caught. What about you and Nick? How did you feel about Louisa?" And now she fell silent again, resolving not to finish his sentences anymore. She had learned a lot from Rabbi Kaplan. Like the rabbi's friend, Mr. Halpern, Emile St. John was more open in the role of storyteller.

"We were all close friends," he said. "We'd gone hungry together, stolen food together. Louisa and Nick used to bicycle into the countryside to raid the crop fields."

"But you weren't in love with her? Either of you?"

He smiled and waved one hand, as if to ask how he should put this. "My mother would've said that Nick and I were musical."

"You're both gay?" This did not square with Prado's credit report listing alimony payments to four ex-wives.

"Well, I should only speak for myself. I'm a homosexual. Nick was merely a slut. And he'd tell you that himself. He's quite proud of it. In those days, he'd go home with anybody. Girls, boys—he didn't care. During the occupation, he never had a relationship that lasted more than a night. Nick couldn't even commit to one gender. Oh, you should've seen him when he was young—a beautiful boy."

"And he still sees himself that way."

"You must take him for a fool, a second-rate flirt, who can't see how ridiculous he is to a girl your age."

She nodded.

"But when he was young, Nick was an uncommon seducer, the best there ever was. He had a Spanish accent in those days, and his hair was coal black. Even his eyes were darker then, and he used them to strip women naked in public. They *loved* it. I know Faustine did. Nick was her favorite boy. He learned a lot of tricks in that old woman's bed. He could seduce anyone, even men who weren't bent that way. If you talked to him for six minutes, or if he only lit your cigarette, you'd be left with the impression that you'd just had sex with him."

"Did he ever take a German soldier to bed?"

"He might have. He got a thrill from risks like that. But what if he did? Nick had no politics, and decadence was his only ideal. He spent every night in a different bed. Sometimes it was simple practicality to save him the cost of breakfast. And his room in back of the print shop didn't have a bathtub—there was that to consider."

"I've seen Nick's forgery—nice work. Suppose the Germans found out about that little sideline of his—assisting political refugees over the border?"

"You think prison worried him? Promiscuity would've gotten him into a worse fix. Even the Germans who waffled between genders were exterminated. Remember, we drank with soldiers every night. We heard the stories about the traveling gas vans. But Nick was fearless—just an enterprising, apolitical teenager with a phenomenal libido."

"You don't think much of his character."

"Nick is what he is—the greatest, most versatile whore that ever lived. A gigolo king and the queen of queens. He was born to run a public relations firm. There's nothing he won't do for publicity."

"You don't like him much, do you?"

This startled him, and suddenly Mallory realized that she had misunderstood everything.

"I love Nick. He's unscrupulous, but I'm his friend until he dies." St. John turned away to flag down the waiter for a check, and he missed the surprised look on her face. But then, it was the same expression she used for peeling onions and loading her gun.

He signed the bill with his room number, and the waiter left them again. "I'm afraid Nick's character will never improve. He still flirts with everything that moves. Male, female, it doesn't matter. Breathing is Nick's only known criterion."

"Did you ever sleep with a German soldier? You claim you were in the Resistance. But lots of people said that—after the Germans left town. Maybe you were a collaborator?" He would never see her next line coming.

"No, Mallory, on both counts. Never slept with Nick either, though I was tempted. During the occupation, I was something of a monk. I still am."

"I know you were an executioner on a Maquis firing squad." She had surprised him that time. Smoke drifted from his open mouth. He had forgotten to exhale.

"That doesn't fit well with monk's robes." She set her wineglass to one side. The socializing was done, the underbelly was laid open for her, and now—down to business. "My college history professor lived in France during the occupation. He said it was a bloodbath right after the liberation. So tell me—how many people did you kill for the Maquis?"

She had touched on something old, but painful still.

"Did Charles tell you that? Yes, it had to be him. Odd that he would remember that old conversation. He was only six or seven years old. I could've sworn he was asleep. Max and I had taken him to a magic show and a late supper. Charles was curled up on the rug by the fire, completely exhausted. Max indulged the child when his parents were out of town. No vegetables and no fixed bedtime. The boy just fell asleep wherever he dropped, and then Max would put him to bed."

No side trips, St. John. Back to the war. "So you told Max about the firing squad."

"I had to talk to someone. I was going through a difficult time—a period of adjustment after the war. It lasted for many years. I was still struggling with it that night. I knew Max would understand. He'd killed in the war. But the people I—" He toyed with his glass for a moment. "Those people were helpless when I shot them, tied up to posts and blinded with pieces of cloth. The squad didn't observe the tradition of one gun with blanks. All the bullets from every man's rifle went into human flesh. There was no chance for self-deception, for the possibility of clean hands."

"Thousands were arrested—a few hundred survived to stand trial."

"Yes, it was like that in the first few months. My compliments to your teacher. The mobs killed a great many people for real and imagined crimes. But this Maquisard unit was executing convicted war criminals—French citizens so eager to please their masters, they went the Germans one better. Their crimes had such zeal and cruelty. Two of them had gouged out the eyes of a living woman and filled the sockets with cockroaches. Getting caught by the Germans wasn't the worst thing that could happen to you in occupied France."

"The trials were drum-barrel justice."

"A military term. That's from the American Civil War, isn't it? A drum overturned on the battleground, an instant court and a swift execution. Yes, right again. I think an abattoir, a bloody assembly line would be a better analogy for the early trials. After the liberation, it seemed that every man and woman in France was part of the Resistance movement. Or so they all claimed—the accused and their accusers. I always suspected the ones who wanted the most blood, the loudest witnesses in court. I have no idea how many innocents were shot by the firing squads." He pushed his chair back from the table. "Since then, I've led a celibate existence, doing penance."

"A monk and an executioner." She raised her open hands, as if she were weighing these words, one against the other.

"You don't think I took any pleasure in those executions?"

She nodded slowly. That was exactly what she thought. "You had to volunteer for a job like that."

"I did volunteer." He puffed on his cigar, comfortable in the knowledge that the waiter would not bother him with regulations about smoking in public—the privilege of money and lavish tips. He exhaled and watched the gray plume twining upward. His eyes searched the smoke. "All around me there were men with too much relish for that kind of work. I believed killing should always be done with deep regret. And so, regretfully, I picked up my rifle and shot helpless humans with their hands tied behind their backs."

He bowed his head to examine the dregs of his wine, a small pool of red at the bottom of the glass. When he spoke again, his voice was too calm. There was no rise and fall of inflection, no emotion at all.

"The best method is a pistol, close to the head. But we were very young gunmen. So inexperienced at efficient killing. We used rifles, and we stood some distance away from—the targets. In an error of compassion, we avoided the head shots that would have given them a quick death. The bullets we fired into their breasts ruptured their hearts and lungs. Done wrong, it's a death of internal hemorrhaging—not an instant kill, as you might suppose. I've made a great study of this over the years."

He looked up from his glass, and she wished that he had not. Later, she would remember his eyes as somehow broken, full of sorrow and so at odds with this dry recital of facts.

"Each round creates a cavity a hundred times larger than the bullet. You see, the heat of impact boils away the blood and the fat of the tissue." His hands clenched tightly, knuckles whitening. "So every bullet acts like a fist reaching into the body, rupturing skin, shattering bones. I was close enough to see the people trembling as they were tied up to the posts. With the first round, they dropped quickly, sliding down the poles, dragging the ropes of their bound hands. But they were still *alive*. I kept punching bullets into their bodies until they stopped screaming to God, so crazy with fear and pain. Until they finally *stopped* moving, and the insanity—stopped."

Eighteen

JUDGING ONLY BY THE WILDLIFE OF COCKROACHES IN THE SINK and pink-flamingo statuary cavorting on dead grass outside his window, Franny Futura had never imagined that squalor could be quite this tacky. He wept for the chipped furniture and the noise the plumbing made when residents on either side of his motel room used the toilet. Years ago, the cracked and dirty walls must have been painted a brighter hue; now they were the color of an aged salmon dying of natural causes.

Franny walked to the only window and looked through a hole in the curtains. He counted the flamingos. One pink plaster bird might have been considered kitsch, an interesting statement. But this flock of four was a deliberate and frightening attempt at decor.

So this was New Jersey.

Nick had told him not to leave the room, but the telephone by the bed had no dial tone. He stared at the public booth on the other side of the parking lot, an upended glass coffin exposed to the traffic of a busy highway—a million pairs of eyes a minute.

It was dangerous to leave the room, or so Nick had said. Franny believed it, for he was always willing to be frightened at the least provocation. He had read somewhere that fear was a genetic thing, that some people were wired from birth to be less brave than others—not his fault.

But he was not a complete coward. In recent years, all

civility had ended, and he had been heckled, hissed and booed by the crowds. There had been times when he feared they would rush the stage and pull him down. Yet he had always remained to finish his act, hands trembling and tears passing for flopsweat. And now he had traveled for thousands of miles, for years and years—for what?

If he could only get through to Emile St. John, everything would be all right. Emile would come to fetch him in a stretch limousine, and they would travel back to New York City, drinking good scotch from the limo bar and smoking Cuban cigars. Rehearsals could resume this afternoon.

He put one hand on the doorknob, then drew back, as if the metal had been hot to the touch. What was the worst thing that could happen to him? What was worse than the terror of anticipation? Well, Nick would be angry. And there was all that highway traffic—all those eyes on him.

Franny stood in front of the door, hands at his sides. Once, long ago, he had done a brave thing. Surely he could walk that stretch of parking lot to the phone booth.

He heard a metallic creak, footsteps stopping outside his door. A knock on the wood and then another. A key was working in the lock. The knob was turning. Franny was backing away, slow-stepping, falling, crawling to the wall.

When the door opened, a large woman in a uniform walked in, her arms full of fresh linens and towels. She gaped at Franny, perhaps surprised to see him huddled on the floor, hands covering his face—crying softly.

✢   ✢   ✢

The building was surrounded by all the traffic noises of the busy midtown theater district, but not even the siren of a fire engine could permeate these walls. Soundproofing had been an important consideration in his selection of performance space. The gallows illusion would be ruined if the audience was distracted from the ticking of gears, the creaks of wood and the cries of the hanged man.

Emile St. John checked the apparatus one last time. Every rehearsal had gone smoothly. Oliver had gotten this one right.

He glanced at his wristwatch as he slipped on the hand-cuffs. His assistant was due back in a few minutes. He had hired the young man for the trait of compulsive punctuality.

Timing was everything.

Thirteen steps above him, the stage of the gallows was very small, only room enough to hang a man. The narrow platform had a ramshackle look about it, crooked lines and rough board that concealed an iron framework. Its appearance was tenuous, as though a child had slapped it together with a handful of rusty nails. Visually, the structure threatened to fall apart at the first breeze created by applause.

He walked up the steps, just as Max Candle had done so many times. His foot was heavier on the last step, so it would crack and break at the hinge. And now he stretched his leg to step up on the tiny elevated stage. Emile shifted his weight, and the entire structure wobbled with precisely six inches of tilt in the superbly engineered framework. Standing beneath the noose, he watched as the line began to lower, pro-grammed by clockwork gears to cast its deadly falling shadow on the curtain behind him. When it was level with his head, the line moved back. So far the mechanism was work-ing smoothly. Oliver had done a wonderful job calibrating the noose by Emile's own height and mass. The metal arm of the hydraulic lift locked on the metal vest beneath his suit.

He slipped the cuff key in the lock. The rope began to pull and tighten; the noose was constricting under his chin, pulling, straining.

And now he heard the sound of splitting wood beneath his feet. His hands were still locked in the manacles. When the structure fell out beneath him, he did not float. He did not fol-low the well-rehearsed routine of removing the noose and descending by invisible steps to the stage below.

He dropped like a stone, a dead weight, and his still body turned slowly, twisting round and round at the end of the rope.

✛   ✛   ✛

When Franny had fumbled the correct number of coins into the public telephone and finally connected with the theater, a young Frenchman's voice answered the phone. It might have been Emile half a century ago.

"Oh, yes, Mr. Futura. I'm his assistant. I'll fetch him right away."

Franny listened to the sound of feet walking away from the telephone. And next he heard the young man's screams.

Apparently, Nick had been right. Emile couldn't help him anymore. Franny hung up the phone. The late-afternoon sun slanted across his contorted face wet with tears.

✛   ✛   ✛

Outside the door of the lockup, NYPD was humming with new cases. Mallory sat at a square table scarred with water marks from soda cans and the carved initials of bored felons and cops. She was the orphan of the Special Crimes budget. Slope's release of Richard Tree's autopsy had killed every hope for additional manpower, and Heller was not available for any more tests or television shows. Her anger was exacerbated by the grinning man who stood between two uniformed officers.

"Prado, if I prove you put that arrow in the body, you'll be prosecuted for mutilating a corpse—not great publicity for the festival. And then there's your public relations firm. All those wealthy clients might decide to take a walk."

"Ridiculous," said Prado. "*All* publicity is good. Do you mind if I start that rumor myself?" He nodded toward the second-floor window overlooking the SoHo street. Reporters were milling on the sidewalk below, creating a litter of coffee cups and sandwich wrappers. Others were behind the fast-food truck, waiting in ambush. "I'll give you a credit line if you like."

Behind her, a moan came from the junkie on the floor of the wire cage.

"Hey, knock it off." Officer Hong brought his truncheon down hard on the wood frame, but failed to get the prisoner's attention. "I think this guy's gonna throw up again."

Mallory looked over one shoulder and caught the eye of

the boy huddled on the floor behind the wire. He was small and skinny and sick.

"Don't piss me off," she said.

The junkie slumped against the wall and lowered his head to his chest.

She turned back to Prado. "I need your movements for Thanksgiving Day. Oliver's nephew was still wearing a tux when I found the body in the platform. So I figure he died a few hours after the parade."

"Franny went to the police station with Richard." Prado slung his coat on the table. Uninvited, he pulled up a chair and sat down. "He told the detectives how he rigged the crossbow stunt, and then they let the boy go. I wasn't even there."

"I know that," said Mallory. "Futura left the station and went directly to Charles's house. But you arrived an hour late. Your movements can't be traced during the parade either. I've been over every camera shot. You're not on any of the film."

"I went to a deli on Columbus Avenue to get coffee. It was a cold day, and the float wasn't due to move for another thirty minutes. It's all in my statement."

"But you never came back with any coffee. And I checked that deli. They don't remember any magicians, no silk hats, no tuxedos."

"They wouldn't remember a Martian. The place was packed and the line for coffee was a very long one. After a while, I decided to pack it in. I went back empty-handed."

"And then what happened? Where were you when the balloon got shot? Were you on the rocks with a rifle?"

"Now there's another good rumor. Wait till the world finds out that I'm willing to shoot puppies and mutilate corpses for my clients. You can't buy publicity like that."

"Help me put you in the clear. Just tell me—"

"You're not paying attention, Mallory. I don't want to get clear of the charges. Now, can I tell the reporters what I'm accused of? Maybe we could both put in a little appearance on the sidewalk. Me in handcuffs—your prisoner."

"I haven't charged you with a crime—not yet."

"What do I have to do to get arrested in this town?" He looked at the uniformed officers, then turned back to Mallory. "And why send strange cops to arrest me? In my fantasy, *you* put the handcuffs on me."

Mallory turned to the two officers in uniform. "You cuffed him?"

"No, we didn't," said Pete Hong. "We told him he wasn't under arrest. It was more like an invitation to come downtown. He offered us a hundred bucks apiece to put handcuffs on him in front of a reporter. I said that was a bribe. And then Mr. Prado said it was a performance fee. I still don't know how to write it up."

"Up to you, Mallory." Hong's partner was staring at the clock, waiting for the hour hand to mark the end of his shift. "Sergeant Bell said it was your call."

Mallory nodded. "Sounds like a bribe to me."

Prado put out his hands. "So *now* you'll cuff me?"

"No," said Mallory. "We never do that if we think the perp might enjoy it."

She stood up and walked over to the wire cage. The sole occupant was a boy wearing blue jeans and vomit on the front of his T-shirt. He was awake again and shivering, huddled on the floor and mumbling foreign things. Mallory could not even identify the language, and still she knew the boy was over the edge and rambling. His skin was slick with sweat, and the long dark hair was matted. Weak and suffering from stomach cramps and nausea, he was in some other world, hardly aware of her anymore.

"Let's see—a bribe or not a bribe." Mallory turned back to the two uniforms. "I suppose we could put Mr. Prado in the cage while we get an opinion from the DA's office. That might take a while."

Prado left his chair and moved closer to the cage for a better look at the small, slight boy on the floor. "So you think your little friend and I might fall in love while I'm waiting?"

"He doesn't want your body. He wants a needle." Mallory looked down at the wasted prisoner with the rolled-back eyes. A thirteen-year-old girl could beat him up in a fair fight. "But he might take a shot at you if you irritate him." She looked at Prado and shook her head. "No, old man, you wouldn't last two seconds with a sick junkie."

Prado was so startled, Mallory half expected him to check his testicles to make sure that she had not snipped them off.

She was getting to that.

After kicking a chair out from the table, she waved him to it. "Have a seat, Prado."

"I think I'll stand." His voice was firm.

Mallory turned to the uniforms. "Sit Mr. Prado down."

They were moving toward him when he decided to take a seat at the table. His movements were stiff.

Mallory nodded to the officers. "You can go now. Oh, wait." She turned back to the boy in the cage. "You're sure he doesn't speak English?"

"Yeah, I'm sure," said Hong, and his partner added, "But the perp's still got eyes, Mallory."

It would be hard to miss the implication that she should not brutalize her suspect in front of a witness—a second opinion on Prado's declining manhood. She watched the man's hands clench into fists.

Now what could she do to make his head explode?

"If I'm not under arrest, I don't have to talk to you."

"You got that backward, Prado. When we arrest you, you'll have the right to remain silent. But right now? You answer questions or I nail you for obstructing a homicide investigation."

"You can't prove Oliver was—"

"Oh, yes I can. It was hardly a perfect murder. But I have so many homicides to choose from. Louisa's—that one's provable, too. And what about Franny Futura? Should I put him on the list of dead bodies? What did you do with him, Prado?"

He held up a cigar. "May I? Oh, wait, there are laws against smoking in public buildings." Prado rose from the chair and collected his coat. "I'll just step outside."

He was moving toward the door when Mallory threw up the window sash. "You can smoke on the fire escape."

She grabbed his arm and swung him back. He was off balance and moving toward the window with the force of inertia and very little effort by Mallory. Prado lost his footing, and his head was thrust out the open window. His hands froze in a death grip on the sill. His mouth hung open, and then he began to shake. One hand went to his chest, and he was fighting for breath.

His heart? No, this was something miles more interesting. In only three seconds, the man had progressed from surprise to a full-blown panic attack. When he moved away from the window on shaky legs, his distress lessened, but Mallory blocked any further retreat.

"Don't be afraid," she said, with too much sincerity to be believed. She pointed down to the street below. His eyes followed this gesture with equal parts of fascination and fear.

"Look, Prado. You can see right through the grate. With all those reporters down there, what are the odds I'm going to push you off?"

If he kept biting into his lower lip, he was going to draw blood.

Perhaps it was something on the sidewalk that frightened him. Mallory leaned out the window and looked down through the grate as Shorty Ross's wheelchair zoomed out the front door of the station house. All the reporters were stampeding one another, hailing taxis and climbing into vans and private cars. Others were pouring into the subway.

A uniformed officer opened the door of the lockup. "Hey, Mallory. That guy you wanted us to pick up—St. John? He hung himself."

✛   ✛   ✛

Charles Butler carried a bouquet of flowers down the corridor and walked into a heated conversation between Mallory and a very large nurse.

A few steps beyond these two, a uniformed policeman stood with Malakhai. Behind them, a door opened and Nick Prado stepped out, looked around at the assembled company, then turned on his heel and sped down the hall toward an exit sign.

Nick had good instincts. Charles wondered if he should pay his respects to Emile St. John some other time.

The woman in the white uniform was yelling at Mallory, "What the hell do I care what you want? Mr. St. John is *not* a crime victim. You got that? It was an *accident.*"

Not Mallory's favorite words these days. "I have a problem with that." She pulled out her badge. "So few people accidentally hang themselves."

The nurse never even glanced at the gold shield. "Mr. St. John says it was a mistake in a magic trick. That's his story, and his assistant backs him up. Now if he wants to see Mr. Prado, or Mr. Malakhai, or anybody else, it's fine with me. But not you. He was real specific about that."

Charles watched Mallory regroup with a tactic short of gunning down the nurse. She pulled a notebook from her pocket, only *showing* the woman a glimpse of the holstered weapon. Her eyes and tone of voice went farther, to tell the nurse how badly she really wanted to draw blood. "I need a statement from—"

"The *hell* you do!" The nurse pointed to the officer standing by the door of the hospital room. "And that guard has no business here. He's gotta go."

Malakhai leaned against the wall of the corridor, enjoying this exchange. He nodded a greeting to Charles, and then turned back to the defeated Mallory. "So you think Emile will have another accident while I'm visiting? Maybe Nick's already done him in. Shouldn't we check?"

Charles perceived a volatile atmosphere between Malakhai and Mallory. If not for the extreme difference in their ages, he might have called it a sexual tension. All the signs were there in a subtle dance. Mallory stepped forward, as if she meant to touch him, and Malakhai bent down to her—in anticipation of what? A caress?

Not likely.

Charles thought she was going to strike the man. At least she had this in her mind, even as she backed away. She was drawn to Malakhai, repulsed by him, angry and fixated, all the symptoms to sister psychoses of love and hate.

The nurse held the door open and spoke to Malakhai. "You just go on inside, and I'll take care of the guard." And now she cast an evil eye on the uniformed officer stationed by the door. When the door had closed behind the magician, Mallory drew Charles down the hall and away from the nurse, who held an uneasy guard duty standing toe to toe with a policeman.

"Let's say a man is afraid of heights," said Mallory. "What are the odds he'd live in a penthouse?"

"And of course, it's just a coincidence that Nick Prado lives in a penthouse."

"Charles, I'm not asking you to turn on a friend. I'm trying to eliminate suspects, too. A fear of heights might explain why he wasn't on that parade float when the gun went off. Now, is he afraid of heights?"

"I have no idea."

"Charles, think back. Futura said Prado wouldn't get up on the float—like he refused. Prado was wearing a tux that morning. He was supposed to be part of the act, right? But did he ever get up on the top hat float?"

"Well, no, but I assumed he was explaining the crossbow stunt to the cops who arrested Oliver's nephew."

"No, Futura did that. It took ten minutes. So Prado was never on that float?"

"Well, no, but that doesn't imply—"

"Could he live in a penthouse if he was afraid of heights?"

"Yes, he could even fly an airplane. As long as he's in an enclosed space, there's no problem. You see, it's the only phobia that carries a fear of physical injury. He'd have to be near the edge of a precipice, or maybe standing on a ladder. But if there's a protective barrier, like window glass—there wouldn't be any anxiety."

"The crown of the top hat float was what? Maybe ten feet high? There's no way he'd ever get up there, right?"

"Right. *If* he was afraid of heights, you wouldn't catch him on a stepladder. But there's no way to verify it."

She looked at him with such grave suspicion. Did she think he was lying? Probably. But he knew this was nothing personal. It was almost flattering that she believed he *could* lie.

"Mallory, you could know someone all your life and never be aware of a phobic disorder. People with phobias always avoid every situation where it might be a problem. So what are the odds you'd ever witness a panic attack?" And an egoist like Nick would never admit to a weakness.

Down the hall, the door to Emile St. John's room was closing. Malakhai walked toward them with an easy smile and a leisurely strolling gait—both good signs that Emile's condition was not at all serious.

"Sorry," said Malakhai. "He can't have any more visitors. It was a rather nasty accident."

"Yeah, right." Mallory had undoubtedly been making the same assessments of his body language, and she had come up with a lie.

Malakhai smiled at her. His face said, *I have a present for you, and you're going to hate it.* "Something went wrong with the illusion, but it's easily correctable. Emile asked Nick to step in and do the act." He leaned close to Mallory and whispered, "Looks like Oliver bungled the plans for another trick."

Charles had one confusing moment when he could not tell if these two were going to kill one another or embrace.

✛   ✛   ✛

Mallory walked into the den and sat down at her desk to write the goodbye letter. Three generations of cops in the Markowitz family had done this before her.

But who would she address it to?

Charles? No, he was a secondhand friend, passed down from her late foster father. And when it came to choosing sides, he might not pick hers. She had gone to great lengths to prevent him from failing this test.

Riker? Or one of Markowitz's old poker cronies? No. Like the pocket watch, they were also hand-me-downs from the old man, the one they really loved.

Mallory looked down at the white paper and overlaid it with images of Sacred Heart Academy. Helen Markowitz had enrolled her foster child with the nuns upon discovering that young Kathy had begun life as a Catholic. This experiment had ended badly. The little girl had proved a natural athlete and a true competitor, yet her classmates did not want her on their teams. She saw them again on the playground, edging away, eyes full of suspicion, sensing that there was something wrong with Kathy Mallory.

The business of choosing up sides had been so important to her then. And now? Well, now that the Markowitzes were dead, she had learned not to care about standing alone.

Yeah, right.

In any case, she *was* alone.

Mallory stared at the blank sheet. So what was the point of this?

The old pocket watch sat at the corner of the desk. Inside the cover, beneath the engravings for the old man and his forefathers, all believers in tradition, her own name was the last line of script.

In the manner of a schoolgirl dutifully attending to a homework assignment, Mallory bowed her head over the paper and wrote, "To all of those whom it may concern." She tore up this sheet and began again, less formal and more realistic in her expectations. "To anyone who cares—"

And that was as far as she got. The light was failing, but she did not turn on the desk lamp.

Louisa's letter had been dated to the day she died, and the writing had obviously consumed all the time she had left. It was a beautiful goodbye, a woman's naked soul rendered on paper. But no one would expect such a letter from Mallory the Machine.

Once more, she labored over the opening salutation. If this was to have any meaning at all, her goodbye must belong to one person. Her foster mother would have called it an act of love to lessen the tears of those who were left behind.

Mallory's pen hung in the air. Her head tilted to one side.

In the absence of love and without any expectation of tears, what was the point of this?

✛   ✛   ✛

Franny Futura woke up with a start, hands batting at the narrow enclosure of glass on all sides—the coffin. And the footlights were moving, traveling across the stage at incredible speeds.

No, he was not on stage. He had never made it back to New York City. Squinting through the grimy glass, he could make out the familiar tableau of four prancing pink flamingos.

So he was still inside the public telephone booth by the highway, and now he was fully awake and full of dread. When he stood up, his knees buckled, and there were searing pains in all his joints and muscles. He slumped against a transparent wall, pressing his forehead to the glass.

When had he ever been so hungry and tired—so cold? What was he to do? The motel room was just across the parking lot. Franny's eyes never left the door as he winced at fresh pain from an Achilles tendon. The door was a hundred miles away for one who lacked the good legs to carry himself across that dark patch of ground.

A pair of headlights entered the lot. The car was aiming straight at him, rushing toward the telephone booth and blinding him with brilliant light magnified in reflections on four walls of glass. Two thousand pounds of steel and chrome stopped just short of the booth, with a squeal of brakes and tires spitting gravel.

Which one of them was playing with him now—torturing him? This was too cruel. Was it Nick Prado or Mallory?

Nineteen

ON THIS DARK MORNING, LIGHTNING SPLIT THE SKY OVER THE
treeline of Central Park. The stone steps of the fountain were
wet with mist, and Mallory's hair was netted with fine pearls
of water. Across the wide driveway that separated the hotel
from its courtyard, a high wind rustled the multinational flags
that decorated the landmark facade.

She could not have orchestrated nature any better.

Another gift to the cause was a crowd of animal-rights
activists ganging along the sidewalks. A small army of angry
people held up giant photographs of wounded animals. Others waved signs defaming a hotel guest, a film star who wore
furs in public.

A bellboy was loading suitcases into the trunk of a long
black limousine. When the chauffeur walked to the rear of
the car to settle the tip, Mallory sprinted out from the cover
of the fountain and pushed her way through the crowd on the
sidewalk. She opened the driver's door and slid in behind the
steering wheel. On the other side of the glass partition, Emile
St. John was the lone passenger in the backseat. Mallory
turned around to smile at him. Hers was not an expression of
warmth—more like a promise of something nasty. And St.
John was taken by surprise.

She depressed a button on the dashboard. The door locks
clicked shut all around the car. Another button rolled down
the glass wall that separated them. "Good morning." She

managed to make this sound like a threat as she turned the key in the ignition and fired up the engine.

"Is this a kidnapping?" St. John had recovered from his jolt, and now he seemed merely amused. "Nick will be so envious. Where are we going?"

"Nowhere." She maneuvered the long car across the lanes of the driveway. Grille and bumper nearly touched the parked cars at both curbs and effectively blocked the flow of traffic. The engine idled as she turned to face him, not smiling anymore. "You were a good cop for a lot of years, St. John. It's not your style to run away."

"I'm afraid I've aged into a coward. I'm too old to do Max Candle's routines." He waved one hand in the air to say, *It's that simple.*

The chauffeur was politely tapping at Mallory's window. She ignored him. "You asked Nick Prado to take over the hangman act. He's about your age, isn't he?"

"But Nick isn't aware of that. I never had the heart to tell him he was getting old." St. John turned to the side window to see a red sedan pulling up to the limousine's broadside. The car's windshield faced the limo's side windows, and the driver was waving at them, flicking the air in a shoo-fly gesture, as if this would clear away the tons of metal stretched lengthwise across his path. St. John held up two fingers to the driver to tell him this wouldn't take long, only a few minutes.

He was wrong about that.

The hotel doorman was knocking on the rear passenger window, trying to get St. John's attention. The luxury limousine was well padded against city noises, and the man's voice was little more than the buzz of an insect, but Mallory could guess what he was saying. The opposite side window gave her a view of the driveway curving back to the busy artery of Central Park South. A cab had pulled up alongside the red sedan, its headlights a foot from the side of the limousine. As these vehicles were disgorging passengers and baggage, two cabs and another private car were queuing up behind them, locking them into the driveway.

The courtyard lit up with a flash of lightning.

She paid no attention to the more insistent rapping at both windows. Her tone was casual. "The doctor said your *accident* amounted to a nasty rope burn." Actually, the doctor had refused to say anything. A raid on the hospital computer had been more helpful. "Now what about Franny Futura? Is he dead yet?"

The bang caught up to the lightning bolt, louder than gunfire.

St. John turned to the window pocked with a smattering of raindrops. Another man was knocking on the glass and gesturing toward a yellow cab sandwiched between the limousine and the other cars.

Mallory tuned out the knocking man. "Where is Futura?"

St. John only shook his head, distracted by the men at the windows. The chauffeur retreated, but the doorman did not, and the cabby had escalated to the sexually graphic gesture of one extended finger, a traditional New York traffic signal directing St. John to insert his car into a dark orifice. Outside the baffle of thick glass, the chauffeur engaged the cabby in a dumb-show shouting match. More cars were pulling into the driveway.

"Where is Futura?" There was no pressure in her voice. She had all day for this. Other drivers were gathering around the cabby and the chauffeur. Round eyes, Asian eyes and every shade of skin could be seen through the rain-streaked glass.

"Mallory, I'd tell you if I knew where Franny was."

"Sure you would."

The cabby had driven off the chauffeur with a raised fist, and now he renewed his attentions to the window, hammering on it with his fist. Though the law forbade the nonemergency use of car horns, Mallory ignored the lawbreaker who leaned on his horn in a continuous shriek. The line of cars was now stretching into the street. Backing up into traffic was not an option for any of the enclosed vehicles. Nor could they jump the curb thronged with activists. One of the protesters waved a giant photograph of an animal's chewed-off leg left in the metal jaws of a trap. The mist had changed to a light rainfall, but none of the animal people showed signs of leaving. They had become an audience for the angry motorists assaulting the car.

"You're not afraid, St. John. That's not why you're running back to Paris. You just don't want to be here when another man dies."

More drivers were carting bags from the back of the line and glaring at the limousine. Other men had joined the cabby, who was hammering on the hood with both fists, frustrated, eyes popping with an implosion of anger, trying to get at this rich bastard who was *ignoring* him. Other drivers were warming up their fists on the windows and the trunk of the car. Their mouths opened and closed with screams that broke through the barrier of thick glass. The words were muffled and some were foreign, but the sentiments were clear. It was easy to lip-read the word *asshole* and its many translations.

A gridlock of traffic blocked two lanes of Central Park South.

St. John was finding it more difficult to keep his tone civil as the windows were assaulted with more hands and angry faces pressed to the glass. "Mallory, this is old business that should've been taken care of long before you were born. In the war, I resolved the killing with my religion as—"

"You never resolved a thing. You still carry it around with you." She had hit home. It was in his eyes, the pain of a stab in the soft spot.

One of the cars at the end of the drive tried to back into the street and hit a carriage, freeing the horse from its traces, and now the old brown mare was running down the sidewalk and scattering pedestrians. Cheers from the animal-rights people penetrated the glass. The overturned horseless carriage cut off more traffic, and now the line of immobilized vehicles extended past the intersection.

A man in a gray suit was pressing his identification to Mallory's window. Without turning to look, she knew he was hotel security. Now the gray suit was being roughly elbowed out of the way by men who were not so well dressed. On all sides, the car was being hammered by fists on the glass and metal. The animal people along the curb appeared to be rooting for the cabbies and supporting the illusion of a full-scale riot.

"I know why you're leaving." She smiled pleasantly. Yes, it

was shaping up to be a fine New York morning, full of confrontation and street violence. "You don't want to watch this murder go down. Like that makes it all right, being somewhere else when a man dies."

More car horns were penetrating the window glass.

"I know you want me to stop this. That's why you locked me inside the platform, isn't it? It was a message just for me. Cop logic. Coincidence is always suspicious."

A man in a turban danced on the hood, then made a jump to the roof of the car. The crowd went wild with applause.

"And hiding the dead body in the platform? That was your work, St. John. You wanted me on this case—officially. You *handed* it to me with that dead body. But now you won't help me stop a murder. You can't choose up sides, can you? Fine, but don't make me chase you down. Stay here and watch a man die. We'll call it penance for the executioner."

"In the war—"

"Don't start with me. You're pathetic, all of you. Old men playing war games. Futura's dead, isn't he?"

He winced, and she knew this was the truth, or it soon would be. A cheer went up from the animal people. St. John looked up to the roof of the car where feet were stomping on the metal.

"It's a hard call. Will Malakhai die?" Her words were in monotone. "Or will he get Prado first? You know I'll get the last man standing, and maybe I'll have to kill him. Is that what you want?"

The car was moving, rocking. Angry hands were pushing it in both directions. The crowd had spilled into the unobstructed half of the driveway for a closer view. They were waiting on the promised destruction of the long black limousine. The man in the turban made another leap to the hood and began a violent dance, denting the metal with his cowboy boots. And now he kicked at the windshield, but the thick glass would not give.

Only Mallory was serene as she studied St. John's face. Was he reliving days of Maquis justice, the mobs, the killing mobs? *Welcome to my war zone, New York—Fun City.*

She could hear the sirens coming, only a shrill whine piercing the glass, but it was building in pitch. The lightning flashed and the bang was an instant behind it; the strikes were closer now.

"The day Louisa died, you told her the Germans were printing up posters with her picture. So they didn't know where she was—not until someone informed on her. Isn't that why Malakhai was wearing a German uniform when he shot her? He knew they were—"

"Yes, yes!" The car was nearly rolled on that pass. St. John clung to the armrests to keep his balance. His face showed no overt expression of fear, but he could not control the sweat of his upper lip, the whitening knuckles. Fistfights were breaking out among the drivers and the people in hotel uniforms, treating St. John to the sight of real blood as the men outside the car were going off like bombs.

Mallory's voice was almost a whisper. "The informer—was it Franny Futura?"

He only stared at her, as if she were insane to be so calm in the center of this human storm. At any moment it would spill into the car—or they would be dragged out. A bloodied face was slammed into the window by St. John's head, and he jumped in his skin. It was not fear in his eyes, but pain. This was the flip side of the Maquis, the target's view of the mob—new insight, fresh hell.

"Was Futura the informer?"

The limousine rocked with renewed violence. The sirens were louder now. The vehicle settled down on all four wheels as two police cars pulled to the curb.

"No, it wasn't Franny." St. John's head lolled back on the upholstery, eyes fixed on the blood-smeared glass. "Informing on Louisa was Oliver's job."

"His *job*? You *all* killed Louisa?"

✦　　✦　　✦

"I liked the other setting much better," said Nick Prado. "More atmosphere. That caged drug addict was a priceless prop." He stood before the mirror at the far end of the formal interview room, brushing nonexistent lint from his tie as an excuse to be closer to his own reflection. "So, Mallory, what became of your little pet?"

"The junkie?" She closed the door and locked it. "We shipped him off to a bigger cage, and someone put a shiv in his back. The other cons will tell you all about it when you get there."

He smiled at the mirror and tapped its surface. "It's a window, isn't it? A one-way glass? Are people watching us right now?"

"No, Prado. Whenever you have that uneasy feeling that you're being watched—that's usually me." Mallory sat down at the table. A theater ticket lay on top of her thick manila folder. A messenger had delivered it to her desk in the squad room of Special Crimes, wrapped in a recently printed publicity flyer.

So Charles Butler was going to perform the Lost Illusion at Carnegie Hall. This tribute to the late Max Candle was scheduled to follow Malakhai's performance.

And whose idea was that?

Prado pulled out a chair on the opposite side of the table and sat down. He reached out to tap the flyer. "I see you've heard the news. Brave boy, our Charles. Not too many people are surviving his cousin's illusions these days." There was a swagger in Prado's voice. His words strutted up and down in inflection.

"Ready to arrest me?" His face was half a grin, half a leer. He stretched out his hands to be cuffed. "Pity you don't wear a uniform. In my fantasy—"

"I'm not that far from a warrant. Don't push your luck." She set the ticket and the flyer to one side. "How do you plan to get out of doing Emile's act—the gallows trick? Thirteen steps to a small rickety stage, right? Given your fear of heights—"

"My what? I don't know what you mean. I've already done one rehearsal this morning. Ask Emile's assistant."

No, she could not be wrong about this.

Mallory leaned far forward, the better to see his eyes when she flashed a hand across his face. He never blinked, and the irises were slow to react when the strong light from the window was blocked. She tossed him a pencil, and he fumbled the catch.

"So, how many sedatives did you have to take just to climb the stairs of the gallows?"

His expression of pure hate only lasted a moment.

Mallory lowered her eyes to the stack of folders. "All right, Prado, let's talk about the homicide of Oliver Tree." She didn't look at him as she riffled the sheets of the first folder. "You're the only one who knew how he was planning to do that trick."

"I see you're still obsessed with the Lost Illusion."

"Not anymore. Oliver gave away every trick he worked out—gifts to his old friends." She pulled out a small notebook and flipped back the pages. "Thanksgiving at Charles's place." She looked up at Prado. "You said you got your props and instructions months ago. But you're the only one who didn't plan to perform in the magic festival."

"I'm doing all the publicity. It's very time-consuming."

"No, you were the one who got the solution for the Lost Illusion. Originally, Oliver never intended to perform that trick in public. I think he knew his shortcomings. He had a lot of respect for the rest of you—the real magicians. The post loops were set too high for a man his size. He made the platform for a taller man, someone Max Candle's size—your size."

She uncovered what she had been searching for. The material was pressed between the sheets of paper. "Oliver invited you to share the bill with Franny Futura. But you turned him down. You convinced him to perform the trick himself—a publicity stunt to kick off the festival."

"How did you arrive at that?" There was nothing in his face to tell her if she had guessed right.

"Oliver's will didn't mention the platform. I always had a problem with that. Then I realized he'd already given it away—to you. Now that's important, nailing down premeditation. You brought the cuff key to the park. You shined it up to look like new." She tossed the green velvet key bag on the table. It was encased in a plastic cover with the attendant paperwork of evidence. "You substituted the bags. This one is yours. It's the one I took off Oliver's body."

Actually, it was the one taken from Charles's tool chest.

Prado looked down at the velvet bag with mild curiosity. "All of Faustine's apprentices had those bags."

Mallory bent over her notebook. "So you're admitting that you had the green bag." This was not a question, and she gave him no time to contradict her. "You don't mind contributing a blood sample, do you? I need it for the DNA tests. I also need the suit you were wearing that day in Central Park. I have to match it to the clothing fibers on the bag." Fat chance Lieutenant Coffey would give her one more dime for a forensic test.

Mallory looked up at him with a show of surprise that was not intended to fool a half-bright ten-year-old. "No? You don't want to cooperate? Well, after I charge you, the best criminal lawyer in town can't stop me from draining off a little blood."

She turned her attention back to the pages of her folder. "Now Louisa's death was more involved. I underestimated you, Prado."

"Thank you. And may I return the compliment? You're beginning to think like a magician."

"No, thinking like a magician is a waste of time. It was harder to get into the mind-set of a ditsy teenage boy—but more productive. The plot to kill Louisa was all you, Prado. Gross stupidity. Too complicated—too much flash. It's like you hung a neon sign on her corpse. I don't know how you survived as a juvenile delinquent in Paris. Now *that* was impressive."

"I prefer *faint* praise, Mallory."

"I caught so many screwups, the jury is gonna laugh till they cry."

"Enough compliments. I'm blushing."

"If Louisa hadn't died that night, the French police

would've laughed their tails off. And then they would've rounded up all of you. Futura would've cracked first. He was always going to be a problem. Is he dead yet?"

"And what evidence—"

"Louisa knew about your little forgery business." She held up the old passport. "Irrefutable evidence of motive. Futura and St. John were in the Resistance. Looks like she had something on all of you, even Oliver. He gave shelter to an escaped prisoner. None of you could afford to let the Germans get her back. That's how you got the rest of them to cooperate in staging the murder of Louisa Malakhai."

He folded his arms; his smile was patronizing.

She held up a fax from the British War Office, then set it down on the table in front of him. "After she died, you became a soldier—licensed murder. Did Louisa give you a taste for it? What a rush. Didn't you love the war?" She tapped the sheet. "You have to kill a lot of people to get this many medals. Between you and Malakhai, you must have wiped out a whole city."

"You were born too late, Mallory. It's a rare woman who would appreciate—"

"I'm betting Futura's still alive. You can't afford one more accidental death. So you just took him out of the loop for a while. You knew I'd break him down. And St. John? That little accident with the hangman's noose was entirely too convenient."

"You think I tried to murder him?"

"No, that was St. John's idea—and not the first time he staged an accident. I know he had a part in Louisa's murder. Oliver betrayed her to the Germans. That was his job the night she died. Timing was critical. If he brought them to the theater too soon, they would've arrested Louisa on sight. Their entrance had to be timed to witness her accident on the stage. You should've given the informant's job to Futura. He would've been *my* choice."

Prado shook his head slowly and smiled. "Franny would've wet his pants if he had to talk to a German soldier."

She leaned forward. "That's why I would've picked him.

He would've been so believable as an informer." And then, as if she were generously excusing the clumsiness of a child, she said, "But then, I'm the pro and you're the amateur."

"You're an interesting young woman." He waved his hand in concession. "All right, a bit of miscasting. But Oliver—"

"Miscasting? Everyone tells me Oliver's timing was bad. Giving him that job was a major screwup on your part. But you lucked out. That night he got the timing right. Then, you needed a doctor to pronounce Louisa dead. That was Futura."

"Franny was born with worry lines in his face. It aged him quite a bit. No screwing around with stage makeup."

"And you needed a French policeman on the scene, so he could take over the *accident* report. That was where Emile's day job paid off. And the last player was you. You were the one who carried her into the back room. And then you murdered her."

"How clever, but—"

"I hope you're not talking about yourself, Prado. It was an incredibly stupid plot. So many holes in it. Too many people involved. Just the sort of thing a brainless teenage boy would come up with."

His smile was faltering, but she still had more chipping to do before he caved in. St. John had only given her the bare bones of the night Louisa died, refusing to call it murder.

"And no one told Louisa what you were planning. That was your idea. You wanted authenticity, real blood, real surprise. All those combat soldiers in the audience that night. You couldn't afford a bad acting job."

He said nothing to contradict her, and he seemed pleased that she had appreciated this fine point of his plot.

"That was another screwup, Prado." Well, that jarred him a little. A chip here, a chip there. "It was a trademark you held on to. You used it again the day of the parade. Charles didn't know the crossbow stunt was staged. And that was your idea. He was an amateur performer, and you needed authentic surprise."

Prado glanced at the mirror.

Looking for solace in his own reflection? No, she guessed he was not able to shake the idea that someone was standing on the other side of the glass. He was smiling for whomever he imagined there.

Mallory rapped the table to call him back to her. "So the Germans showed up to arrest Louisa. And there's Malakhai on the stage. He's wearing the uniform of an SS officer and aiming a crossbow at a defenseless woman."

Mallory opened a folder and pulled out five sheets of Polish text. This was the contribution of a patrolman named Wojcick, who could not read Polish but thought this might be his grandfather's will. Another donation to the cause was the aged photograph clipped to the first page. Though the subject was of German descent, he bore a slight resemblance to Mr. Halpern's portrait of Louisa Malakhai, and that was why she had selected his snapshot from Detective Riker's family album.

Mallory held up the sheets so Prado could see them. Even on the off chance that Polish was a second language, she knew he would not be able to read a single word. She had found the bifocals when she picked his pockets at Oliver's wake. He would never wear that pair of glasses in front of a woman and admit to a weakness of aging eyes.

She tapped the photograph. "Louisa's father died in custody. He never gave up any names. That's why the Germans wanted his daughter so badly."

No reaction from Prado. He knew no more than she did. So it was true Malakhai had never told anyone about Louisa's history.

"There was a bounty on Louisa and wanted posters with her photograph. No exit visas were being issued, so your forgeries would've gotten her arrested at the border. All the papers were being cross-checked by phone and cablegrams. There was no way out. She had to be declared dead. Then she'd only have to stay in hiding till the Spanish frontier was open again. Isn't that how you sold the plot to Malakhai and the rest of them?"

"No flaws in your logic. Not bad for an hour's work, wouldn't you say? That's all the time I had before the show."

"Not *bad*?" She almost laughed out loud. And people said she had no sense of humor. "A chimpanzee could've come up with a better plan. So how did you convince the rest of them it could possibly work? Maybe you showed them the death certificate with the signature of a doctor."

Mallory pulled out another sheet, a document in French. But she concealed this one quickly, sliding it back into the folder, because it was a Haitian policewoman's baptismal certificate with a heading of very large type. "Bad job, Prado. Anybody can tell it's not the same handwriting as the real doctor."

"Everybody's a critic. Let me remind you that no one has questioned that document in more than fifty years."

Mallory went on: "Emile carried it off pretty well. But then he looked more German than the Germans did. They were happy to leave it in his lap—after he convinced them that he didn't plan to trace the runaway SS officer. Obviously an accidental death, a magic trick gone wrong. The Germans liked that, didn't they? So neat, so efficient. And risk-free— because you had an authentically dead body to show them. That was your part."

"You'll never prove that, Mallory."

"If she'd been captured, she would've told them everything she knew. Most people did."

She tidied her stack of folders. "I have all this physical evidence. Juries love things they can hold in their hands. If you save the taxpayers the cost of a trial, you can avoid a death sentence—again. This is a onetime offer. It's today or—"

"I'll take my chances in court. Side bet? I say you can't get a grand jury to indict me."

"You're a prosecutor's dream. French or American, those bastards are all political animals. Careers are made on cases like this one. It's a murder with a little something for everybody—war, romance, betrayal—it'll make great press. But I can't give you to the French. They might not send you back to die for Oliver's murder in New York.

"Last chance, Prado." She waved another folder for her finale. "More evidence. But I don't have to show this one to your lawyer until I've got the indictment."

It contained the mayor's new guidelines for ticketing citizens who did not wash their tinfoil before they recycled it with their bottles and cans. She stacked it neatly in her pile of useless paperwork. "Malakhai missed his shot that day at the parade. But I'm pretty sure he still wants you dead. I could give you protection."

"I don't need your protection, thank you."

"But you're doing the hangman routine—stoned on drugs. Now *there's* a murder in the making."

She held up a slip of paper with a doctor's name and address printed across the top. "Recognize it?" This was the sedative prescription she had taken from his pocket the night of Oliver's wake. "There's already been one accident with the hangman illusion. And you're going to be stoned out of your mind for that performance. There's no other way you can stand on that gallows and watch it collapse. That's what happens, isn't it? The gallows will fold, and you'll be swinging thirteen steps off the ground with a rope around your neck. It's already failed once. Are you sure it's not a setup? Are you very sure you don't need my protection?"

He was pulling himself together, rebuilding his facade. And now she could see that something had just occurred to him. He was smiling again, self-possessed and confident.

"Malakhai *is* a killer. You got that much right." Prado picked up the flyer for Carnegie Hall and waved it in the air like a small flag. "So here's something else to think about. Charles isn't handsome like his cousin. But I promise you that every time Malakhai looks at him, he sees Max Candle's face."

"So? Max and Malakhai were friends."

"Were they?" Prado turned to the mirror and fiddled with the knot of his tie. "Malakhai spent years torturing his old *friend* with the Louisa illusion. He brought his dead wife into Max's home and sat her down at the man's dinner table. Max was very much in love with Louisa. He took her death very hard. And then, there she was, back from the grave and sitting right beside him at the table. Interesting? And then there's Charles. Max loved his little cousin like a son. Did you know that? It's a pity you never worked out the Lost Illusion, just to be on the safe side. When Charles performs at Carnegie Hall, he shouldn't be taking any help from Malakhai."

"Malakhai would never hurt him."

"Are you willing to bet Charles's life on that?" Prado glanced at the mirror before he sat down again. "Hours before Louisa died, I dropped by Oliver's apartment. It was early in the afternoon. Louisa and Malakhai had the room upstairs. We could hear them up there, going at it like animals. They rocked the bed on its feet and made it dance all the way across the ceiling. Poor Oliver turned bright red and pretended it wasn't happening. So provincial. What an American he was. But it wasn't Louisa's husband in that bed with her. You see, Malakhai walked into Oliver's room while the bed was still dancing upstairs. Oh, the look on his face when he stared at that ceiling. He was devastated. No—he was *destroyed.*" Prado leaned across the table, smiling. "Are you quite sure Malakhai didn't mean to kill his wife that *same* night?"

"You're lying. Max and Louisa told him about the affair. That's how he found out."

"Is that what Malakhai said? Well, maybe they did confess. But I promise you, Mallory, that dancing bed was the first he knew about the affair. Don't let Charles—"

"He won't hurt Charles."

"No? Don't you wonder why Malakhai wouldn't help you work out the Lost Illusion? How long do you think he's been planning to share his stage with Max's cousin?" He spoke to her, but he played to his imagined audience in the mirror. "Well, maybe Charles will survive. You never know." He picked up his hat. "You'll excuse me? I have to rehearse Emile's routine. I may need to hang myself ten times. Practice makes perfect."

"Dangerous trick, Prado. And strung out on drugs? Maybe when St. John bowed out, he was helping Malakhai set you up for the kill."

"What of it? I know you'll be there tomorrow night— watching my back. You can make my finale after Malakhai's act. But you'll have to hurry, Mallory. Timing is everything."

He waved one hand in the air, still performing for the watchers he believed were behind the mirror. And now he was unlocking the catch on the doorknob.

"Prado!" She rose from the chair and leaned over to press her hands flat on the table, allowing her blazer to open and show him the gun. "If Franny Futura turns up dead, I'm going to kill you. And it won't be a bullet—not a quick death. You'll never guess the day I come for you. It might be a month or a year. I'm real patient that way."

Now that should assure him that there was no one behind the looking glass.

✛   ✛   ✛

Jack Coffey sat alone in the dark room behind the mirror. Mallory's interview was done, and he knew he should leave now. Yet he remained in his seat, watching her through the one-way glass as she sat down and covered her face with both hands.

He was past the point of a supervisor overseeing a case. This was borderline voyeurism. Coffey shifted in his front-row chair, so like a theater seat. Though he knew he was alone, he turned to check the elevated row of stationary chairs behind him.

But why should he feel guilty? Mallory was the one who just made a death threat against a suspect. Maybe she had only intended to rattle Prado. But then Coffey had to wonder if he should believe every word. He hoped Prado had believed her. It might keep Futura alive awhile longer.

Every good instinct told him to take Mallory off the case. But who else could have done so much with damn little help? Riker's evaluation had been correct. Inspector Markowitz had been the best of cops in his prime, but his child was better.

She was also dangerous.

Coffey wondered what Mallory was thinking, sitting there still as death. He wished he could see her face.

As if responding to this thought, her hands fell away, and she slowly turned her head toward the one-way glass. Hers was not the vague, roaming glance of Nick Prado, who had only suspected a watcher. Mallory was staring into his eyes. Coffey took little comfort in the knowledge that she could not see through the mirror. This was only her paranoia tuned to a fine instrument for fun and terror. She knew he would take the center chair and where his eyes would be.

What would Lou Markowitz do if he could come back from the dead and see his daughter now? Would he laugh or cry?

As if she were reading his mind, Mallory smiled—just like the old man, a Markowitz smile.

Jack Coffey closed his eyes and continued to sit in the dark after Mallory had abandoned the interview room. He listened to her footsteps in the hall. She stopped at the door and tried the knob. Now he heard her working the lock. He was bracing for the confrontation. He would be caught in the act of a voyeur watching a lone woman in the interview room.

The door opened by only an inch. Mallory never looked inside.

What for? She already knew he was there.

Her footsteps continued down the hall. Was she laughing? Or was that Markowitz?

✢   ✢   ✢

A newspaper lay on the floor, headlines screaming about the hanging of Emile St. John. Franny Futura lay back on the pillows. He had not left his bed since the maid brought him the morning paper. The woman had accepted a cheap ring as payment, for he had no money to bribe her.

He had not changed his clothes since his arrival. The suitcases were in the closet, unopened—a neat stack of symbols for his entire existence, always packed and ready to run.

Franny watched the shadows crawl from one side of the room to the other, slowly edging across the walls, and some crawled along the ceiling. Now that darkness had fallen, the headlights of cars in the parking lot created more diverting dark shapes and jerky flashes, dashing across the walls to take him by surprise. Every pair of lights announced another visitor to the motel.

Any moment now.

He had lived his entire life rehearsing for a knock on the door. In dreams, it always happened at night. As often as he had imagined the moment, he could never see beyond the point when the door began to open. On the other side, something awaited him.

Another pair of lights splashed one wall, veered sharply onto the next one, then died off to leave him in the dark. His fear was a hulking thing, crafty and cruel. It sat on his chest with real weight, haunches tensing, crouching, set to spring. Franny listened to the opening and closing of a car door. He followed the sound of steps in the parking lot. They passed him by, and he thought to breathe again.

Locks and bars had been unnecessary adjuncts to his jail. He could never leave this motel room. He would miss the curtain for his Broadway show, and he must reconcile himself to that loss.

He sat up on the bed and stared at his reflection in the mirror over the dresser, looking there for the younger Franny from Faustine's Magic Theater, hiding in the brilliant spotlight of the stage, the only place where he felt truly safe. Even today, if not for his sporadic stage career, he would never leave his rented rooms. But he could not explain this to his agent, who had urged him to retire many years ago.

There was someone behind the door. He was sure of it.

Franny lay back on the pillows, eyes wide with anticipation. He had waited for more than half the century, a million minutes ticking by, building to this moment.

Nick Prado didn't knock. He let himself in with the key.

Twenty

THE YOUNG MAN BENT OVER A NEWSPAPER, INTENDING TO CLOSE his eyes for a nap while passing for a serious reader. This time slot was a death sentence of sleep deprivation. But the hotel manager could not see beyond mere appearance, and so the desk clerk was doomed to the graveyard shift until his skin cleared up.

He smelled her perfume first. A gardenia, the flower of high school prom corsages and a sad reminder of the stag line.

When he turned around to face the desk, he was staring at a tall blonde with full, ruby lips and a tuxedo. A long leather coat was draped over one arm, and her entire body sparkled with black sequins. He thought the silk top hat was marvelous. It marked her as an escapee from a vintage black-and-white movie. In a further audacity, she wore sunglasses at midnight.

"I'm Louisa Malakhai, room 408. I need the key card."

"Madam, I thought you were dead."

The blonde inclined her head, apparently not getting the joke. "I beg your pardon?"

"I'm sorry, Mrs. Malakhai." One hand fluttered up to cover his gaunt face, where brand-new pimples were surely blooming before her eyes. "It must've been a misprint." He dropped his copy of the *Times* on the floor.

"My husband filled out our registration card."

"Of course." He turned to the computer keyboard and

typed in the room number. Louisa Malakhai was indeed a registered guest. He sorted through the box of cards, then pulled one out. Yes, the gentleman had signed for a second occupant, his wife. But according to the newspaper, she had died more than half a century ago.

Pretty damn dead.

He looked up at her face, evidently staring at her too long. Her red fingernails were drumming on the mahogany.

Well, it was an uncommon burglar who showed up in sequins and a top hat. But still—dead was dead. A simple call to the gentleman's room would—

"My husband is asleep. I'd rather you didn't wake him." She laid one soft hand over his to prevent him from picking up the phone. The clerk froze in the attitude of a soldier standing at attention; his insides were flapping like a duck.

"My bag isn't heavy. I can carry it." She held out her hand, palm up and fingers curling to show him the dangerous tips of long red nails. "Give me the key card."

"I'll need to see some identification."

Her mouth dipped on one side, the most subtle indication that she was outraged. This reaction spoke well for both burglar and legal guest, for there was no such thing as hotel security in New York City. It was a lame criminal who could not finesse a victim's key from any desk clerk in town, striking in the busy daylight hours when the clerks were under pressure and easily conned. But it had never been known to happen in the dead hours of a night shift. He bit down on his lower lip and called himself an overzealous ass.

Apparently, she had anticipated just such an ass. She held up an open Czech passport. The photograph was recent, agreeing with what he could see of her face. But didn't the page look a bit yellowed, somewhat older than the picture? Her fingers covered the dates of issue and expiration. Was that deliberate?

"The key card." Her voice had an edge to it.

They were done with pleasantries. This was an order she was issuing, and nothing in his lifetime of erupting pimples and dateless Saturday nights had prepared him to challenge a tall blonde.

He gave her his most ingratiating smile as he handed her the electronic card. "Your English is flawless, Mrs. Malakhai."

✝   ✝   ✝

The narrow beam of her penlight played over his face as Malakhai lay sleeping, all the effects of gravity undone. The light moved on, traveling from wall to bedroom wall. Everything was exactly as the maid had described it this morning. The desk clerk's skepticism had taken her by surprise. The rest of the hotel staff was under the impression that a woman occupied this suite.

Mallory entered the bathroom, but she did not find the anticipated red hairs in the brush or the comb. And contrary to the maid's experience, tonight there was no lipstick-stained tissue in the wastebasket. Louisa was fading away.

She whirled around at the sudden brightness of another light.

Malakhai stood behind her in the glow of the bedside lamp, wearing a long black robe. His back was turned to her with utter disregard for any threat that she might pose. Her suitcase lay on the bed, and her gun was inside, stored there because the fitted tuxedo jacket would not close on the bulge of her shoulder holster.

The lock clicked, then he held up a copy of Faustine's rod of key plugs. "It's the original, if you're still curious about that. I never go anywhere without it." Malakhai's hand grazed the contents of the small valise. "Not the typical young lady's overnight case."

He pulled a cloth sack off the wine bottle she had raided from the basement. "Ah, you New York girls. Very chic." And now he unwrapped the linen covering two wineglasses. When he dipped back into the case, his hand passed over her revolver in favor of the pearl-handled corkscrew.

Mallory had lost the element of surprise and the opportu-
 ̀v to do real damage. She was not in control here—not yet.
  ̀he came up behind him, her voice was full of accusa-

tion. "You arranged for Charles to do the Lost Illusion at Carnegie Hall."

"Charles was invited to do a tribute to Max Candle." Not the least bit defensive, he smiled as he worked the corkscrew into the mouth of the bottle. "I gave him some of Max's old warm-up tricks—not a death finale. The Lost Illusion was Charles's idea. He's doing it for you, Mallory."

Malakhai inhaled deeply. "Your perfume is a bit overdone. Louisa was more discreet." He appraised the close-fitting tuxedo and the top hat. "But apart from that—not a bad impersonation."

She sat down on the edge of the bed. This was not going well. "Did you tell Charles how the illusion was done?"

"No, he worked out his own solution." Malakhai finished uncorking the bottle and poured red wine into the crystal glasses.

"But it's not Max Candle's solution?"

"Come to the show." He handed her a glass. "Judge for yourself."

"You wouldn't hurt him?"

"Of course not." And now he was unsettled, incredulous. "I watched Charles grow up. How could I—"

"He looks a lot like Max Candle, doesn't he?"

"If he were only as handsome as Max, he wouldn't have to risk his neck to impress you." Malakhai sat down on the other side of the bed and lifted his glass. "It's not going to work though, is it? He's not your type. I think I'd be afraid of the man who was."

He sipped his wine, not catching the dark look that passed across her face.

Mallory was staring at the pillow on the unwrinkled side of the bed. "You forgot the mint."

He turned to see the gold foil resting on a pristine pillowcase. Did this sadden him? Yes.

"Time to give it up," said Mallory. "She's gone, isn't she?"

He shook his head as he stared at the pillow.

Mallory pressed this one small advantage. "Oh, you know who she was. And you still have a lot of the stories. But it's getting harder to see her, isn't it? What will you lose tomorrow? If you kill Nick Prado, I'll put you away. And after a while, you won't even remember why I did that to you."

He disappointed her with a slow smile. "Would that take all the fun out of it, Mallory?"

"Yes. I'd rather nail Prado for Oliver's murder. What do you suppose he did with Franny Futura?"

"No idea." He leaned back to rest against the headboard.

Mallory swirled the wine, then set the glass on the bedside table. "You know he has to kill Futura." She looked at Malakhai, hoping to impress him with her contempt. "Prado needs somebody to take the fall when the body turns up. You're the perfect patsy—certifiably insane. Your home address is a *hospital*."

Malakhai swallowed the last of his wine and lifted one shoulder to say, *Yes, so?* He turned to the window of city lights and the glowing streams of midnight traffic. "I really have no idea where Franny is. I wouldn't lie to you."

"But you won't help me either."

Mallory was planning to punish him with another blow to the Louisa illusion, but now she noticed that the hotel mint was gone, and his wife's pillow bore the deep impression of a human head. A shadow was crawling along the wall at the corner of her field of vision, but she wouldn't give Malakhai the satisfaction of staring at it.

Done with distractions, she wondered if she could bludgeon him with something else and hit him in another soft spot.

The shadow was closer, larger, massing upward as if to strike her. Before Mallory could stop the reflex action, her hand hovered in the air, moving toward the open suitcase and her revolver. "Was Max Candle a war lover like Prado?" Passing over the suitcase, she reached for the glass instead of her gun.

Malakhai took this as a request for a refill and leaned across the bed to pour out more burgundy. "No, Max never loved the war." He topped off her glass. "The killing sickened him."

"You told me the war was sublime."

"The sublime can be wonderful or horrible, but it's always

an exalted thing. For Max, the war was a chance to find out what he was made of. He acquitted himself heroically, and he kept his medals locked in a drawer."

She sipped the wine, tasting it this time. "What about Oliver?"

"He was shipped back to the States for basic training, and the army kept him there. They made him a supply clerk. Poor Oliver. He wanted action, but it never came his way." Malakhai cradled the bottle in his arm. "Every one of us went off to a different war. Nick did fall in love with it, but Emile saw it as a simple matter of honor and duty. And it was all Franny could do just to survive it."

"And you?"

"I thought I'd killed my wife. That was the biggest event of my life. Nothing could surpass it. The war was simply going on around me."

"But after the war, when you saw Emile, he told you what really happened to Louisa."

The water glass on the night table had lipstick on it now. When had he done that? The ashtray held a smoking cigarette with the imprint of ruby lips.

"A very stylish interrogation, Mallory." He sipped his wine and sighed. "So this is police brutality. I can't imagine why anyone complains. But you don't know—"

"I know everything. Louisa had no idea what the rest of you were plotting. Her plan was to make a run for the border after the show was over."

"How did—"

"Louisa thought she was going to do the act the way she did it every night. When you drew blood, she wasn't faking the shock."

"No, she never expected me to hurt her—not ever."

"Prado's idea, right? She thought Max Candle was going to do the routine with a wire and a ribbon, not a real arrow. It was Max's act, but he couldn't go through with Prado's plan."

"Max couldn't stand the idea of hurting her. He loved Louisa."

Not as much as you did.

"There was no way out of France," said Mallory. "And Louisa couldn't stay. The Germans had to believe she was dead. There were combat soldiers in the audience, and they knew the genuine article when they saw it—blood and shock. Nothing would scare Louisa more than that uniform. Now that was your idea. You knew all her soft places."

"Torturing people is your gift, isn't it, Mallory? I wonder where you learned that."

"The wound had to be authentic—*real* blood. Her life depended on it. It should have been Max Candle on that stage. But he couldn't go through with it. That's why you did his act that night, and why you wore that uniform. You were the one who loved her enough to frighten her and hurt her— so she could survive."

Malakhai stared at her with naked surprise. Perhaps he had never suspected her of having the humanity to work it out.

"And while she was dying?" Mallory leaned closer. "You must know what went through her mind. Your wife gave up the fight too soon. You know it's true. You've seen more death than I have. You know what it takes to kill a human being. And you know why she stopped fighting? All the while that bastard was murdering her, she thought she had it coming. Louisa thought you *wanted* her dead."

So much for humanity. She had made him drop his wineglass.

He dabbed at the red stain on the sheet. "You're the most ruthless woman I've ever met."

She sat back, somehow disappointed, waving her hand to ask, *Is that all?*

"But whatever you are," he said, "I suppose I'm a hundred times worse. I was doing monstrous things when I was only eighteen years old."

"I can top that," she said. "I was diagnosed as a sociopath when I was *eleven* years old." Did that sound competitive? This was all about control now.

"You're lying, Mallory. *Ruthless* is the only compliment you get."

In a case with no hard evidence, so much depended on topping him at ripping human beings to shreds. "It's true. I've

got everything it takes to nail that bastard. You can trust me to
do the job right."

He shook his head to say he didn't believe her.

"Helen—my foster mother—she tore the psychiatrist's
report into a million pieces. That's how bad it was." The violence of that tearing and shredding had piqued a child's
curiosity. Long past the bedtime of a little girl, she had
retrieved all the scraps from the garbage pail. Behind her
locked bedroom door, young Kathy had been wearing the
hated ducky pajamas, bright yellow baby birds on a field of
ocean blue. She had pretended to love them because they
were a gift from Helen's loving hands.

The child had patiently worked through the night, taping
all the torn bits of paper, restoring each page to precise right-
angled corners and perfectly straight edges. Then she had
read the diagnosis of an eleven-year-old girl. The summary
page had been written in simple language so that no one
could escape its meaning—not even a child.

She recalled the pages falling to the floor, then staring into
a mirror, eyes wounded by an assault of words on paper,
slowly coming to grips with the idea that a monster could
have blue pajamas with yellow ducks.

"I still remember that test." The doctor had said there were
no right or wrong answers, only choices. Later it turned out
that he had lied about that. "I think I only got one question
right." One response had been circled in red ink—probably
as a consolation prize for her foster mother. Dr. Brenner had
known that Helen was a sucker for wounded animals.

"He asked me to choose between a bag of money and a
mangy old cat. Which one would I carry out of a burning
building? I picked the cat—because it was *alive*." And
because that response would have pleased Helen.

"Then you didn't get that one right either," said Malakhai.
"The rest of us would've taken the money." He turned to the
window. "It's raining again."

She leaned toward him. "Give Prado to me. All I need is a
statement. I'll get even for Oliver and Louisa. That's my job,
and I'm good at it."

Better than you—twice the monster. As Emile St. John had said, she was born to do this work.

Malakhai looked at her across the expanse of the bed. "I'm trying to picture you as a baby sociopath." He turned away from her to pour another glass of wine. "I don't see it."

"I can bring Prado down. You want him to suffer? I can arrange that too."

Was he laughing at her? She could not see his face.

Mallory crept across the bed, coming up on his blind side with a new idea for earning his absolute faith in her monsterhood. "Didn't you think it was odd that Max never got a goodbye letter? He would've told you, right? He told you about his diaries. You never wondered about that?"

"No, not at all. Since Max was running away with Louisa, she wouldn't need to say goodbye to him."

"It wasn't that kind of goodbye, and you know it. She didn't think much of her chances for getting across the border alive." Mallory held out her glass. "Do you really believe she was planning to get Max killed, too?"

Now he was paying attention.

She knelt on the mattress beside him, very close, and he filled her glass with more wine. "Your wife sat down to write that letter *after* her confession in the park." And now, so softly, the hook. "There was only time for one letter. It was beautiful. I think Louisa worked on it for all the time she had left. Then she hid it away in the toe of a shoe. She didn't want you to find it, not till she was across the border—or dead."

His smile was sad and wry. "Where are you going with this?"

"Louisa was more devious than you thought."

"You can't possibly know—"

"Max was in love with her. It wasn't hard to get him under the sheets. She planned it very coldly on the dancing bed—that's what Prado called it. You knew she cheated on you *before* that confession in the park."

"Don't do this, Mallory."

"You walked into Oliver's room while your wife was upstairs, rolling around your bed with another man. She was rocking the whole damn floor with the sound of sex. Louisa wasn't trying to hide it—she was *announcing* it. I'd bet even money she timed it so you'd catch her in the act with Max. You're always telling me that timing is everything."

"That's enough." He grabbed her arm. "I don't want to hear Louisa's name in your mouth anymore."

"But you didn't go up there, did you, Malakhai? No, you just walked away. And you never would've called her on it. That's why Louisa had to make the confession in the park. She even brought Max along as proof."

He tightened his grip on her arm. He was hurting her, but damned if she would show it. She smiled instead. "Emile told her Paris was dangerous. Louisa couldn't go back to the prison camp, the interrogations. When she wanted to make a run for the Spanish frontier, you told her that was suicide."

"The border was closed down and the frontier police had her photograph." He pushed her away with enough force to roll her to the other side of the wide bed. "It *was* a suicide run."

"But Louisa already knew that." Mallory crept back across the mattress for another turn at him. "Emile would've told her the same thing. And still, she was game to make that run."

His hand was rising for a strike at her face. She ignored it. "But first, Louisa had to make sure you wouldn't run after her and die with her. She had to make you *hate* her. So she slept with your best friend. Louisa was planning a suicide run, but she wanted you to live. That was *her* plan."

Malakhai's hand dropped away from her face. His head moved slowly from side to side, his mouth forming a silent *No.*

"You shot her with an arrow so she could survive. In a way, she did the same thing to you."

He was slowly doubling over, as if Louisa had indeed shot him. He covered his face with both hands. The rain poured down the windowpane in a solid sheet, obscuring everything beyond the glass, starlight and city lights, heaven and earth— all gone.

Twenty-one

A THIRTY-PIECE ORCHESTRA JOINED IN THE APPLAUSE FOR THE man in the white tuxedo and top hat. Malakhai stood above them on the smaller stage of the platform and cast his shadow on the drawn red curtains hanging from the crossbar. High on the back wall of the Carnegie stage, a video screen made his image several times larger than life.

The audience rose to its feet in screams of *"Encore! Encore!"* Feet were stamping, hands clapping.

At Malakhai's bidding, the men and women of the orchestra stood up to accept their own bravos. The magician had come out from behind the platform curtains five times to answer his encores with a deep bow. And now the audience shouted as a single entity, amplified with three thousand voices, *"Louisa, Louisa, Louisa—"*

Mallory stood in the dark, watching through a narrow opening in the stage doors. The magician turned her way, one hand outstretched and beckoning.

To her? No, of course not.

"—Louisa, Louisa—"

She stepped behind one door as the other one slowly opened and a shadow appeared on its lit surface. The edges of the dark silhouette were soft and the form was indistinct, but it moved, it even seemed to breathe, and Mallory was wary of it—wary of *her.*

"—Louisa, Louisa, Louisa—"

Mallory's eyes went everywhere, to the overhead bank of

lamps and cables, then to the balcony lights, looking for the works and wires to make this happen.

The conductor's baton was rising, and the crowd fell silent, straining to catch each note as the orchestra began to play again.

The silhouette darted onto the stage, encircled by a bright spotlight that failed to kill her dark form. The string section made light running notes as Louisa raced along the back wall. Then her shadow elongated on the platform staircase as she climbed the steps to thirteen soft strokes of the drum and rhythmic notes of oboe and cello that made her heart beat. When she reached the top of the elevated stage, Louisa's shadow stood beside Malakhai as she took a last bow with him. Their shadows were holding hands.

The audience was rising to a stand in waves that began in the front row and rippled toward the seats in the back of the theater, then up through the balconies to the ceiling, accompanied by the rumbling thunder of madly clapping hands—all for the dead woman.

The music shifted its shape, changing cadence away from the classical form of *Louisa's Concerto.* The musicians played with only a few instruments—strings and soulful horns. So Riker had been mistaken; one could dance to this music.

Louisa did.

Malakhai turned to her and their shadows melded on the red curtain. The cheers nearly drowned out the music, as the pair turned in slow steps.

The solid man melted back behind the curtains. His shadow remained with Louisa. And now her silhouette was sharpening into a finer form; the profile was young and elfin. The stage walls deepened to indigo, and cymbal tings dropped into the music—the sound of falling stars.

And Mallory guessed it must be a year in the early forties, a very good year for wine and life. The boys were all together, and Louisa was still alive. The magician's shadow had changed his top hat for a cap, and he was a boy again, dancing with his young wife. One by one, the musical instruments fell silent. The lovers turned slowly, gracefully, moving closer together in the bluesy riff of a single horn. The last note faded.

The audience went wild, filling the vast space with a deafening roar of cheers and the higher notes of whistles. And when the spotlight was killed and the shadows had died in the dark, the screams went on and on.

Mallory watched the center panel on the side of the platform, but no one appeared at the door to the interior room. Was Malakhai inside or standing behind the curtain?

A brief intermission was announced. The patrons were leaving their seats and moving toward the back of the hall. Mallory passed through the stage doors and fought against the opposing flow of workers carrying chairs and music stands toward the wings. Max Candle's Lost Illusion would be accompanied only by the ticks of the clockwork gears on the crossbow pedestals.

Mallory walked along the stage wall for a better look at the back of the platform curtains. The magician was not up there. She walked to the center panel and put her hand on the pressure latch. The door opened on the lit interior room, but Malakhai was not there either. Crossing over to the other pair of doors, she followed the last musician out of the hall.

The backstage area was lit by two monitors and a shielded bulb over the abandoned lighting console. The man who worked at this post was headed for the 56th Street exit, pulling out a cigarette as he walked.

Where were the uniformed officers she had posted at the doors?

She heard voices in low conversation close by. Rounding a pillar of stacked furniture, she found Malakhai. He had changed into a dark suit and tie, and now he was talking with Officer Harris.

Well, at least one of the uniforms had not botched the job of guarding the stage exit. "Harris, where's your partner?"

Malakhai answered for the man. "Officer Briant is over there." He pointed toward the open stage doors, and Mallory turned to see Charles and the second uniform installing pedestals in the wells of the platform step. Malakhai put one hand on the shoulder of the man beside him. "And Officer Harris has to join his partner before the intermission ends."

"He's not taking orders from you," said Mallory.

"Or you." Harris was not even trying to conceal impatience. "We were invited for the magic act, Mallory. Nobody said anything about guard duty." He walked off through the stage doors, heading for the platform.

Mallory looked at her watch. Would Riker be downtown yet? She estimated twenty minutes of bad traffic between Faustine's to the north and the theater district fifteen blocks south of Carnegie Hall.

Malakhai was standing by the doors, watching the uniformed officers carry the oval target to the top of the platform. "You can't blame Harris for being testy. He's an artist now, isn't he? How many cops get to play Carnegie Hall?" He smiled at her. "Would you like a few minutes in show business, Mallory? Charles could use an assistant tonight."

"You said Max Candle always worked alone."

"But Charles is only a gifted amateur." He was looking at the clock behind her. "So, what's the news? Did Franny show up at Faustine's?"

"No, Riker said another magician went on in his time slot. The stage manager hasn't heard from him since he disappeared."

"What a pity. He's waited so long for a chance like this. Franny must be devastated."

"No, he's probably dead." She watched his face for signs of disquiet, but there were none. "Do you want Prado to get away with that? Hasn't he done enough killing? Help me. Give me something I can use on that bastard."

"All right." He waved one hand toward the platform. "I'll tell you how I knew Oliver botched the Lost Illusion."

The platform curtains had been pulled back and the oval target was suspended between the posts. The two officers were climbing the stairs with the demonstration dummy as the audience flooded back into the hall. When the crowd was seated and silent, Charles stood at the edge of the stage, crediting the crossbow act to his famous cousin, Max Candle.

Malakhai spoke close to her ear to be heard over Charles's recital on the history of the Lost Illusion. "Oliver could've avoided three of the arrows. Max always made a great show of struggling with the manacles while he was shifting his body to dodge the first three. But Oliver didn't even try. When the cuff key jammed, he knew he was going to be killed by the last arrow in the heart."

"Tell me something I *don't* know." She looked through the stage doors. The officers had finished chaining the dummy to the target with their own handcuffs, and they were descending the staircase.

He was staring at the platform. "Watch the policemen loading the arrows into the magazines. There's nothing to block the shots. They will all fire."

Charles nodded to each pedestal in turn, and the officers cocked the weapons and pressed the buttons to start the gears. The volume of the ticking increased as each pedestal was set in motion, wheels turning, red-flagged pegs rising toward their triggers in the crossbow pistols. The audience was dead silent, mesmerized by the sound.

Malakhai pointed to the demonstration dummy spread across the face of the target. "Let's make the problem more personal. Say that's Charles up there. Assume the act is rigged to kill him. You want to save him, but you can't interfere with the first arrow. That would throw off his timing, and he'd take it in the neck—like Oliver did."

The first arrow flew. The dummy's throat was ripped open and spilling sawdust on the floorboards of the platform stage.

"If you can't stop the act before that first arrow flies, then I suggest you move between the second arrow and the third one. You only have seconds to run between the shots."

The ticking lessened by one more pedestal as the second arrow hit the dummy's right leg. "You'll keep him alive if you can pull up the crossbow at the near corner of the platform. That's the one that kills. You have to lift it off the pedestal. You can't just pull out the trigger peg—not without a wrench. Charles wedged it in that tight."

Another bow fired and the arrow pinned the dummy's left leg.

"How does any of this help me nail Nick Prado?"

"It doesn't. But it might keep Charles alive." He turned his back and walked toward the exit sign, heading for the stairs down to the street. "I told you he might need some help, and I can't stay for the rest of the act."

The final arrow tore open the dummy's chest.

"Malakhai, you're not going anywhere."

The officers were climbing the stairs again to retrieve the gutted burlap body.

Malakhai looked at the clock on the wall. "Nick should be finishing his act soon. The finale might be worth catching. I really have to fly."

She grabbed his arm. "You're not going after Prado. You leave him to me."

He turned on her, and before she could react, he was holding her face in both his hands, gently bringing her close to him. There was no time to pull back. His arms enfolded her, and his lips brushed her hair. He kissed her cheek and held her in a tight embrace. Though unaccustomed to contact and warmth, she did nothing to end it. Then, with both hands on her shoulders, he held her at a distance. "That's just in case I can't remember you when we meet again."

"I'll be right next to you. I'll remind you."

"No, Mallory. You have to stay here and keep Charles alive. I promise you, there's nothing in those magazines to block any of the arrows."

Charles was standing at the base of the staircase.

"You expect me to—"

"Believe it, Mallory. All the arrows will fire, and he'll never get out of those manacles. I got this idea from you— last night, when you asked me if I'd hurt Charles. If not for you, it never would've occurred to me. Remember, Charles is doing this to impress you, so it won't be easy to talk him out of it. You may have to shoot him."

She turned to the stage. The officers were bowing to the audience. So what were the odds they would come running when she called? "You wouldn't hurt him."

"No, I love Charles. In your own strange way, I think you're also rather fond of him."

"I'm not buying it, Malakhai. I don't believe you'd let him die."

"I never lied to you, Mallory." He turned his back on her.

"Stop! You know I'll shoot you."

"Remember, if you can't stop him from mounting the platform, you have to pull the front crossbow off the pedestal." He was moving under the exit sign.

She pulled out her revolver and aimed low to shoot a leg out from under him.

What the hell?

The revolver was too light. She fired off a click. The prop gun wasn't even loaded with a charge.

The kiss. He had taken her gun with a kiss and left a toy in its place. And now he was gone. The doors closed behind him.

Charles was walking toward the first crossbow with the officer who would set the gears in motion. Standing between the doors to the stage and the doors to the street, she damned Jack Coffey for shorting her on manpower.

"Wait!" She ran onto the stage and grabbed Charles by one arm. "You can't go on."

He glanced over one shoulder to look at the three thousand expectant faces behind them. "Well, actually, I *am* on." There was tittering in the audience, though his voice had been low. Now he removed her hand from his arm, saying, "So you'll excuse me, Mallory, but—"

"Malakhai rigged your act. If you go ahead with it, you'll die."

More laughs came from the audience. And now she saw the microphone on Charles's lapel.

He looked down at her, saying in a louder voice, "Mallory, it's a solo act."

And the audience was laughing again. His foolish face was no good to him in a poker game, but it did lend itself to comedy.

She put her hand over his microphone. "You can't go through with this. Your cuff key won't work."

Charles grinned. "Malakhai told you that, did he?" As he turned to face the audience, his voice was booming, needing no amplifier in the perfect acoustic realm of the great hall. "She doesn't want me to go through with the act. Thinks it might be dangerous."

And now they were all laughing at her. She could feel the heat rising in her face. "If you go up those stairs, I'll dismantle the crossbows. I don't have time to screw around, Charles." She moved toward the deadliest weapon at the corner of the platform.

"Do you mind?" He gripped her wrist to stop her from pulling the crossbow off its pedestal. "Perhaps we could discuss this another time." Charles picked her up and put her over one shoulder, as if she weighed no more than a sack of screaming, pounding feathers. He carried her to the side of the platform. And now the door was opening in the wooden wall.

"No!" she screamed, beating her fists, forgetting that this would be akin to flies landing on the back of a man Charles's size.

And the audience was roaring.

"No!" Mallory was deposited on the floor inside the platform. She landed on the empty back pocket of her jeans, where her cell phone used to make a bulge—but no longer.

Damn Malakhai.

The door slammed shut. The tin lampshade cast a bright pool of light on the floor, and the ceiling was in shadow. Mallory was on her feet and banging her fists on the wood. "Let me out!"

The crowd fell silent, and she could hear the loud tick of the first pedestal gear through the baffle of the walls. Seconds later, the next one was armed. The ticking grew louder with each pedestal set in motion. She heard his footfalls halfway up the staircase, and screamed, "Stop now! Go back down, or you'll die!"

He stomped his foot on the middle stair, and she heard his amplified voice saying, "Quiet! You'll break my concentration."

The audience was laughing again. She was an even bigger joke. "Charles, you have to stop the act!"

He was on the small stage at the top of the stairs, stomping on the floor. "Enough!" he yelled.

More laughs.

Mallory looked up at the shadows on the ceiling. Charles had said there was no way out except for the knobless door, but there were two exits from the prop room in Charles's basement. Malakhai had said that Oliver's copy was made too well. This original might have a weakness.

The ticking was loud. The trapdoor dropped open in the nine-foot ceiling, and the lazy tongs were rising up through the square hole in the stage. She could see a flash of Charles's trousers as he stepped away from the cape supported by the metal skeleton. Before she could climb the wall ladder, the door had snapped shut. She could not reach it from the wall, but the other trapdoor behind the curtain was at the top of the ladder. She pulled on the spring that kept the door from falling open. It would take a more powerful man than Charles to work it manually, and the operating levers were on the stage above her.

By now Charles's body would be spread across the face of the target, his ankles bound by leg irons and his wrists in NYPD manacles. The lazy tongs were lowering through the trapdoor beyond her reach. The ticking was louder. No—that was a trick of her mind; panic was magnifying the noise.

She heard the audience's collective gasp. The first arrow had flown, and Charles was yelling, "Wait! Something's gone wrong!" Max Candle's famous lines.

Or had Charles just discovered that his cuff key didn't work? The front rows were filled with magicians and Charles's poker cronies. They all knew the trademark words; not one of them would help him. And the two police officers would prevent any Good Samaritans from climbing onto the stage.

The audience gasped again. Had he avoided the second arrow to the leg? He was still screaming for someone to help him. She had twenty seconds to get to the crossbow.

How did Malakhai get out? His exit had to be at the ground level, yet he had not used the side door. She climbed down the ladder and stood before the rear wall, pressing on the slats around the center panel. Charles was screaming. Another arrow had flown, and she started as though it had hit her.

Easy, now. Don't panic, don't— And now her fingers found the pressure lock, a give in the wooden slat. The door opened to the bright lights of the stage. She was out and running, looking up as she flew around the platform. Charles's eyes were wide with fear, but in his face, tragedy passed for comedy. He was still bound by leg irons and both hands were cuffed to the iron post rings. Only one pedestal was ticking now. His right hand balled into a fist and lunged forward, ripping the loop from the post, where she had weakened it. His hand came away with a splintered section of wood.

Mallory's eyes fixed on the crossbow that was going to kill him. She flew toward it, almost there. Charles was almost dead. Her hands closed on the crossbow—too late. The string released before she could unseat it from the pedestal.

Charles screamed in pain.

She turned to see the arrow buried in his chest as he rolled away from the target and stopped struggling. He was not holding an arrow in place this time. He sank down, dangling by one manacle, eyes closed.

And Mallory's whole world took on the dreamer's quality of walking underwater. Sound was dulled, and her movements were slow. She was unaware that she still held the pistol grip of the crossbow. The uniforms were racing up the stairs. Dr. Slope had left his wife and child in the front row, and he was climbing over the edge of the stage. Now he was also running past her on the staircase. All the rest of the world was moving faster. Her legs were so heavy. Each step was a great effort. Her hands were frozen, wrapped tight around the grip of the crossbow pistol.

It was another replay of Oliver's final act—different actors. The policemen lowered Charles to the floor of the platform stage, handling him gently, as if he were not beyond pain. Edward Slope knelt beside the body, pressing one hand to Charles's throat, desperate to find a pulse that wasn't there.

Mallory reached the top step and looked down on the corpse. No magic here. This was the very real death of Charles Butler.

Dr. Slope stood up and turned to the audience. In a loud voice, he announced, "Well, that's showbiz."

What?

The audience was clapping and cheering as Charles stood up to take his bow. He pulled the arrow out of his chest. The shirt was torn where he had ripped a button free, and she could see a flash of the chain-mail vest and the tube that had held the arrow.

Her hand unconsciously opened and dropped the crossbow to the floor.

Edward Slope leaned close to her ear. "I've been rehearsing that line all day."

Mallory slapped the doctor's face so hard, she left the red imprint of her hand on his flesh.

Everyone laughed but Edward Slope. He was shaking his head, eyes saying, *Sorry, so sorry.* "Mallory, I thought you knew. I thought you were part of the act."

The splintered piece of the broken post was dangling from the manacle on Charles's wrist. And now she saw the peg in the wood. She looked up at the post to find the peg's receiving hole in the damaged section. So Malakhai was right; Oliver had made his own replica too well, missing this one feature.

A damn breakaway post.

It left just enough maneuvering room to avoid the final shot. So Charles had pulled the arrow from the target and fitted it into the tube in his chest.

"That's *it?*" She was outraged. The audience was ecstatic. Her voice was still being amplified by Charles's microphone, and her angry face was magnified by the video screen on the wall. "That's *all?*"

Charles turned to her with his loony smile. And now the laughter masked his words for everyone but Mallory. "Well, *you* couldn't figure it out." He raised his hand to dangle the wood in front of her. "Malakhai was putting you on. The handcuffs were never supposed to open. That was Oliver's mistake."

She heard Robin Duffy's voice calling out to her from the first row, where he stood with the rabbi and Mrs. Kaplan. She turned to look down at Robin's adoring face as he said, "Kathy, you were wonderful."

Mallory turned on the uniformed officers standing at the side of the small stage. She yelled, "Give me a *gun!*"

The audience roared, and so did the men in uniform. She tried to take a gun from Harris's holster. He laughed and held it high in the air. She turned to Patrolman Briant. In the spirit of a playground game of keep-away, he also held his gun out of her reach.

This was humiliation on a scale she had never known before, yet she resisted the urge to kick Officer Briant's testicles across the room; not a good idea in front of three thousand witnesses, almost as serious as shooting a sick rat.

Mallory bent down to the floor to pick up the crossbow pistol. This sent the audience into helpless shakes and quakes of laughter. And their screams of hilarity increased with every arrow she pulled from the target.

✢   ✢   ✢

Well, Malakhai had not lied to her. The crossbows had all fired arrows, and Charles had not escaped from the handcuffs.

Mallory gave the driver the address for Nick Prado's performance in the theater district. The cabby was nodding, driving slowly and not paying any attention to the street. He was fixated on the rearview mirror, eyes wide open and showing entirely too much of the whites as he watched her loading arrows into the crossbow magazine.

Perhaps the cabby was lamenting the fact that his car had no bulletproof glass between him and his passenger, a fool's economy measure in New York City. And oddly enough, by this lack of protection, Mallory pegged him as the cautious type, only picking up the safe passengers—nuns, Girl Scouts and upscale theater patrons. Who knew a crossbow would turn up on a fare from Carnegie Hall?

Her next theory was that the driver might be carrying a pistol. People who owned guns traveled in a false bubble of security, always believing the weapon would be at hand when trouble happened. It never was. Lots of dead cabbies had carried guns.

The last arrow fell into the crossbow magazine. Mallory leaned forward. "Give me your cell phone!"

The driver plucked the phone off the dashboard and threw it back over his shoulder, not wanting any contact with her. Mallory dialed Riker's number and counted two rings.

Riker, answer me.

Why had Malakhai waited so long? There had been other chances to kill Nick Prado.

She looked at her watch. It was nearly time for the hangman finale. Prado would be stoned on sedatives to get him through an act on a high narrow stage. He would make an easy, slow-moving target.

"Yeah, Riker here," said the voice in the cell phone.

"Riker, is Nick Prado still on stage? Do you have him in sight?"

"Naw, he was gone before I got here. I don't think—"

"Gone?"

"Yeah, they changed the time slots. He went on when I was still uptown at Faustine's."

Damn Lieutenant Coffey. With only one extra man, she could have covered all three theaters.

"Riker, see if you can find Prado backstage. Malakhai is headed your way, and he's got a gun."

"Jesus."

"I'm on the—" The cell phone went dead. *Oh, great, just great. A perfect evening.* She tossed it over the seat of the cab. "You need new batteries."

This was getting too complex, not Malakhai's style at all. More like Prado's sense of spectacle for maximum effect, his convoluted planning. It was almost as if the publicity king had orchestrated everything.

Of course, he did.

"Turn this cab around! We're going uptown."

"Anything you want, princess."

The cab pulled over to the curb and she waited while the traffic crawled by. Finally, he made the illegal U-turn, and they were moving north toward Faustine's.

She leaned close to the back of his head. "Do you have a gun?"

The cabby turned his head to look at her. He was more surprised than afraid, and his New York attitude was rising to the surface from sheer force of habit. "Lady, you're already loaded for bear with your own damn—"

Mallory held her gold shield inches from his eyes. "When I ask to see your weapons, you show them to me. That's how it works."

"A cop. Well, why didn't you— Aw *shit.*" His hands loosened their white-knuckle grip on the steering wheel. "Freaking cops."

He reached over to the glove compartment and opened it. The city lights were crawling by the windows of the slow-moving car. Scattered raindrops hit the glass as the man pulled out his inventory. "I got a lead pipe, a razor, a knife." He showed her an aerosol can. "This is mustard spray, but it's real old stuff." He pulled out a second can. "Here's the pepper spray. But no gun. Satisfied?"

In a city with two lethal weapons per person, you could never find a gun when you needed one.

"Speed up. And you can go through all the red lights. That's your tip." She threw two twenties over the front seat. "That's the fare. I don't need a receipt."

And now the cab accelerated. Money always worked better than a badge in Manhattan.

✦   ✦   ✦

A young man stood outside the stage exit of Faustine's Magic Theater. He wore an old-fashioned usher's uniform and a matching green pillbox hat. As he dropped his cigarette on the sidewalk, his mouth hung open, and he never even considered trying to stop the running woman with the crossbow pistol.

Inside the theater, a man in coveralls was doing last-minute repairs on a newly installed window when she burst through the door with a push that sent the knob into the wall with a crash of breaking plaster. And this man was equally reticent to get in her way as she raced toward the wings of the stage.

Mallory paused by a dustbin, and looked down the dark corridors created by layers of giant plywood screens. There were boxes and cartons everywhere, too many hiding places. She walked past the edge of the closed curtain. Now she had a clear view of a man in evening attire standing before the audience with a microphone in hand. He announced the next performer, Franny Futura.

Mallory was not surprised.

The audience clapped with more than polite applause for the overhyped act they had all come to see. This was a sporting town. Who had not played the conspiracy game of every daily newspaper? True New Yorkers, the audience had probably made book on a man's life: Would he show or not, was he dead or alive? She could almost see the money changing hands out there in the dark.

Nick Prado was standing in the wings when she came up behind him, soft-stepping across the wood.

A man in coveralls was crouched on the floor nearby, frozen in the act of bending over his toolbox. The streetwise workman rose slowly and backed away from Mallory with no sudden movements, abandoning the toolbox in his haste to avoid witnessing anything that might require a court appearance.

Mallory tapped Prado on the shoulder and stood back out of reach. He turned around, only showing slight surprise.

"Mallory, how are you this evening?"

This might have passed for a normal encounter, except for the crossbow she was aiming at his eyes.

He was stoned again. His reaction time was too slow. How

many pills had it taken to get him through the hanged man routine in the downtown theater?

Prado nodded at the weapon. "I like it. Suits you even better than a gun."

She glanced at the people gathering behind the curtain. A long black table was being assembled by two stagehands. Another man was moving a large upright rectangle of clockwork gears into position at the rear of the stage.

"So Franny's still alive," said Prado. "Are you crushed, Mallory? I hope you didn't have any money riding on that theory of yours."

She looked up beyond the valance of the curtain to the catwalk, a bridge of wooden planks and metal handrails. Her eyes traveled to the vertical rod of steel hanging over the stage. The end of the stalk held a silver crescent razor, a cruel-looking thing, nicked—and familiar. "That's not a replica. It came from Charles's basement."

"Yes," said Prado. "A loan from Charles. Franny didn't want to risk another one of Oliver's botched tricks."

"You won't feel safe until he's dead, will you, Prado?"

"You think I might've tampered with Franny's act? Can't be done. He's not doing it Max's way."

"Because he doesn't know how. Oliver didn't send him the plans for the pendulum. He gave Futura the Lost Illusion— the platform and the crossbows."

"My compliments, Mallory. Yes, that was a particular bit of sweetness on Oliver's part. Franny had such a tired act. The Lost Illusion would've made him a headliner. Of course, Franny never had the guts to go through with it. Turned it down. Poor Oliver was such a bad judge of character. He gave everyone credit for his own large heart."

Mallory nodded. "Oliver *was* a brave little man, wasn't he? So it was easy to talk him into doing the illusion himself. I know you arranged the Central Park show—just like you arranged that old man's murder. You even wrote the invitations. The wording wasn't Oliver's style—everyone said so."

"Franny murdered Oliver." His words had a tone of disparagement. "I assumed you understood that."

"And Louisa?"

"Also Franny's murder. Emile will back me up. I only carried her backstage, a few spots of blood on my shirt. Franny was covered with her blood."

Interesting that he was so forthcoming with Futura's guilt, though she knew he was being truthful. "Scaring Futura, getting him to kill Louisa—that was the *only* smart thing you ever did."

Prado didn't like that. He wanted *pure* praise.

She relaxed her bow hand to point the weapon at his heart. "You knew Malakhai would come tonight. His second chance—last chance. He has to do this execution while he still remembers *why* he's doing it. You stashed Futura so you could go on working the wires, the timing, orchestrating everything."

"Perhaps you give me too much credit." Though his smile said she had not given him credit enough—not nearly enough.

The curtains opened and Franny Futura was joyously grinning in the spotlight. Behind him were six people in scarlet capes, their faces shadowed by hoods. Mallory was intent on bits of anatomy exposed with the movements of these men. The hoods made their height misleading, but they were all close to the same average stature of the magician in the tuxedo, none tall enough to be Malakhai.

"Such a frightened little man," she said. "Hard to imagine him killing Louisa. But you told him a fake death would never fool the Germans. And you were right about that. So you got him all worked up, crazy with fear, hysterical. Did you tell him Louisa knew about his connection to the Resistance movement?"

Prado was enjoying this. "You know, at the time, I didn't even know Franny was in the Resistance."

"But you knew St. John was connected. I know you're the one who gave him up to Futura. You exposed your best friend to up the ante. When fear wasn't enough, you made a woman's murder into an act of patriotism."

His eyes flickered and his mouth opened in dumb surprise—wordless, stunned. It was more than the stupefying effect of drugs. She had guessed right.

Mallory turned to scan the audience, searching for Malakhai's face. Young men in workmen's clothes and old men in tuxedos were clustering in the wings at the opposite end of the stage. She motioned Prado to walk ahead of her and beyond the backdrop curtain.

"Prado, I know you're running this show. You want Futura to die while all those people are watching. That's part of the kick, isn't it? Did you rig his act? Or did Malakhai do that?"

"I'm not here to—"

"We're going up there." She waved the crossbow to the ladder for the narrow catwalk. "No witnesses. Most people never look up."

Prado stared at the ladder. His reflexes might be dulled by drugs, but the anxiety of acrophobia was surfacing. His head snapped back, as if she had shot him seconds ago and the arrow had just caught up to him. "Mallory, if you really think Franny's act is rigged, why not just stop the show and check his props?"

"That's not as easy as you might think. *Move!*" And now Prado had confirmed that she would find no evidence of tampering. If she did stop the show, she would only become the butt of a joke for the second time in one night.

And the threat would not come from the direction of the audience either. She knew Malakhai was not out there planning to risk another long-range shot, not with a revolver. He had stolen her handgun for something up close, point-blank and fatal.

Prado rested one tentative hand on a rung of the ladder. She prodded him with the crossbow. He climbed slowly toward the suspension bridge that stretched across the stage. Eyes shut, he gripped the ladder so tightly, it was an effort to uncurl his fingers from one rung to the next.

Mallory followed him, inching one hand along the rail, aiming the crossbow at his backside. He stepped off the ladder and onto a small metal platform. Mallory stood behind him. "Keep moving."

His eyes opened in disbelief, head shaking in denial.

Were the drugs wearing off?

She put the crossbow into the small of his back. Gingerly, he put one foot on the wooden planks, and the suspension bridge moved beneath him. He gripped the handrails. Mallory prodded him again, and he moved forward. The wooden planks swayed with every step. He froze to make the motion stop, and Mallory shifted her weight to make the bridge move again.

"All right!" He edged forward.

When they were over the center of the stage, Mallory said, "Stop here." She looked down at the floorboards. A glass coffin rested on the long black table. Futura was standing by a microphone as the six assistants carried a burlap dummy in the fashion of tap-dancing pallbearers. Recorded music blared out of amplifiers in the wings. It was a second-rate show tune she could not name.

"Canned music and chorus boys," muttered Prado. "Franny hired *chorus* boys."

He gripped the rails and lowered his head to look down. She had not expected him to do that. The thing that terrified him also fascinated him. "That dummy is all that's left of a beautiful illusion. Franny wanted to use a pumpkin for the demonstration. Can you imagine that?"

"So you *did* help him with the act." She had caught the false notes in his voice, a catch in the throat as he made a hash of forced bravado. She studied his face and found it wanting in terror. How many pills had he taken to get him through the hangman illusion?

"You should've told Emile you were afraid of heights. He wouldn't have asked you to do his act."

"I am not afraid—"

She shifted her weight to rock the catwalk from side to side. Prado's hands wrapped around the rail in a death grip. His eyes were wider now, looking down with the expression of someone witnessing a train wreck in the making. In his mind, he was already falling.

On the stage below, the cloth dummy lay inside the coffin, and Franny Futura was separating the halves of the glass box to expose the midriff of burlap. The pendulum began to move, lowering as it swung. She could barely hear the well-oiled clockwork gears running up the base in a flow of wheels, levers and springs to operate the swing and fall of the crescent razor.

Prado's jaw was locked; he spoke through closed teeth. "No sign of Malakhai."

"He's here." Her eyes searched a backstage cluster of workmen and stagehands. Malakhai would not risk a shot from the wings.

Prado's smile was grim, almost sickly. Delusions of grandeur were warring with the fear of falling. His sedatives were robbing her. This was not the full-blown phobia, not all the fear she wanted. Mallory made the bridge sway, but only a little this time. When she had his attention, the movement stopped. She was teaching him rat-lab protocol. If he did as he was told, she would not terrify him—much.

Below her, the pendulum was picking up speed as the arc of the razor widened. "I thought Emile was the one who told Malakhai how his wife really died. But I was wrong about that, wasn't I? You got to him first." She shook the bridge and Prado reacted a bit faster this time.

His nod was exaggerated, saying, *Yes, whatever you like.*

"After the war, you wanted Malakhai to kill Futura. That would've tied up your only loose end for Louisa's murder."

The pendulum had sunk to the level of the coffin. Four of the chorus boys were dancing and flapping their scarlet capes in a circle around the magician in the tuxedo. Two of them covered the separated halves of the glass coffin with drapes, hiding all but the cloth dummy's midsection.

Mallory leaned close to Prado, knowing he'd never release his hold on the rail to go for her weapon. "Futura was born frightened, wasn't he? He read Oliver's invitation and nearly lost his mind. I've got the phone records," she lied. "I know he talked it over with you."

Had she guessed wrong this time? Between the drugs and the fear of falling, his face was unreadable. Mallory waited until he had taken a few deep breaths. "I know you planned Oliver's murder." She could not be wrong about that part.

"And I know you did it just to make a motive for this one. That's your style, too complex, too messy—still plotting like an idiot teenager."

Prado seemed genuinely indignant. "I never killed—"

She shifted her weight again. The bridge moved with a wider pitch. His face was flushed, and his breathing was fast and shallow. When she was done with his punishment for lying, she stopped rocking her body. "So it takes two murders to cover up what you did to Louisa? You couldn't afford to let her run that night, not with your forged documents. You had to come up with a way to kill her in Paris."

"*Franny* killed Louisa!"

She rocked the bridge again, and he sank to his knees, his hands still wrapped around the rails, eyes shut tight.

"Everyone was in danger," he said. "Emile was—"

She rocked the bridge with violence, making it swing from side to side. His eyes opened and rolled back to solid whites.

"No, Prado. St. John has the reputation of a cop with good instincts. He always knew Louisa was a risk, a hunted woman. He never gave up any secrets. *You* did. First you tried to scare Futura. And he wanted to run away, didn't he? That's when you told him Louisa would betray St. John if the Germans got her alive."

Prado moaned, and she made the bridge sway again. When he was at the point of vomiting his dinner, she stopped the movement.

"Then you sent Futura into that back room to kill a woman who was crying and wounded and helpless. You told him it was going to be so easy, a quick job—just hold the pillow over her face." What did Futura know about killing? What did any of them know? They were only boys. "When Louisa fought back, that must have scared him out of his mind. Two frightened people, one killing the other." Pure terror for both of them. And right outside—German soldiers at the door.

The pendulum was swinging between the glass boxes. The sawdust was flying in both directions. Mallory shook the bridge again, then stopped to stare at the spreading wetness on Prado's crotch. He stank of urine.

"Get up!"

Prado was slow to stand. His head was bowed to hide the humiliation in his face.

"Futura didn't kill her to save his own skin," said Mallory. "He would've run away if he felt threatened. I know his type." The lesson of urban warfare—rabbits run. "So when fear didn't work—then you exposed St. John. You cut it close. The Germans were there—no time to think. Maybe you reminded him that Malakhai's wife had a bad record for betrayal. And *then* that terrified little man marched into the back room and killed Louisa. He probably cried while he was doing it. Poor bastard. He thought he was doing the right thing—a brave thing."

When Prado finally raised his face to hers, he was putting on a good show of composure. "But Franny *did* kill Louisa. Don't you wonder why Malakhai waited so long for his revenge?" He held this out in the air between them, as though it were his chip to withhold or bargain with.

"No deal, Prado. I already know."

The pendulum was rising again, and the arc was narrowing as it withdrew behind the cover of the curtain's valance.

"After you told Malakhai what really happened to his wife, it must have driven you nuts when he didn't kill Futura—when Malakhai forgave him for Louisa's murder." She watched his eyes for an indication that she had made an error, but he was genuinely stunned. "Then Oliver was murdered, and that changed everything. Malakhai felt responsible—you made sure of that. That's why Malakhai tried to shoot Futura during the parade."

There had been an identifying marker in Malakhai's method of execution, a companion quality to forgiveness—almost mercy. Franny Futura would never have seen the rifle. There would not have been any time for him to be afraid.

"Mallory, if I had a hat, I'd take it off. You might be the best cop in the world."

He would have to say that. A lesser cop could not be responsible for undoing the great Nick Prado—not in his own mind. His ego was surfacing again, driving off the anxiety.

"You really worked on Malakhai, didn't you?" She rocked

the bridge to prompt him. "You told him if he'd only taken care of business after the war, Oliver would still be alive."

"Yes, and I failed—but *you* didn't." He did not fall to his knees this time. He was intensely focused on her face. She was his tormentor, but also his visual anchor.

"I couldn't have done it without you, Mallory. You're the one who told him how Louisa died, how much Franny hurt her—all that fear and pain. Yes, I told Malakhai she was murdered. Then he went after Emile for more details. Emile told him it was a quick death, no suffering. If Franny hadn't killed Oliver—"

"He *didn't*. You made the key switch that day in the park." She stared at him, waiting for any sign that she had guessed wrong. The drugs had slowed all his reactions, but also his ability to mask surprise. She was right—he was the one. "Futura didn't even feel threatened by Oliver's invitation, did he? The war was over for everyone but you. Fear didn't work this time. Another screwup, Prado?"

His face had the slow beginnings of a smile.

"Not quite it?" No, she had gotten something wrong. "I'm betting you only used that invitation to sell the murder to Malakhai. You never even mentioned it to Futura."

Yes, that was it. His smugness died away, and his hands slid back along the rail, leaving a slick of sweat on the metal.

"Did you tell him Futura was afraid of Oliver? I bet you planted that idea before the magic show in the park. Better to let Malakhai work it out for himself." She shook the bridge again and made it rock wildly, turning its planks from side to side, approaching right angles to the stage below. "Why did Malakhai mess up that shot at Futura? If he'd missed, he would've taken more shots. But there was only one."

Prado gripped the rails but his hands were greased with more sweat. He lost his handhold and his footing, coming down hard on his knees, while Mallory kept the perfect balance of a creature with paws and claws.

He shut his eyes and yelled, "Enough!"

She ceased to rock, and waited for him to get control of himself. Below her, the chorus boys were dancing.

Prado wiped his palms on his suit. His breath was rapid, and now one hand clawed at his tie. "I was watching Malakhai when he put down the rifle. He just lost the heart for a killing. I don't know why. He was going to walk away from it *again.*"

He was rallying, catching his breath. The hot flush faded off, and his smile was stealing back. "And then you worked on him, Mallory, and you never let up. Finally, he came back to me—that lovely boy I used to know. Last night, he was weeping and angry—ready to kill the whole world. You deserve half the credit."

The pendulum was still, and she had a clear view of the dummy's midsection torn in two. The assistants were lifting it out of the coffin. Mallory checked the backstage area again. "He's down there with a gun. That wasn't part of your plan, was it? In *your* version, Futura dies in the act, right? Cut in half by a razor?"

Yes, the gun was a surprise to him.

She trained the crossbow down toward the stage. From this perspective, she could not tell a tall man from a short one. Coming up here was a mistake.

Prado was also looking down again, perhaps only to prove that he could. "What if you do spot Malakhai? You can't just shoot him without—"

"But that's what you want, isn't it? You just don't want me to get the killing out of order. If I take out Malakhai first, Franny will talk. Oh, God, how he'll talk."

The pendulum was in motion again and slowly lowering toward the stage.

"I wouldn't risk a shot to wound him," she said. "And that's a matter of respect."

Prado flinched. He understood that he was only alive because he fell into a less respected category.

Mallory set the crossbow down. He was slow to register shock as she grabbed his arm and rammed it up behind his back. She maneuvered him over the steel rail, smashing his paunch into the metal and knocking the breath out of his lungs. The suspension bridge swayed and threatened to drop both of them off. The crossbow hung off the edge of the planks, and she kicked it back to the center of the bridge.

"You're out of shape, old man. This silly idea that you can beat me in a fair fight? You can't. But Malakhai could. That's why I have to kill him on sight." She wrenched his arm tighter. "Have I made my point? If you help me stop him, you still have breathing room to weasel out of this or disappear."

Mallory released him and picked up the crossbow. Prado was taking deep breaths and looking down—flirting with the fall. Perhaps the drugs were kicking in again. Below him, the assistants were helping the magician to climb inside his glass coffin.

"What happens now, Prado?"

He looked up at the crossbow as she pointed it toward the stage. His voice was close to calm. "I'm sure you don't want to kill a chorus boy. *Anyone* can do that."

The assistants separated the sections of the glass coffin to expose the black cummerbund of Futura's tuxedo. And now they slipped the magician's hands and feet through the holes in the glass and manacled him by wrist and ankle.

"The cuffs are breakaways," said Prado. "No problem with a key this time. Franny wouldn't even risk that much."

The assistants draped both halves of the coffin with red cloth.

"He'll be out of the coffin in another minute or two," said Prado. "Now, if he was a limber young boy, he'd snap the breakaways on his legs and curl up in the front box. That's another tired old cheat."

One of the assistants blocked the audience view of the space between the separated glass sections. The man took a thick log of black cloth from under his cape and placed it in the coffin.

"That's a cheat to make the audience think he's still in the box when the razor comes down. It matches Franny's tuxedo."

A bundle of red material was pushed into the front half of the coffin.

"And that's another cape for Franny. He'll put it on before

he rolls out the back side of the coffin. The rear walls are hinged. Then he'll blend in with the chorus boys."

A man in a long red cape was coming out of a crouch by the front section of the coffin.

"That's Franny," said Prado. "Now count the assistants. There are seven on stage right now. The act started with six."

The pendulum began to move again, back and forth over the slot between the boxes.

"There's a microphone in the front half of the coffin," said Prado. "In a minute, a machine will send a layer of fog across the stage. That hides the wire while an assistant plugs it into the coffin. Very cheap sound equipment, almost as old as Franny. When you hear his voice on stage, he'll be in a back room screaming into a speaker."

The pendulum was dropping closer.

"When Max did this act, he didn't drape the coffin. You could see him in there beating the glass while he screamed. You watched the razor shred his cummerbund. No fake blood, nothing crude. But people swore they saw Max's blood dripping rivers onto the stage. Franny's version is second-rate all around. Boring as a closed-coffin funeral."

Prado was suddenly much too talkative, too helpful—stalling for time. With her free hand, she reached down, gripped his collar and pushed his head forward over the planks. "You won't walk away from this if he dies."

He twisted his head up to smile at her. Sweat poured down his face, his eyes bulged—the smile persisted. "I thought you'd be more understanding, Mallory. You're in the justice profession."

"No, that's someone else's job. I'm only the law. If I wasn't, I'd toss you off this catwalk right now. Justice is easy. What I do is so much harder."

For all the fear, his smile was broadening into the genuine article. Was it the drugs? Or was he aiming her like a gun? Yes, he was only trying to control the timing. It was important that Futura died first.

The seventh man was leaving the stage. The six assistants stayed to dance while the pendulum dropped lower. A door closed backstage. Was Futura already in the back room? Was Malakhai waiting there? She had missed something. That was why he smiled.

Mallory turned and ran toward the end of the catwalk and started down the ladder. What if the gun was only misdirection? Did Malakhai plan to kill Futura the same way Louisa died—in a replica of the same room?

The microphone version of Futura's voice was screaming from the coffin, "Wait, something has gone wrong!" And simultaneously, she heard the same voice from the back of the theater, muffled by walls. Four rungs from the floor, she jumped from the ladder and drew a bead on the caped figure heading toward the back room. "Malakhai! Stop! Or I'll drop you."

He moved behind a round plaster column. The illusion of transformation was perfect. His red cape had disappeared when he emerged on the other side of the pillar in a dark suit and tie. Her stolen revolver was dangling from his right hand.

The voice from the stage was crying out for help. Low clouds of machine-made fog rolled across the floorboards, covering the wires. She could hear Futura in the back room where he felt utterly safe shouting fear into his microphone.

"It's not going to happen, Malakhai. I've got three arrows in the magazine. I want my gun back. *Now!* I *will* shoot you."

"Yes, I know. You would've been astonishing in the war. Oh, wait—wrong period. Sorry. The other night, Riker told me you were raised on cowboy movies."

He held out the gun on the flat of his hand.

She used the crossbow to gesture toward the floor. "Put it down."

He set it on the floor in front of his shoes. "So how did you like Charles's act?"

"Kick it over to me." The stereo yelling was ongoing. The pendulum must still be dropping. She never looked toward the stage; that way lay misdirection. "Kick it over. *Now!*"

He sent the gun scraping across the wood with the tap of his foot. It came to rest in front of her. She held the crossbow on him and dipped low to retrieve her revolver. In a split second, she had checked the visible chambers, each one packed with a bullet.

"Always wise to check the whole cylinder." He leaned back against the post and folded his arms. "I might've taken out the first round. Were you disappointed in the Lost Illusion? You didn't say."

"Charles didn't get it right either, did he?"

"No, but Max would've been proud. I watched Charles's rehearsal. That was quite a risk he took—and all for you. Whenever I think of the two of you, I see ghosts."

"You knew I'd never be able to talk him out of it."

"Not if you held a gun to his head."

"Something could've gone wrong."

"That's true. And Charles knew that. Max's effect was actually less dangerous, but more stunning. How did you know Charles did it wrong?"

"It wasn't—enough. Just an escape routine, no magic. There should've been magic."

"So my tutelage has paid off. Well, Charles made the best of it, opting for comedy. But Max did the impossible and made everyone believe in it. I could show you, but I'd need the crossbow."

"Yeah, right."

"So skeptical, Mallory." He held out his hand, believing that she would actually give it to him. "Why the hesitation? You have the gun. Surely a bullet is faster than an arrow? Your cowboy movies must've taught you that much. If you still want to know how the Lost Illusion worked, I'll show you. If you wait till tomorrow, I might have another stroke. And then you'd never—"

She shook her head. It was not going to happen.

"But, Mallory, you *like* the edge so much. What's the worst thing that could happen? A duel? A showdown? Give me the crossbow. If you want to know how the trick is done, it's going to cost you something—a risk."

"No way."

"I'd never hurt you, Mallory. I've never lied to you."

The idea was seductive. Her reflexes were better, faster.

And she did not believe that he wanted her dead, but neither was she a practitioner of absolute faith. Training her revolver on his heart, she turned the crossbow upside down and three arrows fell to the floor. Now she held it out to him.

Malakhai accepted the weapon. "But I need the arrows." He knelt down on the floor and reached toward them, looking up at her, eyebrows arched to ask, *May I?*

"Sure," she said. "But if you try to cock the crossbow, I'll kill you."

"Understood." He set down the crossbow and loaded the arrows, slowly dropping them into the slot of the wooden magazine. "Max always stocked three arrows. You wondered about that."

He stood up, and she raised the muzzle of her revolver to his face. Though she had been trained to fire at the wider target of the chest, aiming at the head was a more deadly reminder that she was prepared to kill him.

Behind her, the music ended, but the chorus boys continued to tap-dance to the screams of Franny Futura. She heard the hiss. And that must be the pendulum slicing through the air. Her finger touched lightly on the revolver's trigger to feel the cold metal, but no pressure, not yet.

He held the crossbow by the shaft and offered it to her. "Here. The trick is all set up. You only have to cock the bow and shoot me in the heart."

"Of course," she said, clearly meaning, *Not a shot in hell.* It took two hands to cock the bow, and she would not holster her gun. She took the crossbow in her left hand. Her right hand kept the revolver trained on his face.

"You can do it," he said, as though encouraging a child in first steps. "If you want the solution, you'll have to shoot me to get it."

Chiming in with Futura's yelling was the squeal of the microphone feedback. Malakhai looked toward the closed room. "That's the problem with technical cheats. Now the whole effect is ruined." He turned back to her. "Ready for *real* magic?" He spread his arms to offer her a clear aim at his chest. "I'm waiting on my arrow, Mallory." He smiled so gently. "You can't do it? Well, in that case, I have some unfinished business to take care of. I never needed your gun for this."

He was turning when she extended her gun arm. "You move—I shoot you with a bullet. It's like that." But she was not aiming to kill, not willing to become a mechanical prop of Nick Prado.

Malakhai raised one hand to show her a dark metal file. He tossed it in the direction of the open toolbox abandoned by the workman. "I told you I never needed the gun. You should have paid more attention to my shell game. I am sorry about the damage to your revolver, and of course I'll pay for it."

Mallory knew what she was going to see before she looked down at the pulled-back hammer. He had filed down the firing pin.

She raised the crossbow as she holstered the gun.

"That's better," he said. "But I don't think you *can* shoot me. Well, I'm off. Killing only takes a few seconds when you know how. And I do."

"Malakhai!" She cocked the bow, bringing down the lever to pull the string tight. "You know I'll shoot."

"Will you, Mallory? In the back? How will you explain that? I'm unarmed." He was almost to the door of the back room. "Maybe you're overconfident in your monsterhood. Personally, I don't think you have the makings."

"Stop!"

"Franny's act is almost done. I have to hurry."

Mallory didn't aim to wound him; she picked that place where the shaft would travel into his back and rupture his heart. She squeezed the crossbow trigger. The bowstring released with a twang, and in that same instant, he whirled around. His hand flashed out and caught the arrow in midair.

Impossible.

She knew the velocity of the arrow. He could not have done that, yet there was an arrow in his hand.

"Apparently I misjudged you." He came strolling back to her, smiling, taking his own time. "Sorry. No hard feelings?"

"You palmed that arrow." She looked down into the magazine. A misfire? She cocked it again and raised the sights to his chest.

He kept coming. "It won't work this time either." He was closing the gap between them. Futura was still shouting for help from his little room.

She fired the weapon at his chest. The string released, but the arrow did not fly. "You jammed the magazine? That's not the way—"

"*Just* the way Max did it. Felt a slight kick though, didn't you? Oh, I see the confusion. How could the arrows fly for the dummy, then jam for the human target? Well, you're really going to hate this part."

He held up the arrow and twisted the metal tip. It screwed up and down on the shaft. "This elongates the arrow. Only the first one drops straight into the bed—that's for the test shot on the dummy. When you load the second arrow, the long one, its tip digs into the wood of the magazine as you press down on the other end. And the third arrow? That kept the audience from seeing that the second arrow never fired."

"But cops loaded the magazines in both—"

"Not when Max did the routine. The policemen only handed him the arrows, all identical, all the same length. *He* loaded them. Oliver and Charles got that part backward. So as Max loaded the second crossbow, he twisted the tip."

He put the arrow into her demanding outstretched hand.

"So that's all there was to it? Max rigged a crossbow?"

"Oh, no," said Malakhai. "He rigged *two* bows. Now Charles's solution was good, but when Max did the illusion, the effect was brilliant, electrifying. He evaded the first two shots, and the tension was unbearable while he struggled with the handcuffs. Then he broke the post, and the audience screamed—they howled. The crossbow fired—then the arrow was in his hand, caught in midair to thunderous applause. And the last shot? It appeared that his timing was off, that he had failed to catch the last arrow before it pierced his heart. Max died there on the target. When he came back from the dead to pull the arrow out of his own heart, a man in the front row fainted."

"So he had two arrows hidden in his jacket."

"Right. It was a thrilling effect."

"But the jammed arrow could've been dislodged by the kick when the first arrow fired."

"That actually did happen in a rehearsal with the dummy. It was always a possibility. When I saw Max take the arrow in his heart that night, I wasn't sure. Only someone as tall as Charles could've avoided the fatal arrow. Even with one free hand, Max didn't have that much room to maneuver. Still, Charles risked his life. You don't see that kind of courage every day. That's why Max's routines were never stolen."

Malakhai smiled as he watched her use an arrow to push the jammed one into the shaft, still determined to shoot him.

Behind her the music began to play again.

"And now, the best for last." He tugged on his shirt cuffs and showed her his empty sleeves. Then he held up two closed fists for her inspection.

His fingers slowly uncurled, and Mallory heard the distant scream of real pain coming from two directions at once, the stage and the back room. She listened to the audience reaction, the great white static of a hundred whispers all seeking reassurance in the dark. The screaming grew louder as his hands opened wider, as if Malakhai were working the other man's pain like a ventriloquist.

She turned to the stage where the pendulum was swinging in a wide arc between the glass boxes. The edge of the crescent razor was stained red. "Max Candle didn't use blood in the act."

"No, Mallory. Neither did Franny."

"Not a microphone in the box."

"Oh, yes there is—but so is Franny." He caught up one of her hands as she was rushing the stage. When he swung her back to his side, the crossbow clattered to the floor. "It's the sound equipment you hear in the back room. Nothing to cheat you and disappoint you—not this time. It's all quite real."

She tried to pull away. Her leg was rising and she needed space for the groin shot. He wrenched her wrist sharply, and she was wrapped in his arms.

"The pendulum won't stop for you, Mallory." He spoke so

softly, so reasonably—*this* from a killer. It was the voice of reason that chilled her, as if he could believe that this was a sane act.

"It's not a device you can switch off," he said. "It has to play out the movements of the gears. That machine doesn't care if you're a cop."

She tried to break Malakhai's hold, writhing in his grasp until she faced the stage. He held her closer—like a lover, like a jailor, imprisoning her hands in his, arms binding her tighter than ropes.

Futura's pain was a continuous shriek. Malakhai's voice was at her ear. "You wanted to know what I did in the war? Then watch."

"No! Stop it!" She called out to the dancing boys, "Move the coffin out of the way!" Mallory's shouts mingled with Futura's screams. The assistants faced the audience as they danced at the edge of the stage, ignoring cries for help, and the music played on. Her heart was banging in a sympathetic rhythm with Futura's terror, his bleating and his bleeding.

And Malakhai was whispering, "Rare justice, Mallory. For Louisa, for Oliver."

The pendulum was splattering the stage with blood, drops of it landing on the costumes of the dancing boys. Their backs were turned on the coffin as they kicked their feet in unison.

Malakhai tightened his embrace. "See those people at the back?" Two shadowy forms were rising in the dim light of the audience. "Those men are coming to save Franny. They'll be too late, of course, but they're coming. Only two of them. Look at the rest."

A lone woman's scream rose above the sound of shrieking pain in the coffin.

"Mallory, think of Oliver Tree—all those arrows. He was your Oliver, too, wasn't he? You always called him by his first name."

Blood splattered the edge of the stage. The pendulum swung in a wider arc, and red drops hit the dresses of two women in the front row. Only one woman was screaming as loud as Franny Futura and with the same pain. The rest of the audience sat in stunned silence, except for the two men who had made their way to the center aisle. Now they raced toward the stage.

"Only two rescuers," said Malakhai.

There were spots of blood on a woman's dress in the second row. The pendulum swung out again, red and wet. And now a man in the front row had a trickle of blood streaming down his face, as did the man next to him. The two rescuers were climbing onto the stage.

"Mallory, look at the people in the front rows. They know it's gone wrong—never doubt that. They know Franny's dying, and they can't take their eyes away. Now *this* is theater—a small window on World War II, the way it *really* was. A leftover minute of horror."

The two rescuers could not reach the coffin. They were surrounded by flapping red capes in a tight formation of tap-dancing chorus boys. Blood pooled beneath the table.

One desperate woman's scream harmonized with shrieks from the glass coffin, echoes from the back room, and a shrill electronic squeal of sound equipment.

And then the screaming stopped—Mallory's and Franny's.

The pendulum continued to swing in silence, to cut the flesh and break the bones, not knowing or caring that the man was dead. The blood was lessening, trickling only, with no more coming to fuel the spillage.

The dead did not bleed.

Malakhai released her. "And now you've been to war, Mallory. Wasn't it sublime?"

The music ended, the dancing stopped—all silent now as the caped chorus boys and the two men in suits slowly approached the coffin.

Mallory sank down to the floor. Though spent and drained, she would not let go of the rage. She beat one clenched hand on the floorboards until the pain flooded her eyes with tears.

Malakhai knelt down beside her, and Mallory turned her face away to hide it.

"You're a fraud." He caressed her hair gently. "You have more compassion than those people out there with blood on their faces—the ones who only watched."

She shot out one fist.

He was faster, catching her balled hand and engulfing it in his own. "Of course, you did try to kill me. No one can ever take that away from you. And I do think you're ruthless—if that's a consolation." He stood up slowly, releasing the uncurling fingers of her fist, which had lost its power. "But, Mallory, we can't all be monsters. As I said—you don't have the makings."

Head bowed, she drew up her legs very close to her body and listened to his footsteps leaving her, then the closing of a door. Over the babble of the audience, she heard the sirens wailing on Broadway, coming closer by the second, louder now, almost there. Mallory closed her eyes and hugged her knees, rocking, rocking, shell-shocked and wounded by her minute in the war.

Twenty-two

EVEN AT THIS DISTANCE FROM THE STAGE, THE AIR WAS DANK and clammy—all that blood. And there was a stink of defecation and the dead man's dinner, undigested before he was cut in two.

Detective Riker had arrived to find Mallory leaning into the glass coffin. She had allowed him to wash the blood off her hands, but pushed him away when he made a mess of her cashmere blazer, smearing and spreading the red stains with wet paper towels.

Now she sat at a desk near the stage door. A lamp cast her rigid shadow on a nearby wall of message boxes. She seemed unaware of the odors and the heavy traffic of patrolmen and detectives, the medical examiner's investigators and the district attorney's man. Her eyes were blind to everything in the immediate world.

Riker knew she was replaying Franny Futura's death in her mind, repeating the images over and over, hunting for the imperfections in her work.

And that must stop.

He accepted a paper cup from a stagehand and gave the man five dollars for his trouble. Mallory eyed the container with mild suspicion, and Riker took that as a sign that she was feeling more herself.

He placed the cup in her hand. "It's water."

She took one sip. "It's not."

"Oh, that's the booze you're tasting. But there's water in

there, too. Drink it all down, kid. You need the vitamins." Riker thought she might also need a blood transfusion. He glanced toward the stage where two men were lifting the body from the coffin. When he turned back to his partner, her paper cup was drained, and she was crumpling it in a tight fist. Another good sign.

"They suckered me, Riker."

This was true, and they would probably get away with it, but he would never throw that up to her. He pulled out his notebook. "The first cop on the scene took statements from the old guy's assistants. They all thought the voice in the coffin was a microphone."

She nodded. "A two-way feed. The sound equipment is in the back room. It worked like an intercom with a stuck button."

"These magicians all swear they saw Futura leave the coffin before the pendulum dropped. How could—"

"They're not magicians," said Mallory. "Just a pack of chorus boys. What they *saw* was a man in a red cape. That was Malakhai. He ducked under the coffin drapes and came out again on cue. The boys were so busy dancing their little brains out, none of them noticed that Malakhai was taller." Her face lifted, and she was staring at the suspension bridge overhead. "I would've caught that if I hadn't been up there on the catwalk."

"Don't beat yourself up." He held out a copy of Faustine's rod with a single key plug screwed into the end. "Look familiar? We found this near the body. It looks like Futura dropped it before he could unlock his cuffs."

She only glanced at it. "That's probably Malakhai's key. Franny didn't plan to use real handcuffs. Malakhai switched the breakaways for real ones. That's how he killed the old man."

"So then Malakhai *planted* a key? Pretty slick. We'll never prove murder."

"I never saw Malakhai go on stage, never saw him duck under the table. Prado's job was misdirection. If I can't nail him for Oliver's murder, I'll get him on conspiracy for this one."

"I don't think so, kid. Malakhai did the hands-on murder. There's nothing to tie Prado to conspiracy." Riker pulled up a wooden chair next to hers and straddled it, resting his folded arms across the back. "We can't even make a case for motive."

"I should've shot Malakhai on sight," said Mallory. "And I *knew* that. Another mistake."

Riker looked over his shoulder to see Jack Coffey walking toward them with a damp raincoat slung over his shoulder. Had the lieutenant heard that last remark?

Coffey stopped in front of the desk. He wore his bad-news face as he looked down at Mallory. "I just finished with Prado. He claims you contributed to the accidental death of Futura. He says you actually prevented him from assisting the—"

"Prado engineered that homicide," said Mallory. "The act didn't need any help. It worked just fine. Franny Futura is really, really dead."

Riker put one hand on her shoulder to keep her from leaving the chair. "Easy, kid. Nobody believes it's an accident. But Prado just killed the case. The newspapers will say it was your fault. Then they'll crucify the whole department."

Coffey sat on the edge of the desk. "Prado says he isn't going to put that version in his formal statement. When he told me that, it had the smell of a deal. I'm taking your side on this, Mallory, but we can't arrest either one of them. They both walk away."

Mallory's voice was too calm. "Did you take a close look at what they did? That didn't make you sick?"

Riker was staring at her hands, folded tightly over one another to hide the slight tremor. This was not a symptom of frayed nerves, but a warning sign that she was close to losing her temper, her judgment and her job. She was containing the anger, but how long would that last?

Lieutenant Coffey nodded toward a man standing near the ladder of the suspension bridge. He was in his late twenties with a dark raincoat and a pasty-white face. "That's Crane. He's an assistant DA and a real jerk. But he's the man on this one, and he says it's a flat no. The DA's office won't even look at the case."

Crane joined the small party of three, but stood a pronounced distance from Coffey. The man looked down at Mallory, as if from some lofty height. And Riker gathered that this was supposed to put the detective in her place.

But she was making her own assessments, openly appraising the lawyer's cheap raincoat commensurate with the starting salary of an ADA. Even Riker could see that the sleeves were miles too long. Mallory's tailor would have spat on that coat.

The man's voice was an annoying nasal whine. "I understand *all* of Max Candle's illusions were dangerous. And these people you're accusing? Decorated war heroes, both of them. Their character reference is Emile St. John, a former bureau chief for Interpol." The assistant district attorney placed both hands on the desk and leaned entirely too close to Mallory. "You screwed up royally, Detective. If anyone sues the city for your part in this death, I'm going to throw—"

The assistant DA lost his place in this spiel which smacked of rehearsal. Though Mallory hardly moved, even a dense fool like Crane must realize that she really wanted to hurt him, and pain could only be moments away.

The lawyer pulled back and stood closer to Coffey as he made a show of straightening his tie. Then Crane's lip curled up on one side, and Riker wondered if that little gesture of contempt had been perfected in a shaving mirror.

"It was a clear accident," said Crane. "The man dropped his handcuff key. Any *idiot* could see that. So why do I have to explain these simple facts to a cop? The next time you drag me out on a crime scene, you get your facts straight. Use your head. *Open* your eyes. Do you *understand* me, Detective?"

Tomorrow morning, Mallory would become the joke of the district attorney's office. This time, she would eat the humiliation—or maybe not. She was rising off the chair, but Riker had a tight grip on the back of her trench coat.

Jack Coffey's expression was close to evil, almost a Mallory smile. "Riker, what do you think you're doing? If she wants to deck the weasel, that's her call."

Riker's hand dropped away, and he turned his eyes upward to study the neon sign over the door, as if the word *EXIT* might be a difficult read.

And now it was Mallory's turn to smile.

"Wait, I changed my mind." Coffey stabbed the assistant DA with two fingers to the man's chest, pushing him back a step. "You're a real screwup, Crane. I saw the evidence—*all* of it." He jabbed the man's chest again for emphasis. "I say she's got a case. You're too stupid or too scared to run with it."

The lawyer's face was going slack. He was sliding into shock, and with good reason. In the hierarchy of cops and prosecutors, this should not be happening to him.

"This is obviously your first day on the job," said Coffey. "So I'm not gonna list your mistakes in my report. If I did, your boss would ask me why I didn't kick your sorry ass."

What mistakes?

Riker knew the district attorney would never side with Jack Coffey. Come morning, the chief prosecutor would be all over the lieutenant for this transgression. It was policy and common practice to use cops for punching bags when the young princes of the DA's office were thwarted or merely miffed. And a seasoned lawyer would know that. So it probably *was* Crane's first day on the job.

And now Riker recognized this tango of brazenly shifting guilt and leading with a mouthful of lies. Lieutenant Coffey was taking lessons from Mallory.

They were all doomed.

Coffey glanced at his watch. "Tell you what, Crane. I'm gonna give you a ten-second running head start."

The lieutenant moved toward the lawyer, and Crane retreated, no longer puffing out his chest in a last-ditch effort to convey the idea that he was still in charge. He was clearly confused, probably wondering what he had missed, what error he had made—the hallmark of a green ADA. Lieutenant Coffey had pegged the lawyer right; he *was* a weasel, and now the man was slinking away, gently closing the stage door behind him. In Riker's lights, this was a good omen. If Crane intended to get even, if revenge was in his mind, the door would have slammed.

A clear win.

Coffey was facing the stage as he spoke to Mallory. "You've got nowhere to go with this case. It wasn't a perfect murder, but damn close." He watched the medical examiner's men reuniting the body parts in a long black zippered bag. "You got zero chance of Prado confessing to conspiracy. And no physical evidence of murder. Now Malakhai's a certified card-carrying lunatic. Suppose you got a confession from him? A madman's testimony is no good, not against himself or anyone else."

Mallory's hands unfolded and relaxed on the arms of the wooden chair. Her voice was listless. "If we could get this case in front of a jury, I could diagram the whole thing."

Coffey shook his head. For the first time, he seemed reluctant to win an argument with her. "It all hangs on your testimony, Mallory. Nick Prado will kill your credibility if he hangs this death on you." He pulled on his raincoat as the gurney moved past the desk, pushed along by the medical examiner's men. "I'm sorry you couldn't save that old guy. I'm glad you tried." The lieutenant watched the progress of the rolling body bag until it had cleared the stage door. "Mallory? If I'd given you the manpower you wanted—"

"It wouldn't have made any difference." She rested her head on the back of the chair. "It wouldn't have changed a damn thing."

Coffey turned away from her and walked out the stage door.

Riker inched his chair closer to Mallory. "You really blew it, kid. If you'd said it was Coffey's fault, you could've used that on him down the road. Nothin' like guilt in the bank." He put his hand on her forehead. "Are you feeling okay?"

She brushed him away.

"No fever," said Riker. "Well, your old man always said you'd grow up to be a class act. I guess that's the only explanation."

So this was her idea of payback for nailing the weasel. And

Jack Coffey had done that with style, a smooth *beau geste* without a drop of sweat or a blink—all to save Mallory's face. It was damn near romantic.

Of course, the stress would make the rest of Coffey's hair fall out overnight, but he would still be beautiful to Riker in the morning.

Mallory pulled her gun from the holster and set it down on the desk. "What else have we got? Anything? I bet no one remembers seeing Malakhai in the theater, right?"

"No one can put him on the scene." Riker never took his eyes off her gun. A suicide watch was standard practice for a cop involved in a bloody killing, but Mallory would get no such service for an accidental death. "What about motive for the first one? You think Oliver Tree really knew how Louisa died?"

"No, he was just a nice old man." She picked up the gun and turned it over in her hands. "But he was brave, wasn't he? All those arrows."

"Yeah, he was." Riker understood how much Oliver Tree had meant to her. But she was already on a first-name basis with the new corpse, Franny Futura, and that worried him. There was a possessive quality to the way she pronounced his name.

She was not done yet.

"You did good. It's not your fault that—" And now he watched her pull back the hammer on her revolver. "Mallory, you know Coffey's right. There's nothing more you can do."

Certainly nothing legal.

His eyes were still on the revolver in her hands. Even without his glasses, the damage to the firing pin was obvious. Though he would wonder about that for a long time to come, he would never ask how it had happened. He put one hand on her shoulder and squeezed it lightly. "You're only human, kid."

Mallory smiled. "But you're not really sure about that, are you, Riker?" She slid the broken gun into her holster. "Drive me home?"

"Sure thing. You wanna change clothes?"

"Something like that."

✛   ✛   ✛

The long room was paneled in dark wood. Plush red leather couches and chairs were arranged in conversational groupings, and the far wall was lined with bottles and a long mirror above the mahogany bar. For lack of customers, a cocktail waitress passed the time in low conversation with the bartender. They were too far away to be overheard.

Mallory stood near the archway of the lounge, facing the wide dining room entrance across a narrow hallway. She watched the waiter's progress through the many tables set with crystal and linen, wine and food. The man had not yet found Malakhai among the patrons at this private party.

It was a window on another time. Fur wraps were draped on the chairs of women who showed no fear of assault by political spittle. Illicit smoke curled upward from long cigarette holders, and bright jewels flashed sparks of light from bracelets and rings. Champagne corks were popping, and the music of another era swelled up and floated back across the divide of the hall. Two people were slow-dancing between the tables, and other outlaws were rising to join them in this unlicensed, untaxed pleasure.

And behind her, the December rain was drumming on the glass.

Malakhai emerged from the dining room and walked toward the lounge. He was happy to see her. Perhaps he misunderstood her visit, taking it as a graceful gesture of defeat.

She felt lighter in the body as he drew closer. And there was a quickening in her chest where the most vital organ should be, but none other than Dr. Slope had said she did not have a heart. An ache was rising in her throat. She knew what that was; it came with sorrow, but she could not understand it—not here, not now. And so she put it down to the frayed nerves of closing on endgame. She was here to call Malakhai out and finish him off.

"Mallory, I hope you'll let me pay for wrecking your gun."

"Don't worry about it." She unbelted her trench coat. "I

have lots of guns." She opened her blazer to display the .38 in her holster. "This one works just fine."

He was standing very close to her. Her pulse was racing. And this excitement going on beneath her skin? Nerves, only that. Such a long night. Almost over.

"Come to the party?" Malakhai glanced at the dining room for a moment. "Or were you planning to make an arrest for illegal dancing?"

Mallory looked into the other room. "I thought they might've canceled it—because of the *accident*."

"Most of these people were at Carnegie Hall tonight," said Malakhai. "No one's come in from Faustine's yet. I may have forgotten to mention the incident."

"But you remember killing a man. You know I'll get you for that."

"Ah, the arrest—that's the main thing, isn't it? Nick says there won't be one. But I have more faith in you. Of course, by the time you make a case, I probably won't remember *why* you're arresting me. I hope that doesn't spoil it. I hate disappointing you." Perversely, he seemed sincere in this. There was no sarcasm in his voice. He was moving closer.

Mallory did not back away, but she did warn him off with the slow shake of her head. "I think I can get a warrant before your brain turns to soup."

He smiled as if this were a great joke. "The strokes are coming faster now. Years are disappearing. Entire decades are mostly smoke."

"So I was right, wasn't I? Louisa's gone?"

"She's been gone a long time."

"But she was there when you took a shot at Futura. Louisa wouldn't let you do it, would she?"

He shook his head in mild confusion.

So this was one more mystery she would never have the answer to—like the way he had worked a dead woman's shadow. Curiously, Mallory had more faith in Malakhai's wife than he did. If Louisa had not died a second time, Franny might have lived.

He put out one hand to touch her hair. "Right now, this

moment—it's just you and me." He bowed his head, bringing his face closer to hers. "I hope to die before I forget you, Kathy Mallory."

She listened to the rain drumming on the windowpane behind her. One moment strung into the next. His arm moved around her shoulder, and he was leading her toward the dining room.

"So come to the party." His voice was stronger now. "We'll break the law while I still remember how to dance."

Mallory pulled back, shook him off, and still he was not seeing her as an opponent—a good time to slip in a knife. What would it take to convince him that he had murdered the wrong man? Nick Prado was standing on the other side of the narrow hall, and she knew the same idea was crossing his mind as he watched their conversation with great interest.

With just the right words, the right timing, she could aim Malakhai at Prado and commit a perfect murder with proxy hands.

Prado was a serial killer—three deaths. He was so good at this. She had underestimated him—another mistake. But now she could do the same thing better, quicker—and get clean away with it. Prado would die, and Malakhai would be effectively destroyed when he knew he had killed the wrong man. A little justice for everyone.

Her trench coat was parted. The holster was exposed as she casually drew the blazer material to one side. Malakhai had already had some practice in taking her gun tonight. She only had to point him toward the target standing just across the hall.

This is going to be so easy.

But now, slowly and with deep regret, she closed her coat, hiding the gun and cinching the leather with a hard tug on her belt. Justice had nothing to do with her job. She was only the law.

Prado drifted back into the party. Opportunity was walking away from her.

She turned her face to Malakhai, ready to begin his slow destruction. This would be done the long way, the right way—with lies upon lies.

He must have taken the cinched belt as a signal of goodbye. His eyes were full of disappointment as he stared at her across the gap of three steps. She was aware of every detail of the night, shimmers from a sea of sequins in the room behind him, wavering flames of candlelight. She heard the clink of glasses. A bottle crashed to the floor and freed bubbles of bright laughter floated up with the music.

His head tilted to one side, trying to understand her, as if he could. "I'll never see you again, will I?"

"You'll see me when I come to arrest you in the morning. The paperwork will hit my desk at nine," she lied.

"There's no case for—"

"Because Prado said so? He thinks like an amateur, plots like one too."

"You have no evidence."

"I do—a very strong case for Louisa's murder." *A very weak case.* "That's your motive for the killing you did tonight."

"But you can't prove her death wasn't an accident."

"I can. I've got your testimony from the poker game and a postmortem interview conducted by a medical examiner, Dr. Slope. Expert testimony is admissible evidence." Not likely, but it had the ring of a true thing. "I have physical evidence—your cuff key from Faustine's. I bet it was Nick's idea to leave it near the body—stupid move. I ordered lab tests for DNA. It comes from the oil on your fingers." Heller would fall down laughing at that one.

She turned away from him. "You can plead insanity. You can trot out Louisa, have her do a few cheap tricks in open court. But then I get to tell them how Franny died."

Malakhai reached out and gently turned her face back to his. "You called him by his first name. You don't care about Franny's crimes anymore, do you?" His voice was incredulous. "It's all changed now."

She brushed his hand away.

Malakhai's hand slowly dropped to his side. "Franny was that damn cat in the burning building, wasn't he?"

What is he talking about?

He was reading this question on her face.

"That psychiatrist's report," he said. "The one test question you got right—the one little piece of you that you're really proud of. You wanted to carry your damn cat out of the fire—only because Franny was a living, breathing . . ." His words tapered off to nothing. He stared at her, as if she had somehow betrayed him with this one small thing she had gotten right.

"I'm sorry, Mallory."

"Sorry doesn't get it. This is nothing to do with me. A man died tonight." *The wrong man.* "And you're going to pay for that." *All that blood.*

"You know it'll be a year before this comes to trial. The doctors say I'll be dead by then."

"I know." *But there was all that pain. The screams.* Franny would not stop calling out for help.

"Then what's the point, Mallory?"

"I'll still have Nick Prado and Emile St. John."

His hand gripped the back of a leather chair, as if he might need this support.

She moved closer for the final shot. They were almost done. "I'm going for a triple indictment, naming them as coconspirators. It makes a stronger case with three of you. You can't *all* plead insanity. But Prado never saw that far ahead—freaking amateur."

"Emile had nothing to do with this."

"I know that. You think I care? If he had cooperated with me—" *If he had betrayed every friend—* "He withheld information." He had understood why Franny killed Louisa. Mallory had given him the motive when she told him about Prado's betrayal. St. John had elected not to destroy the survivors with the truth. Mallory had no such qualms about destruction—and yet she stopped short of telling Malakhai he had killed the wrong man.

Malakhai was already badly wounded—they both were. Mallory could not shake the images of a pendulum's slicing razor.

"St. John was a first-rate cop," said Mallory. "He was always the strongest one—and the weak link—too moral for cold-blooded murder." She could still hear Franny screaming. "St. John's part was so passive he could walk if he turned state's evidence. But we both know he'll never do that. I'll get *all* of you." She forced a smile and gave equal weight to each word of the bluff. "I can't lose."

"You're wrong, Mallory. Emile is innocent."

"He had guilty knowledge. That's all I need for conspiracy." Blood streamed down the faces in the audience. "And here's the kicker." *Malakhai, can you hear the pendulum hissing through the air?* "I won't even have to prove it. St. John will write out a full confession and save the state the cost of a trial. And since he's taking the fall anyway, he'll take it for you and Nick. He'll go to jail for you, maybe die for you." Penance for the executioner of the Maquis.

"He's innocent."

Franny screamed again. *All that pain.*

"What do I care who goes down?" said Mallory. "As long as somebody pays." She was seeing the blood as it flew off the pendulum and struck the faces in the audience. "I don't have any more time to waste on you. I'll do my deal with St. John." She turned her back on him and walked toward the door, and Franny went with her, crying out for help, bleeding from his wounds.

"Mallory?"

Malakhai came up behind her and put his hands on her shoulders to keep her from leaving him. She felt his face pressing into her hair.

The blood, all that blood. This was her mantra.

He whispered, "Suppose *I* save the state the cost of a trial? If I confess, you don't need Nick or Emile, do you? They don't even have to know about this conversation."

Mallory saw the shadow move across the wall, but there was no one to cast it. She closed her eyes, so tired, seeing things that were not there. Franny was crying.

"What do I care?" *All that blood.* "So long as somebody pays." One conviction was better than none. "But there are conditions."

Mallory was thinking ahead to the defense attorney who would demolish the case before it ever went to court. Did she smell gardenias? Had she ever been this tired? She could hear

Riker say again that she was only human. His voice was drowned out by Franny, who would not stop crying and screaming.

This had to end, and quickly.

The attorney—right. With documentation of insanity, any first-year law student could nullify a signed confession.

"Conditions." She opened her eyes. There was no shadow on the wall, and the interior screams had stopped. "You'll waive your right to a lawyer when you write out your statement. There won't be any case for extenuating circumstances—no medical reports, no psych evaluations."

She could feel his warmth behind her, so close. His breath was in her hair.

"You'll make a second confession in open court. After sentencing, you'll be taken into custody." Something dark was moving in the corner of her eye, a shadow rising up the length of the wall, ready to strike.

No, there's nothing there.

"Then you'll go straight to prison. No postponements, no legal games to buy you any time." There was no woman to make that shadow. Louisa had died more than half a century ago.

"Agreed," said Malakhai. "Tomorrow morning I'll write it all down. And tonight we'll close the deal with a drink—one last glass of wine."

His hands fell away from her shoulders as she turned around to face him, saying, "I won't drink with you."

Malakhai stepped back. "No, of course you won't." He was finally altogether broken. It was in his face, more sorrow than she had ever seen. He inclined his head in the ghost of a bow, a gesture of good night, then turned away from her and strode across the lobby to cut a solitary swath through the partyers. She watched his back until he was swallowed by the crowd.

"You won't drink with me either, will you?" The front door was swinging shut as Emile St. John walked toward her. He carried no umbrella, and the rain ran off the brim of his hat when he tipped it in salute, saying, "It's about choosing up sides."

She nodded.

"You're a good cop, Mallory." He turned away from her and walked into the dining area, where Charles Butler rose from his chair to slap the man's back in a warm greeting. A young brunette sallied over to Nick Prado with a wineglass in her hand. He swept her up under one arm and ran with her across the room, stepping in time to music—upbeat, *alive.* The wine spilled, the smoke swirled. Mallory could hear the high notes of laughter across the narrow divide.

Life was always going on in another room.

Epilogue

CHARLES BUTLER HAD NOT BEEN INVITED TO THE FUNERAL. HE would be slow to forgive her for that, but he was no good at covert things. Mallory had prepared for this death long in advance, determined that Malakhai's interment would not become a mass media event.

She had traveled to the prison with her entourage of undertakers and collected his body in the dark hours of early morning. The coffin was airborne before the first reporters converged on the prison gates.

Mallory wanted no flights of doves, no tricks, nor a legion of magicians in white satin. She had hurried Malakhai over the ocean and into this foreign soil. Now she stood before the monument ordered from a French stonecutter months before the death. Once the grave was filled with dirt, this slab of marble would cover husband and wife, reunited in a common grave.

She could not have done this without the influence of Emile St. John. Long ago, this historic cemetery had been closed to any more traffic with the dead. St. John had dealt with the officials and cut through reams of paperwork to expand Louisa's plot and lay Malakhai beside her. He took no credit for his work, modestly explaining that the French would always favor lovers over bureaucracy.

He stared at the blue Paris sky, then slowly bowed his head to read a passage from the Old Testament. He had also done this service for Franny. And after today, St. John and Mallory could stop meeting like this.

The cover of his Bible opened to a rush of wings as two doves appeared to fly from the pages. St. John looked up from the book with a deep apology on his face, for this was not what they had agreed upon.

"Old habit," he said. "They just slipped out." He turned his eyes down to the text of Solomon, and read aloud from the Song of Songs.

Mallory followed the flight of the doves, never hearing these words; they meant nothing to her. She had also been deaf to the prison chaplain when he argued that Malakhai should be left in a state of ignorance—he had called it grace—so the prisoner might go to God with a clean soul.

Mallory had no soul, or she had heard rumors to that effect and seen it writ in the shredded pages of a child's psychiatric evaluation. And she was not a believer in God, though she did have personal knowledge of a living hell, its flames and its agony.

After a massive stroke, Malakhai had awakened to look around his prison cell, bewildered and as innocent as the boy from 1942, not understanding what crime he was paying for. Though justice was someone else's job, and Mallory was only the imperfect machine of law, she had been there to explain it to him—every visitors' day until his death. She had brought him Mr. Halpern's portrait of Louisa and given him back his own love story in every detail he had given to her. Mallory had carried the frightened boy through all the years of his life to rebuild the man—to keep him sane.

She had carried him out of the fire.

Long after St. John had departed from the cemetery, the gravediggers stood in the distance, leaning on their shovels and waiting for the young American to finally let go of the dead.

A reporter appeared at the iron gates—the first fly on a fresh corpse. And then another one turned up, and another, buzzing, buzzing, cameras clicking.

✢   ✢   ✢

In a darker time zone half the world away, Nick Prado stood by the window looking out on the city lights of Chicago. Behind him, a television broadcast recapped the death of the man who had butchered Franny Futura.

Fools.

The reporters never got anything right. Malakhai had been one of the greats, and he deserved a better press release. In a further heresy, the news media had upgraded Franny from a tired hack to a legend among the magic men.

Ah, Fame—what a twitchy bitch you are.

He glanced at the telephone. He longed to speak with his oldest friend, but Emile St. John was not accepting his calls anymore. The past six months since Franny's death had been one prolonged meal of ashes.

Mallory's banquet.

Would she call again tonight? No, he thought not.

So many times, he had seen her on the street. At first, he had thought this was only an illusion—her face in the crowd—for Mallory did not belong on the sidewalks of Chicago. But each time she had appeared, the dates corresponded with first-class airline tickets and limousines charged to his personal credit cards.

Amusing child.

He had paid the bills without complaint.

But of course, she's quite insane.

He had also been a good sport when a large sum of money was criminally transferred from corporate accounts to pay for Franny's funeral expenses. Mallory did have exquisite taste in upscale cemeteries with lake-view mausoleums. Franny would have adored his fine marble house by the water.

Graciously and quietly, he had replaced the corporate money with his own personal funds.

In another act of creative accounting, she had emptied out several client accounts. With skillful computer trading, she had purchased a good selection of stocks for his own portfolio. A battery of lawyers and accountants had shuttled the illegally commingled money back to its rightful owners to thwart an embezzlement charge. But his own well-intentioned bribes to affected parties had brought on new charges for obstruction of justice and witness tampering. He had spent the entire day dodging the bearers of warrants for his arrest.

More stunning damage had been for a lesser amount, payment to a French stonecutter for a monument purchased long before Malakhai's death—just a little memo from hell to tell him that an old friend was wasting, dying in prison, while Nick breathed the rarefied air of a penthouse mansion in the sky.

Lest he ever forget that, Mallory had awakened him every night with a silent reminder. He knew it was her, though she never spoke and no source number was ever caught by caller-identification equipment or phone-line traps. And whenever he traveled out of town, the calls had come directly to his suite, with no record of passing through a hotel operator.

Ghost calls.

Did she know how much they affected his sleep, his dreams? He suspected that she only called to hear the sound of his voice, a response to her silent inquiry about his health—What? Not dead yet? Click.

Actually, she always slammed down the receiver—still angry after all this time.

Now he took pills to make him sleep, and yet he always woke up tired. So there were more pills to get him through the days.

This morning he had found an envelope on the table by his bed. It contained receipts for his own funeral expenses. Mallory had selected a pauper's plot, an apt metaphor for a man with no more friends. He had recognized her perfume in the air. Fortunately, he had not opened his eyes to catch her there.

He had not quite recovered from her last covert visit to his bedroom. That night, he had awakened to find her sitting close to his prone body, her green eyes glittering, so intense. All the fanged and clawed predators stared at their living, writhing meals in that same manner. A moment later, the lights had gone out, and Mallory had vanished. And that time, she had not charged her plane tickets to his credit card.

Had she really been there? Had he imagined her perfume this morning?

Perhaps his houseboy had taken the envelope from the hand of a common messenger, then left it on the bedside table while his employer lay sleeping.

Nick would never ask.

He looked at his watch. By now Malakhai must be lying deep in the earth of France, asleep beneath the City of Light. *Good night, old friend. My regards to Louisa.*

The reporters would not come until just before dawn. He stared at his own image floating in the night-dark glass, and over one reflected shoulder, he searched the room behind his back.

On one of her visits to Chicago, Mallory had suddenly appeared behind him in the mirror of a shopwindow, where he had paused awhile to admire himself. She had not spoken to him that day. He had stared at her reflection in stunned silence, only watching her hands curl into talons, rising slowly, as if she meant to rake his back—or push him through the glass. He had closed his eyes for a quiet moment of terror—and then she was gone. He had not turned his head to watch her disappear into the crowded Chicago street. His eyes had been fixed on the shop mirror, looking at himself with new clarity of vision and cruel daylight—seeing lines in his flesh never noticed before, veins in the whites of his eyes and broken capillaries beneath the paper-thin skin. The boy from Faustine's wasn't there anymore. Nor could he find his handsome young self anywhere in this sky-high mansion of many mirrors.

He had continued to look for Mallory in every crowd. *Such a pretty face, but so cold and crazy.*

Now he turned back to his first love, his own reflection in the penthouse window glass.

When beauty dies—what then?

Hours passed as he watched the sky lighten. Then the telephone rang on the table beside him—and that would be Mallory. Apparently, she had taken no time for sightseeing in Paris. He picked up the receiver and listened to the expected silence at the other end of the line.

Still checking for a pulse, my dear?

He only heard the background sounds of traffic on a busy

street. Was she calling from a cell phone or a pay phone? Finally he spoke into the void, "No, Mallory, I'm not dead yet."

He heard the receiver crash down on its cradle at the other end of the wire and recognized her phone-slamming style.

Nick ran to the front door and checked each one of the five locks—just on the off chance that she had come back for another visit. Three of the locks were new and guaranteed pick-proof, but he suspected that she had already gotten past two of them on previous occasions. He also toyed with the idea that she tapped his phones, though none of the security experts had found any trace of electronic bugs. But they had also failed to catch her phone calls.

Nick sauntered back to the front room, opened the terrace door and stepped outside. It was a rare calm night for a town called the Windy City. He walked toward the retaining wall and looked over the edge. Even through a fog of drugs and booze, he could still feel the vertigo, the sensation of falling while standing still, the irresistible pull of the earth so far below.

It had taken him a month only to approach this ledge. And now that he had hit on exactly the right dosage of sedatives and bourbon, he was free to look down at the insect life on the pavement, tiny people straggling along the sidewalk in the predawn hours, leaving night-shift jobs or rolling out of after-hours bars. From this distance, he could not distinguish between hookers and newsboys.

He turned to look over his shoulder.

She wasn't there.

Mallory had been right—her job was the hardest one. And he had given her credit for that. The memoirs of the great Nick Prado lay on his coffee table. Within those pages, Mallory was mentioned as a corroborating footnote for three perfect murders. He had gone on at length about his greatness—so the world would fully appreciate how hard the young detective's job had been—and why she had failed.

The manuscript was neatly packaged in an envelope addressed to a prominent literary agent. His cover letter detailed the reasons for his upcoming publicity stunt—to kick off the book auction of the century. He had included a press package. The glossy black-and-white photographs had all been taken when he was young and beautiful. He had spent hours selecting the best of them and burning every lesser image in his fireplace. All his imperfections were gone now. In his favorite portrait, he was only nineteen years old, and this one lay on top of the envelope so the reporters would have a picture to run with his obituary.

He looked down at the street again. Almost dawn. He had selected this hour in deference to the cameras. The sky would be light enough for a backdrop, but not too bright.

Timing is everything.

All the daily papers and local TV stations had been alerted in time for the morning news. The first reporter and camera-man had arrived on the street far below. Nick put on his glasses, the better to see one of the tiny ants emerge from a toy van with his video equipment. The headlights of another van were pulling up to the curb. And more of them were coming to the party in private cars. When he had counted one crew for each news channel, and a smattering of more ants to represent radio and the print media, he removed his eye-glasses.

He was never photographed with bifocals.

So they had all turned out, and right on time. Nick had not disappointed them once in all his years as the king of hype. He had promised them a stunt to rival the great Max Candle.

The terrace ledge was broad enough for a larger, wider man to walk with ease around the entire building, but from the street it would appear more dangerous. Back east in New York, Mallory would see him on television, for this act would certainly go national, maybe international with live coverage by satellite. Television executives would salivate over him. His show would crank up the figures for advertising sales beyond their wet dreams of profit. Throughout the hours of his ordeal, broadcast journalists would speculate on the rea-sons for his protracted stroll in the clouds, and not *if* he would jump, but *when.* They would probably put the cause to outstanding warrants for his arrest and his prospects of dying in prison.